THE BEST ADVENTURE
AND SURVIVAL STORIES
2003

THE BEST ADVENTURE AND SURVIVAL STORIES

2003

EDITED BY NATE HARDCASTLE

Thunder's Mouth Press
New York

THE BEST ADVENTURE AND SURVIVAL STORIES 2003

Compilation copyright © 2003 by Clint Willis
Introductions copyright © 2003 by Nate Hardcastle

Adrenaline ® and the Adrenaline® logo are trademarks of
Avalon Publishing Group Incorporated, New York, NY.

An Adrenaline Book®

Published by
Thunder's Mouth Press
An Imprint of Avalon Publishing Group Incorporated
161 William Street, 16th floor
New York, NY 10038

frontispiece photo: Skier outrunning avalanche, Copyright © Lee
Cohen/Corbis.

Library of Congress Cataloging-in-Publication Data is available.

ISBN: 1-56025-506-4

Book design: Sue Canavan

Printed in the United States of America

Distributed by Publishers Group West

For Clint Willis,
who has been a mentor

c o n t e n t s

introduction

The stories in this book recount two types of dangerous experience. The first type tells of mountain climbers, explorers and other risk-takers who get themselves into potentially dangerous situations for reasons that range from thrill-seeking to résumé-building. These stories usually follow a familiar pattern: A person or group pursues a particular goal fraught with danger, and along the way encounters obstacles and either overcomes them or suffers the consequences. The familiarity of that structure can make the stories comforting to read, hair-raising moments notwithstanding.

The thrill-seekers' stories sometimes convey exuberance. Joshua Cooper Ramo's profile of aerobatic pilot Kirby Chambliss is one example in this collection. Other intentional adventures make for funny stories—see Terry Grosz's anecdote about a survival-training session. Still others inform us (Peter Canby's "The Forest Primeval") or portray courage (the excerpt from James Mawdsley's book *The Iron Road*).

The second type of survival or adventure story is about people who encounter danger when they are going about the business of everyday life. Those unexpected adventures can be unsettling to read about—

they remind us that we live in a dangerous world: Terrorists attack; cars crash; snakes bite. People confronted with events such as the destruction of the World Trade Center or the bombing of Bali's Sari Club are thrust into survival situations, often with little or no preparation.

It's a cliché to say that we turn to adventure stories for artificial, voyeuristic thrills now that danger has been regulated and litigated away from our daily experience. True enough. Good adventure and survival stories are terrifically entertaining, in part because they describe real danger and the people who struggle to overcome it—a reliable recipe for convincing drama. And overcoming danger has sex appeal. Ask professional bull rider Justin McBride, who in Chris Heath's article "This is Not a Rodeo Story" explains his vocation this way: "'We found a way to be cowboys and still make a great living, and to be way cooler than anybody in the world.'"

We also read these stories to become acquainted with danger, so we can try to understand it and prepare for it. Most Americans live with more fear now than they did a few years ago. Fear is a powerful feeling, and like other powerful feelings—love, say—it stimulates curiosity. We want to see how other people have dealt with danger so we can learn from their experiences. The knowledge we gain from these stories can mitigate our fear. People trying to understand love or wisdom or death turn to stories. Why should fear and danger be any different?

—Nate Hardcastle

Little Sister, Big Mountain
by Michael Finkel

Michael Finkel has compiled an impressive résumé of adventures, from paddling the previously unexplored Chinko River in Central Africa to crossing the most remote part of the Sahara Desert. His sister Diane is a climber and ultra-marathon runner. The two in 2001 tried to become the first brother-sister team to summit an 8,000-meter peak. This story appeared in National Geographic Adventure.

I am not a particularly superstitious person, and neither is my sister, but we both thought that what happened to the Korean climber was about as bad an omen as one could ever encounter. What happened to him was that his brain grew too big for his skull. This is one of the risks of life at high altitude.

His symptoms were not much different from those of a person who has suffered a severe head injury in, say, a motorcycle accident, only with the Korean climber these symptoms progressed in slow motion. He was gripped by a throbbing headache; he felt drowsy and weak; he lost his appetite.

At this point, descent of a few thousand feet is the ideal treatment, but though his teammates were concerned, the Korean climber hunkered down in his tent and refused all medical attention. After a few days, the pressure within his head was so great that his brain was being squeezed through the small opening, called the foramen magnum, at the base of the skull. His brain was literally crushing itself to death. He soon had difficulty speaking and walking. His face seemed drained of color. He began to hallucinate. He did not eat.

It wasn't until he lost consciousness that his teammates finally took action. They zipped him into a warm sleeping bag and draped him over a yak. A couple of Sherpas guided the yak down the trail. By the time they arrived at the nearest dirt road, after a full day's walk, the Korean climber was dead. His name was Kim Su-Ya. He was 34 years old.

His body was placed in the back seat of a Toyota Land Cruiser, which navigated the bumpy road for a few hours until it reached the closest village, a tiny outpost on the Tibetan plateau called Tingri. This is where we were waiting—waiting, in fact, for a Land Cruiser. We'd been informed of the death via field radio, and we remained in our rented room while the Korean's body was put onto a cargo truck to be transported to Kathmandu and then flown home. Later, I learned that we'd all been thinking of ill omens, but at the time, nobody said much, and the four of us stepped somberly into the Land Cruiser and the driver turned around and headed back up the dirt road to base camp, so that our climb could begin.

The mountain is called Cho Oyu. It's the sixth highest peak in the world, 26,906 feet above sea level. This converts to 8,201 meters, meaning that Cho Oyu, which straddles the border of Nepal and Tibet, is one of the 14 members of the much obsessed upon and much mythologized 8,000-meter-peak club.

The four of us who attempted to climb Cho Oyu last fall included a photographer from Boulder, Colorado, named Beth Wald; my younger sister and only sibling, Diana Finkel; Diana's longtime boyfriend, Ben Woodbeck; and me. I went to the mountain for only one reason: My sister was going to the mountain.

We have an unusual relationship, my sister and I. We are not especially close. Until we began planning this trip we seldom talked on the phone, and though we didn't live too far apart (Diana in southern

Colorado, me in western Montana), we almost never visited each other's homes. Yet when it comes to athletic pursuits, we have a profound understanding of each other's limits, and how to push the other beyond them. I can't quite explain why, but there is no one else—not a friend, not a coach—who can motivate me athletically the way Diana can. Three years ago, for example, I entered a hundred-mile run. A pacer was allowed to join me for the final 38 miles; Diana eagerly accepted the job, coaxed me to the edge of my ability and then further, and brought me to the finish just under the elusive 24-hour barrier.

A year after my run, Diana also entered a hundred-mile race, and I paced her. My sister, who is almost exactly three years younger than I am, has a long history of surpassing my performances. She finished the race in a little over 21 hours. In another ultra, soon after, she set the course record. Her boyfriend, Ben, calls her La Torita—the Little Bull.

Our hundred-mile runs were unexpectedly bonding. They made us want to spend more time together, both as teammates and, it seemed, as friends. And so we began pondering other tests to tackle.

Diana is a moderately accomplished climber; she and Ben have made several first ascents in the Coast Mountains of Alaska and have completed demanding routes in the Cascades and the Canadian Rockies. I am a far less skilled alpinist, but I do have a stubbornness that is suited to the rigors of big-peak climbing. Diana and I had climbed together a few times—most notably on a successful push up Mount Rainier—and we began to talk about trying another mountain. The more we talked, the bigger the mountain became, until soon enough we were talking about the Himalaya, and then, inevitably, the 8,000-meter peaks.

The decision to attempt such a mountain was not made lightly. It really couldn't be. Climbing an 8,000-meter peak is both expensive and dangerous. With all the permits, fees, and guides to pay, even the most economical trips can cost in excess of $6,000 per person; an Everest climb can easily exceed $60,000 each. Despite the media-generated impression of crowds up high, climbing an 8,000-meter mountain is not a common pursuit. From 1950, when the first of the 14 was climbed—Annapurna, in central Nepal—until the day of our departure, fewer than 3,000 men and 200 women had ever summited an 8,000-meter peak. This includes Mount Everest. At the same time, about 600 people have died, which means that for every five climbers who have reached an 8,000-meter summit, there has been one death.

Diana discovered, after a bit of research, that of the 200 or so women to reach the top of an 8,000-meter mountain, not one had done so with a brother. None of the men, therefore, had summited with a sister. We could attempt to become the first brother-and-sister team ever to climb an 8,000-meter peak. This fact thrilled us—we could be the Hillary and Norgay of sibling alpinists!—and, at the same time, pretty much convinced our parents that they would lose both their children in one fell swoop.

Our own concerns, at least initially, were less about danger than about finances. Here, though, we had a piece of luck: Shrewdly playing the brother-sister first-ascent angle, we applied for and won a $25,000 grant from the National Geographic Expeditions Council. None of the four of us had ever attempted an 8,000-meter peak, and only Beth had previously even seen the Himalaya, so we also paid for a guide and a two-person support crew, whom we met up with in Kathmandu. The expedition's total cost came to $61,915.

We chose Cho Oyu for several reasons. Most significantly, it is considered one of the least dangerous 8,000-meter peaks (one death for every 36 summiters). It's about as popular to climb as Everest, and there was no way we were going to try Everest on our first trip to the Himalaya, though other people have. Also, Diana and I wanted to climb without oxygen—we were both attracted to the purer challenge of going on our own lung power, succeed or fail—and Cho Oyu, which is 2,100 feet shorter than Everest, is demanding but feasible without oxygen. And so Cho Oyu it was.

The Land Cruiser dropped us off at the end of the road, a place called Chinese Base Camp. The Himalaya are generally pristine and gorgeous, but Chinese Base Camp is not a highlight. It's located at 15,450 feet on a muddy, wind-scoured spit along a shallow river. Save for the bald humps of the Himalayan foothills, there's not much of a view.

Yak herds frequently pass through, and their owners often set their handwoven yak-hair tents amid the climbers' candy-colored ripstop-nylon domes. The yak herders sleep in long, double-ended bags that look like rolled carpets—two persons to a bag, feet in the middle, a head poking out each end. During our stay, the herdsmen's kids nosed around our camps and stared at our gear and giggled. I swapped a chocolate-chip Clif bar with one young girl for a glass of sour yak milk; afterward, neither of us seemed in a rush to change our diet.

We'd arrived at the beginning of the post-monsoon climbing season, August through October, and though we'd left as early as our work schedules would allow, we were a few days behind most of the other expeditions. Except for a couple of stragglers, the teams had all moved up to Advance Base Camp, at 18,750 feet, which is where the Korean climber had taken ill.

At Chinese Base Camp, we caught up with our guide and two Sherpa assistants, who, already used to the altitude, had taken the car up a day ahead of us to begin making camp. Hiring a guide was, for us, a difficult and confusing decision. There are at least half a dozen reputable outfitters that offer trips to Cho Oyu—Mountain Madness, International Mountain Guides, Adventure Consultants, among others—but we eventually passed on all of them. We'd talked with many people who had climbed with commercial expeditions, and though nearly everyone expressed overall satisfaction, we heard complaints ranging from being assigned a horrible tentmate to being part of a group with wildly incongruous skills. "You're treated like a child," one person told me. We wanted a little more autonomy than these groups seemed to offer, even if it meant a lower chance of success.

After several weeks of Internet research and phone interviews, we settled on a guide named Jamie McGuinness, an energetic 35-year-old from New Zealand. Jamie was relatively inexperienced as a big-mountain guide: We were only the second team he had led on an 8,000-meter peak. (His first clients, both of whom had summited, had given him a solid recommendation.) He was reasonably priced, he supported our plan to try the peak without oxygen, and, perhaps most important, he was willing to guide the four of us as a private group.

Jamie had hired our two-person support crew—a cook and a climbing assistant. The assistant was 43-year-old Pasang Phurba Sherpa, who had summited Cho Oyu three times. Why Pasang himself wasn't our guide has a lot to do with marketing and tradition; Sherpas are just now starting to operate guide services, and if I ever return to the Himalaya I plan to bring my business directly to them.

Pasang was older than most Sherpa climbers—his face, frost-nipped and sun-wrinkled, charted a legacy of life in the high mountains—and there was about him the gravitas of an elder statesman, though one with a fine-tuned sense of humor. He spoke workable English and enjoyed teasing my sister. Diana is a vegetarian and has a habit of asking what is in every meal. Whenever she'd ask this of Pasang, he'd give her a serious look and say, "Everything meat!"

Our cook was a 24-year-old newlywed named Namgyal Sherpa. He was a tiny man, and the bottom third of his ears stuck oddly outward, and he styled his hair in a boyish bowl cut—in other words, he looked a little bit like an elf. His salary, he said, was $5 per day, plus a $500 equipment allotment. He ferried loads up and down the mountain, cooked our meals, carried tea to our tents, would not allow anyone to so much as scrub a dish, and never, in five weeks, appeared to be in anything less than the sunniest of moods. I miss him terribly.

We spent four nights at Chinese Base Camp. What did we do there? Well, we acclimatized—which is just a fancy way of saying we did nothing. When it comes to 8,000-meter peaks, most of the climbing is about not climbing. It's more about solving an impossible mathematical equation: How can three complex, often contradictory variables—acclimatization (the more time spent at altitude the better); health (the more time, in most cases, the worse); and weather (wholly unpredictable)—best be juggled?

We concentrated on the most controllable of the variables: our health. We kept precise tabs on colds and coughs and headaches. We chain-sucked throat lozenges. We drank as much water as we could, then drank some more. "Hydration," said Ben, "is our religion." We discussed, inordinately, the quantity of our urine and the consistency of our stool. We tried to eat as much as possible, since at high altitude one's appetite is naturally curbed and the body burns excess calories merely to breathe. Of the four of us, only Diana lost less weight than I did, but despite Namgyal's endless portions of *dal-bhat*, by the time we left the mountain I'd dropped 21 pounds.

Fifteen yaks were rented to help ferry our supplies to Advance Base Camp. The hike took two days. On the second, we crested a small ridge and beheld, for the first time, Cho Oyu. Jamie had warned us that Cho Oyu was not a pretty mountain, and in the classic sense he was right— it certainly doesn't pierce the stratosphere like a Matterhorn. Cho Oyu, quite simply, is enormous: a huge, humpbacked knot of glacier and granite, white-capped lesser peaks massed about its flanks like supplicants. The most common translation of the mountain's name is "Goddess of Turquoise," but another way to translate it, "Mighty Head," now seemed more apropos. Cho Oyu is so high that its top often intersects with the jet stream, which shifts latitudes from time to time. Extreme winds slamming into a stationary object create a froth of clouds; at the moment, the clouds streaming off Cho Oyu's summit looked like the tail of a galloping horse. It looked cold.

Almost immediately, a nervous, tingly feeling came over me. It felt like fear, but it wasn't quite. If you're a mountaineer, you know what I mean—that undeniable tug, triggered by the sight of mountains, of needing to ascend. By the time we reached Advance Base Camp, I was so wound up I nearly forgot I had a headache.

Advance Base Camp was a fascinating place, horrible and wonderful at once. It looked like a traveling circus—a jam of tents packed vestibule to vestibule on a boulder-strewn moraine pinched between a glacier and a foothill. There were 35 expeditions from 24 nations, as well as a resident herd of yaks. Population 250, I'd guess (not counting the yaks), with almost as many tents. If there'd been a NO VACANCY sign, it might have been lit. Our small group alone erected seven tents: a sleeping tent for me; another for Beth; another for Jamie; another for Diana and Ben; another for Pasang and Namgyal; a large dining tent with a table and plastic chairs; and an even larger cook tent.

From almost any spot in camp, I could hear the babble of a dozen languages and detect the smells of a dozen variants of dal-bhat. E-mail could be sent for $10 per message; satellite phone calls were $10 a minute. Strings of colorful prayer flags hung everywhere, like at a used-car dealership. There was even a bar, sanctioned by the China Tibet Mountaineering Association and housed in a canvas army tent, that sold tea, soda, beer (Pabst Blue Ribbon, from a factory in China), whiskey, and goat-meat stew—and, it was rumored, the favors of the two Tibetan women who worked there. The camp was probably 90 percent male, with an average age, I'd estimate, of 40.

Except for a few clumps of butter-colored lichen, the place was devoid of vegetation. Overhead, continually circling, were gangs of ravenlike *goraks*. Their name is onomatopoeic—the sound they make is *Gorak! Gorak! Gorak!*—and they were not at all timid about swooping in uninvited and helping themselves to a bit of our lunch. People slept at all hours of the day, as in a college dorm, and at night, if you didn't walk carefully, you were likely to trip over a dozing yak.

I spent a few days wandering around camp—acclimatizing, of course, and meeting my fellow climbers. In the center of everything, forming a sort of town square, was the immense Norwegian encampment. There were eight climbers on the team; the oldest was 31. They'd apparently been sponsored by a Norwegian investment bank, which seemed to have opened the vault to them. Their dining tent could have housed a tennis court. They'd brought with them two gas-powered generators, a DVD player ("Do you want to watch *Vertical Limit*?"), a stocked liquor cabinet, a bunch of funny wigs, a 25-foot flagpole, and a television film crew, which was shooting a documentary about the team.

Next door, in a tiny red tent, lived Boldbaatar Luvsandash. Bold, as he liked to be called, was trying to become the first Mongolian to scale an 8,000-meter peak. He was already the first Mongolian atop

Kilimanjaro and Mont Blanc. He was 42. "I sold everything I own to pay for this," he said. "I sold my car; I sold my TV. I don't have a camera because I sold that, too."

A few tents over from Bold, I met Hibi Elko, 59, a grandmother of two. She was attempting to become the oldest Japanese woman to climb an 8,000-meter peak. "I am very afraid," she told me.

I met an Italian named Pino, who planned to hit a golf ball from the summit and thereby gain entry into *Guinness World Records*. I met a Sherpa named Jangbu, who was the first person to climb K2 twice in one year. I met a snowmobile dealer, an airline pilot, two doctors, three lawyers, and a professor of computer science from Stanford University. I met a man who told me his name was Slate and that his occupation was "warrior."

I met Sergio Martini, also from Italy, who said he'd already climbed every 8,000-meter peak but was returning to Cho Oyu because his view from the summit on his previous trip was "no good." I met a 21-year-old Japanese climber and a 72-year-old American. I learned which camp had extra Kit Kats, and where I could get free popcorn, and who had a supply of red licorice. I stood in line for an opportunity to flirt with a blond-haired, long-legged Canadian named Michelle.

Eventually, Diana and I walked over to the Korean camp to express our condolences. The evening we stopped by, it so happened, was the evening before the remainder of the team planned to set out for the higher camps. We poked our heads into their mess tent and were promptly pulled inside, where we were seated at a table and each handed a beer, a shot of whiskey, and a cigarette. Just about everyone was drunk. Apparently it is something of a Korean tradition to hold a party before a big climb.

Koreans, I'm sorry to report, do not have a very good reputation in the climbing world. More than one person at base camp summarized their mountaineering philosophy thusly: Reach the summit or die trying. The dead man, I learned, had been the team's leader and its most experienced climber.

I smoked and drank with the Koreans—what the hell—and though nobody seemed particularly upset, Diana and I tried to offer some comforting words. After a while, one of the climbers figured out what we were attempting to express. "Leader?" he said. I nodded yes, my face a mask of compassion. "Dead!" he shouted, running a finger across his throat. Then he threw his head back and laughed. "Leader—dead!" he repeated, and everyone in the tent laughed and laughed and laughed.

The air in the high mountains, some Sherpas still believe, is poisoned. The higher you go, they say, the more toxic it is. In essence, the Sherpas are right. Thin air is deadly. This is why there are no permanent human settlements above 17,000 feet. Altitude can trigger embolisms, it can paralyze you, it can blind you. Symptoms can progress gradually or strike suddenly. You can climb ten mountains without a problem, but on the 11th you can abruptly fall ill. Many outfitters, after you pay for a climb, send you a "body disposal election form," in which you indicate whether, in the event of your death, your corpse should be tossed into a crevasse, cremated at a local monastery, or, for a hefty fee, shipped home.

Before flying to Nepal, my sister and I had often discussed how much we were willing to risk to climb Cho Oyu. The fact that people frequently die on 8,000-meter peaks is, we both admitted, one of the perverse allures of such a climb. We wanted to succeed where others had fatally failed. Diana and I were not willing to die, certainly, but we did want to reach the top. Our aim was to ascend as a complete team, at the pace of the slowest climber. On the flight over, the four of us had tabulated, not jokingly, how many digits we were each prepared to sacrifice in order to summit. Diana was willing to give up two toes—preferably, she said, the little ones. I ponied up one finger and one toe. Ben tithed a finger. Beth was not willing to lose anything.

Now, on the mountain, Diana was the one who was poleaxed by altitude. Her sickness came on strong. We were still at Advance Base Camp when she woke in the middle of the night with head pain exponentially fiercer than the low-simmer ache that is a fact of life up high. Her lips were blue. Ben, sleeping next to her, administered an altitude-sickness prophylactic called Diamox, but it did not significantly ease her symptoms. Diana fell back to sleep, but her breathing was erratic, sometimes ceasing for up to half a minute at a time. Periodic respiration, as this condition is called, is common at altitude but still scary.

In the morning, she looked ragged. I asked how she felt. My sister, you should know, is one of the world's great positive thinkers. If she tells you that a movie is merely "fantastic," it's probably wise to stay away; "the best ever" is only slightly better. So when she answered, using our typical scale of one to ten, that she was feeling no better than eight, Ben and I were alarmed. Diana an eight? We'd never imagined such a thing.

Then we learned why. We'd brought with us a small electronic device called a pulse oxometer, which clips onto the end of a finger. It measures the percentage of blood cells that are saturated with oxygen—a good indicator of how well one is adjusting to altitude. At sea level, most of us are at 95 to 97 percent; a measure below 92 can be cause for concern and sometimes hospitalization. High in the Himalaya, readings in the 80s are typical, and a measurement in the 70s, while disquieting, is no reason to stop climbing. Once the oxometer reads in the 60s, an internal alarm should sound—if you're feeling terrible, you can be fairly certain you're suffering from acute mountain sickness, an illness that can swiftly progress to pulmonary edema (fluid in the lungs) or cerebral edema (swelling of the brain), which is what killed the Korean climber. A percentage in the 50s can indicate an emergency.

That morning, Diana, her lips still blue and her skin pale, registered a 48. "I have never heard of a reading that low," said Tod Schimelpfenig, the curriculum director of the Wilderness Medicine Institute in Lander, Wyoming, when I spoke with him after our climb. "I would think that patient would be incredibly sick, and possibly not conscious." Luis Benitez, a guide for Alpine Ascents International who has twice summited Everest, put it more bluntly: "I've never heard of anyone being alive with that reading."

At this point, it is clear, we should have ended the climb. Diana had many of the same symptoms that had preceded the Korean's death. Her mood was dour; she had no appetite. The rest of us measured at least 20 points higher on the oxometer.

Diana admitted that she did not feel right but insisted she was well enough to keep climbing. "I know my own body," she said, "and I know I can go up." We gave her a few tests for ataxia—loss of physical coordination—which is a sure sign of severe sickness. She passed all of them easily. Jamie, our guide, supported her desire to continue.

My sister, I told myself, was the Little Bull; if anyone could defy the odds, she could. I knew how badly she wanted to climb, and I knew how badly I wanted to climb with her. We'd traveled halfway around the world and spent a small fortune. We'd accepted grant money; we'd taken time off from our jobs. It would have been devastating for our team to quit having never left Base Camp. And so, without any real debate, we made our decision. We decided to go up.

On our fifth day at Advance Base Camp, we held a ceremony called a *puja*, in which a lama blessed not only us but also our boots, crampons, ice axes, and harnesses. Then we loaded our blessed gear into our backpacks and headed higher. We followed a trail of cairns over the rubble-covered Gyabrag Glacier until it met with the western flank of Cho Oyu. Here we camped for the night beneath a steep scree field sometimes referred to as Hell Hill.

I didn't mind Hell Hill. It was a relief, after all that waiting at Advance Base Camp, to finally climb. I moved slowly—ten steps and a rest, my breathing heavy but controlled, my body warm and welcoming the challenge. The numbers on my wrist-watch's altimeter crept higher, and soon, for the first time in my life, I was above 20,000 feet. Atop Hell Hill was Camp I, really just a narrow ridge hung between a cliff and a crevasse—no place for sleepwalking. Until this point, we'd climbed only on rock and gravel. Now, just over a vertical mile from the summit, we'd finally reached snow.

For much of the hike, I followed my sister. We repeatedly tested her with the oxometer, and her readings never broke 60. Even so, she seemed much recovered, though with Diana you can never tell. My sister is a professional hiker. She and Ben work for the Minnesota Department of Corrections, escorting groups of 10 to 12 teenagers who have been convicted of nonviolent crimes (drug offenses, mostly) on three-week forays into the northern Minnesota backcountry. Wilderness therapy, it's sometimes called; I call it Hoods in the Woods. Diana's business attire includes a 90-pound backpack and a pair of handcuffs. Often she removes items from the teenagers' packs to ensure she's carrying the heaviest load. Diana is five-foot-four, when she's exaggerating only a little; her weight barely reaches triple digits.

Diana and Ben have an enviably strong relationship, grounded in the happy meshing of profound personality differences. They form a natural good-cop, bad-cop duo. Diana is preternaturally bubbly—she was a cheerleader in college—while Ben, it seems, has an acute case of misanthropy. On the mountain, Diana's coffee mug was emblazoned with a sticker that said GIRLS KICK ASS; Ben's mug said PEOPLE SUCK.

When they're not escorting juvenile delinquents through the woods, Diana and Ben tend to guide themselves. In addition to distance running, my sister loves rock climbing, ice climbing, bicycling, canoeing, kayaking, and cross-country skiing. She is good at all of them. She is good at almost everything she does.

She can also be stubborn to the point of irrationality. She does not like cities. I can count on zero fingers how many times I have seen her wear makeup. She feels uncomfortable when dining in a restaurant fancier than a Denny's. Give her a couple of Power-Bars and a sleeping bag and she's fine for weeks. Over the last decade she has slept outside an average of 250 days a year.

In fact, until recently the house Diana and Ben rent in Colorado did not have a bed. They simply slept on the floor, on their camping pads. Now, though, they have a bed. A friend gave it to them. "We've spent $20, total, on all the furniture we own," Diana told me. This did not seem believable, so I asked Ben. "No, she's wrong," he said. "It's not $20. It's more like $15."

• • •

An 8,000-meter peak is almost never climbed in one continuous ascent. Instead, to allow the body to become accustomed to extreme altitude, climbers typically make at least one trip partway up the mountain and then return to Base Camp for a rest before heading to the top.

After several days at Camp I, we retreated to Advance Base Camp. The weather was beautiful. Glacier glasses replaced goggles; it was warm enough, at midday, to take a quick bucket bath. Teams were starting to mass at Camp II and Camp III. Summit fever swept across the mountain; it was impossible not to catch it.

We didn't spend long at Base Camp—the weather and the summit rush made us too jumpy. Diana was still recording oxometer readings in the 50s and was still obstinate. The rest of us were reasonably healthy and solidly acclimatized. The variables seemed aligned. So we prepared our packs for a trip to the summit, and Namgyal baked us a cake. He wrote on the top, in icing fashioned from vanilla-flavored Gu, GOOD LUCK CLIMB.

Back we trudged across the glacier. Back up Hell Hill, back to Camp I. From here, the ascent became more serious; we changed into plastic boots and crampons and swapped hiking poles for ice axes. The route took us along a steep, narrow rib, with a scary drop-off on both sides. Sherpas from several expeditions had worked together to string thousands of feet of rope along the rib, anchoring the lines in place with ice screws. We each clipped into the rope with a carabiner attached to our harness; if we slipped over the edge it'd be unpleasant, no question, but likely not fatal.

We passed 21,000 feet, then 22,000. "Thin air," I realized, seemed exactly the wrong term; if anything, the air felt absurdly overweight. It was as though I had to physically shove the air out of my way, as if trying to move through a crowded bar. My heart slapped in my chest at a lunatic beat. The strain of the climb and the heat radiating off the snow had me down to my T-shirt. I could never quite catch my breath. A friend had once told me that a good way to train for altitude is to jog with a plastic bag tied loosely over your head. I ignored him then, but I have to say now that he may have been right.

On the standard route up Cho Oyu, there is really only one section that demands technical climbing skills, and we'd finally reached it. The obstacle is a wall of ice that looks somewhat like a life-size sculpture of a cresting tsunami. There was a rope in place, but it was badly frayed and dubiously anchored—nothing you wanted to entrust your life to. This was not a good spot to fall.

The climb was magnificent. I kicked steps; I hacked grips; I cursed audibly. I moved up the wall, affixed to Earth only by the tines of my crampons and the pick of my ax. The ice was tinted a perfect iridescent blue that I could imagine being painted on the walls of heaven.

I made it to the top of the wall, and Diana did, too. We all did. For the first time since we'd arrived, I truly thought we would all reach the summit. I envisioned, vividly, Diana and me embracing at the top, the first brother-sister team ever to do so. We strode into Camp II with the confidence of veterans.

Camp II on Cho Oyu is 23,400 feet above sea level. It's just a field of snow speckled with a few dozen tents. Facing west, I could see an ocean of mountains; north, the brown-green carpet of the Tibetan Plateau. I could view another 8,000-meter peak, the three-headed Shisha Pangma, but I could not see Everest. On Cho Oyu's standard route, you can't see Everest until you are a few feet shy of the summit. I'd never seen Mount Everest; the idea of a glimpse of it nearly eye to eye was, for me, one of the enticements of the climb.

At Camp II, where we rested for two nights, we saw climbers from other teams returning from their summit attempts—some who'd made it, others who hadn't. It was largely a parade of horrors. Even the healthy and strong had faces damaged by windburn and sunburn and frostbite. One of the members of the Norwegian team was forced to turn back because of retinal hemorrhages—bleeding behind his eyes. Hibi, the Japanese grandmother, made it to the summit, but on the descent she could stagger forward only with the aid of two Sherpas and an oxygen mask. Bold, who had sold all his belongings to fund the climb, did indeed become the first Mongolian to reach 8,000 meters, but he encountered a windstorm a few hundred feet shy of the top and was forced to turn back. Pino, the Italian summit golfer, did not, alas, manage to drive a ball off the top (though he did drive one from Camp II, the highest point he reached). Several of the Koreans were successful, though on the way down one could walk only a few shaky steps between collapses.

Ginella, a climber from Sweden, apparently suffered a stroke on the way up—she was blind in her right eye, had no use of her right arm, and could not speak. She was carried down on a makeshift litter. Marcel, from the German-Swiss expedition, was found a thousand feet from the summit, lying fetal in the snow. He was blind; blood was pouring from his nose; his left leg wasn't functioning; he had lost his gloves. The middle finger of his right hand had turned the color of a rotten banana. During his rescue, he kept asking why everyone was carrying fishing equipment.

While we waited at Camp II, our own health started to disintegrate. Our stomachs went sour, our throats turned raw, our heads throbbed. Even Pasang, our seemingly invincible climbing assistant, was fighting a cold. I began to cough up flecks of dried blood—my sinus glands, said Jamie, were probably bleeding.

We became moody and short-tempered; any semblance of team unity appeared to collapse. Little things began pissing me off—the know-it-all tone in Jamie's voice, the sound of Beth blowing her nose. We could hardly eat: Diana could stomach only peanut butter; Beth could eat only tuna; I could take only ramen noodles; Ben was limited to Pringles and dips of chewing tobacco. Everything else seemed to make us queasy. Ben's supper bowl, which he hadn't cleaned in weeks, made me nauseous; Beth's tuna made me nauseous; the smell of my long johns made me nauseous.

At night everything was worse. Nighttime high on a mountain is a 12-hour survival test. You can't go outside for more than a minute without feeling a full-body chill. There's little to distract you from your ailments. I kept dreaming I was drowning; I woke repeatedly, frightened and gasping for breath. My headaches escalated from the pinprick kind to the vice-grip to the boom-boom-boom. From surrounding tents came a chorus of hacking coughs, punctuated by an occasional arpeggio of vomiting. I kept a ZipLoc bag by my head in case my own stomach decided to follow suit. My flatulence was frequent and horrid. I swallowed a Pepto-Bismol, a Bayer, a Tylenol, a Cipro, a Diamox.

I shared a tent with Diana during our second night at Camp II. Ben needed a break, and I soon understood why. It was, to say the least, an upsetting night. My sister appeared to be fighting demons, tossing and turning and crying out—"Oh God, oh God, oh God, oh God." She alternately shivered and boiled, and when she woke, the look on her face—a pinched forehead, a sour grimace—was that of someone throttled with pain.

I didn't know what to do. I was panicked, but also helpless. I'd always thought of Diana as tireless and spirited and invincible. Now I was afraid that she'd suddenly stop breathing and not resume. So I stayed awake, making sure her sleeping bag rose and fell, and for most of the interminable night I couldn't shake the feeling that I was watching my sister slowly die.

And yet, in the morning, we continued up. Again it was Diana's decision to go, and again none of us argued with her. She was slow getting dressed, though, and I left before her, working my way up a steep, open bowl toward Camp III, just below a layer of crumbly rock known as the Yellow Band. The sun was up, the sky was clear, the night had been survived. We were nearing the top of the world. I could hear only the sound of my breathing and the crunch of my crampons. Snow sublimated out of the air, the flakes winking in the sun like spangles. My head floated in the strange, thought-free zone that often overtakes me when I'm climbing. The steady pace lubricated my legs and lifted my spirits, and I felt optimistic, once again, about our chances for success.

I was on a rest break, sitting on my pack, when it finally happened. I watched the whole thing from above. Later, Beth related what had occurred. Diana had left camp at a sluggish pace, repeatedly shaking her hands to combat the chill. Beth, hiking next to her, gave her a pair of overmittens, and the two continued on. But after a minute Diana was shaking her hands again.

"Hey, Di, are you OK?" Beth asked.

"I'm so cold, I'm so cold," Diana answered.

At this point Diana was hardly moving. Beth gave her an extra parka. She put it on, fumbling clumsily with the sleeves. Her eyes, Beth said, seemed unable to focus. Ben and Jamie and Pasang, who'd been the final group to exit camp, soon caught up with them.

"How do you feel?" Ben asked her.

"I feel cold; I just feel blah," she said.

The altitude sickness had finally caught up with her. There was little reaction. There were no tears. Diana just turned around and started back down. Ben, who told me later that he hadn't been having fun for weeks because of Diana's illness, went down with her. He sacrificed his own climb in order to minister to my sister. There, I thought, was the definition of love. Beth, Jamie, and Pasang continued up.

It took a while to register: My sister was no longer climbing. I watched her descend for several minutes; then I pushed myself to my feet, turned my back on her, and resumed my ascent. I wasn't sure how I felt. Upset, yes; disappointed, yes. But there was also something more sinister. Some part of me, I have to admit, felt strangely glad that Diana had turned back. It dawned on me that perhaps this wasn't completely a brother-and-sister climb but something of a brother-*versus*-sister climb. Maybe, in truth, my sister and I can push each other so well because we are actually the other's fiercest competitor.

I hiked to Camp III and waited for Beth and Jamie and Pasang. Our plan was to rest for a few hours and start for the summit a little after midnight. We lit a stove and melted snow for drinking water; we choked down a couple of energy bars. We didn't sleep, but we did lie still, which is as close to sleep as you can get at 24,600 feet. That night, though, the weather changed. The two-week window of beautiful conditions abruptly slammed shut.

It was a windstorm, and not just any wind—the jet stream was lashing against our tent. The violence of the gale was alarming. The tent poles creaked and bowed, and I could feel the wind beneath me, and I wondered if the tents would be ripped from their moorings and the lot of us blown away. It's happened before on 8,000-meter peaks.

I wanted to climb anyway. I didn't care about the danger. By this point I'd spent 27 days on Cho Oyu, and I was right there, just half a day from the top. My health, miraculously, had held up. I'd acclimatized well. I'd committed my money and my time and my utmost effort. But the weather variable was wrong. At that moment, I hated 8,000-meter peaks. I hated the whole expedition. Climbing a big mountain, I realized, is no way to seek clarity or improve a relationship. Rather, it seems to foster confusion and indecision. It breaks up teams; it harms friendships. It was, I decided, an extraordinarily selfish pursuit.

We retreated to Camp II, fighting our way through the storm. Beth and I dove into one tent, Jamie and Pasang into another. There was nothing to do. It was brutally cold. We just lay in the tent and stared at the ceiling. We stared so long that Beth eventually took a picture of it. We were now in whiteout conditions; the mountain seemed no longer to exist—my world was reduced to a tent shaking so violently in the wind it made me seasick.

I missed Diana. With her gone, the climb seemed pointless. She was at Advance Base Camp, safe and recovering—I could speak with her on our radio—while I was fighting illness and exposed to serious avalanche danger. I don't think I'd ever felt more distant from her. It dawned on me, as I stared at the ceiling, that I hardly knew who my sister was. Athleticism was our only argot, and it was a limited one. I'd been awed by Diana's achievements, by her talents, by her physical prowess. I felt like I knew *about* her, as with a celebrity, but didn't actually know her. We'd spent nearly a month together on Cho Oyu, but there were few moments, if any, of real bonding. This made me sad. It was then, in my tent, with the wind howling, that I thought: *I would really like to get to know her.*

In the post-monsoon season of 2001, 28 of the 35 teams that

attempted Cho Oyu placed at least one climber on the summit. Eighty-eight people reached the top. The Korean, Kim Su-Ya, was the only fatality. There still has never been a brother-sister team to climb an 8,000-meter peak. I waited at Camp II for three nights, until the storm finally broke and the sun reemerged. A few climbers began working their way back up the mountain, trying for the top, but I started down. I was headed all the way to Base Camp, so that I could say hello to my sister.

from No Visible Horizon
by Joshua Cooper Ramo

Journalist Joshua Cooper Ramo holds two U.S. airspeed records. This chapter from his 2003 book features Kirby Chambliss, one of the great aerobatic pilots.

Kirby Chambliss was thinking. There was a lot to think about. He paced the whole impossible act off in his head. For a moment he ran the flight down as if he were perusing a check-list: get in the airplane, jerk free of the runway, accelerate to 170 miles an hour or so, and fly through a hole in a cliff. You had to stop and scratch your head at that last item. *Fly through a hole in a cliff.* He could already hear the roar of the 150,000 Chinese who were gathered for the spectacle. They stretched from the runway here all the way out to the hole itself. Flying planes through cliffs was big news in China, a big act of faith. The Chinese called the hole Heaven's Gate, but it wasn't really much of a gate. It wasn't some thin two-dimensional thing you could just pop through, like the drill team at homecoming grin-popping through a piece of painted paper. No, the hole was a tunnel. A 150-foot-long rock tube screwed out of a ropy red sandstone cliff face by millennia of erosion. It was ninety feet wide at one point. Fifteen planes, flying through one after another. Fifteen accidents waiting to happen, one after another. Live on Chinese television. Heaven's gate? Maybe. Act of faith? For sure.

Kirby was standing on a hot, black-tarred runway about five miles from the hole. There was a dervish of a breeze, lightly tickling his brown-blond surfer's cut from every corner of the compass. He was a center of attention; the Chinese were riveted by him, a high priest of American aerobatics. Everything about him said it: the blond hair, the blue eyes, the aw-shucks gait that syncopated his spare six-foot frame as he paced around his plane. Kirby looked like he had just peeled himself off of some Southern California beach, kicked off his flip-flops, and slipped into a parachute. He was a fast pilot, he flew aerobatics with razored precision, but personally nothing keyed him up. He could sit in the plane and do extreme things because his mind was more or less beach-ready at any moment. You could almost hear him humming to himself as he flew. He was going to get bumped around on this flight, he knew. So what? The approach to the hole would be speckled with little eddies of air, invisible until they started juggling his 1,300-pound plane like a paint mixer. Kirby's plane was thirty feet from wingtip to wingtip. A bad bump could jam him into the rock before he had time to recover.

Then there were the Chinese. Jesus, they were everywhere. One hundred thousand at the airfield alone. Another 50,000 packed along the sides of the cliff near the hole, all fodder for a flying prop or crashing plane. The seating was strictly old-school Commie, with the most powerful officials jammed right up against the front of the hole smiling and chattering as they slurped down mao-tais from canteens. One small mistake, one unfortunate gust, and Kirby would smash right into them, using several dozen local apparatchiks to absorb the screaming shock of his plane. Kirby figured he'd walk away from any problem. But he didn't think he'd walk very far from that problem. Not with 150,000 (less a few dozen) pissed-off Chinese right there.

To be totally honest, Kirby *was* a little troubled. Not by the chance of a wreck, though. That was never enough to stop the humming. Not here, not back home in Arizona, not during the summer a few years back when a friend had been killed every single weekend, a year when he could almost set his watch by the bad-news Sunday night calls. You could burn yourself up with worry if you wanted. What was the point? No, what was itching at Kirby this morning was the problem of what the hell he was going to do *inside* the hole. It wasn't enough to take three weeks off from his job hauling tourists and businessmen and families and mail for an American airline to drag his ass all the way to China, just to fly straight-and-level through a hole. That was like trivial flight-instructor stuff to him, something a kid back in Phoenix might try in a Cessna after one too many Tecates. Kirby Chambliss was a high priest of aerobatic flight. His act-of-faith needed to be extraordinary. So, as he stood on the runway, staring through acrid smog in the general direction of the hole in the rock (it was over there, right?) what perplexed him was this: should he roll through the hole, cranking the plane around in an elegant twist as the rock spooled by all around him? Should he loop into the hole? Or what about a snap roll, a kind of super-violent horizontal spin? A normal human being, sitting in Kirby's brain watching these thoughts play out, might phrase the question as: how can I take something dangerous and make it into a fucking paragon of danger? How can I make the Chinese go home, look up danger in their little Red dictionaries, and see my face smiling back? This was going to be on live TV, right? Ten-million-plus Chinese watching? They needed to know what he knew. There was no better pilot.

What, he wondered, would Jurgis do?

Kirby looked over at Jurgis Kayris, standing near his Russian-built aerobatic plane. Jurgis was an aeronautical prodigy who had helped pencil out the design of the Sukhoi back when he was the top cock of the Soviet team. He was older now, past forty, and an even craftier stick. In Vilnius, Lithuania, one weekend he had flown his plane under ten bridges in a row. Upside down. It was a guerrilla prank; even the government didn't know it was coming. They had tried to act angry. The local police had fined him for "illegal advertising" since his plane was plastered with cigarette logos. But to bust him for the flying? No one would seriously consider it. Jurgis was a national treasure. People talked about him running for president some day. "Every pilot has his own personal limits," one European writer observed after the bridge stunt. "For Jurgis, flying inverted with his tail fin six inches off the water is his personal limit. 'I'm unable to go any lower,' he said." You could almost hear the smirk. But six inches really was Jurgis's limit. And Kirby's? Maybe six inches was too high? At competitions, awed pilots would point to the little marks running up along the tail of Chambliss's plane, places where he had scraped it against the runway pulling up into vertical maneuvers, they gossiped. The nicks said: "My personal limit is zero inches. I am unable to go any lower."

Lined up back along the runway were another dozen wide-winged, over-engined aerobatic planes, Russian-built Sukhois and Yaks, Czech-made Zlins, a German Extra, and Kirby's Edge 540. The names sounded great, little haiku of power and grace. Next to them all, pilots laughing and chattering in a half-dozen languages, all probably thinking along the same lines as Kirby. Roll? Snap? Loop? Zero-inch pilots one and all. But even here, even at the summit of competitive flying, there was a hierarchy, a constant compulsive contest to see who was the best. Just to get here you had to be willing to never back off the edge. The minute you did you became a Cessna driver, you gave up your claim to the brotherhood. But to stay on the edge? That was to hold on to what was magical about flight, to say something about man and machine, about fate and faith. Look at Martin Stahalik over there by his plane.

An absolute aerial genius, Picasso of the skies. An athletic six-footer with dark hair he brushed down in a Little Caesar cut, Stahalik was a past master of risk and recovery. Once, deep into a competition sequence, the prop on his plane had screamed right off the engine, snapped loose like a coffee-stick. (Imagine what those forces did to the man!) And as the prop tumbled to the ground below him, as his plane nearly shook itself apart, Stahalik shut down the engine, finished the figure, drove the plane back onto the runway and, incidentally, won the contest. He'd be dead a year after this China adventure, spun into the soft summer grass of an airfield near Amsterdam, the wrong side of the zero-inch limit.

This was standard aerobatics. Competence wasn't insurance against death. Kind of the opposite. The better you were, the more extreme your flying had to be. Getting better just gave you more chances to kill yourself. There was simply no way to avoid the math. It caught everyone eventually. One way or another you would have to look at an ultimate mistake from your cockpit. Just how costly that mistake was going to be, well, who knew? The sport was merciless that way. Take the first world-class U.S. aerobatic team, circa 1960: Hal Krier, Art Scholl, Bob Herendeen, Charlie Hillard. Some of the best pilots America had ever produced. Yeager-class pilots, men made to fly in the same way most people are made to eat and breathe. The kind of guys who could land propless planes too, just like Stahalik. Guys who grew up flying, who soloed planes when they were twelve, who amassed tens of thousands of hours of flight time. Would the flying take one or two of them in its random violence? Was 50 percent too much interest to ask for a life spent in the skies doing wonderful things? No. Airplanes killed every fucking one of them.

That was the price. Extreme flight was a way of life, in competition or airshows or even just flying in shitty weather, confident that you didn't need more than fifty feet of forward visibility to land safely . . . until some idiot strung a treetop-high power line across the road you were following. You couldn't escape it. You might try to be a reasonable pilot, to avoid the risks. But they would find you. Over some mountain, flying wingtip to wingtip with a friend on the way back from a competition. In clouds. Without instruments. The macho instinct was like anger. It surged in you. Later, after you landed, you might say, "What the fuck did I just do?" But you would do it again. It was, in truth, like being an addict. And it was wonderful, every second. Even the last one.

Competition aerobatics itself is a kind of aerial ice skating, with an international panel of judges who grade each figure. But this isn't ice skating, of course. When was the last time Kristy Yamaguchi burst into flames in the middle of a salchow? No one had ever been killed at a U.S. competition. Bailouts, sure. But no deaths in the United States. Thank God for that, the grandfathers of the sport, the old white-haired guys on the sidelines of competitions, would say to one another. A competition was just too intense to permit the kind of aerial fucking around that would kill you. You came to a competition to win, and that meant extreme caution even along the very edge of what was recoverable. The old white-haired guys at the contests held on to this as a proof of the sport's overall safety. Which would have been okay except for the fact that the old white-haired guys were *the survivors*. They collected dead friends the way most codgers collect golf tees. Between 600 and 800 pilots fly some kind of aerobatics during a year. In a bad year fifteen to twenty end up on the wrong side of the zero-inch limit. One in thirty, one in forty dead.

What was weird about the whole thing, what puzzled even the old guys, was that the sport seemed to be as hungry to kill good pilots as bad. Take the Unlimited jocks like Kirby. The name said it all: no limits. You did everything in a plane that was possible. To fly Unlimited Aerobatics you had to be so deeply familiar with your plane that everything seemed recoverable. Whoa! There goes the prop. No problem. It takes years to get that sort of control, to build the confidence that comes with it. And to hold on to that confidence as you hit the turbulence of dead friends and your own near misses? That doesn't take years. That is innate. You either do it or not. No sport on earth kills more of its participants. One minute you are waxing about the zero-inch limit. The next you are eating it. A medical or personal or mechanical fluff melts your illusions like a fog, and it does it all at once. Maybe one spark plug misfires at the top of a loop. At the wrong moment that can be enough. Between every flight in China, Martin Stahalik and his mechanic pulled every goddamned spark plug from his engine (eighteen of them), cleaned them like crown jewels on coronation day, and put them back in place. He was taking no chances, right? His plugs were probably spotless when he cratered in Amsterdam. On hangar walls around the

United States you'll find an old photo of a biplane that some pilot has smashed into a tree. It has this hortatory caption: "Aviation is not inherently dangerous. But to an even greater extent than the sea, it is terribly unforgiving of any carelessness, incapacity or neglect."

Kirby and the other aces were in China for a paid aerobatics competition. Someone, probably at China TV, had a thought: while the guys are here, why not run 'em through Heaven's Gate? The local aviation authorities loved the idea right away. Great for China, showing the whole country how advanced their aviation system was by, uh, having foreign pilots fly through a hole in a rock! Possibly some would crash. Still, good for China, right? Good TV, at least. Kirby thought this rattling love of spectacle was one of the great things about Asia. It resonated with his own love of a good show, his own itch to put one on for his audience. In the States, every time you wanted to go upside down in a plane you had to consider a phone book of FAA rules. The Feds specified how many degrees of wing-bank you were allowed before you were considered to be flying aerobatics, how far you could move the nose. It was like having your mom on board. But in Asia, local aviation authorities were just so fucking slack-jawed that anyone would do this shit that it never occurred to them to regulate it, to say nothing of stopping it. In Japan, Kirby had flown a whole routine pretty much on top of a crowd. Necks cracked back, several thousand Japanese had cheered as Kirby looped, rolled, and dove the plane right at them. "Aaah!" Kirby liked to say, imitating the way the Japanese had scurried away in horror from his descending plane. In the United States, the FAA set up designated "dead lines" at air shows well away from crowds. Fly over the dead line, lose your flight ticket. In the United States you could wait five years before the FAA cleared you across their paperwork river and into the Promised Land known as ground-level aerobatics. In Japan you could slink off a plane at Narita in the morning and be cranking ten g's over a Tokyo crowd by mid-afternoon.

What would Jurgis do? Kirby looked down the flight line. What

would they all do? There was Victor Chemal, surely among the best
pilots of them all, plotting out his routine. Victor looked as if he
belonged on a Hungarian postage stamp. Handsome, with a graying
pre-WWI mustache, he was known for a gambler's touch on the stick,
a willingness to wait until just the last moment before moving his
plane. Next to Victor was Boriak, the former Soviet champion, now in
his late forties. Boriak was engaged in a typical activity, banging his
Sukhoi back into working order. While most aerobatic planes are built
with the delicate precision of Formula One race cars, the Sukhois were
famous for being built by the Russians in the same way they built
tanks. "Ees traktor," Boriak would say as he worked the engine over.
With a hammer. He had been a test pilot on the Suk before he was
twenty-five. Someone had installed a camera in Sergei's cockpit here
and the pilots had already seen the TV images of handsome Sergei,
straining under high-g loads, pushing his cheeks out and knitting his
brow hard to hold the blood in his brain as he chunked the plane
through one tight figure after another. He looked like a monkey with
a headset. The monkey flew here representing Kazakhstan.

Kirby admired the Sukhoi as a plane, the way a Corvette owner
might see some good points about a Mustang. The Suk could climb
fast. But it was a pig, he thought, heavy and slow to roll. Kirby's plane
was an Edge 540, the best aerobatic plane ever made in the United
States. During the 1970s and 1980s the United States had produced
the finest aerobatic mounts in the world, little two-wing Pitts biplanes
made of wood and fabric. But in the early 1990s single-wing planes
made from extra-light and extra-strong composites began edging the
Pitts out of competitions. The new planes could handle higher g-loads
too, which ostensibly made them safer. In fact, pilots just took the new
g-limits as an excuse to fly harder. The judges loved the new, tight
flying. The Pitts became a relic, replaced by the French-made CAPs and
Russian Suks.

The first credible threat to European dominance was Kirby's Edge,
made of light carbon fiber and hung with a 300 horsepower engine
and a high-torque propeller. The plane was built around a wing that

allowed it to fly as well upside down as right side up, to roll at 540 degrees a second. It could climb at better than 5,000 feet per minute and could pull into a vertical line and fly straight up for 3,000 feet before tumbling away earthward, spent like a racehorse. That agility, with an admixture of pure speed, made the Edge ideal for aerobatics. Jet planes, moving at 300 or 400 miles an hour, take too much space in the sky for aerobatics. Planes like the Edge were a compromise, suited to maneuver in the 3,300-foot-square cube that marks the outline of an aerobatic "box."

There were an awful lot of curious Chinese around his plane, Kirby noticed. Some of them were taking notes. Well, hell, he thought, there wasn't too much for them to learn from looking. The Edge kept most of its secrets buried in the formulas that produced the composite parts and the mathematical models that explained the supercritical wing. There was no high-tech gear in the cockpit that was worth stealing. Who needed the extra weight? Gyros? Artificial horizons? Ten pounds! Pilots were dieting to boost their climb rates.

Heaven's Gate. A long way from home in Arizona, to be sure. Kirby still flew occasionally for the airline these days, when his schedule allowed it, but mostly his life was aerobatics. Though he was one of the company's most senior captains, there was no great seduction in the heavy metal of the Boeings. "Even if I won the lotto, I'd stick around," guys at work would say to each other, sitting up front in the planes with the autopilot on, reading *Yachting* or *Field and Stream* or some other magazine related to a hobby that made you fatter. They liked this life. "If I wanted to fly a seven-three-seven I'd buy one," Kirby said of his imagined post-lotto life. A 747? Fly for fourteen hours at a whack? *I don't think so.* Kirby's real flying was now done in seven-minute chunks, the seven hard minutes of an Unlimited aerobatic routine.

But the Boeings had brought good things to Kirby. The house in the desert an hour south of Phoenix. Two landing strips there and a private box marked out on the ground for Kirby to practice. The fabulous-looking wife, a stewardess. A swimming pool plunked down right under the aerobatic box so Kirby's flying buddies could soak while he twisted and pulled over their heads. And the Boeings brought a lifestyle that let Kirby take the time he needed to keep a fingertip feel for the airplane. Even a week away from the plane and it all felt different, rocky, not quite right.

Kirby had picked up the aerobatics as a result of his first big-time flying gig, driving a Cessna Citation jet for La Quinta Inns. His job was to ferry teams of accountants around on surprise audits to unsuspecting La Quinta managers. "Can we see your books please?" If you looked closely, you could see the managers begin to moisten. Kirby was the only copilot on a three-person flight staff. The captains split the duties three days and two. Kirby flew five. Whenever the plane moved, he was on it. He was twenty. The job had perks. Kirby could stay at any La Quinta, though he and the other pilots registered under fake names, since nervous managers had started distributing lists of the pilots' names as an audit early-warning system. If "Kirby Chambliss" had checked into a La Quinta in Omaha, La Quinta phones would be ringing as far away as Otumwa.

Another perk was the jet time. Kirby was putting about a hundred hours a month into his logbook, triple what he'd see in his airline job. That let him log enough jet time in two years to land the job flying heavy metal. He had selected the airline because it was one of only four that flew 737s, a plane with no flight-engineer position. FEs were the guys who sat *behind* the pilots and wrote down things like what the oil pressure was doing every five minutes. FEs sat in the cockpits of 747s, 727s, DC-10s, L-1011s for about three years before ever getting to so much as taxi a plane. The Boeing 737 had just two slots up front, both for pilots. Perfect for Kirby. No backseat for him. Everyone got laid, if you know what I mean.

Kirby's boss back at La Quinta was a guy named Jerry Anderson. Jerry decided that maybe it wasn't such a bad idea for his pilots to be upside down every now and then. So the company paid for five hours of aerobatics every year. Duane Cole, an American aerobatics legend, would haul down to San Antonio and teach them a few tricks in an old

Decathlon. Imagine finding your life's work in an immediate flash, like getting a mental telegram saying THIS IS WHAT YOU ARE TO DO. The first time Duane drove the little Decathlon wings past vertical, Kirby was done for. In a way it was the kind of distraction you didn't want. But you couldn't stop yourself. After he went to work at the airline, he was one excited dude. He was twenty-four, surrounded by beautiful flight attendants. (That was key because he'd been flying with guys for two years.) He had this super attitude for a pilot. His dream had come true. And then one day, driving back from the airport, his brain started up on him. "Now what?" He bought an aerobatic plane. Within a year the job became an inconvenience.

The pilots at work didn't want to talk much about the aerobatics. Chambliss was a check-airman, meaning he was responsible for giving proficiency checks to his fellow pilots every six months. Everyone at the line knew Kirby had won the 1998 U.S. National Aerobatic Championships. They knew he was among the best in the world. But there wasn't a lot of ass-slapping about the aerobatics. Didn't *everyone* want to fly aerobatics?

There are, Kirby was discovering, two kinds of guys—still just a few women—in the cockpits of those Boeings. Some of them loved everything about flight, dreamed of takeoffs when they went to bed at night, savored landings like wines. And then there were the bus drivers. There were other divisions too. The split, for instance, between civilian-trained pilots and the ex-military jocks. The civilian flyers, who had laddered their way up through flight schools and then jobs like the one Kirby had in his teens flying auto parts through Texas nights, tended to be more interested in aerobatics. The military guys rarely ventured past a macho nibble or two. "How many g's you pull?" they'd ask casually. And then they'd balk at the answer. "No way anyone pulls ten g's and walks away. And ten *negative* g's. Not happening." Negative g's were impossible in fighter jets, which require the constant force of gravity in order to keep fuel flowing. But it did happen. Every flight for Kirby. It was right there on his g-meter. Or it would have been on the g-meter if Kirby hadn't torn his out because after a while he decided he just didn't want to know how many g's he was pulling. Negative g's were what happened when you pushed the plane around instead of pulling, the force of gravity trying to throw you out of your seat instead of keeping you in it. With positive g's, the blood rushed from your head. With negative g's it rushed in, often painfully. The planes are designed for the stress. In Kirby's Edge, you could go from +10 to -10 for as long as your body could take it. After a good flight Kirby would step out of his plane covered in sweat, maybe shaking slightly, his eyes a little red. He could drop a dozen pounds in a hard week of training. After a good flight the military guys could get out of their F-16s and go home without a shower. No wonder they weren't interested.

Learning to fly aerobatics requires a walk away from the world of traditional flight training. The average flying student, soldiering toward a license in a Cessna, rarely sees anything that resembles aerobatics. The initial impression of aerobatics—scary and a little out of control—is enough to take it off the agendas of most flight schools. The retired schoolteachers who populate most flight schools, or the young kids trying to build hours toward an airline job, aren't inclined to risk their planes. I tried to get a dozen teachers to show me a spin when I was learning to fly. None would oblige. Wisely, I think now. They probably could not have reliably recovered.

There's a cost to this ignorance. It comes later, when a pilot suddenly finds himself upside down in the clouds or low-and-slow on final approach. Then the unfamiliarity with how the plane flies outside a limited envelope becomes fatal. Unusual Attitudes, as the FAA calls them, are ghoulish things. They strike at bad moments, by which I mean close to the ground. Their basic aerodynamics demand a different language of flight. The instincts that would save you in many situations can kill you in an unusual attitude. A Cessna pilot on final approach at a big airport slips in behind a 747 to land, for example. A wingtip vortex from the Boeing, essentially a whirlwind, grabs the tiny plane and snaps it over on its back. The vortex is twisting at about 300 degrees a second. The roll-rate on the small plane is about 100 degrees a second. It is badly outclassed. Now our pilot is upside down. His first instinct, as demonstrated to proficiency by many dead pilots, is to pull back on the stick, trying to bring the plane through a little half-loop. He pulls hard. But he never has enough altitude. As the ground rushes up, he pulls harder. Pieces of the plane, now breaking apart under the g-load, rain down like cracker crumbs. The pull is an instinct. Without training to do the right thing, to lean hard forward and force the plane to roll upright, it is a suicidal reaction.

Kirby had come to understand that every pilot has an envelope that describes what he's willing to do in a plane. And most pilots have a damn small envelope. There's nothing wrong with that, of course. But for pilots who have huge envelopes, the narrow envelopes are a puzzle. One aerobatic pilot, who makes his living at an airline, recalls a flight in his early days as a copilot with a captain whose envelope included about 5 degrees of wing bank. This made for some very weird flights. The captain was afraid of his plane. But that could kill you too. Motorcycle racers called it target-fixation. You stare at the thing you want to avoid and, inevitably, you crater right into it. One afternoon, as this captain brought a jet in for landing, his fear almost killed a whole planeful of folks. To slow down a passenger jet for landing, engineers have designed all kinds of stuff to throw into the airflow: flaps, spoilers, air brakes. But at slow speed all these devices can change the turn and roll characteristics of the plane. Beyond a certain angle of bank, the plane can accelerate its roll sharply. It's as if you were turning your car and when you cranked the steering wheel past 20 degrees it had a hundred times the effect. At several hundred miles an hour and just thousands of feet above the ground this kind of snatch can be dangerous. One day, at about 3,000 feet, with his aerobatic-trained copilot watching, Captain Terror gently banked his usual 5 degrees to line up with the runway. But because he had miscalculated for wind or something, he was turning too gently. Slowly he added more and more bank until, suddenly, the plane hit the roll acceleration point and began slipping through 20, 25, 30, 35 degrees of bank. Sitting in the left seat, where the captain always sits on airliners, he just froze as the wing started dropping earthward. He was so far outside his envelope he did not know what to do, even though all that was required was to simply turn the plane the opposite direction. It was like he had been dropped on Mars. Finally, he figured out what his amused copilot had been thinking all along: put in opposite controls.

Few pilots are born with perfect instincts. Kirby recalls going out in his pre-aerobatic days as a flight instructor and leading his students through stall sequences. Handled badly, a stall causes the wing of the plane to drop. Handled really badly that wing-drop can turn into a spin. *Jesus!* Kriby would think as the plane fell. *I have no idea how to get this airplane out of a spin.* Never push the rudder all the way in, he told himself. You didn't know what is going to happen.

Yet the more Kirby flew, the more he thought he did know what was going to happen. He could hear the plane. On good days, he could even tell by the sound of the wind going past the wings what was going to happen next. And so he started to develop a, well, what's the right word for it? Confidence? No, that's not quite solid enough. Kirby just started to know in every nerve that he wasn't going to crash his plane, at least not while he was able to control it. He was learning, especially from his mistakes. After nearly two decades of flying, Kirby thought you could freeze frame the plane at any moment and he could get from there to the ground safely. It wasn't arrogance—okay, maybe there was a little of that—but it was more like a kind of fusion of time and talent. I don't worry, he said like a mantra. His wife, Kellie? *She can't worry all the time, it gets tiring.* "That's not to say that I won't make a mistake. But I worry more about something breaking." It was like when they set off the atomic bomb in the New Mexican desert and the heat turned the sand to glass. The more Kirby flew the more the blaze of his confidence melted the sands of his doubts into something else altogether.

Once Kirby was practicing a routine that involved a rolling vertical climb, essentially a line straight up with lots of rolls as you go. In particular, this sequence required that he fly straight up and do a two-point roll, a roll that would stop after 180 degrees for a fraction of a second before continuing on to finish the complete 360 degrees. Kirby pulled hard to vertical. He jammed the stick left to start the roll. It snapped off in his hand.

"Fuuuuck."

"Well," he thought, "at least I'm going up." That was a good start. Flying the plane with the nub of the fractured stick, Kirby made it back to the ground. Sort of like driving a car with the parking brake, but no steering wheel. At 200 miles an hour. Kirby has also snapped the tail off of a biplane. He landed on a runway that just happened to be right below him. In 1998, he pulled so hard during the World Championships in France that he sheared clean through a three-quarter-inch steel tube in the front of his Edge. He landed fine that time too. "I've heard for years from people that I'm going to die in an airplane," Kirby said. *You know you can die tomorrow doing this,* he said to himself. "There is a sense that if you fly a certain way—aggressive—you're going to die. The guy I hear that about is a guy coming up right now, he flies aggressive. And low. And someone was saying he's going to die. And I said, 'Come on. We've heard that for years. They said it about me.' " A lot of times, Kirby thought, people said that because they didn't want to fly that way themselves. "They're going to have to," he said, "if they want to beat you."

"Is it that much more dangerous to fly aggressive? In 1992 I had twelve friends killed. It was like someone was dying every other weekend. And it was bad. People would ask me about it. I had a good buddy of mine who was killed right near my house, at Eloy airport, that year practicing. And people will go, 'Well you're better than they are.' And I say, 'No, you know what, in this sport you live and you learn or you die and you don't.' And there's plenty of times I probably should have died and I came out and I was just lucky enough and I just missed it."

The Chinese were waiting. Kirby strapped on his chute and climbed into his plane. He pushed forward the small lever that primed the engine and then hit the ignition, sending the prop spinning as the engine kicked to life. Kirby taxied his plane to the end of the runway and quickly checked the controls, putting the stick around all four corners to make sure there were no jams. He ran the engine up, moved the propeller control back and forth. The engine surged as he adjusted the blades. He stretched his head back and forth a half-dozen times to loosen up his neck muscles, which would contract under the high-g loads. Then he taxied into position, hit the power, and rolled down the runway and up into the sky.

The flight to the hole took one minute. As Kirby raced in he could see the thousands of faces below. He watched as a pilot zipped into the hole ahead of him, rolling the plane as he went. Okay, so that trick was out. Kirby shot up to the mouth of the hole, nearing 150 miles an hour. He leveled the plane off and steadied himself against the turbulence. Not as bad as he expected. He was in the hole in a second and, moments later, as he shot out the other end he yanked back hard on the stick and pulled up into a loop. Up and over the hole he arced, and then shot back right into the mouth of the damn thing. A loop! He could almost hear the glee of the Chinese as he screamed past again and pulled hard to get back into the hole, bouncing around a bit. As he pulled up again, a big California grin worked across Kirby's face. "Let them top that," he was thinking. "Let Jurgis fucking top that." But what was lurking in the back of Kirby's mind as he pulled away on that second loop was this: he had heard they might be invited back next year to fly under a 1,000-year-old bridge with twenty-three feet of water clearance. Could he loop that?

Kirby was going about 200 miles an hour when he hit the water. If you talked to the people who saw it they explained how the wings had come off first, turning the plane into a bullet, how the left wing had just barely touched the river and then the whole collection—plane, Kirby, water—had just become a blur of junk. It was as if you had taken reality and put it into a blender. There was just this kind of stew in front of your eyes. It was brown like the water, blue and white in places, like Kirby's plane. Right on the other side of the bridge, just opposite where Kirby had flown under. Nobody could see the pink that must be Kirby's body, but they figured that might be some kind of blessing. Maybe it was just over, over in a hurry for him. And, gosh, it *was* fast. Of course Kirby had always liked it like that: blazing. But this really was so speedy, it was so just gunshot-quick. That was what really stayed with people afterward, this parable of how our world can collide with our hopes and how it can do it so fast we don't have time to shout, or say a prayer, or say good-bye.

The amazing thing, and this really was amazing, was that Kirby was okay. The Chinese raced out to the plane, his fellow pilots raced out, all of them in a furious sprint-swim to the mess lying out there on the water. Blood streaming down his face, Kirby teetered out of the crumpled plane. The Chinese helped him onto a boat.

When he got home, Kirby found that his wife had had the engine taken off his plane. No more flying. But two months later he was back in the sky. Airshow season lingered ahead. It was a team selection year for the United States. He needed the practice. He needed the flying. Let Jurgis fucking top that.

from The Iron Road

by James Mawdsley

Englishman James Mawdsley in 1996 went to Burma to work against the country's military dictatorship. Mawdsley planned to get arrested to draw international attention to Burma's pro-democracy struggle. He recruited a man named Kublai to smuggle him into Moulmein, Burma's third-largest city. This selection finds him entering the city center.

I dug the cassette recorder out of my bag, switched it on, slung it over my shoulder with democratic songs blaring out, and took out a handful of stickers. The stickers showed a picture of Min Ko Naing and called for his release. His real name was Paw Oo Tun, but he had been given the legendary nom de guerre Min Ko Naing, meaning "conqueror of kings." He was a student leader, arrested on 23 March 1989 and sentenced to twenty years' solitary confinement for making "antigovernment" (i.e., prodemocracy) speeches.[*] He had won renown throughout the previous year for his fearless stand against the military. In public speeches to crowds of thousands he had said:

---

[*]His sentence was commuted to end by March 2000, but Min Ko Naing remains in prison today.

Our brothers in the past sacrificed to topple this military dictatorship but their demands were only met with violence, bullets and killing . . . We, the people of Burma, have had to live without human dignity for twenty-six years under an oppressive rule. We must end dictatorial rule in our country . . . If we want to enjoy the same rights as people in other countries we have to be disciplined, united and brave enough to stand up to dictators. Let's express our sufferings and demands. Nothing is going to stop us from achieving peace and justice in our country.

Today, more than twelve years later, he is still in solitary confinement. In his words:

I will never die. Physically I might be dead, but many more Min Ko Naings will appear to take my place. As you know, Min Ko Naing can only conquer a bad king. If the ruler is good, we will carry him on our shoulders.

The sticker I gave out also called for the release of all political prisoners and demanded that the universities be reopened (they had been closed for most of the past ten years) and the students be able to form a student union. One of the first things Ne Win had done in 1962 when he seized power was to dynamite the Student Union building, regardless of who might be inside, shoot dead an unknown number of protesters, and lock up thousands. Ne Win could not cope with any kind of dissent. Only once in his life did he give a press conference. A question came up that was not to his liking. The "president" then overturned his table, stormed out ranting, and never gave a press conference again.

At first I just dropped the stickers and cassettes on the floor, wanting to move quickly. If anyone wanted to pick them up they could. After a couple of minutes I began sticking them on lampposts, careful not to put them on the wall of a house or shop where the owner might be troubled for not immediately ripping them down. By the time I turned into the third street there was a crowd of delighted children skipping after me and begging for stickers. Rather missed the point, I thought, but I gave them a few, then decided I had to conserve the rest. Two disappointed children moped off, then started peeling the stickers down from lampposts behind me. "No, no!" I shouted. They ran away giggling. I arrived at the market and did a few laps of the ground floor, plastering every pillar with stickers and handing them to locals who caught my eye. Half an hour after I had begun I started to worry that I would not be arrested. I sat down, shattered, in the middle of the central courtyard, music still playing, and hollered a few things about freedom.

A large crowd was gathering but still no police. I spoke a little with the people around me and one man ran off to get me cigarettes and Sprite. I drank gratefully.

Then at last a grim character appeared. He looked dirty and exceedingly angry, dressed in plain clothes. I stood up. "Give me one!" he demanded, pointing to the stickers.

"Sorry, chief, I don't have enough left."

He scowled at me and immediately a gorgeous young woman appeared and put out her hand. She was so sweet, and determined to get a sticker. Young, fresh, playful, she was the antithesis of the obscene, joyless, and politically constipated regime which sought to dominate her. I quickly gave her a sticker and smiled unapologetically at the nark. He fumed off. Seconds later uniformed police arrived.

The police wanted me to come with them but I refused. They tried to get the cassette player but I held it at arm's length behind my back. We had a minute's fun like that, then I signaled them to relax. I brought the tape recorder forward, ejected the tape, then tossed it over the heads of the crowd. The police grabbed the machine and tried to grab me. Their anger was very much tempered by a feeling of helplessness. For five minutes I argued: "Am I being arrested? What am I being arrested for? What is the charge? What is the name of the arresting officer?"

"No, you are not arrested. Just come with us. Don't ask questions. You must come with us."

Every now and then a couple of thugs tried to push the crowd back. They would hit the front row fiercely and the crush would reel back on all sides, seeming to go almost horizontal, then immediately spring back into place. What they were witnessing was more than unusual. Several jaws were hanging slack.

At last the police had had enough. They manhandled me out. The second-story balcony of the market was ringed with "spectators." Altogether maybe three hundred people had witnessed it all. Just as I left I shouted out "Democracy!" at the top of my voice. I looked up and another girl caught my eye. She waved quickly, blushing and smiling. That really touched me. Just a small sign but it was confirmation enough that we were all on the same side.

Outside, I was surprised by the number of vans and motorbikes that were waiting, surrounded by milling police. I was directed to the back of a van and we were off.

As soon as the police van drove away from the central marketplace, the smile disappeared from my face. It was important to look cheery while hundreds of Burmese locals were watching, but now it was just the junta and me, and I did not feel brave at all. There were four officers in the back of the van with me. None of them seemed to know what to do. I tried to enjoy the views of Moulmein—the sun setting over the sea, the houses and hills, the few people on the quiet streets—but my mind was elsewhere. Soon we arrived at the police compound.

I was taken to a crumbling brick building, made up of only two small rooms, and told to sit at a table. The bare walls were as dirty as the concrete floor, the wooden desk clear except for a couple of pens. On the other side was the smuggest-looking weasel I have ever seen, with a weak chin and sharp face. He was Than Nyunt, the head of the Thaton division of the MI services, thin, thirty-five, and full of self-importance. About twenty other men were crowded around and outside the room. I was quite a novelty. Than Nyunt asked me who I was and I returned the question. He asked me where I was from and I told him "planet earth." He was not pleased.

One of the other officers had my kit bag. He emptied it contemptuously onto the filthy floor and he and several others began searching through my belongings. There was not much there. I had removed anything which might identify me, cutting the labels out of clothes and even throwing away a pen because it had "made in Australia" written on it. They were surprised to find no passport. They searched me and then became more excited by the absence of any documents.

"How did you get here?" asked Than Nyunt.

"Who are you?" I responded.

"I am police."

"Who made you a policeman?"

"?"

"Where do you get your authority?"

"I am police. You must answer my questions. What is your name and nationality?"

"Have I been arrested? On what charge have I been arrested?"

"No, you must answer my question. Where country are you from? You are American."

"Have I been arrested?"

"I think you American."

More and more men were coming and going. The atmosphere was uncertain but not yet threatening. I took out a cigarette and asked for a light. They let me smoke. I still had half a bottle of Sprite left and set about finishing it off, unsure of where my next drink might come from.

"Tell me your name," Than Nyunt repeated. He was laughing, nervously and angrily.

"I am under no obligation whatsoever to answer your questions. You are not a policeman. You work for anticonstitutional terrorists. I will answer any question put to me by a police officer who has been appointed by Burma's elected government, the NLD. I need to go to the toilet. Can I go to the toilet?"

I did not need to go, but I wanted to find out what rights I still had. They led me out to the extremely dilapidated toilet. There were about twenty other buildings in the compound, all one-story, getting more derelict toward the back. The toilet was filthy and the door would not shut. An officer was waiting outside and kept peering in to see if I was trying to dig an escape tunnel. He hurried me up.

Back in the interrogation room Than Nyunt carried on: "You are from South Africa, I know you are. Where is your passport? You are English."

"Let's talk about human rights. Your soldiers are murdering thousands of Karen civilians. They burn down villages. They tell everyone that they have five days or even five hours to get out of the village and then they burn it down. If people are too old or too sick to move out, they burn them alive in their homes. Soldiers push broken bottles into the vaginas of young girls—"

"You must answer my questions. I am policeman. Where your passport? Where you been staying? What guest house?" He was more confused than angry.

"You are not a policeman. You have not told me if I have been charged—"

Than Nyunt raised his hand above my head to hit me. "Answer!" he shouted. "Where you from?" I flinched, but he did not hit me. "You English. That is sure. You are an American. Where you from?"

"Let's talk about 1988. Thousands of civilians were shot by your regime. Housewives, nurses, schoolchildren, Buddhist monks bayoneted—"

"No! First you must to answer my questions!" His men were still bewildered, but he was beginning to get angry.

"No, 1988 happened before today, so let's deal with the first problem. Later we can talk about today. These were peaceful demonstrators—"

Than Nyunt grabbed a bottle and swung it down past my head as if to hit me. The bottle was plastic, which somewhat spoilt the intended effect.

"You are not a policeman. I have no obligation to answer your questions. I will answer an officer appointed by the NLD."

Than Nyunt gathered his patience. "Please tell me where you are from and how you arrived in Moulmein?"

"Do you mind if I smoke?"

"You can smoke."

"Very kind of you."

There was a pause to light the cigarette. Than Nyunt smiled. His men were searching my bag for the sixth time. They shook their heads—still nothing.

"Now, can you tell me to where you from and why have you cause disruption to our national peace and stability?" (His English was not very good but these were stock phrases from the regime's incessant propaganda.)

I smiled at him, then took a long drag on the cigarette, certain that soon I would not be allowed to smoke at all. "I will answer any question put to me by an officer who is appointed by Burma's elected government, the NLD—"

Than Nyunt shot to his feet. "Stand up!" he screamed, and for the third time drew back his hand as if to strike me. "You must obey. I am government. You are guilty one." He turned to his men and issued orders in Burmese. They surrounded me, told me to hand over my boots, belt, watch, and anything else I had on me. I was surprised that they had not done this straightaway. I had been grateful to have held on to my watch for that long. It was getting on toward about seven o'clock, which meant I had to hold out for another eighteen hours if I was to give Kublai enough time to get away; I reckoned a day's grace would be enough.

Than Nyunt stormed off and the room emptied after him, and my kit too was taken away. A couple of guards stood outside but otherwise I was alone. So far so good. I had enjoyed making the point that the National League for Democracy was sovereign, but I did not know how long the polite approach would last. I now had just my T-shirt and trousers. I sat there full of adrenaline and apprehension, but it was best to act unafraid. I put my head round the door and asked a guard for a smoke. He did not know what to do, but assumed that I would not have asked if it was not allowed. Should he hate me or be polite to me? He gave me a smoke.

Eventually the mob returned. This time a middle-aged, well-fed man sat opposite me. He was wearing very casual clothes. "Good evening."

"Good evening."

Pause.

"Will you tell me your name?" He was very friendly.

"Who are you?"

"I am an NLD sympathizer. I have just—"

"A what?"

"I am an NLD sympathizer. I have just come from the golf course." He beamed. His English accent was good. "Look, you can see that I have just come from the golf course." He waved his hand down his body to indicate the polo shirt and slacks. Certainly very casual, certainly fine golfing clothes, but was this supposed to turn me?

"What do you mean an NLD sympathizer?" I asked. "Do you agree that the National League for Democracy won the election in 1990?"

He smiled uncomfortably.

"Do you agree that they won eighty-two percent of the seats, that they are Burma's rightful government, and that since then the military junta have exiled, imprisoned, and murdered hundreds of Burma's elected representatives?" He reminded me of the "Indian businessman" brought in during my Rangoon interrogation: intelligent and civil, but utterly full of deceit.

"Look, I sympathize with the NLD. Many people do . . ."

"Are you a member of the NLD?"

"No, I am not a member. I am a sympathizer. I have just come from the golf course. I was playing a game of golf. They asked me to come and speak with you." He seemed very pleased that he was a golfer. Golf was the favorite game of the generals, to show how modern they were. "Where is your passport?"

"Do you sympathize with U Win Tin? He is an NLD member, has been in prison since 1989. He is an innocent man. He is now sick, very sick, but is being denied proper medical attention. He could die. Do you sympathize with him?"

The golfer looked at me sourly. We carried on like this for a while and then again the room emptied for a conference of war. The Sprite was finished. I smiled at the guards. They looked away. I sighed, smiled again, and they smiled back.

I wondered how long this would last. Yet another man came. He looked more unsure than the last, and a good deal uglier. He announced that he too was an NLD sympathizer.

"No you're not," I retorted. "I saw you in the next room ages ago. You're one of them." I hitched my thumb toward the bunch of police and other officials. I looked at him sternly but I was half bluffing, not sure if I had really seen him in the crowd. The bluff worked; he plodded out, looking foolish.

Next time the mob returned they were triumphant. "Stand up!" someone barked. "Hand behind your back!" I saw the handcuffs and my stomach churned. They were getting serious. The cuffs were put on painfully tight and I was led out to a cell in another building. There was a pithy sign above the cell door, for some reason in English. It said that the guilty man would burn whether he confessed or not and therefore he might as well confess. Strange.

Inside the cell there was nothing but a bamboo mat. I sat down on it and was relieved to see them all go. Would they leave me now? Of course not. Moments later they opened up the room again and half a dozen men poured in. I had already stood up, I felt too vulnerable on the ground. They told me to turn round and face the back wall. I did so and grew increasingly nervous. There was some activity behind me; one man had a stick. They were doing something, building something or maybe moving some equipment into the room. I could not tell what was going on, but it was accompanied by giggles and laughter.

Eventually they told me to turn round and I wondered what terrible instrument of torture would await me.

In fact, there was nothing. One man had a ruler and—wanting to measure my height—they had been marking off foot-long intervals on the wall. I suppose they started laughing when they got to five foot and then had to do another; Burmese, of course, are not generally so tall. The real fun would have begun when another wit suggested they mark off seven feet.

They worked out that I was six foot one and a bit, but before I could relax they produced a blindfold. That surprised me. Although extremely nervous, I was also curious to know what they would do. Ideally, they would sit me down with a judge and we could argue the toss about sovereignty. That would at least mean there was some sense in the regime; that they were willing to talk, if not to listen. But that was a far-off dream.

The blindfold smelt of petrol, which immediately saps your resolve. It was no longer a question of a dreamer wondering: Could I hold out under torture? Now there was a stark choice: Shall I tell them my name or risk having my face burnt off? I was led out to the front of the compound, sharp stones cutting my bare feet. There was a van with its engine running, and as I was bundled into the back I heard the voice of some Igor-type creature shout "Torture!" following it with a shamelessly melodramatic laugh, which began deep and ended hysterically. I tried to climb onto one of the benches, which I had felt down the side of the van, but was pushed to the cold metal floor. We set off into the night and I have never been so terrified in my life. There was no turning back. This bizarre situation was not a dream. It was real. And I had no one but myself to blame.

I prayed and prayed like a mantra, "Dear God, please be with me now. Dear Jesus, please help me now. Dear God, please be with me now." I wanted the journey to last forever, but it was over in no time. Still blindfolded, I was taken into another compound. As we got out there were lots of voices and footsteps. I was led into what felt like a huge building, but which I later discovered was the very poky reception area of Moulmein prison. We sat down in a side room and the blindfold was removed.

Old faces, new faces, too many for me to keep track of. A senior-looking man, who turned out to be the prison governor, asked me my name and nationality. I gave the usual response.

Then they brought out their trump card. He was an elderly gentleman, dressed in a *longyi* and collared check shirt, with very dark skin below his frizz of white hair. He was the best-spoken person I have ever heard. "Good evening to you," he said in perfect BBC English. "May I have the pleasure of knowing whom I am addressing?"

I fairly laughed. "Could you tell me who you are?" I inquired politely.

"Certainly," he answered with a smile. "My name is U Maung Maung. I am party secretary for the National League for Democracy in Mon State."

That was most unlikely. Not that I would have to answer his questions anyway; so long as I was taking the constitutional line I would say I was still waiting to meet a proper policeman or judge. But if somehow this chap really were NLD I did not want to offend him; indeed, I would want to worship him. So I dragged out the conversation a bit and the situation became clear. He was getting terribly confused between "them" and "us," did not know where he stood, and had absolutely no interest in anything except my name and nationality. He was working for the regime alone, so I told him I did not believe he was NLD.

They were getting increasingly exasperated but were obviously wary of physically hurting me. They would have no such doubts with a local, but interrogating a foreigner was uncharted territory. An official who makes a mistake in Burma is cruelly punished, unless, of course, he can pass the blame on to his underlings and cruelly punish them. Usually both things happen: a storm of rage from the top causes punishments to rain down right to the bottom of the hierarchy. They decided to give it one more try.

This time they brought a young man to me. He was dressed in a white *longyi* and shirt. This was a prisoner's uniform. As a nice touch he was also wearing handcuffs and I was told that he was NLD Youth and, yes, indeed, a prisoner. They seemed to have missed my point about introducing me to someone with authority from the sovereign government, but I was keen to learn as much as I could and to drag things out for as long as possible. It was now approaching nine in the evening. I had to give Kublai sixteen more hours.

I was immediately suspicious because this "prisoner" looked so clean and healthy. He was wearing immaculate clothes and the handcuffs on him were not tight like mine or fastened behind his back, but were two jolly dangling bracelets out front. Supposedly he could speak no English, so U Maung Maung translated with his usual eloquence.

The "prisoner" wanted to impress upon me that he had been foolish to believe in the NLD and that now he saw how the junta were truly the loving leaders of Burma. I asked him what subject he had studied at university. This shook him; he had certainly never been to university, but wanting to maintain his NLD Youth cover, he eventually said history. I thought of asking him a history question to see what he knew, but the syllabus in Burma had been destroyed and twisted by the regime. I asked him what university he had gone to. U Maung Maung had noticed his stumbling on the last question and, not realizing that I understood some Burmese, translated, "What university did you go to? Say Rangoon."

I clapped my hands in delight and told them they were all frauds. It might have been more professional to carry on talking, but I wanted to come across as a straightforward guy. The two sloped out and immediately I heard the handcuffs being removed and the "prisoner" launching into an excited jabbering about what had happened. His demeanor had changed completely; he was obviously talking to colleagues rather than to his gaolers. I could not believe they had even tried such feeble ruses, never mind having botched them so completely. Anyway, they were tired of it too. It was time for harsher methods.

The blindfold went back on. I was told to stand. I could hear them circling me and questions came intermittently from different directions, sometimes right in my ear, sometimes from far away; it was slightly disorientating. "What's your name?" "Where are you from?" "How did you get to Moulmein?" "Where is your passport?"

From now on I answered only, "I am sorry, I cannot answer that question." The British army recommends that you add "sir." The idea is to hold out for twenty-four hours so that the military situation on the ground has changed sufficiently and all information you have is out of date anyway. Although I was not a soldier and Kublai had asked me to give him just forty minutes to get away, I was determined to give him twenty-four hours.

One of the men had a towel, which he twisted into a rope and began flicking next to my cheeks. Then he hit me in the stomach with it and then the genitals. Blindfolded and with my hands behind my back, I felt totally vulnerable, at their mercy. I was not allowed to sit, nor to eat or drink. I was already exhausted from the two-week trek from the border. It did not take long before I began to get dizzy.

Whispered questions and accusations continued. "You are CIA," which surprised me. "You MI6." Did they really think that possible? "You CIA, I know you CIA." Later on it got even more ridiculous. "You KGB, Mossad. Sure, you are KGB." I laughed, but it was a real worry that they could be so stupid as even to think it.

Occasionally one of them would kick the back of my knees to see how weak my legs were. I would gladly have fallen over and pretended to lose consciousness, but I doubted they would stop there. Still not sure if they should hurt me, one of them found a cat and wiped its anus down my arm. This caused them great amusement. I told them to let the poor animal go. Each time the towel flicked into me my body jumped. I wondered what would happen if I fell and soon found out. Fists and feet came from everywhere and I was hauled back up. They were not vicious blows, but they were frightening.

One guard then took a pen and started probing with it between my knuckles. My whole body tensed since I knew what was coming. Torture does not require elaborate medieval apparatus. An accomplished torturer does not even need a pen. I squeezed my fists as tight as possible but eventually the pen was prized between two of my fingers. The guard gripped my fingers in his hand and began slowly to squeeze. I do not know how painful that sounds but the reality is excruciating. Your knuckles are in agony and certainly feel as if they soon must break. And when you are blindfolded you do not want to take one step from where you are, not knowing what will happen if you do. I was rooted to the spot.

As the pressure grew I began talking about why I had come, slamming the junta for human rights abuses and insisting that I was under no obligation to answer their questions. I began shouting louder and louder, and just as my fingers were about to break I hollered out at the top of my voice, "For justice and FREEDOM!" Suddenly the pain stopped. They had become nervous. I had probably woken up a quarter of Moulmein. The pen was removed.

Unable to stand any longer, I passed out. Kicks and punches woke me and again I was hauled to my feet. More blows to the genitals and the guard with the pen kept prodding it into my knuckles to remind me what he could do. He was enjoying it. Later he would just click the pen by my ears so that I could not forget it.

There were light moments. The blindfold kept slipping down. I could feel it loosening and would warn them that it was about to go. Strangely I felt sorry for them that they could not even get that right. Fortunately it meant that I was frequently able to look at the clock and so could focus on how long I had to last. Sometimes I would roll my head around as if in terrible distress but in fact I was glancing out of the bottom of the blindfold at the clock. I was hoping that the BBC had broadcast news of my arrest by now and that they could get my name that way. Then I could begin talking to them, having made a point of not volunteering my name.

Handcuffs make you feel defenseless. With your arms behind your back, every itch becomes a problem. You cannot scratch yourself, you cannot wipe your runny nose, you cannot wipe the sweat from your brow. Not at all brutal, but distressing; you feel helpless.

The night wore on and I passed out again. The next thing I

remember is sitting cross-legged. Again I could just see straight down below the blindfold. There was a huge cockroach on my leg. This was a cause of much merriment for the one who had put it there. He was trying to urge it up my trouser leg. I wondered if I should shake it off, but then they would know I could see. In any case it flew away.

I asked for water and they refused. I was not allowed to go to the toilet. Then began the "iron road." This is a favorite tactic of Burma's MI. The victim sits or lies with his legs straight out and an iron or bamboo rod is rolled up and down the shins with increasing pressure. Done long enough, it will strip you to the bone. In my case a senior officer must have signaled them to stop before it went too far. After that they tickled my feet for half an hour. I could not believe it. Here was the brutal and heartless Military Intelligence torturing their victim . . . by tickling his feet. But as the idea was sleep deprivation it was completely effective. My left foot was being held down and tickled, my right foot was being stabbed with a bamboo cane.

I asked again for water and this time a cup was brought to my lips. I sucked at it greedily but they would not tilt it back, I was gulping only air. Ever so slowly they tilted it back and I sucked away until it was horizontal—still no water. This was just their little joke.

When you are being tortured it is not so much the pain that beats you as your own fear. I was uncomfortable and exhausted but only rarely in pain, and then not often excruciating. But I began to wonder: What if they extinguish a cigarette on me? I could bear it on my body. But in my ear? On my eye? What if they spread my legs and one of them grinds a testicle under his heel? What if they make me squat naked and light a candle under my scrotum? Surely it was not worth keeping back my name in the face of that—after all, the BBC was bound (I prayed) to be broadcasting it soon anyway?

But I did not want to give in. I really wanted to make the point to them that they had no authority, that the junta were illegal and that no one on earth has the right to torture another.

I do not remember how often I passed out. One time I was kneeling down and asked for a cigarette. It was nearly morning and to my great surprise a cigarette was placed between my lips. My heart leapt as I thought they were changing tack again. Perhaps someone in Rangoon had ordered a softer approach. I waited for a few moments until it dawned on me—no light. I considered eating the cigarette just to annoy them, but spat it out instead.

The next thing I remember is waking up in another room. I had insisted on being allowed to go to the toilet and I thought to myself that perhaps this was where I had been taken next. In the toilet there was no water or paper to clean oneself—with pretty unpleasant conse-quences for one's clothes. I was lying on the floor covered in sweat and grime, my trousers soiled with blood and shit. I felt utterly awful. As I opened my eyes I saw two men looking down on me. They were in civilian clothes, MI officers, probably sergeants. As they caught my eye I was filled with dread. I so much wanted to sleep and now I had let them know I was awake. But they did nothing. They let me close my eyes again. They let me sleep awhile.

But I had to get up before the sun and was again made to stand up, although there was no strength left in me. I wondered if it would really hurt for me to tell them my name and nationality. A soldier should give name, rank, and number, but again, I was not a soldier, I was trying to make a political point.

How does torture work? It is not all brutality and pain. Half the task of a torturer is to make you feel irrational for holding out. And sure enough, when you are thoroughly exhausted and desperate for food or sleep, it is hard to think clearly. Sometimes they would sigh and pout, bring in a reasonable fellow who said that all they wanted was my name and nationality, and then they would give me all the food and sleep I wanted. They complain that you are making their lives difficult, that they are tired too, that they have wives and children to go back to.

It was approaching midday. Since dawn they had not really hurt me. They seemed content to just let me stand there, handcuffed and blind-folded. Probably I spent a lot of time sitting down as well. The situa-tion began to seem silly. I began to feel silly too. I was wiped out, I felt alone. Had news got out to the outside world? Did the British embassy know about my arrest yet? How long would it be before they put someone more cultivated than Than Nyunt in charge?

If I could wait just two more hours I would have given Kublai his time. I would be disappointed that I had had to back down on my principle of not giving my name. I would have preferred for them to get it from the media like last time and then I would have said, "OK, let's talk." After all, we had much to talk about and I could not argue the case for democracy with my mouth shut. But my principle now seemed irrelevant and petty. I just wanted something to drink, somewhere to sleep. I could start talking now and easily delay two hours before mentioning how I had got to Moulmein. That was my way out. I began to cry, only for about one or two minutes, but the kind of tears you just cannot stop or control.

I would tell them my name, I said, I would tell them my nationality, if only they would promise that I could then immediately contact my embassy in Rangoon. Certainly, they said. I asked again and again for confirmation. It came from the top. Of course I could talk to my embassy, only first tell them . . .

"James Mawdsley, dual citizenship, Britain and Australia."

Everyone sighed.

Man-Eaters

by Robert Frump

Many refugees who have fled Mozambique during recent years have tried to enter neighboring South Africa through that country's Kruger National Park. The park contains 2,000 lions. Robert Frump wrote this report for Men's Journal.

Neville Edwards was having a bad day in the bushveld. The 40-year-old ranger was escorting two clients on a safari through South Africa's Kruger National Park, in the heart of lion country, in July 2000. The two French corporate VIPs on the seat next to him were out to see their fellow carnivores, but Edwards hadn't been able to show them so much as a rodent.

Finally, he found a herd of elephants and steered his Land Rover within throwing distance. While the VIPs pointed at a magnificent bull ambling across the grand vista, Edwards stayed alert. Elephants usually put on a good show, and the bull was indeed flapping his ears and kicking up dirt. If Edwards got lucky, a mock charge would follow. A good trumpeting always gets the adrenaline flowing.

But Edwards was a consummate pro, with 20 years in the bush, and he kept the Landie jammed in reverse, with one foot on the depressed clutch, just in case the bull actually charged. Instinctively, he scanned the bush around him, snapping back to the elephants at any sign of motion. Thanks to nine decades of conservation management, Kruger, a park the size of Massachusetts in the northeast corner of South Africa, hard against the border of Mozambique, had been transformed into the "Eden of Africa." Each year, a million visitors came to Kruger on safaris to see elephants, zebras, kudu, and herds of lithe, model-thin impala. But most of all, they came to see lions, and it's a basic truth of the bush that what you're looking for often comes from where you aren't looking.

On a slow sweep behind him, Edwards saw a hand rise up from the bush and wave a casual good morning. He snapped back to the elephants, then to the hand. With an odd tremble, it seemed to beckon him forward. Warily, he raised his binoculars to see what the person wanted. He knew there were more than 2,000 lions in the bush, and no one should've been out there on foot. As he got his binoculars focused, a black-backed jackal popped crisply into view. The scavenger was biting and tearing at the body attached to the arm, which danced above, still waving. Then the jackal changed its grip. A human head flopped into view and fell, flopped and fell, impossibly relaxed.

There was a brief moment when lucid thoughts crossed Edwards's mind. A woman's hand, he thought, as the fingers were slender. Probably a refugee from Mozambique. He'd heard stories about them walking across Kruger and falling prey to lions, but he'd never seen any proof until now. The poor woman hadn't been killed very long ago, since her body was still flexible. However many lions had attacked her, they couldn't be far away. They had probably just let the jackal in to clean up.

Then Edwards lost it. The jackal was gulping, as jackals do, gorging all it could in case the lions returned. Edwards fumbled for the radio and keyed the mike. He started to yell to base camp in English, "I need help!"—then thought better of it in case the French might understand. They had not seen the body, and they didn't need to. He switched to Zulu: "Ifuna siza! Ifuna siza!" Then, to the amazement and protest of his clients, he sped away from the only game they would see that day.

Edwards didn't care. At that moment, he and the VIPs were no longer the alpha predators. In the middle of Africa's greatest feat of conservation, humans themselves had become prey.

For more than a century, refugees from Mozambique have illegally crossed the area that is now Kruger National Park in great numbers. For food, for family, for a future, they came first to work in the gold mines and on the farms across the South African border, then to flee Mozambique's war of liberation from Portugal, an ensuing civil war, and a series of floods and droughts. "Going west to Joni" was the way the refugees put it, to Johannesburg, to safety, and to economic promise.

Crossing into the park wasn't always easy. Until the end of apartheid, in the 1990s, the fence along Kruger's eastern border with Mozambique carried a lethal 3,000-volt charge to keep poachers and illegal migrants at bay. But desperation always finds a way, and refugees learned to short out the fence or go through gaps cut by poachers. In the southern part of the park, they walked on the little-traveled roads along the Crocodile River. In the middle section, they cut right through the bush near the campsite of Satara. And in the north, near Punda Maria, the habit was to follow a series of power lines that snaked across the wilderness, resting by day in remote bush country and walking the lines at night to avoid border patrols.

Some walked west on their own, often carrying *muti*, a magic totem such as a hyena's tail, bought from traditional healers. Muti was guaranteed to repel lions, though it was difficult for consumers to collect on the warranty when the totem malfunctioned. Other refugees hired guides, who escorted groups of 20 to 30 at a time across the park. But that method also lacked assurances. If you became sick, if you were carrying a baby, or if you were old and couldn't keep up, you were likely to be left behind. Soon after the heaviest migrations began, park rangers and guides and poacher patrols began to find tattered bits of clothing. Sometimes a shoe, a wallet with Mozambican currency, a lone suitcase, perhaps some blood, and sometimes the human corpse left from a kill.

When a crossing was done successfully, it was done as John Khoza did it. Khoza grew up in a family of herders in a small Mozambican village. His father owned many cattle. Disease—Khoza does not know which—claimed his mother when he was ten and his father when he was 15. Although they were orphans, he and his older brother would have been affluent by Mozambican standards, but the cattle were passed on to their uncle. Khoza would herd all day, and at night there would be only a bowl of cornmeal to eat. Malnourished and futureless, he and two friends, also herders, decided to cross "the Kruger," as they called it with awe and respect.

Khoza was lucky to know a guide who could take them. He was luckier still to be a herder, since he'd come in contact with lions and knew never to threaten or run away from one. So at 2 a.m. on a July night in 1972, Khoza and his small party found where a wart hog had burrowed under the fence at Kruger's border. They wriggled under and set out across the southern end of the park. "You do not take food; you only worry about water," Khoza says. "You do not take a gun, or they will arrest you as a poacher. You do not take clothes or worry about what you will wear. You are starving. You move with purpose through the bush. You stay off the roads and away from the helicopters, the rangers on bicycles, the army patrols, and the tourists." When they came upon elephants or dangerous cape buffalo, they moved cautiously and—ever the herdsmen—threw rocks at the animals to move them along.

Then the lions found them. "I froze." Khoza says. "We all did. I faced the lion in front of me, but I knew there were at least two or three to the rear. Always, there are lions to the rear. We were absolutely still. Ten minutes passed. Fifteen minutes passed. Then we did not count the time." Eventually, seeing no obvious vulnerabilities, the lions moved on to easier prey.

This scene was repeated four times that first night. During the day, they hid and rested under trees. The next night, they moved again, and again the lions found them several times along the way. But the herdsmen always stood firm, careful not to incite an attack. After two days and nights in the park, halfway across it, they turned south to the Crocodile River and swam their way into South Africa. Khoza is now a legal resident and the father of six. He drives a four-wheel-drive truck to and from his job at a game lodge and is wealthy beyond the means of the average Mozambican. But he no longer walks at night.

Success stories like Khoza's enticed even more refugees to cross the border. From 1987 through 1992, when the civil war was at its most brutal, between 250,000 and 500,000 refugees fled to South Africa, most of them through Kruger. Today, ten years after the war's end, they continue to flee, driven toward promise and away from some of the worst human conditions on the globe. Mozambique is the world's poorest nation. Its citizens have an annual per capita income of about $220. They live on average only until age 43, succumbing to violence, starvation, drought, floods, and disease. Mozambique is the only country to sport an AK-47 on its national flag. A land mine might be just as appropriate, since almost two million of them are scattered throughout the countryside.

It was under those circumstances that Johanna Nkuna and her three daughters set out one day, in July 1998, from the small Mozambican village of Shikwalakwala and slipped through the fence into Kruger. They planned to walk to Soweto, where an uncle lived. They would rest in remote bush country during the day, and at night they'd follow the power lines that would take them west.

Nkuna and her girls fared well for most of the trip, but in the bush near Punda Maria, a large, fenced-in camp in the north of Kruger, they heard noises and growls coming from the bush. A pride was hunting. The lions advanced, snarling at the girls, heading instinctively toward the young, testing for vulnerability. Nkuna didn't know the importance of making a stand. She charged the lions, yelling and waving her hands, and the pride took her.

The sacrifice gave her children a chance. They scattered, running for their lives in three directions. The two older girls eventually turned east, following the lines back home. Eleven-year-old Emelda ducked into a small hole in a large termite mound, where she huddled up for the night, listening to her mother's screams, the lions' snarls and growls, and then the more horrible quiet.

The next day, she crept out to find her mother's mostly eaten corpse. She walked aimlessly down a road, in shock. As a safari vehicle with tourists and a ranger pulled even with her, she neither acknowledged them nor fled nor stopped walking. "What are you doing alone in the park?" a ranger asked in the Xitsonga language as they crept along. And slowly the story came out.

No one knows for sure how many refugees make it safely across Kruger, as John Khoza did, or how many, like Johanna Nkuna, fall prey to lions. No records are kept, and no single entity is in charge of keeping count—not the South African or Mozambican governments, not the Kruger police, not the park rangers—and none of them seem anxious to be in charge. Tourism is the number one industry in this part of Africa, and no one wants to scare the customers away. Not that man-eating lions are necessarily bad for business: A well-known private game camp lost a careless tourist to a lion a few years back and feared a slump in clients. Business boomed instead. "People wanted to know the place was real," says Steve Gibson, a guide and the owner of Esseness Safaris, another camp. "It gave the place an authentic feel."

But as refugees continue to migrate through Kruger, ominous evidence continues to accumulate. In March 2002, a lion killed an illegal immigrant from Mozambique just outside Kruger and carried the body through the town of Phalaborwa on a Saturday night. Dr. Willem Gertenbach, the head of all conservation efforts within Kruger, says that only one or two bodies are found each year, but that the number of deaths is almost certainly much higher than that. Shoes, suitcases, and torn pieces of clothing are found on a regular basis, with no explanations and no bodies. "Some people say, Well, perhaps they were scared and dropped these things," says Albert Machaba, the head ranger in Kruger's Satara area. "But how do you drop clothes that are tattered and torn like that? What refugee would leave his shoes? No, I don't think that is what is happening."

What *is* known is that roughly 4,000 refugees are caught each year by 220 Kruger rangers and about 600 South African Army border patrolmen, who operate during the day. At night, when the immigrants are on the move, the officials retreat to fenced-in camps. If they catch 4,000 refugees per year, how many must the lions—on the hunt when the refugees are on the move—catch? To kill 100 humans per year, the Kruger lions would have to catch only 2.5 percent of what the rangers and patrolmen do—a figure that Gerrie Camacho, a scientist and lion advocate in the Mpumalanga province, near Kruger, agrees is reasonable, if not conservative. Since 1972, that would be 3,000 humans killed and consumed by lions. The probability is that this number is low, that the 820 rangers and soldiers, even with the advantage of having jeeps, airplanes, and radios, would not catch 40 times more refugees than the 2,000 lions.

The celebrated Ghosts of Tsavo, two maneless lions that brought a British bridge-construction project to a halt for months, were responsible for killing 130 people at the turn of the last century. A more obscure but far deadlier pride in southern Tanzania killed 1,500 between 1932 and 1947—considered the "all-Africa record," as one writer phrased it. Even without precise statistics, the carnage caused in Kruger makes the kills by the lions of Tsavo and the lions of Tanzania look small, and it qualifies the "Eden of Africa" as the home of the largest lion kill of humans in history.

The only good thing about being eaten by a lion is that it apparently doesn't hurt very much. Dr. David Livingstone, the explorer and missionary, was seized in 1844 by a lion and later wrote, "Growling horribly close to my ear, he shook me as a terrier dog does a rat. It caused a sort of dreaminess in which there was no sense of pain, nor feeling of terror, though I was quite conscious of all that was happening. It was like what patients partially under the influence of chloroform describe in that they see the operation but do not feel the knife. This placidity is probably produced in all animals killed by the carnivora; and if so, is a merciful provision of the Creator for lessening the pain of death."

"That's absolutely right," says Gerrie Camacho. "You do feel everything. It is as if you have been seized by a vise. Such strength! You know you are powerless against it. You feel your muscle ripping and tearing. You feel your meat separate from the bone. You *feel* all that, but you do not feel pain or even really care. You are in a dream state, not unpleasant at all." He speaks from experience, and it gives him a unique perspective on exactly what is going on in Kruger. In 1988, Camacho and other conservationists were attempting to tranquilize and treat a pregnant lioness that seemed to have an infection. They lured her into a large fenced-in area just outside Kruger, but the pride followed, making it impossible to treat her. One day, the pride left the area, leaving the sick lioness and one young male alone within the fences. Camacho and Johan Vander Walt, a colleague, rushed to the area. Vander Walt parked their Land Rover in front of the entrance to keep the pride from reentering. Camacho ran to the lioness, thinking he'd simply scare away the male. Young males are skittish, and when Camacho began yelling and flapping his arms, the lion rushed toward a hole in the fence to rejoin the pride.

But something made him turn. Perhaps he lost sight of the fence gap. Perhaps it was the Land Rover. His escape seemingly blocked, he wheeled and charged back at Camacho. Hoping it was a mock charge, Camacho, who is six feet four, made his stand. He "looked large," hooting and waving his arms above his head. But this was no mock charge, and the lion hit Camacho head-on, knocking him backward as if he were a beer can struck by a flying anvil.

Fortunately, Camacho was thrown up against a tree and remained standing. Had he gone down, he almost certainly would have been killed. The lion seized Camacho's right calf, which he held in his teeth while raking Camacho's upper body with his box-cutter-like claws. When the lion tried to move his grip up for the kill, Camacho began pummeling his eyes with big roundhouse lefts and rights. "It was the only soft spot I could reach," he says. The lion's odor—a sweet and powerful mix of urine and excrement—engulfed him.

Vander Walt watched in horror but was more alarmed when the

pride, hearing the sounds of the attack, began streaming toward the hole in the fence. Vander Walt knew that if they got back in, they would make short work of Camacho. Normally, there would have been a rifle clipped to the dash of the Land Rover, and Camacho sometimes carried a .375 Magnum on his belt. But they had hurried here to seize their chance to isolate the lioness; both the rifle and Camacho's revolver were back at the camp. Vander Walt desperately searched the Landie and came up with a tire iron.

He ran toward the fence, waving it at the pride, making as much noise as he could. The lions, confused and stymied, retreated. Vander Walt then ran to Camacho, yelling and swinging the tire iron wildly. Camacho was still punching the lion frantically. In the end, it was all too much for the young male: the blows to the eyes, the madman with the tire iron, the retreating pride. He let go of Camacho and lit out for the hole, and it was over.

Camacho needed 64 stitches to his calf, upper leg, and arm. After spending several weeks in rehab, he was back in the field, searching for lions—but not vengeance. "In no way could that lion be held at fault," he says. "I was stupid. I caused the attack." Camacho's opinions carry a lot of weight in the region, in part because of the scars he bears from the attack and in part because he's spent ten years reinstating lions into wild areas of South Africa. He's a scientist who knows firsthand the dangers of the bush, and he contends that when lions kill humans in Kruger, they are merely doing what comes naturally.

"What you are saying about the lions and refugees is true, but you must not be sensational and call them man-eaters, or suggest that they have a taste for human flesh," he says. "Man-eaters should be individuals or prides that specialize in hunting humans as prey and that focus on any humans, even those within the safety of the camps. The lions in Kruger do not set out to kill humans. They are opportunists."

It is crucial, Camacho says, to understand that the lion is two animals. Man is diurnal, and the tourists who drive through Kruger on safaris see the lion in its passive daytime mode. At night, however, when refugees walk west through Kruger, the lion becomes a fearsome carnivore that roams the bush in highly organized hunting parties, looking for protein: "If a large group of vulnerable refugees comes predictably through every night, the lions will see that there is easy prey, and they will kill it, and this will stay in their memory."

When around lions, "you are always on a thin edge," Camacho says. But there are two conditions in which humans are likely to become lion prey. The first is when they intrude in the "comfort zone" of the lion. Even a passive daytime tabby will attack if someone in Kruger is foolish enough to leave the Land Rover and stick a camera in its face. Like Hannibal Lecter, lions tend to eat the rude. The second condition is when human behavior "triggers" the lion to attack. These triggers are hard-wired into the lion psyche, and, like kittens to a dangled string, they respond aggressively to certain signals—crying, running, revealing any sign of weakness. "I was in a Land Rover one day just a meter away from a very placid lioness when a small child began to cry," Camacho says. "Instantly the lioness was alert. Lions are experts in spotting weakness. This is how they pick their prey from a herd. They are constantly scanning for vulnerability. So at night, if you are a refugee, the lions will size you up. If you are too small, you are vulnerable. If you are overweight, you are vulnerable. If you limp, you are vulnerable. If you are alone, you are vulnerable. If you are any of these things, then you may trigger a lion attack. It is the same to the lions as if you were a squealing pig."

While in Kruger in 1998, Camacho first saw evidence of how refugees can trigger lion attacks. He was in the bush with documentary filmmaker Greg Nelson (who was producing a series called *Free of Fear*), a camera crew, and two American veterinarian trainees. They had lured lions with bait and hyena calls, but had seen and tranquilized only two of them, even though their methods usually attracted an entire pride. So where were the other lions?

Someone on Nelson's crew said he'd heard what sounded like a human cry a few hundred yards away. There, in the middle of the road, they found the fed-upon corpse of a refugee. It was clear from the tracks what had happened. The refugee had been wearing athletic shoes with a brand name on the soles. He'd been taking casual steps, imprinting "Fila" in the dust of the road, going west to Joni, slowly but surely. A bit farther on, the tracks of a large lioness appeared from out of the bush, as if merging from an entrance ramp. The two sets of prints proceeded unchanged for a while, the "Fila" imprints spaced leisurely, the lion's pug marks following behind. Judging from her gait, the lioness seemed to be curious, open to opportunity but not charging.

Then the athletic-shoe tracks broke into a run—he must have heard her growl or cough behind him—and her tracks showed the trigger point: Instantly, the slow walk became a short, bounding run, then a leap. There was an area that clearly suggested a scuffle. Both the man's shoes were thrown to the side. Then he regained his feet and raced, barefoot, for his life. The lion tracks—now with claws extended—followed for 20 feet, and then there was a great deal of blood. The corpse was little more than a rib cage and a smear of red, its teeth exposed through missing lips in a ghoulish rictus.

Shocked and repulsed by what they'd found, the men pulled the Land Rover over the body to keep jackals and hyenas away from it. Between them they had spent hundreds of nights sleeping in the open bush, but at that moment they were sincerely afraid of lions for the first time. Camacho was so shaken that he staggered away, walking back through the bush to the tranquilized lions. He stumbled on the first one, literally stepping on her, then changed direction and bumped into the other, which was recovering and eyeing him warily. Camacho regained his senses and walked back to the group assembled around the corpse. With too much gear to return home, they had to sleep in the bush. They circled the Land Rovers, pioneer style, and Camacho crawled under his, where he slept fitfully, dreaming of smiling corpses.

Still, reflecting on the incident, Camacho says, "Yet again, this was not the fault of the lion. The lion did not seek the refugee. The refugee walked into her turf and triggered the attack. You cannot call her a man-eater in the classic sense of the word."

Whatever its causes, very little has been done about the lion problem in

Kruger. There have been no anti-lion uprisings, and on a continent where more than 30 million people are infected with AIDS, where genocide by machete cuts down hundreds of thousands, where malaria claims hundreds of thousands in South Africa alone, public officials haven't been spurred to action. In part, this is because everyone understands that the lions are the rock stars of eco-tourism. By contrast, many South Africans view the immigrants as border jumpers who steal jobs, and the lions are a sort of biological razor wire, a way to literally put teeth into the border-patrol efforts. And then there are the lion politics: Should members of a protected species be killed when they are doing what comes naturally? "Some people say. Well, the lions were here first, and man comes in and creates a problem, so why must the animal suffer?" conservation chief Gertenbach says. "That's a difficult statement to make. There are human rights."

And sometimes the lions do pay a price. In 1997, a pride of five was shot in Kruger's northern section. "They had become too aggressive," says Gertenbach. "We could tell they were man-eaters. In one stomach, we found a wallet with Mozambican currency." Kruger ranger Albert Machaba says, "We would've been their next targets. Even though we were fully armed, when we were in the bush, they were watching us and waiting."

The shooting of lions has none of the glory it carried during the days of the Great White Hunter. These are not brave sorties into the bush after fleeing demons. They are executions. The act is anathema to the rangers, who are sworn to protect wildlife. When three Mozambican brothers were attacked in the park in 1998, two came to Machaba and begged him to help the third, as they could not drive the lioness off by themselves. From 500 meters, backed by several rangers armed with rifles, Machaba could see that the lioness had killed the man and was feeding on him. He sighted down the scope of his .458 Magnum, enough gun to bring down an elephant. Heart shots and head shots are the most humane and lethal, and Machaba put the cross hairs on the head. He squeezed, the big gun bucked, and the lion fell dead across its prey. "It was a sad day," Machaba says. "Sad for the man. Sad for the lion. But when we catch them red-handed, we must kill them. There is no looking away from that."

Yet the laws of lion justice are loosely written and even more loosely enforced. "When we know a lion has become a man-eater, we must shoot it," Gertenbach says. "But if it isn't absolutely clear, we give it the benefit of the doubt. Besides, we are not equipped to solve this problem. We're already short-handed in performing our primary duties—patrolling for poachers and snares, and maintaining the park for the animals and the tourists."

Which is not to say Gertenbach hasn't tried. In 1998, he suggested that buses be set up on the border and visas issued. But the South African home office balked. He also helped establish a barter system with refugees along Kruger's border with Mozambique. The refugees would provide crafts, which the park would sell in gift shops. They would be given food in return and would agree to stay in their home country. But the program ran afoul of South African customs policy, and, at best, it was tangential to the problem.

Machaba has taken a different tack. When he arrived in the Satara area, in 1998, he began crossing the Mozambique border each month to visit the local officials. "You must educate the refugees," he tells them. "Travel in large groups. Use guides. Do not set fires to keep warm." His education program may be working. In the central Satara area, Machaba hasn't found a corpse in more than four years. But problems in Mozambique persist. A flood in 2000. A horrible drought this year. "If the drought continues, I expect there will be even more refugees," Machaba says. And as long as there are refugees, there will be man-eating lions in Kruger. "Even if conditions in Mozambique get better, there are many families and tribespeople who are separated by the park," he says. "They will always cross."

The only legal way to step one rung down on the food chain is on a sanctioned night drive through Kruger in a big safari vehicle with staggered stadium seats that can accommodate 20 tourists at a time. Instructions are brief: Stay inside the open vehicle. Do not break the profile of the truck and show your human self. No noise. Do not talk. If you do, we are told, the game will run.

Handheld million-candlepower spotlights bleach the roadside. The blackness of the African night swallows them just a few feet into the bush, but they can scour the near terrain, catching the eyes of all the creatures. A set of green eyes: kudo. A rock that moves: elephant. Yellow eyes: a serval cat. We peer into the bush, looking for lions.

When we see them, however, they are on the road, a hunting platoon of 11 males and females moving languidly in ordered single file. Lithe and powerful, they swagger, all balls and confidence, like an urban gang patrolling its turf.

We pull even with them and are among them. Motor drives whir. Camera strobes freeze the cats. They stare at wheel level but ignore us, an arm's length up and out from them. What happens then perhaps is seen through a lens of too much information, too much listening to Gerrie Camacho and his talk about comfort zones and trigger points. Yet we see what we see and hear what we hear.

The coiled potential for violence begins to undo the passengers. There are lions everywhere, just a few feet away. Human invulnerability has been stripped. First, it is a woman in the back. In a tremulous voice, she says, "Driver! Please. Turn back. I am afraid they will jump in the car!"

An older man joins in. "Yes! Yes! Turn back, please! They are too close!"

Then, on the brink of tears, rattled badly by the adults, a young girl of about eight says in the shakiest of voices, "Let's do go home. Please! I am very afraid. They are going to jump onto us."

There is no response from the driver, but the lioness nearest us twitches and instantly looks up. She has been angling toward the vehicle. Perhaps she truly sees it for the first time, and that is the cause of her alertness. Or perhaps she has heard the trigger of the child. Her face looks both piqued and confused. She stares up and backs onto the downward slope of the road, her back legs feeling for footing, coiling under her. The spotlights shine in her vision, and within the beams she hears more fear. Her hind legs bend more as she backs away. Footing?

Or preparing to leap? It's impossible to tell. But there's no doubt that she is searching.

More of the adults are chorusing now, asking the driver to leave. Some stalwarts half-shout, "No. Stay!" and blaze away with their cameras. All of them are breaking the rules. The girl sniffles and begins to sob. The lioness again twitches in response. Her face is intent, fearless.

"There, there," the girl's mother says. "They're just as scared of you as you are of them, my dear. There is nothing to worry about."

There is no indication that this is true. The lioness is stone-faced and resolute, still interested, ripped with coils of muscle. But the woman's voice seems eternally invulnerable, and it calms us all. As the driver begins to pull the vehicle away, the lioness backpedals down the shoulder of the road. There is an embarrassed silence, but a moment later it's as if the panic never even occurred, as if we did not briefly feel like prey. We ascend confidently back to the top of the food chain and accept the myth that there was never anything to worry about. Yes, the lions were scared of us.

As we drive away, the platoon troops down the road again in single file. Then they do something I recognize from my pheasant-hunting days back home in rural Illinois. As kids, my friends and I would go out in groups, proud that we were trusted with shotguns. We'd find a field of standing corn. Walking single file along one side, we'd space ourselves out to cover the most ground, and with a signal or a nod, we'd enter the corn to begin driving the game before us.

The lions move to the bush alongside the road, and at some silent signal, they space themselves. Some look from side to side to gauge the span, while others trot ahead. When they are comfortable with the intervals, when they are spread out to cover the ground, they move as one and lope into the bush. They are on the hunt now, looking for easy prey, heading east, toward Mozambique.

This Is Not a Rodeo Story
by Chris Heath

Chris Heath profiled a group of professional bull riders for Men's Journal.

Bull riding is simple enough. You get on the back of a bull that's penned in a chute in which it cannot move. Your bull rope is tied round the bull's midsection, a little behind its front legs, and is wound round the fingers and palm of your riding hand. There is no handle; no closed loop to hang on to. Only the tightness of your grip—and the sticky rosin applied between rope and glove—prevents the rope from releasing and your handhold from evaporating.

When you give the nod, the chute is opened, and the annoyed bull launches itself into the arena. There is something on its back, and its instinct is to dislodge it violently. Bulls bred for bull riding weigh up to 2,000 pounds and are especially good at bucking off presumptuous humans. They can leap in the air, buck, and spin in either direction, in unpredictable combinations and with remarkable force and velocity. You may touch the bull only with your riding hand and by gripping with your lower body; the rest comes down to whatever mysterious mixture of balance, strength, anticipation, and skill that allows a very few men to be able to ride bulls some of the time.

Nobody can ride bulls all of the time. If you stay on for less than eight seconds after the chute opens, you have failed. No score. If you stay on for eight seconds, a buzzer announces that the ride is over, and you will receive a mark out of 100: up to 50 for the bull's performance, up to 50 for yours.

Whether you dismount voluntarily after eight seconds—no easy task, as the bull, not surprisingly, is unaware that the ride is over—or have already been thrown off, you must then avoid being stomped on or mauled by the bull's horns. If you fail to do this, you can be injured. You might even die.

Even the most successful bull rider is unlikely to ride atop a bull for more than 15 minutes in any year. You will be lucky to make ten minutes. If you stay healthy, and fortune smiles on you, then you may ride bulls for a total of two hours in your life, and it will be the experience you live for.

Justin McBride is 23 years old today. He is one of the honest young stars of professional bull riding, a cowboy who finished last year ranked third in the world and has so far earned nearly $650,000 in career prize money. He grew up in Nebraska, where his father (who also rode bulls, though not so successfully) was a farm manager. His parents recently moved to a ranch not far from Elk City, Oklahoma, and that is where Justin also lives for the moment while his first house is being built on some ranchland a few miles away. Even though his mother works at a local bank, these are not people who much believe in loans. Justin's father tells me that the house gets built according to how each bull-riding event goes: If Justin falls off, work slows down.

He's not big on preambles or extraneous information, Justin. People are who they are. When I arrive at his parents' ranch, it takes him a while to catch my name, and it's several hours before he bothers to ask which magazine I'm from. I am here at his home, the sun is shining, everything is fine, and he wants to know only one thing. "You want to go riding or fishing?" I choose fishing, because being unable to do that may be less obvious and also less potentially catastrophic. He talks on the phone the whole way there, chatting with a friend. "I got some awesome hunting boots for my birthday," he says into the phone. "Now, I want to know when them elks'll be ready to hunt." Justin turns off the dirt road and into the open countryside, traversing an uneven slope, and points the truck toward a pond with red mud banks.

He asks me to catch grasshoppers while he readies our rods. On his first cast, he lands a catfish. We fish—more catfish, perch, bass—until we get too hot and they stop biting. McBride doesn't say much. Later he tells me that he likes to fish here alone, in the middle of the week, to clear his head and to think. I ask him what he thinks about when he comes here.

He smiles. "Riding bulls," he says.

Riding bulls is all Justin McBride has ever dreamed of doing, even before he can remember dreaming it. "I've seen pictures of myself trying to ride the dog when I was two years old," he tells me, "with my boots and diaper and hat on." Not long after that, his father saw an unwanted dwarf calf, red with a white face, for $3 at market and bought it for Justin. "I'd get on him, and he'd buck around a little bit." Justin built bucking bulls to practice on by suspending barrels from trees with ropes and springs, and he had a pet donkey called Chile Pepper that would try to buck him off. Justin wasn't just going to be a bull rider; he was going to be world champion. "Hell," he says, "I remember giving world-title acceptance speeches to myself when I was eight years old." He would study films of the famous bull riders of his day: Tuff Hedeman, Jim Sharp, Michael Gaffney, and Ty Murray, who would become arguably the most famous cowboy of all time by winning an unprecedented eight all-round rodeo titles. McBride figured that if he could take what was special from each of them, maybe he could become the best bull rider of all.

Many people think that bull riding is synonymous with rodeo, and for a while it was. Traditionally, bull riding was the seventh and final event of a rodeo, and until the Professional Bull Riding tour was formed, in 1992, most bull riding took place at rodeos run by the Professional Rodeo Cowboys Association. Riders would travel to as many as 125 events a year, trying to earn enough money to survive and to qualify for the annual finals, where bigger money could be earned. The bull riders felt they weren't being treated fairly. They felt underpaid and exploited, and the quality of the bulls was so inconsistent that the finest bull rider could travel a thousand miles only to ride a butt so sluggish that no one could possibly have won money on him.

In 1992, 20 of the top bull riders met in Scottsdale, Arizona, and agreed to break away from traditional rodeo and form their own rider-owned bull-riding organization. They put down $1,000 each. (Just under 90 percent of the PBR is still owned by the riders.) Their first event was in 1994. They contracted for only the best bulls and put all the earnings into prize money for the riders. They tried to shed rodeo's hokey image, replacing the brass bands with rock 'n' roll and introducing fancy pyrotechnics and lights. "We want to distance ourselves from rodeo," says PBR's CEO Randy Bernard. "We look at that as a place you take your kids to show them a tradition that's dying. We want to ride NASCAR's shirttails, not rodeo's."

These days, PBR events make regular stops in markets far from the traditional western-heritage strongholds, appearing in Detroit as often as in Oklahoma City. Bernard says that he knew things were working the evening they sold out an event—in a snowstorm—in Worcester, Massachusetts.

Bernard claims that, since 1995, only three events have lost money: Birmingham, Alabama, on the day Michael Jordan retired from minor league baseball (his AA team was based there); Vancouver, during the 1998 Olympic gold-medal hockey game; and Detroit, the week after September 11. Things are going so well that the PBR recently bought back its TV rights—given away in its early years in order to be able to get any TV exposure—for $6.2 million. As well as having 29 events a year on cable, the PBR has just had an event on CBS, and this

November 17 it has the first of six events on NBC leading up to next October's finals. (The organization even advanced the start of its new season by six weeks so that the first NBC event could premiere after NASCAR.) This is the beginning of the PBR's next big push, to make bull riding the cool new spectator sport—the push that it hopes will make riders like McBride more famous than even he'd imagined.

PBR events take place over two days—45 riders tackle different bulls each of the first two nights, after which the top 15 riders ride a third bull in the final round. This week, the riders learn which bulls they've drawn for Saturday only when they arrive at the arena, but their Friday ride is announced earlier. On Wednesday, a few hours after we return from fishing, Justin's mother looks up his ride for Bullnanza Oklahoma City, this weekend's event, on the Internet. Justin has drawn Buzzard Bait. It's a good draw. In the bull-riding world, bulls are either "rank" (nasty and spirited, which is good) or "a dink" (too sedate, which is bad). Buzzard Bait is a rank bull, but not unridable. Justin was on him twice last year. The first rime he scored a 90.5. (Anything 90 or higher is an impressive score.) The second time, Justin says, "he drilled me."

"I just hate his horns," says Mrs. McBride with concern.

"Me, too, Mama," Justin answers, teasing her. He taps out "Happy Birthday" on a keyboard, backtracking once or twice. "I've been practicing all week," he says. His girlfriend, Michelle Beadle, appears. She's one of the PBR's TV announcers. Justin picks at some brisket on the stove, opens a Bud Light, and waits for his birthday party to start. His best friends in the bull-riding world are all invited here tonight. "Ain't no telling how many's coming, when they'll get here, how long they'll stay," he says with a grin.

Justin's birthday also coincided with the Oklahoma City event last year, and it was not a quiet affair. If you look on pbrnow.com, you will learn that Justin broke his hand at last year's Bullnanza. This isn't quite the full story. Although he did leave the arena with a broken hand, it hadn't really been right when he arrived—most of the damage was done in Elk City late on his birthday night. Justin is reluctant to spell out too many details, but amid all the other fun there was a fight. "We were just being cowboys," he laughs. "Hell, we was just having a good time. It was some guys we didn't know." He maintains that the hand wasn't really broken until after his first bull—one that, for the record, he rode well enough to win the round.

Today, Justin still has a big bump between his third and fourth fingers, a callous left after his hand was fixed. He couldn't have it plated, because he would have missed too much time and lost ground in the title race. Instead, doctors just threaded a rod through his ring finger and he was riding three weeks later. "It hurt like hell," he says, "but it couldn't break."

A woman from next door comes over to give him a pie she has baked for his birthday and to wish him well for the weekend. "I'm gonna ride them all," he tells her. The workmen who are building his house come round, and he takes them onto the back porch for a drink, then sings them a song, strumming his guitar. "I got a 12-inch dick," he begins, "a dozen roses, and a pickup truck, hubba hubba hubba . . ." He stops playing. "That's all I wrote, because I figured that's all I'd need."

The workmen leave, and the riders begin to trickle in. "Goddamn, I'm glad you boys are here," the host says. He shows them his horses, but rejects their taunts that he should get on one that's not yet broken. "I ain't doing any bucking shit today," he says. Instead, they sit down by his mother's goldfish pond, lazily trying to catch goldfish with their hands while they drink beer, chew tobacco, and talk rodeo business.

I settle next to three of them—Justin, J.W. Hart, and K.J. Pletcher, who is injured, but here anyway—and ask a few simple questions.

Why, I inquire, do they ride bulls?

" 'Cause women like bull riders," says J.W. "And we like women."

"The best thing I know to say," says McBride, "is that it's the only thing we know how to do."

"Too lazy to work, too nervous to steal," mutters J.W.

"You know," says McBride, "we grew up being cowboys. We loved old westerns, John Wayne movies. We grew up being cowboys and then we found a way to be cowboys and still make a great living, and to be way cooler than anybody in the world. You show me a sport that challenges a human being against a 2,000-pound animal.

"You know, you might find a rich kid that rides bulls really good," continues McBride. "But mostly we're all the same people. I mean, look at [PBR legend] Tuff Hedeman. He's a poor kid growing up—an ugly, stupid idiot, and he'll tell you even worse just so it sounds good. He didn't have a shot at life other than working for eight dollars an hour—it was his best hope. And now he's one of the most popular cowboys who ever lived."

Most of these cowboys are joyously drunk before sundown; after dark their drinking accelerates. The last to arrive is Justin's closest PBR buddy, Ross Coleman, whom he's known since they were 15, when they met in the high school rodeo finals. The two rode together on the UNLV rodeo team and have leapfrogged each other ever since. Last year, Justin came in third in the world championship, and Ross came in fourth; this year, Ross is sitting in second, Justin fourth. Coleman catches up with the rest of the party pretty quickly, with its drinking games, tasteless jokes, bawdy songs, and general cowboy hilarity. Some of the riders head into town, in search of fun and women, but this year Justin stays home. In the morning, many of the PBR's finest talents are spread, comatose, over the McBrides' living room floor. Outside, there are clothes scattered over the ground and the bushes. On the surface of Mrs. McBride's goldfish pond floats a single dead fish.

The apparent danger involved when a man climbs onto a bull is not an illusion. In 1998, one of the PBR's founders, Jerome Davis, was hit in the head, thrown off, and paralyzed from the chest down. Then, two years ago in Albuquerque, a rider named Glen Keeley was on a bull called Promise Land when he came off and the bull stepped on his chest. He seemed hurt, but not seriously. "He walked out of the arena, and I was right there," Coleman says. That evening, Keeley died in the hospital, and the PBR had its first death.

"When I got there at seven in the morning," recalls PBR chief Randy Bernard, "the lobby was just full of cowboys crying." All the riders decided to ride the following night. "It was a real weird mood that next night," McBride remembers. "It's hard for the crowd to drink beer and have fun and cheer and holler when they just watched somebody die." But some catharsis came of it. In the short round, a rider named Owen Washburn drew Promise Land. Every cowboy was watching, cheering him on as he stayed on their friend's accidental killer, got 95 points, and won the event.

All of this is, anyway, part of the sport's appeal. Every person I spoke to in the PBR says the same thing: "Everybody likes to see a wreck." They know that its danger is one of its principal marketing pegs, though Bernard will say, with appropriate gravity, "It's a dangerous game—and I'm sure, unfortunately, there's going to be more deaths." He pauses. "You know, I just heard that the insurers Lloyd's of London has called us the most dangerous sport in the world."

On the night after Justin's birthday, and the night before the Bull-nanza's first round, Justin and Ross share a drink with Jim Sharp at the Oklahoma City Lone Star Steakhouse. Sharp, 37, is one of the tour's veterans. In the past couple of years, he has started hanging out with Ross and Justin, and his career has rebounded. (He is third, right between them, in the points race.) Sharp, who has a dry, understated way about him, credits them with making him feel 15 years younger.

"If I went to bull riding, I'd want to see a wreck," Sharp mutters while Coleman and McBride are across the room. "I don't want to see anybody get hurt, but I'd like to see somebody get run over."

"But," I say, "you don't want to be a wreck."

"Oh, yeah," he agrees. "I don't want to be a wreck. I'd rather Justin get in a wreck." He laughs. "I don't want him to get hurt, just maybe get rolled around a little bit. 'Cause he probably deserves it."

A bit later, Coleman answers the phone, then clicks off. "Whores already calling me," he says, smiling. Coleman says he's going to turn in early. ("I got a call a bit later," he explains the next day, "so I had to . . . deal with something." He grins.)

There is never a shortage of women around riders whenever they step into public. These ladies are known as Buckle Bunnies, because they're drawn to the winning cowboys—each big win brings its own belt buckle—though Coleman says that term's a little old-fashioned. "Some call them pro hos," he says, then adds apologetically, "but that's kind of rude."

McBride has already suggested to me that if I want to know about this part of the bull-riding subculture, Coleman is the man I need to speak with. "There are very many beautiful girls out there," Coleman explains. "And I know that every one of them got a TV. Girls like popular guys that are making a little money and on TV every week. I'm sure someday I'll have a family or whatever. But I'm 23 years old, and I like to ride bulls and drink Bud Light, have fun, enjoy my life while I can."

He says that sometimes the girls like them to bring bull riding into the bedroom. "They like to wear the hat," he says. "Sometimes they want you to put the chaps on. And the girls like to wear the chaps sometimes."

And you're happy to oblige?

"No problem."

Some bull riders are superstitious. Won't eat peanuts. Won't wear yellow. Won't put their hat on the bed. Riders like McBride and Coleman have no time for that. "If you think about that superstitious shit, you're already outsmarting yourself," says Coleman. "I'm just a fricking cowboy."

Coleman and I meet for Friday lunch in his hotel. He can hardly wait for the night's event: "It's, like, the most exciting thing you could ever imagine. It's like letting a bomb go off inside of you, the biggest adrenaline rush you could ever imagine." As he sees it, tonight is the start of his run, with five events to go, to winning the world championship. "Every day, I look at what it'd be like to win it. To have that feeling, that belt buckle."

Later, Coleman and I wander over to the pens at the back of the arena where the bulls are gathered together. "They're just crazy, mean, wild untamed animals, pretty much," he says. "But in the back pens they're just kind of docile, like we are." Most of the bulls are standing still, some sitting. Ross can recognize the ones he's ridden. "Look at the size of that fucker," he says, pointing at one that's thrown him off before. He points to another. "I rode that black bull there. Slick Willie. He's awesome. Got a 92 on him. I've been on a bunch of them. I was 93 on this one, 92 on that one . . ."

As the crowd files in, I speak with Tuff Hedeman, who retired in 1998 and is now both PBR president and anchor of the tour's TV coverage. During the event, he sits with McBride's girlfriend, Michelle, on a platform by the bull chutes, which is where he offers his opinions on Coleman and McBride. "I see them as two different types of riders," he says. "You look at Ross and he's a guy who, to me, doesn't look like he has a lot of natural ability. He's a little bigger. Riding has probably come harder for him than it has for Justin. Justin's a guy who seems to have a lot more natural ability, but Ross is a guy who's just an overachiever—he's successful because he puts out twice the effort, three times the effort. I think Justin's desire could be and should be stronger. To me it's frustrating, and I'm harder on him than probably anybody, because I see a guy that has loads of talent and could be maybe the best of his generation, but it doesn't matter how much talent you have. You have to want it when you get jerked down and you get your teeth knocked out and you're bleeding and you're dragging a leg—you still have to want it. I'm not saying Justin doesn't, but he doesn't show it as much as Ross does."

McBride hasn't got much time for this kind of talk. Even before I met Hedeman, he had told me: "You could ask Tuff and he'd say, 'He's a natural; he's got talent.' To me, talent's a myth. Talent is an *excuse.* Bullshit. I spent my entire life learning how to do this well."

At the beginning of the Bullnanza the lights go down, and the riders are introduced one by one. Each runs out into the center of the arena's floor, where he stands, lines of flames burning in the dirt around him. This controlled sense of drama is not one that can be maintained for the bull riding itself. For one thing, the lights are brought back up: You don't do something like this in the dark. For another, it is the rider who decides when he is ready for his chute to be opened, which may be in the middle of the commentators' introduction, and so the commentary and score updates always seem slightly out of sync with the action. In the flesh, the rides are brief and terrifyingly fierce. When they go wrong, the riders are simply tossed aside, and scamper, often clearly panicking, for the safety of the arena railing while the three bullfighters—whose risky job it is to distract the bull while the rider escapes—do their best to urge the bull through a gate into the corral. So far tonight, few riders seem to be staying on, setting things up perfectly for Coleman, McBride, and Sharp to mount their challenges on the year's points leader, Ednei Caminhas of Brazil.

Sharp goes first. He is bucked off before the eight seconds, and when you watch it in real time it all seems impossibly fast. Then I stand by Coleman's chute, watching him pull his rope as tight as he can, pumped and determined. The chute opens, and his bull turns back to the right and doesn't kick much, and then it spins and, as the riders say, drops him in the well—their term for when a rider begins to fall off a bull and into the hole in the middle of a bull's spin, the most dangerous place to fall, and the hardest to recover from. Coleman can feel the bull sensing him slip down there, and then moving to finish the deal, and then he is gone—4.7 seconds after the chute has opened, he is striding off, his face fixed in a furious grimace.

The stage is set for McBride, the home-state favorite. Buzzard Bait goes left, rocks him to the right, then takes a jump, and McBride almost gets back where he needs to be—balanced on top of the bull, in tune with its motions—but then the bull suddenly veers left and it's all over: 4.4 seconds. "He turned out of there really slow, and I just fell off of him," says McBride later. "I felt so stupid." Right now, he goes to be by himself for a while, sitting in the far corner of the locker room, trying to figure out what he did wrong.

At around a quarter to 12, Coleman and McBride walk into the hotel bar together.

"Annoying day?" I say to McBride.

"Yeah," he mutters, staring at the carpet, and changes the subject. The only consolation is that they can redeem themselves tomorrow. There were not many successful rides, so a good ride in the second round can still qualify them for the final round.

They chat with one of the livestock contractors—quite literally talking bull—for a while, and order some bar food. As it is with many modern athletes, diet is everything, and so it would be wrong to end the day without a few beers and a quesadilla.

The next morning, I pop into McBride's hotel room. "Last night me and Ross both sucked horribly," he says. "We looked like we'd never done this shit before. That wasn't nobody's fault but our own."

I mention how amazing it is that all the closest title challengers failed.

"We all fell off like girls." He laughs dryly. "It's a pretty weird leader board right now. It ain't going to end up that way."

I find Ross backstage in the early evening. "Tonight's gonna kick ass. I've got a good bull. A bull I rode in the finals called Juice." He winks. "I'll do better tonight."

Jim Sharp is up early. Justin is there by the chute, helping him prepare. Sharp comes off quickly, and the bull skims his head, shaving a little skin off it.

"Goddamn," says McBride.

McBride goes later, and he comes off more quickly than last night. Coleman follows, and he, too, never finds his balance, crashing to the ground after 3.8 seconds, the bull's horn hitting him in the leg.

Back in the dressing room, Coleman knocks a beer over in fury, then begins to take his chaps off. By intermission, 30 of the riders know that their night is over, and it is their mood that dominates in the dressing room. One holds an ice pack to his head. J.W. (2.3 seconds) throws a bottle of water across the room. McBride sits with his arms wrapped around his body, a beer in one hand. Ty Murray, who retired early this season but is in town for a PBR board meeting, consoles another rider: "You had that son of a bitch. I don't know where it went south on you."

I go over and sit with Coleman. "Last night I was pissed, but not as pissed off as I am tonight," he says. Tonight he had a perfect bull: "The kind of bull I want every time. But one mistake and you're off." He exhales. "Pretty much the shittiest weekend I could have this time of year. That's bull riding, pretty much. One day you're gonna be the happiest guy in the world, the next day you're the most pissed-off guy in the world. But no matter how good you are, or how good you think you are, you're going to get your ass kicked."

"It didn't feel good," reflects McBride. "It doesn't feel good to be a loser."

Soon he'll be back at the fishing pond. Nothing to disturb him, apart from his thoughts. Running it through his mind, over and over. The bull turning back to the left, his upper body getting too far back. "I somehow managed to fall off," he says. "That's the bottom line. I just fell off." So he'll sit there, thinking about bulls, about what he did, and what he should have done. About how this time he fell off, and how next time he won't.

from American Ground
by William Langewiesche

William Langewiesche had unrestricted access to the Ground Zero cleanup crew during the months following September 11, 2001. Here he gives an account of the events that occurred immediately after the attacks.

The rush to find survivors was hopeful at first, and then less so. Sam Melisi later described for me the wild-eyed urgency of the initial search. Speaking of the lost firemen, who throughout the months to come provided a focus to the recovery efforts, he said, "These were people you had worked with, and they were maybe alive. You knew they were trapped in there, and there was a sense of franticness, and it was personal. I remember crawling through the steel—it would have probably been by the hotel. There were some spaces that let you get below and take a look around. It wasn't regulated at all. The first couple of days, anything went. It wasn't like somebody was saying, 'You can't go in there, you can't do this, you can't do that.' It was more like 'Hey, if you think you can get in there, go ahead.' All bets were off. It was just 'Go and bring somebody home.' "

At age forty-three, Melisi was a small, wiry man who had a disarming way of suggesting his opinions rather than asserting them. He had a nasal voice and a big moustache. He was obviously somewhat shy. Within the wolf-pack world of the Trade Center site he became known at first simply because his diffidence was unique. Still, he was a fireman through and through, with strong allegiances to the department and a blue-collar history that was fairly standard for the type. He grew up on Staten Island as the son of a diver with a small marine-salvage business, and he excelled in high school before heading to college in Oregon, where, cut off from his roots, he floundered. After dropping out of school, he hired on at a sawmill for six months, and then returned to New York, went to work in heavy construction, and eventually became a licensed equipment and crane operator. At the advanced age of twenty-seven he joined the Fire Department because of the generous time off ("Like being on permanent vacation," he told me) and only then discovered the job's power to mold people's lives, including his own. So far he had put sixteen years into the service—in various ladder and rescue companies, and most recently as an assistant in the engine room of the city's 1938 fireboat, called the *Firefighter*. Because of his heavy-equipment experience and additional training, he also served on a specialized collapsed-building team, which had responded to the 1993 bombing of the Trade Center and had been dispatched to the subsequent bombing in Oklahoma City and to a hurricane disaster in the Dominican Republic. He lived with his wife and two young children on Staten Island, in a surprisingly rural setting—a small wooden house from the 1840s with a large back yard bordering on a forest preserve and littered with old construction equipment, including a small crane. (One day at the site he said, "People here keep saying how strange it all looks, but I dunno, it kind of looks like my back yard.") In a shed at the end of his yard he had built a welding and machine shop. The jobs he did there helped him to supplement his modest salary. Sometimes he moonlighted as an electrician. Sometimes he was a plumber, sometimes a carpenter, too.

When the first airplane hit, Melisi put down his reading in the *Fire-fighter's* engine room and prepared to get under way. When the second airplane hit, he understood it meant war, and he had the strange impression of feeling every possible emotion all at once. When the South Tower fell, the boat was plowing at full speed across New York Harbor, and the twin diesels were roaring. When the North Tower fell, the boat was pulling up to shore, and the diesels were still so loud that Melisi did not hear the thunder. The boat docked just north of the North Cove, along a riverfront promenade. Melisi emerged from the engine room and helped the deck crew drag hose to the fire-suppression teams on the northwest corner of the site. He returned to the boat and helped to engage its pumps, which delivered enormous quantities of harbor water to the ruins over the following two weeks. Aware of Melisi's training in collapsed buildings and rescue operations, his supervisor then cut him loose. He said, "Just go. See what you can do." This turned out to be more than a little thing. Melisi's maritime career had come suddenly to a halt.

He joined the scramble through the smoke and debris, searching for cavities in which people might have survived. This was a collapse unlike any he had seen before, and not only in size. Though the top layer of the pile was jagged, it was also fantastically dense, and it offered little in the way of natural shelters, or of access to the underground. Melisi circled to the north side, where fires raged and Building Seven threatened to fall, but the devastation was less severe. Handicapped by the lack of a flashlight, he joined a rescue team that descended through a crater in Building Six and made multiple attempts on the North Tower basements, but was blocked each time by smoke and heavy debris. Back on the surface again, he moved down West Street, squeezed under the ruins of the north pedestrian bridge between the hulks of crushed fire trucks, and spent the afternoon with a shovel, digging for survivors and uncovering only the dead. He arrived in the site's southwest corner that evening at about the same time that Ken Holden, Mike Burton, and the unbuilding crew first came walking through. Melisi neither knew nor noticed them then, but he shared some of their construction expertise, and he had drawn conclusions similar to theirs—that the bucket brigades he saw operating on the pile were ineffectual, and that if victims were to be found alive, it was essential to bring in large cranes and grapplers that could lift the fallen steel columns and expose cavities below the surface. Typically, Melisi did something practical about it right away. He worked to clear an access route from the south, directing front-end loaders to shove cars and toppled lampposts aside, opening a path that detoured around the heaviest obstacles. A perverse pattern then prevailed; the fast-moving small equipment was the first to arrive, and time and again it had to be dismantled or laboriously moved out of the way in order to allow the larger and more effective pieces in; because of the quantities of debris, space was simply not available for both. The delays were frustrating for Melisi, who through his actions and expertise was unintentionally already involved in the management of the site. The greater frustration came later, however, and it was the near total lack of survivors.

The lack was partly definitional, since it excluded the 15,000 people who were able to walk away, in some cases even after the buildings fell. Their survival, however, did not diminish the reality that thousands remained unaccounted for, or the terrible feeling in those first confused hours and days that time was running out. It went without saying that the survivors who mattered were the ones who might now be lying trapped in the debris. They turned out to be rare: over the subsequent months of retrieval it became obvious from the condition of the bodies that few if any of the victims had perished while awaiting rescue. By the final count, in a place where nearly 3,000 had died, only eighteen people were recovered alive. Two of them were injured policemen discovered on the first day in the underground concourse, a shopping area east of the South Tower that had been speared and pummeled by falling columns but not completely crushed. The remaining sixteen were all found among the ruins of the North Tower. Fourteen of them—twelve firemen, one policeman, and one civilian office worker—came through largely unscathed in an intact stairwell section between the second and fourth floors, sandwiched between collapses. When they were rescued, also on the first day, they emerged from the ground as if from the bowels of hell, and cheering broke out across the site.

But only two other people were ever found alive. Both were Port Authority employees caught at relatively high elevations in the North Tower. They did not "surf" the collapse, as a couple of Port Authority cops were falsely rumored to have done in the South Tower, but they lived through falls that should have killed them. The first of them was a thirty-two-year-old staff engineer named Pasquale Buzzelli whose job involved overseeing work on the George Washington Bridge— including Rinaldi's project of decorating the span with lights. Buzzelli was riding an intermediate-stage elevator to his office, on the sixty-fourth floor, when the 767 slammed into the North Tower far above. The elevator shook violently and briefly dropped before catching itself and returning slowly to its starting point, the "sky lobby" on the forty-fourth floor. When the doors opened, Buzzelli was confronted by a confusion of shouts and thick black smoke (presumably from burning jet fuel that had poured down other shafts). He retreated into the elevator and, with no way to go but up, instinctively pushed the button for his familiar sixty-fourth floor. It was a slow ride. When he got there, the floor looked well lit and calm, and it was almost smoke-free. Most of the workers had already left, but more than a dozen remained, and were dutifully awaiting instructions from the authorities below, as apparently they had been asked to do by Port Authority and Fire Department officials on the phone. Because the group included Buzzelli's supervisor, a man named Pat Hoey, Buzzelli decided to stay too. He said, "What happened, Pat?"

Hoey said, "I don't know, but I was just about thrown out of my chair."

"Really? I thought it was some kind of elevator thing." Hoey kept calling downstairs to the Port Authority communications center and was unable to get clear information. He seemed edgy, but more from frustration than fear.

Buzzelli got on another phone and called his wife, who was seven months pregnant with their first child. He said, "Don't be alarmed or anything like that. I'm okay. Just put on the TV. Tell me if something has happened."

He waited. After a while she came back and said, "Oh, my God, Pasquale! There's a plane in your building!"

Buzzelli lived up to the reputation of engineers as unflappable. He said, "All right, all right. Don't get excited." (When he recounted the conversation later, he explained, "She was getting all worried and stuff.") He said, "Just can you please tell me where it is? Did it hit high, middle, or low?" ("Because she doesn't really know the floors and stuff.")

She said, "Well, it looks pretty high up in the building."

This was of course good news. Buzzelli had been through the 1993 World Trade Center bombing, and was not overly concerned. He said, "Okay. Well, just so you know, I'm okay, and we're here, and we're going to figure out what to do."

It took them a while. They learned that the South Tower, too, had been hit by an airplane—but they neither heard nor saw the impact. Their offices occupied the northwest corner of the North Tower, as far from the South Tower as could be. They were surprisingly isolated, and were unaware that their upstairs neighbors were jumping from windows and falling by outside. They stuffed wet coats under the doors against the faint smoke that was drifting through the elevator lobby. Apparently their reactions were slowed by a sort of collective inertia: believing they had been told to stay, they worked the phones looking for someone who could give them a schedule for the evacuation. They delayed for more than an hour, during which Frank Lombardi, who would have told them immediately to go, climbed down the stairs from his office overhead, but of course without checking in on every floor. At 9:59 they heard muted thunder and felt the building vibrate. It was the South Tower collapsing, an unseen and unimaginable event. They attributed the commotion to something less, maybe a piece of airplane breaking free and sliding down the outside. They did not go to that side of the building and look through the windows. However, they did notice that the smoke in the elevator lobby was growing thicker. Buzzelli and another man unblocked the doors and went out to check the nearest stairwell, which they found clear and well lit. They returned to the office and reported the news. The time had come to leave, with or without permission. At last the group started walking down from the sixty-fourth floor.

There were sixteen of them. They moved at different speeds and eventually spread out over at least nine floors. The stairway descended with left turns, in a counterclockwise direction, and it was of course windowless and completely cut off from the outside. About a third of the way down (in the forties) Buzzelli began to encounter exhausted firemen, some of whom were sitting on the steps and resting. They knew no better than he that the South Tower had fallen or that their forces had been ordered to retreat. They were calm, and said, "Just keep going down, clear run. Keep going down, clear run."

Buzzelli had just passed the twenty-second floor when the North Tower gave way. It was 10:28 in the morning, an hour and forty-two minutes after the attack. Buzzelli felt the building rumble, and immediately afterward heard a tremendous pounding coming at him from above, as one after another the upper floors collapsed in sequence. Buzzelli's memory of it afterward was distinct. The pounding was rhythmic, and it intensified fast, as if a monstrous boulder were bounding down the stairwell toward his head. He reacted viscerally by diving halfway down a flight of stairs and curling into the corner of a landing. He knew that the building was failing. Buzzelli was Catholic. He closed his eyes and prayed for his wife and unborn child. He prayed for a quick death. Because his eyes were closed, he felt rather than saw the walls crack open around him. For an instant the walls folded onto his head and arms and he felt pressure, but then the structure disintegrated beneath him, and he thought, "I'm going," and began to fall. He kept his eyes closed. He felt the weightlessness of acceleration. The sensation reminded him of thrill rides he had enjoyed at Great Adventure, in New Jersey. He did not enjoy it now, but did not actively dislike it either. He did not actively do anything at all. He felt the wind on his face, and a sandblasting effect against his skin as he tumbled through the clouds of debris. He saw four flashes from small blows to the head, and then another really bright flash when he landed. Right after that he opened his eyes, and it was three hours later.

He sat up. He saw blue sky and a world of shattered steel and concrete. He had landed on a slab like a sacrificial altar, perched high among mountains of ruin. He was cut off by a drop of fifteen feet to the debris below him. He saw heavy smoke in the air. Above his head rose a lovely skeletal wall, a lacy gothic thing that looked as if it would topple at any moment. He remembered his fall exactly. He assumed that he was dead. He waited for a while to see if death would be as it is shown in the movies—if an angel would come by, or if he would float up and see himself from the outside. But then he started to cough and to feel pain in his leg, and he realized that he was alive. He was trapped high on the altar, injured, and covered with a slick powdery dust. He shouted for help and called out the names of the people who had accompanied him down the stairs, but heard only silence in response, and saw no movement of a human kind. Where the Twin Towers should have stood he saw only smoke and sky. Somehow an entire huge building had passed him on its way to the ground. Somehow also he had landed just right. Buzzelli was a Catholic, but an engineer, not a theologian. For an hour he sat trapped on the altar trying to reason things through.

Conditions were still precarious. The altar itself was unstable, threatening to capsize or collapse. Buzzelli was too badly injured to climb down. He worried that if he rolled off his perch—simply allowed himself to drop—he would be impaled on the twisted steel below. Increasingly he had trouble staying calm. He was alone. He was helpless. And when the silence was finally broken, it was not by the sounds of rescue, but the crackle of an approaching fire. The fire came from an area behind him, which from his position he could not see. He worried that the fire would weaken the skeletal wall and cause it to topple onto him—or, worse, that the flames would burn him alive. Judging from the sound, the danger was growing rapidly.

Then he heard someone call, "Richie!" It was a fireman climbing unseen through the rubble nearby, attempting to locate the fourteen stairwell survivors, one of whom had established radio contact and was guiding in the rescuers.

Buzzelli did not know this. All he knew was that there was a human presence. He started shouting, "Help, help! I'm up here!" Eventually the fireman materialized below the altar. He looked up at Buzzelli and said, "Oh. Do you need a rope to get down?" He seemed to think Buzzelli was a fellow rescuer who somehow had gotten stranded on top of the slab.

Buzzelli said, "I'll jump if you want me to, but I can't climb down alone."

Apparently, this was not what the fireman expected to hear. He did a double take and said, "Oh, my God. Guys, we've got a civilian up here!"

Other firemen arrived and began to discuss how to get Buzzelli down. It was not an obvious thing. They were worried about the instability of the debris slopes as well as the precariousness of Buzzelli's perch. They were also worried about the fire. It was not just a fire, it was an inferno. Indeed, just then the flames flared up, and came on so aggressively that the firemen had to retreat. As they disappeared, one of them yelled, "Hold on! We'll get back to you!" The promise was of little comfort to Buzzelli, who figured, probably correctly, that they would not have left him if there was any way they could have stayed.

Buzzelli by now was thoroughly terrified. The fire was roaring, popping, and setting off small explosions just behind the altar. He still could not see the flames, but he could feel the heat. Now he heard a new, more intimate sound, which he took to be the groaning and sizzling of overheating steel. This was the end. Desperate at least to assume control over his fate, he groped around and found a sharp metal scrap with which to slash his wrists. He had it firmly in hand and was about to cut himself open when, strangely, just as suddenly as the fire had grown, it subsided and died. A few minutes later the firemen reappeared. One named Jimmy said, "All right, we'll get to you somehow." He circled clockwise around the altar, disappeared for a stretch of dangerous climbing, and pioneered a route to an alcove high in the rubble mountains above and behind Buzzelli. Somehow he clambered down to the altar. Three others followed. The firemen then fashioned a rope cradle, got it around Buzzelli, and lowered him to the debris slope below.

The group still had 400 yards of difficult terrain to go. Despite the severe pain in his leg, Buzzelli managed to walk about halfway before beginning to lose consciousness. The firemen put him onto a plastic stretcher known as a Stokes basket, and they passed him down the pile in the manner of the bucket brigades.

In the ambulance a kindly attendant lent him a cell phone to call his wife. She was at home, surrounded by friends and family. It was late in the afternoon. She said, "Oh, my God, I can't believe . . ." He heard an uproar in the background. He said, "Yeah, I'm alive." He was taken to Saint Vincent's Hospital, where the other patients were firemen or cops—rescuers who had been lightly injured in the debris. The staff assumed that Buzzelli was just another one of them. He had some cuts and bruises, and a broken right foot—that was all. They told him to go home or sleep in the cafeteria if he liked, because they were still thinking triage then, and standing by for the rush that never occurred.

The Forest Primeval
by Peter Canby

Peter Canby is the author of The Heart of the Sky: Travels Among the Maya *and is the head of fact-checking at* The New Yorker. *He went to the Republic of Congo in 2000 to accompany biologist Stephen Blake on the last of Blake's nine "long walks" through the utterly wild Nouabalé-Ndoki forest. This story appeared in* Harper's.

I've just reached Makao, the most remote village in the Republic of Congo. I'm traveling with Stephen Blake, a British wildlife biologist, in a thirty-foot, outboard motor-powered pirogue—a dugout canoe—following the muddy, weed-clotted Motaba River north from its confluence with the Ubangui River. At first, after leaving the Ubangui, we passed small villages hacked out of the forest, but for a long time we've seen swamp interrupted only by the odd fishing camp: small bird nest-like huts and topless Pygmy women in grass skirts waving their catch forlornly as we motor by.

But now we've arrived at Makao, the end of the line, the last town along the Motaba. Ahead is pure, howling wilderness. Makao has a population of perhaps 500, half Bantu and half Bayaka—among the most traditional Pygmy tribes in Africa. The village long had a reputation as a poaching town, one of the centers of the extensive and illegal

African "bushmeat" trade, which, in the Congo basin alone, still accounts, annually, for a million metric tons of meat from animals that have been illegally killed. But since 1993 the poaching in Makao has all but ceased, and the village has taken on another significance: it is the back door to the Nouabalé-Ndoki forest. Nouabalé-Ndoki is named for two rivers, only one of which actually exists. The name of the existing river—Ndoki—means "sorcerer" in Lingala, the lingua franca of much of the two Congos. Nouabalé doesn't mean a thing. It's a misnomer for another river, the Mabale, inaccurately represented on a geographer's map in the faraway Congolese capital, Brazzaville.

Nouabalé-Ndoki is now a 1,700-square-mile national park known chiefly for having the least disturbed population of forest life in Central Africa. No one lives in the park, or anywhere nearby. Nouabalé-Ndoki has neither roads nor footpaths. It contains forest elephants, western lowland gorillas, leopards, chimpanzees, forest and red river hogs, dwarf and slender-snouted crocodiles, innumerable kinds of monkeys, and nine species of forest antelope, including the reclusive sitatunga and the supremely beautiful bongo. The southwest corner of the park is home to the famous "naive chimps" that sit for hours and stare at human intruders. Until biologists arrived just over ten years ago, few of these animals, including the chimps, had ever encountered humans.

Blake studies elephants. A self-proclaimed "working-class lad" from Dartford, England, Blake read zoology at the University of London; he is now working on a doctoral thesis about the migratory patterns of Nouabalé-Ndoki forest elephants at the University of Edinburgh. Thirty-six, fit, and lean, Blake is known as a scientist who likes the bush and is not afraid to go where wild animals live. But he's also con-sidered audacious, a biologist who thinks nothing of crossing wild forests clad in sandals and a pair of shorts. Richard Ruggiero, who runs the elephant fund for the U.S. Fish and Wildlife Service and worked with Blake just after the park was established, compares him to nineteenth-century explorers: "He's someone who could walk across Africa, turn around, and then be ready to go back again." Another colleague described encountering him as he emerged from a long stint in the bush. "He was wearing torn shorts and a tattered T-shirt. He had a staph infection but seemed completely happy."

As part of his research, Blake has taken a series of what he calls "long walks"—foot surveys that start in Makao and follow a web of elephant trails up the Motaba and Mokala rivers to the park's northern border, cross the park from north to south, and then emerge from the headwater swamps of the Likouala aux Herbes River below the park's southern border. (The gorillas of the Likouala aux Herbes were the subject of Blake's master's thesis at Edinburgh.) Each of these treks—and Blake has made eight—covers about 150 miles and takes about a month. When I joined him, Blake was preparing to embark on his ninth and final trip along his survey route. I had heard of Blake's work from Amy Vedder, a program director at the Wildlife Conservation Society, which, along with the U.S. Fish and Wildlife Service and the Columbus (Ohio) Zoo, funds his research. Vedder and I had been discussing the toll that the region's wars have taken on its wildlife when she told me about Blake's long walks. I signed on to accompany him on his last one. At the time, it seemed a rare opportunity to see the Earth as it was thousands of years ago, at the moment when humans lived side by side with the great apes from which they evolved.

But now that I've reached Makao, I'm wondering why I made no special preparations for this trip. All the perils, which seemed theoretical before I left, have become disturbingly real. Not only don't we have phones or any means of communication; we also face threats of dengue fever, deadly malaria, the newly resurgent sleeping sickness, and even AIDS and Ebola, which are believed to have emerged from the forests of this region. I'm also afraid of army ants, ticks (eventually one crawls up my nose and inflates just at the top of my nasal passage), swarms of flies, and, above all, snakes. When I let slip that I am particularly nervous about snakes, Blake tells me about the Gabon viper, a fat, deadly-poisonous snake with the longest fangs of any snake in the world. It often lies in ambush on Nouabalé-Ndoki trails. "The Gabon viper always bites the third person in line," Blake says glibly. "That's your slot."

• • •

The Wildlife Conservation Society maintains a field station in Makao, and we spend several days there assembling a crew. One morning, as Blake and I bathe in the Motaba while a cloud of blue butterflies swarms around us, he explains how his recruiting policy has been determined by local economics. Bushmeat, he tells me, was a staple of the Congolese diet and, for many, the only available source of income. In Makao, the W.C.S. provides jobs to people who are now forbidden by law to hunt; Blake himself has also sought to hire the best former hunters in order to keep them off the market. Practically speaking, this means recruiting the Bayaka, who live not just in Makao but also north and east of the park. Unlike Pygmies elsewhere in Africa, who are increasingly removed from hunting and gathering, many of the Bayaka still go into the forest for months, or even years, at a time, living off the land with little more than spears and homemade crossbows. Blake hires them because they know the forest intimately. "I often think every Bayaka should be awarded a doctorate in forest ecology," Blake says. "They know what's going on."

But Makao is ruled by Bantus, who, while dominant, know much less than the Bayaka about the forest. Blake would rather travel only with Bayaka, but, because of the dynamics of the village, he also hires Bantus. The relationship between the groups is complicated. The Bayaka Pygmies are small forest people—the men in Makao seem to average around five feet three—and presumably the original inhabitants of Central Africa. The Bantus, who are taller, are fishermen and slash-and-burn cultivators who migrated to the region several thousand years ago. The Bantus control Bayaka families; the Bayaka are expected to hunt for their Bantu owners and to work their manioc fields. In return the Bayaka get metal implements, notably cooking pots and spear points, made from automobile leaf springs; having acquired these things, they light off to follow a nomadic life in the forest. This arrangement is changing, however, as many Bayaka now live in the village year-round. Not all of the Bayaka still know how to make crossbows, recognize plants, or use spears. They can no longer survive in the forest.

Several of Blake's Bayaka recruits have accompanied him on earlier treks. They include one of Blake's oldest Bayaka friends, Lamba, who is named for a stout vine that winds helix-like up into the canopy trees, and Mossimbo, who is named for an elephant-hunting charm. But this time Blake is excited about a new recruit: Zonmiputu. Zonmiputu comes from one of the most traditional bands of the Makao Bayaka. Blake had met him on one of his early trips after a chance encounter, somewhere outside the park, with Zonmiputu's father's band, which had been living off the forest, following the ancient, intricate Bayaka way of life, for more than a year.

"They were carrying spears and homemade crossbows," Blake recalls. "They had one cooking pot, no water jugs, and a lot of baskets they'd made out of forest vines. Their clothes had worn out, and they'd gone back to wearing bark fabric."

As the first person ever to have employed the Bayaka, Blake is changing their lives. "Before they worked for me, their wives had to scrape for yams using sticks. Almost all their food was baked in leaves. Now one of them works for me for a month and makes enough money to buy a machete, a few clothes, a pot, and some fishhooks." Still, after returning from a month in the forest, Blake has frequently been confronted by Bantu patrons demanding the money he is about to pay "their" Pygmy. They react with incredulity when Blake won't give it to them.

As Blake and I talk by the river, I hear what I take for a birdcall. It's soon answered by a similar call—but at a harmonic interval—and then a third. Soon the river valley is full of strange syncopated harmonies. It's as if the trees themselves were singing. "Pygmies," Blake says when he sees my puzzled expression. "They're working the fields."

By the next day we've assembled our team—Zonmiputu, Lamba, Mossimbo, four other Bayaka, three Bantus, Blake, and me. Our walk begins another six hours up the river. We pile ourselves and our gear into the pirogue. Our "tucker," as Blake calls our food, comes from a market in the town of Impfondo along the Ubangui. It consists of sixty cans of tomato paste, two hundred cans of Moroccan sardines, forty cans of Argentine corned beef, twenty pounds of spaghetti, one hundred pounds of rice, several bags of "pili-pili"—the very hot, powdered African peppers—and large quantities of cooking oil, sugar, coffee, and tea. ("What's an Englishman to do in the forest without tea?" Blake asks.) We've topped off our supplies with three fifty-pound sacks of manioc flour and two baskets of smoked Ubangui River fish, bought from a fish merchant in an Impfondo courtyard.

We cast off early one morning. Above Makao, the riverbanks are uninhabited. It's late February—the end of the dry season—but the twenty-foot-wide river courses swiftly between marshy banks. We pass African fish eagles, perched on overhanging branches. Hornbills wing their way overhead, making otherworldly cries and beating the air with a ferocity that evokes the original archaeopteryx. Around ten in the morning an eight-foot, slender-snouted crocodile surfaces next to the boat and glances dispassionately at us. Our disembarkation point, from which the boatman will return the pirogue to Makao and we will begin walking, is near a fallen tree just below the juncture of the Motaba with one of its tributaries, the Mokala. I step ashore, look down at my pale, tender feet clad in rubber sandals, and wonder how I'm going to survive this expedition. In front of me, hearts of palm have been peeled—evidence of gorillas. Behind me Mossimbo spots fresh python skin, assumes the python is nearby, and leaps back in panic. Pythons here can grow to twenty feet; they strangle everything from antelopes to crocodiles. Everyone roars with laughter at Mossimbo's expense. The laughter covers the whir of the pirogue's motor as it pulls away, and when the Pygmies quiet down I hear the pirogue disappearing back downriver. My heart sinks.

Ten years ago the Nouabalé-Ndoki park didn't exist. The land was set aside after a decade of mass slaughter of elephants. During the 1970s a Japanese vogue for ivory signature seals, a consequent tenfold increase in the price of ivory, and a continent-wide collapse of civil authority combined to set off an orgy of elephant destruction.

Poachers wielding AK-47s massacred entire herds for tusks, and then sold the ivory through illegal networks presided over by potentates like Jean-Bédel Bokassa, the cannibal emperor of the Central African Republic, and Jonas Savimbi, the murderous Angolan warlord. At the height of the slaughter, poachers were killing 80,000 elephants annually. In the 1980s almost 700,000 elephants were killed.

In 1989 conservation organizations intervened. The Convention on International Trade in Endangered Species (CITES), a widely supported treaty that regulates trade in endangered species, put African elephant ivory on its list of most restricted commodities, thus effectively banning its international exchange. The market collapsed and conservationists rallied to save the remaining elephants. Africa has two types of elephants: *Loxodonta africana africana*, the bush elephant of the savannas, and *Loxodonta africana cyclotis*, the forest elephant. Biologists know a great deal about the savanna elephant, the world's largest land mammal, which is easy to spot and easy to monitor. But the forest elephants that Blake studies are smaller, more elusive creatures. Only recently identified as their own species, forest elephants live in Africa's impenetrable jungle, and their behavioral patterns—even their numbers—are almost entirely unknown.

As part of a continent-wide elephant census that began with the conservation efforts, the Wildlife Conservation Society and the European Economic Community contracted to estimate the elephant population in the north of the Republic of Congo. The north was then almost entirely unexplored but had recently been carved into forest blocks designated for European logging interests. Michael Fay, an American botanist and former Peace Corps volunteer who was studying western lowland gorillas, was hired to conduct the survey. Today, Fay is known for having made a 1,200-mile "megatransect," a trek from Nouabalé-Ndoki to the coast of Gabon. But in 1989, Fay was just an adventurous graduate student and Nouabalé-Ndoki merely Brazzaville's name for an unexplored logging concession. Fay traversed Nouabalé-Ndoki with a group of Bangombe Pygmies. In the interior they found large numbers of forest elephants, western lowland gorillas, and chimpanzees that were unafraid of humans. Chimps are hunted everywhere in Africa, and their lack of fear in this instance led Fay to conclude that he and his team were the first humans they had ever seen. He decided that Nouabalé-Ndoki—unspoiled, vast, and teeming with wild animals—would make an ideal national park. Working with Amy Vedder and William Weber, directors of the Wildlife Conservation Society's Africa program, Fay wrote a proposal for a park that W.C.S., the World Bank, and the U.S. Agency for International Development agreed to fund. In a dramatic gesture that pleased conservationists, the government of Congo withdrew Nouabalé-Ndoki from the list of logging concessions. In December of 1993 it became a national park, with Michael Fay as its first director.

Early in his tenure, Fay recruited Blake to study wildlife at Nouabalé-Ndoki. In 1990, Blake had come to Brazzaville to work in an orphanage for gorillas whose parents had been killed in the bushmeat trade. In those days, Blake hung out with a group of De Beers diamond merchants. His best friend ("a cracking bloke") was an arms trader. He drank a lot of vodka, raced the orphanage car around Brazzaville, and ran a speedboat up and down the Congo River. But by 1993, Blake was ready for a change. When Fay asked him to work in the new park, Blake quickly accepted. He started as a volunteer. Fay remembers that he showed up "clad from head to toe and carrying an enormous green backpack that must have weighed five thousand pounds." In contrast, Fay had evolved a style of jungle travel that involved bringing Pygmies and packing light—one pair of shorts, Teva sandals, no shirt; he would wear the same clothes every day, wash them every night, and wrap blisters and cuts with duct tape. Blake rapidly adopted Fay's style and soon became, as Vedder puts it, Nouabalé-Ndoki's "wild-forest guy."

On his early surveys of the new park, Blake explored an elaborate network of elephant trails that crisscross the forest. Some trails were as wide as boulevards, and each seemed to have a purpose: one led to a grove of fruit trees, another to a river crossing, another to a bathing site. These trails existed only where there were no humans around to disrupt the elephants' lives. Outside the park, where there were human settlements, the trails vanished. Blake became certain that in the trail system was a map of the ecological and psychological mysteries of forest-elephant life. In 1997 he enrolled in the Ph.D. program at Edinburgh and began his thesis on the elephants of Nouabalé-Ndoki. "Elephants are kingpins of forest life," Blake says. "I have come to feel that if you could understand elephants you could really understand what was going on throughout the forest. Here's this bloody great big animal. It's disappearing, and we know bugger all about it."

In the years since he began his study, Blake's work has acquired a new sense of urgency, and this is one of the reasons he's invited me to join him on his long walk. In 1997, just as Blake was beginning his research, a civil war erupted in Brazzaville when the then president, Pascal Lissouba, sought to disarm a tribal faction from the north. Protracted firefight leveled what had been one of Central Africa's few intact cities; 10,000 to 12,000 people were killed in Brazzaville alone. The violence also spread to rural areas, where a third of the country's population was displaced and uncounted numbers were killed. Many Congolese fled their villages and hid in the forest, where they died of disease or starvation while trying to subsist off wild game.

"People did a lot of atrocious things and got away with them," Blake says. "Every Tom, Dick, and Harry had an AK-47. You'd go into a tiny village and half a dozen sixteen-year-olds would come strutting down the street with bandannas and automatic rifles." The war led to more hunting. Although the park itself was spared, largely because of its remoteness, the surrounding elephant population, as Blake puts it, "got hammered."

This history has contributed to Blake's conviction that the isolation—indeed the very existence—of places like Nouabalé-Ndoki is imperiled. As we've traveled, I've noticed a certain desperation on his part, as if he were convinced that whatever he doesn't learn about the elephants on this trip will never be learned—and that all there is to know about forest elephants will be irrevocably lost.

• • •

"Fresh dung!" Blake exclaims. He sheds his daypack and pulls out his water-proof notebook. With a ruler, he measures the diameter of the dung pile (which looks like an oversized stack of horse manure), cuts two sticks, and begins to separate seeds from the undigested roughage.

We're four days up a wide-open elephant trail along the Mokala River. The trail is thick with dinosaur-sized elephant prints. There are also hoof marks of red river hogs; the seldom seen giant forest hog, which grows to 600 pounds; and a pangolin, a 75-pound nocturnal consumer of ants and termites that is covered in dark-brown scales that look like the shingles on a roof; as well as leopard prints and both rear foot and knuckle prints of a big gorilla. Overhead, troops of monkeys chatter and scold: spot-nosed guenons, gray-cheeked mangabeys, and the leaf-eating colobus. In spite of all the tracks and animals we've come across, however, we've found little evidence that elephants have been here recently.

We travel each day with one of the Bayaka acting as a guide while the other Bayaka and Bantus, who tend to be boisterous on what for them is a junket into the wilderness, cavort well behind us so that they don't scare away the animals. On this day, Blake's old friend Lamba has taken the lead, followed by Blake, and then me in the Gabon-viper slot. Lamba crouches over the dung pile while Blake isolates four types of seeds in it. Three of the four, he says, are dispersed only by elephants. One of these is the seed of a bush mango.

Lamba tells Blake that we're not seeing elephants along the trail because they've left the river for the hills, where the wild mangoes are bearing fruit.

"Most fruits are produced in fixed seasons," Blake says to me. "But there seems to be no pattern here with mangoes. They fruit whenever. It would be great if we could find lots of fruiting mangoes and lots of elephant signs. That's the kind of thing we're looking for, a few indicators of what moves elephant populations."

The most obvious explanation of what moves elephants is food, and Blake's research involves making a thorough study of the plants we encounter as well as chasing down feeding trails. We stop every twenty minutes so that he can make botanical notes. In order to create a definitive survey, Blake always follows the same route, varying it only when he makes side trips down feeding trails. He carries a Global Positioning System, a handheld device that translates satellite signals into geographic coordinates and which Blake uses to record the exact location of his observations. The Bayaka take care of navigation. Blake also carries a palm-sized computer, into which he enters his data. The use of such technology is new in wildlife biology. As Richard Ruggiero puts it, "[Blake]'s the first to use GPS and satellites to successfully look at the long-term movements of elephants in the forest. He's collected data no one else has looked at before."

But none of this matters if we don't see elephants. Despite Blake's estimate that as many as 3,000 elephants use the park, the animals themselves elude us. They're hard to see because they are agile and fast: Forest elephants grow to nine feet at the shoulder and weigh up to 8,000 pounds but move with surprising stealth, thanks to a pad of spongy material on the soles of their feet, which dampens the sound of breaking branches. The elephants also communicate by using infrasound, a frequency below the range of human hearing. Once elephants have determined that intruders are present, they can warn one another over significant distances—without humans detecting the exchange.

Blake has attempted to make elephants easier to find in a number of ways. In the fall of 1998, he received a grant from Save the Elephants, a foundation run by noted elephant conservationist Iain Douglas-Hamilton, to outfit several elephants with GPS collars. Blake and Billy Karesh, a Wildlife Conservation Society field veterinarian, went deep into the forests of Central Africa with a high-powered tranquilizing rifle; they managed to sedate two elephants near Nouabalé-Ndoki and put collars on them. One of the collars never worked, but the second, placed on a female, worked for a month, long enough to trace the elephant's movements outside the protected forest.

The fewer signs we see of elephants, the more restless Blake becomes. "Amazing, isn't it," he muses. "Absolute bugger all."

On the fifth day, as we're walking along a ridge above the Mokala,

Blake hears a branch snap. Zonmiputu is our guide. He is a quiet man, about five feet tall, an inch or two shorter than the rest of the Pygmies, and perhaps forty years old.

"*Ndzoko,*" Zonmiputu whispers. Elephant.

Quietly he puts down his pack, indicates the elephant's direction with his machete, and leads us at a crouch through the thick underbrush. After thirty-five yards, Zonmiputu stops and points out a shadowy shape looming twenty yards away. It is a young-looking bull, about eight feet at the shoulder, with deep chocolate-colored skin. I can see its brown tusks waving as it reaches up with its trunk and rips branches out of the surrounding trees. We approach. Blake hands me his binoculars. The elephant is now fifteen yards away, and I'm focused on its eye—a startling sight, sunken in the wrinkled skin, bloodshot; it seems to peer out from another epoch, as if it were looking forward at some huge, unfathomable span of time.

"A young bull," Blake whispers. "Perhaps twenty years old."

The bull senses that we're near, lifts its trunk toward us, and crashes off into the forest.

In the evening, sitting around the camp after dinner, I ask Blake to ask the Bayaka if any of them has ever killed an elephant. I know that Pygmies have traditionally hunted elephants with spears. As Blake relays the question, the Bayaka stiffen. It's illegal to kill elephants. They don't know why I'm asking, and they all say no—unconvincingly. All, that is, except Lamba. Blake refers to Lamba as "Beya," the Bayaka word for giant forest hog, because he has, as Blake puts it, "scabby habits." Having made this trip several times together, Lamba and Blake are perpetually laughing at each other, and, in front of Blake, Lamba doesn't bother to dissemble. He's killed three elephants with his spear, he tells us. He stalked the elephants and speared them in the gut. When necessary, he'd spear one a second time in the foot to prevent it from running.

For one of these elephants, which a Makao Bantu hired him to kill for its tusks, Lamba was paid an aluminum cooking pot. For another, he received a pair of shorts.

"This for a hunt that would have taken him weeks," Blake says hotly.

I ask Lamba whether he has any fear while hunting an elephant.

No, he doesn't, he responds, even though elephants can kill hunters. Gorillas, however, scare him. A mature male—a silverback—can grow to over 400 pounds. He knows three Pygmies who've been killed while stalking gorillas.

"And do the Bayaka kill *people?*" Blake asks.

This elicits nervous laughter. Cannibalism is not unknown in this region, though no one has ever accused the Bayaka of eating people. But we're not far from Bangui, where, in modern times, Emperor Bokassa is said to have served human flesh at state dinners. Blake tells me that the first Frenchman to arrive in Makao in 1908 was eaten. "We found records of it in the colonial archives in Paris," he tells me. (Later, when looking in vain for a copy of the document at park headquarters, I turn up a similar complaint from another colonist whose son had been eaten in a nearby village.)

When the laughter dies down, we hear a roar in the hills. It's a gorilla beating its chest.

Talking to my fellow travelers requires several stages of translation. Most of our conversation is in Lingala, which Blake, the Bayaka, and the Bantus all speak. In addition to Lingala, however, the Bayaka speak Kaka, the Ubangui language of Makao Bantus, and Sango. Their own language—Bayaka—is Bantu-based, and if the Bayaka ever spoke an independent, non-Bantu language, it disappeared after the Bantu migration into the region thousands of years ago. As we progress farther into the forest, the Pygmies use words for plants and animals that are so specific they may be relics of an older Bayaka, the ancestral language of a forest-based people.

"There are 4,000 to 5,000 plants in this forest," Blake says one day. "I know the botanical names of perhaps 400. Mossimbo knows the Bayaka names for probably twice that. Zonmiputu knows even more."

What the language gap means is that if I want to ask the Bayaka a question, I have to first ask Blake in English, who then translates it into

Lingala, which often sets off a discussion in Bayaka, which is summarized in Lingala to Blake, who finally gives it back to me in English. Meaning is distorted—lost—in the process. My frustration rises as I gradually realize that not only do the Bayaka speak several human languages but they can also summon wild animals.

We are walking under a troop of monkeys one day when Lamba begins to whistle, a loud, repeated screech in imitation of an African crowned eagle, a canopy predator. The monkeys are already screaming at us, but Lamba's sound throws them into a state of agitation and draws them down to the trees' lower branches. Soon the forest resounds with the thrashing of limbs and the cracking of branches, as well as grunts, whistles, and alarmed chattering, as the monkeys react to being caught between the imagined eagle above them and the indefinable hominids below.

On another occasion, Lamba crouches down and makes a nasal call that imitates the distress call of a duiker, a type of forest antelope that has adapted to the lack of browse on the tropical forest floor by eating fruit, flowers, and leaves dislodged by canopy monkeys and birds. Immediately a blue duiker—only a foot tall, one of the smallest of the forest antelopes—charges out of the undergrowth. It has big eyes and a small, round nose. When it spots us, it pulls up short, then turns around and bolts. But it can't resist Lamba's call. It returns, stops, bolts again, and comes back—until Lamba finally breaks the spell by laughing at the antelope's confusion.

Later, we come across a herd of fifteen red river hogs rooting and grunting around the forest floor. These hogs grow to 250 pounds and have small, razor-sharp tusks. Our presence makes them skittish, but they don't flee. They may never have seen men before. We stalk until the closest hog is five yards away, just over the trunk of a fallen tree. Mossimbo then begins a wheezing-pig call. The pigs freeze, dash away, and then, spellbound, return nervously, almost compulsively. Mossimbo keeps calling until he has the biggest boars lined up across the trunk from us. Staring, entranced, their faces look extraterrestrial—tufted ears, long snouts, big sensitive eyes ringed with white; they seem unable to fathom just what they're looking at. Mossimbo squeals—an alarm. The pigs' eyes bug out, and they race off into the forest as Mossimbo erupts in laughter.

To me these episodes are fragmentary glimpses of a world in which humans and animals share a symbolic language. The Bayaka take great pleasure in their mastery over the animal world, and nearly every episode of their summoning animals ends in guffaws. It's not benevolent laughter. If Blake and I hadn't been present, each of these animals would certainly have wound up in a Bayaka cooking pot—and there's something about this nasty, exhilarating confidence that is quintessentially human.

We've come to a point where we must ford the crocodile-rich Mokala. The current is swift, the river bottom sandy, and the water up to our chins. We hold our bags above the water level and, shortly after we reach the far shore, wade across a tributary and enter the park. As we climb up the bank, we enter an area of closed canopy forest where the understory is more passable and the butts of the trees are eight and nine feet in diameter, with straight boles that explode into kingdoms of filigree high above. Zonmiputu is again in the lead when he stops stock-still, turns back to us, and whispers, "Koi." Leopard.

Through a gap in the underbrush, we make out a pattern of dark rosettes on a brown background. The impression gradually resolves into the abdomen and haunch of a large leopard. As we watch, it glides out of the frame, its snaky tail trailing behind.

Zonmiputu crouches, clears his throat, and makes a duiker call to try to fool the leopard into coming to investigate. Through another gap, I see the leopard hesitate, then break into a run. It's gone.

Although leopards are not commonly believed to attack humans, the Pygmies claim they do. Several days earlier, Mossimbo had pointed out a pile of leopard scat filled with reddish-brown hair. Blake poked around in it long enough to discover a strange brown cylinder the size and color of a cigar butt. Using a stick, we rolled it over. I leapt back in horror. It was the top half of a finger, the nail still intact.

"Chimpanzee," Blake said.

• • •

The eerie discomfort of the forest is beginning to overwhelm me. One night, I'm inside my tent in the grips of a dream. I'm being suffocated by vines, buried until only my face is exposed. Slowly I'm being pulled into the earth. I awake with a start, pull out my flashlight, and check my watch. It's four-thirty in the morning. The air inside the tent is thick and stifling. Outside, water drips from leaves, unseen creatures scurry, branches snap, beasts hoot and squeak. Overhead, I feel the claustrophobic weight of tropical foliage. Tonight's dream is one of a series that has become vivid—houses I used to live in, offices I've worked in, visits with friends—and I wonder if this is what it's like to be dead. My restless spirit is haunting the places I loved.

Dawn is filtering down to the forest floor. I hear the rest of the camp stirring: the Pygmies whack their machetes into dead branches and clang our battered, soot-covered aluminum pots over the fire. I hear Blake yawning in his tent. He calls out to ask how I've slept. I lie and tell him I've slept well. But now, at six in the morning, this trip has become oppressive. Breakfast arrives: a mound of glutinous white rice covered with Moroccan sardines and the leftovers of last night's smoked-fish stew. Gloomily, I tuck in. Blake asks if I find the forest claustrophobic. I lie again and tell him no, but it's a bad line of thinking, because today in fact I do. Neither am I heartened by the fact that today we're not moving camp. While Blake goes off to do some elephant-feeding studies, I'll have to spend the day alone with the Bayaka.

The Bayaka and I leave camp around eight, cross a stream, head up into the hills, and wander, foraging for wild mushrooms, yams, seasonal fruit, a bark that tastes like garlic, a bark that serves as an antibiotic, a bark containing quinine, an edible vine in the legume family, a sapling that is said to act like Viagra—in short, whatever the forest will provide. With Blake, we follow elephant trails and walk purposefully in single file. With the Bayaka we maintain no consistent direction. My compass becomes useless. I cling to my guides.

My first Bayaka encounter occurred as Blake and I stepped from our pirogue into the waiting crowd at the riverside. A kindly-looking old

Bayaka in a torn shirt stepped out from the back of the crowd and headed straight for me. He grasped my hand, stared curiously into my eyes, and wouldn't let go.

"He just wanted to see what kind of a person you are," Blake explained, once I'd pried my hand free.

It was almost as if the old Bayaka recognized me. If he had, it wouldn't have been entirely far-fetched. Douglas Wallace, the geneticist who has made a career reconstructing human migrations around the globe through rates of change in mitochondrial DNA, believes that the Bayaka are descended from a small group of Paleolithic people who once roamed across eastern Africa. Wallace and several others argue that a population genetically very close to the present-day Bayaka were the first modern humans to leave Africa some 50,000 years ago. "We are looking at the beginning of what we would call Homo sapiens," he wrote recently.

In other words, I live in New York, but I'm also the long-lost cousin of the Bayaka, the depigmented descendant of their ancestors who hiked over the horizon and never came back—until now.

Strolling through the forest, I've noticed that my cousins appear to be in a perpetual Wordsworthian idyll; they often gaze dreamily upward, as if contemplating the god that has provided them with such sylvan abundance. At one point, I convey this impression to Blake. He corrects me. "What they're looking for is not divinity but wild honey. Although, for them, it's pretty much the same thing."

Sure enough, my day with the Bayaka devolves into a honey hunt. There are several kinds of wild honey in the forest; one belongs to a stinging bee. Mossimbo doesn't take long to spot what he takes for a stinging-bee hive high overhead, sixty feet up, in a hole in a tree branch. The Bayaka rapidly build a fire and extinguish it. Mossimbo wraps the coals in a bundle of leaves, straps the bundle on his back, grabs a machete, and effortlessly shinnies up a liana along the branchless tree trunk. Soon he's vanished into the foliage, and all we can hear is his machete hacking into a tree branch. Finally he descends with two dry honeycombs.

"*Chef,*" he says, drawing on his minimal French for the first time. "*C'est fini.*"

The hive has been abandoned.

After several more hours of wandering, the Pygmies spot a more accessible stingless sweat-bee hive, climb the tree, and soon revel in honey that tastes watery, smoky. I sample it, but to me it's an off-putting soup of bark, twigs, grubs, and dead and dying bees. I leave it to the Pygmies.

After we leave the hive, the sweat bees pursue us vengefully. We're squatting down in front of a pile of bush mangoes, shucking the seeds out of the hardened pits, when I'm suddenly overcome with helplessness. A large part of my frustration comes from the language. Blake is not here to translate my questions. But I'm not just deprived of speech today; I'm also faced with the fact that the forest, which is such a source of bounty to the Bayaka, is, to me, an undifferentiated mass. I don't have the vocabulary to break this environment down into parts. There's nothing I can parse, nothing I can usefully understand. I'm completely at a loss without words. The Pygmies see that I'm wilting.

"Papa," Mossimbo says, affectionately, handing me a mango seed.

By the time we get back to camp, it's thick with tsetse and filaria flies. Tsetse flies carry sleeping sickness. Filaria flies can deposit the larva of parasitic worms in a human's bloodstream. (Blake later comes down with fly-borne elephantiasis.) One of the Bantus slaps a tsetse that is feasting on my back, leaving the dead insect lying in a pool of my blood. I think of what Blake told me when I'd been bitten earlier by a tsetse. "No one can tell me those flies can't transmit AIDS. All you need is a few viral cells. We're in the Congo, after all, and the AIDS problem is huge."

As the afternoon ends, I'm not fit for anything but crawling inside my tent.

The flies disappear at sundown, and I re-emerge for dinner. Smoked fish again. This time it's served with manioc, a cloying flour made from the tuberous root of the cassava plant. After our meal, the Bayaka pull out *djamba*—marijuana—a substance that the Bayaka value only slightly less than wild honey. As they have on many nights, the Bayaka roll the marijuana in forest leaves and inhale deeply. Tonight the ensuing hilarity seems greater than usual. Since all the jokes are in Bayaka or Lingala, I ask Blake for explanations. The Pygmies have asked him if I'm rich, he says. Obligingly, he has told them that I am the richest man in the world.

"You're their new culture hero," he says.

I try to imagine what might have led the Pygmies to speculate about my wealth, and remember that, in addition to the Tevas I wear most days (we're constantly in and out of water), I have two pairs of sneakers, one of which I haven't even worn. Three pairs of shoes! Extravagant, prodigal—*rich*.

I retire to my tent and, crawling in, notice that the ground under the tent floor is blotched with patches of light. I have smoked the *djamba*, and the tent floor looks like a city at night seen from an airplane. Until I figure out that it's a phosphorescent fungus, this vision offers consolation, if only because it reminds me that there is a city out there, somewhere in the world. I fall asleep and have another strange Ndoki dream. A woman appears and teaches me the supernatural art of being in two places at once.

We've reached the line of *bais* stretching from north to south that defines the center of the park's elephant life. The word *"bai"* is derived from the French *"baie,"* but it has escaped into local usage to describe a miniature savanna maintained by forest elephants in the middle of the forest. "If elephants are lost from an area," Blake says, *"bais* quickly grow over."

One afternoon, Blake and I follow the elephant trails to the Bonye River *bai*. The *bai* is big, the size of three football fields, and it's the first open terrain we've seen since leaving Makao. The afternoon light is soft and golden, playing on the riffling surface of the river as it winds through the clearing. In the water, about seventy-five yards away, are nine forest elephants—four adults and five young, three of them infants. As we watch, an old matriarch ambles out of the forest, followed by two more young and another adult female. The matriarch reaches the riverbed, kneels, drills her trunk into the white sand, and gurgles as she sucks mineral-rich water out of the streambed. When she pulls her trunk up, she sprays river water into her mouth. Upstream, a wading bird picks at the riverbed while three red river hogs browse on the marsh grass, trying to avoid the playful charges of one of the baby elephants. On the far margins a sitatunga, with its distinctive wide, splayed feet, feeds quietly.

During the next hour and a half there is a constant coming and going until we've seen thirty elephants in all. The young ones prance around and engage in mock fights, and the adults spray themselves and their children, as the sunlight flashes in the water droplets. Blake looks blissful. He creeps forward to the edge of the *bai*, quietly sets up a video camera, pulls out his notebook, and begins sketching what are the most distinctive and identifying features of individual elephants: their ears. He'll exchange these later with Andrea Turkalo, a forest-elephant researcher who is studying the social structures of elephant herds in a Dzanga Sangha *bai* across the border in the Central African Republic.

I sit on a fallen tree trunk, relieved, enjoying the light. Elephants are members of the ancient, highly successful order of Proboscidea, which, historically, has contained almost 200 different trunked and tusked species, including mastodons and mammoths. Beginning 50 million years ago, and as recently as the late Pleistocene, 10,000 or so years ago, proboscideans roamed the globe. Mastodons and mammoths grew up to fifteen feet. But there were also pygmy elephants. (A four-foot-tall elephant, *Elephas falconeri,* survived on the Greek island of Tilos until a little over 4,000 years ago. A dwarf mammoth lived on Wrangel Island off Siberia until 1700 B.C.) Then, toward the end of the Ice Age, elephants died off en masse, and today only two species survive—the Asian elephant, *Elephas maximus,* and its bigger cousin, the African elephant, *Loxodonta africana.* Both of these species evolved in Africa, but *Elephas* moved into Asia and then became extinct in its home range. Some argue that only then—about 40,000 years ago—did

Loxodonta africana, which had been exclusively a forest creature, emerge to seize the open savanna.

The mass proboscidean die-off was part of the mysterious and more general Pleistocene extinctions. Sometime between 10,000 and 25,000 years ago, all mammals weighing more than a ton—as well as many lighter than that—disappeared from Europe, Asia, and the Americas. This is an old story. But the other story is that some elephants survived— as a miracle, emissaries from the prehistoric world.

From Bonye *bai* we head south to Little Bonye *bai*, Mabale *bai*, and, ulti- mately, Mingingi *bai*, the epicenter of elephant life in the park. Blake points out the various fruit trees associated with elephant trails. The most conspicuous of these, he says, is *Duboscia macrocarpa*, a large tree with an almost gothically fluted trunk. Virtually every duboscia we see stands at the intersection of several elephant trails, gracefully alone in a clearing made by fruiting-season elephant traffic to the tree. Another regular tree along the trails is *Omphalocarpum elatum*, which has fruit growing out of the side of its trunk. The fruit is encased in a heavy, hard-shelled ball— the size of a medicine ball—which the elephants like well enough to dislodge by ramming the tree with their heads.

"The importance of fruit trees for forest elephants has only recently been acknowledged," Blake says. "And that's because almost all ele- phant research has been based on savanna elephants, which eat very little fruit. In fact, many conclusions drawn from savanna-elephant research are simply not applicable to forest elephants. It's always amazing to me that elephants get lumped in categories the way they do."

As we walk, Blake confesses to me his obsession with the rocker Chrissie Hynde, and in particular with her song "Tattooed Love Boys." And one evening, after we arrive in camp, Blake spots Lamba sprawled across his bags, Blake takes his daypack, lifts it over his head, stands over Lamba as if to hurl it down, and recites:

> Run to the bedroom.
> In the suitcase on the left,

You'll find my favorite axe.
Don't look so frightened.
This is just a passing phase,
One of my bad days.
Would you like to watch TV?
Or get between the sheets?

Lamba is baffled but, with the rest of the Bayaka, laughs nervously. "'One of My Turns,' by Pink Floyd," Blake explains to me. "You never heard *The Wall* concert they played in Berlin, did you? There's that whole debate about stadium concerts, I'm not that big a fan of stadium concerts, but that was a great concert."

As we're ducking under some vines, we see our first snake. It's in the branches overhead—a big, evil-looking thing nearly five feet long. Blake can't identify it, but it's not one of the famously poisonous snakes of this region—not a boomslang, not a black mamba, not one of the several cobras. The Bayaka give us their name for it, say it's bad, and seem anxious to get away from it. "Can you imagine how many others we haven't seen?" says Blake.

Shortly afterward we scare a leopard off a fresh-killed duiker. The duiker's entrails are ripped out, but it's still warm. The Bayaka tie up the duiker and take it along for our dinner.

We're wading in the sandy shallows of the Mabale River when we discover a dead baby elephant. It's a gruesome and disturbing sight; the elephant, the size of a pony but stouter, is half submerged, covered in flies, and leaking blood from its trunk.

At this same spot last evening, we saw one of the elephants Blake had collared two years earlier now standing in the river, still wearing her nonfunctioning transmitter. Considering the size of the park, this was quite a coincidence. And not only did we see her yesterday but we saw her with a young elephant following close behind her; at the time she was collared, she had been pregnant, and this young elephant looked about a year old—the appropriate age. Now, it seems, that baby is dead.

"Hell of a thing," says Blake, pacing back and forth. "Hell of a thing." He picks up the baby elephant's trunk, lets it flop back into the water, and examines the tiny tusks and the toenails on each foot. He picks up a stiff leg and turns the little creature over, looking for some telltale sign of what killed it, but he can't find anything except a group of puncture wounds on the animal's chest. With snakes on my mind, I suggest that the wounds might be the result of Gabon-viper bites—and that the elephant may have died of hemolytic bleeding. Blake is unimpressed but seems distressed that he can't come up with an explanation. He frets, hovers, pulls out his notebook and takes notes, gets his video camera and shoots pictures. He is reluctant to leave.

Looking over the little creature, dead of unknown causes, I'm struck again with a sense of being dead—the idea that this lifeless body could be mine. After a quarter of an hour, I persuade Blake to give up his forensics, and we start up a trail—only to turn back ten minutes later. He has decided the puncture wounds are the result of a leopard attack.

"If we could demonstrate that a leopard could kill a baby elephant, it would be quite a thing," he says.

We wade back into the river. Blake pulls out his knife and makes precise incisions along the puncture wounds, two of which go straight through the elephant's chest and into its lungs. A punctured lung could be the source of the bleeding through the trunk. The elephant could have drowned in its own blood. Blake's hypothesis about the leopard suddenly seems plausible.

"Hell of a thing. Hell of a thing," Blake repeats to himself, still agitated, but in much better spirits now that he's arrived at a theory. It occurs to me that science is formidable, and not merely for its accomplishments but because faith in reason leads people to brave treacherous environments like this one.

We camp along the Mingingi River, a mile or so below the *bai*. The day is sultry, buggy. Thunderclaps rumble across the distant forest, and late in the afternoon we're drenched by a brief downpour. But the weather clears overnight, and I awake at three in the morning to gorilla calls echoing up the valley, elephants trumpeting from the *bai* above, and moonlight illuminating the side of my tent.

In the morning we head up to the *bai*. The approach paths are wide and parklike, and the landscape has been designed by elephants. They have dug bathing pools out of the hillsides. The underbrush has been cleared of patches of forest, and tree trunks are swollen to exotic shapes from elephants having picked away their bark. We find a meadow surrounding a highly polished termite nest—an elephant rubbing post surrounded by the marks of heavy traffic and worn down so far that it looks somehow like a public monument.

We creep forward toward the edge of the *bai*, a huge open space of marshy grassland and isolated clumps of trees. A shower has just passed and the mist is lifting off the forest all around. Swallows are dipping in the river. A white palm-nut vulture with its hooked yellow beak is perched on a dead tree limb. A single bull is drinking from a pool.

Just as we're preparing to walk out into the river, nine bongos—large forest antelopes—emerge out of the underbrush and wade into the middle of the *bai*, tails flicking, sides adorned with vertical white stripes, their celestial-looking horns curving gracefully skyward.

Lamba hears what he says is a yellow-backed duiker, the largest of the duikers. We're beyond Mingingi, in the center of the park. We squat while Lamba calls. No response. He calls again. A stick snaps. Silence. Lamba calls a third time. Another stick snaps, off to our right. I wheel around and see two heads duck quickly behind a termite mound. It's a strange, stealthy gesture. The heads are humanlike. We're not the only ones stalking; we're being stalked. Chimpanzees, thinking they're going to find a wounded duiker, have instead found their nearest primate cousins.

"It's just the lads," Blake says, "checking us out."

Along with baboons—and of course humans—chimpanzees are the only primates who regularly kill other mammals. In Nouabalé-Ndoki, chimpanzees set methodical ambushes for the leaf-eating colobus monkeys and even for duikers. They also scavenge other meat—

including pigs—and Blake tells me that in the past he has called in chimpanzees by hiding behind tree roots and making duiker calls.

"When they respond to the duiker call, they come for the kill," Blake says. "The males are quite a sight with their hair standing on end. They come whipping around the tree root, see us, and just deflate. They've never seen humans before. I've had one sit and stare at me for five minutes."

In his book *The Third Chimpanzee*, the physiologist Jared Diamond argues that humans are close enough to chimpanzees to properly be thought of as a third chimpanzee species (after chimpanzees and bonobos). The DNA of chimpanzees is 98.4 percent the same as ours, and of the remaining 1.6 percent, most is insignificant. The meaningful genetic differences could be focused in as little as one tenth of one percent; they account for the genes that lengthened our limbs (allowing us to walk upright and use tools) and, more importantly, altered, as Diamond puts it, "the structure of the larynx, tongue, and associated muscles that give us fine control over spoken sounds." Indeed, a group of scientists have recently isolated a single gene that may underlie the human ability to speak. These scientists are presently trying to determine when this gene evolved. One theory dates it to only 50,000 years ago—around the time the ancestral Bayaka left Africa and set out to explore the world.

We're in chimpanzee territory now, and after our stalking encounter we find signs of chimps everywhere. We hear them pounding on tree trunks and howling like coyotes out in the forest. We see their skillfully made nests in the trees and the ingenious traps they've set at termite nests, but we don't see the chimps themselves. Noticing that I've become preoccupied with spotting a chimp, Lamba volunteers that the Bayaka make a chimp-hunting charm, but when I ask him about it he averts his eyes. The next day one of the Bantus speaks up. *"Chef,"* he says to Blake, "Lamba was lying. There's no chimp-hunting charm—only a gorilla-hunting charm."

A few nights later, Zonmiputu strips a liana down into fine strands and dries the strands over the fire. ("It's *Manneophyton fulvum,* the liana they use for making hunting nets," Blake explains.) Zonmiputu tosses the mass of shredded vine to Manguso, another of the Bayaka. Taking the mass of vine with him, just at sunset, Manguso climbs into the lower branches of a tree. He makes gentle sounds, gorilla sounds—imploring noises, soft exclamations, sounds of surprise—all the while weaving whatever he's expressing into a rope.

"You do it this way," Zonmiputu explains, "so you can get the gorilla up in a tree."

It's the gorilla-hunting charm.

"Not every Bayaka knows how to make this," Blake says to me. "These people are disappearing as fast as the elephants, and their knowledge is disappearing with them."

Two days later, I'm wearing the charm bandolier-style across my chest when Zonmiputu sees me. He looks alarmed. He's made the gorilla charm for me, but one of the other Bayaka is supposed to wear it. Such things are supposed to be worn only by initiated Bayaka—but we can't, of course, talk to each other, and I only learn about this prohibition later. Zonmiputu sends one of the Bantus to explain that if I come across an elephant, I must take it off. Otherwise the elephant will become mean.

We smell the gorillas before we see them. There's a dusky odor along the trail. The gorillas are just ahead of us, and apparently they smell us. There's a loud crash of tree branches, and a silverback barks, then ignominiously flees. A female with an infant on her back and two juveniles are caught in the trees. For the next ten minutes, they try to muster the nerve to descend and flee. Eventually, the mother, the infant, and one of the juveniles make death-defying leaps to the ground and run off into the underbrush. The remaining juvenile stays behind, defiantly pounding his little chest until we move along and leave it in peace.

"They're in for a shock when the loggers get here," Blake says.

We're now out of the park and in the Pokola logging concession, which is leased to the German-owned, French-managed company

Congolaise Industrielle des Bois (C.I.B.). Blake, who was jubilant while in the forest, now seems depressed.

"Our wilderness walk is over as far as I'm concerned," he says. "We're now in the realm of man."

The prospecting line, however, is only the first sign of what Blake refers to as the park's "biggest land management issue"—industrial logging. C.I.B. now has the rights to two of the three concessions surrounding the park, and over the next twenty years the entire forest surrounding the park will be selectively logged. What this means, Blake says, is that in twenty years the only intact forest in the north of Congo will be Nouabalé-Ndoki.

Logging itself is not the most dangerous threat to wildlife. Loggers in the region generally confine themselves to removing only two species of African mahogany that bring high enough prices on the European market to justify the expense of transporting them. (A single African mahogany log might bring $4,000 on the dock at a European port.) The additional light brought to the forest floor as trees come down may even promote the growth of ground ferns favored by many large mammals, including elephants, and logging may *increase* densities of certain animals. But by building roads, bringing in thousands of foreign workers, and creating a cash economy, logging has invariably led to uncontrolled killing of animals—poaching. C.I.B. is working with the Wildlife Conservation Society and the Congolese government to develop wildlife management within logging concessions and to control poaching, but it remains an ominous situation.

"The big issue," Blake told me, "is for the logging companies to take responsibility for hunting in their concessions. It's not a feasible argument for us to say they shouldn't be here—Congo needs revenue, and we'd be laughed out of the country. Controls on hunting, the prohibition on the export of bushmeat, and the importation of beef or some other source of protein are about the extent of our demands on the company."

We descend the Bodingo peninsula, an elevated ridge of land south of the park's border that runs down into the Likouala aux Herbes swamps. We soon discover that more than a prospecting line has been cut through the forest. C.I.B. has surveyed much of the peninsula, marking off the commercially valuable trees with stakes in the ground. The prospectors appear to have been accompanied by a party of Pygmy hunters. We see abandoned snares and places where trapped animals have struggled to free themselves by digging holes in the ground and raking trees with their claws in attempts to escape.

The forest has been cut up in a grid, letting in light, leaving it curiously thin. Taking in the devastation around us, I realize that what's lost when a forest is cut is the weight of evolutionary history, the whole sequence of life, all the voices that the Bayaka can still understand— the voices that existed in nature before we other primates found a way to describe, and circumscribe, the world around us.

Blake is studying an African mahogany that's been marked for harvest. Its dense trunk, which is ten feet in diameter and has oaklike bark, soars upward toward the canopy. "That tree may be 900 years old," he says. "Soon it will be gone. Just like that."

We continue down the peninsula and launch off into the swamps. Tsetse flies are in evidence, along with sword grass, thorn forest, army ants. We sprint through the ant columns. We sleep on patches of raised earth, bathe in mud puddles, and drink coffee-colored water out of stagnant pools. One day Lamba finds a greenish-water-filled excavation—the home, he explains, of an African dwarf crocodile. He squats down and makes a birdlike sound. Soon eight little crocodile heads nervously broach the algae-green surface, their elevated eyes popping up like bubbles.

I am walking behind Zonmiputu when I look up and spy a spider the size of a dessert plate crawling up his back toward his hair and his collar. "Putus!" I shout, using his nickname. Zonmiputu freezes. This is distressing. Zonmiputu is supposed to be invulnerable. I run up behind him, intending to brush the spider off. But the spider has a furrowed, lethal-looking body and strong hairy legs that are tensing as if it is preparing to leap. I grab a stick and whisk the spider into the bushes. Zonmiputu turns around, looks at my spider pantomime, grimaces, shudders, and hurries back along the trail.

In Nouabalé-Ndoki there is always the unnerving sensation that something is watching you. A mongoose creeps through the underbrush; a tree snake twirls along a branch. Today, as we scramble over root snarls, plunge thigh-deep through pools of mud, and approach Terre de Kabounga, the end of our walk, we come across the fresh trail of a crocodile and then hit something that really stops us: a human footprint in the mud. It's so fresh that it's still filling with water. Someone has spotted us, and he's hiding.

The Bayaka find the trail and follow it. We hit dry land and soon hear a woman singing, a meandering, flutelike voice. A tall, graceful Bantu woman, clad in brightly colored wax-print African fabrics, her hair in cornrows, is gathering firewood and, though she has seen us, defiantly continues her song. Before long a husband emerges. He's a square-shouldered, handsome man, the schoolteacher, he tells us, from the nearby town of Bene. He hasn't been paid in three years, so he closed down the school and left his students, the future of Africa, to fend for themselves. He moved out into the swamps, along with a good part of the rest of this region's shattered population, to smoke fish and hunt bushmeat.

We follow the schoolteacher and his wife to their camp. It's filled with fish and hung with shotguns. Other relatives come out of the forest to stare at us in wonder. They direct us to a path that leads, an hour later, to the cut-over edge of the forest. We emerge onto a red-clay road, blinking and squinting in the harsh, flat light of the open road. The heat, unfiltered by the forest, hits like a blast furnace. We shake hands in a gesture of shared congratulation, but the triumph feels hollow. We've been dreaming of the human world, but now that we've arrived it's disorienting.

We walk for hours. Late that afternoon a big, flatbed Mercedes drives up. The driver is so drunk he can barely stand. The ten of us find space in back among twenty-seven other passengers, sacks of manioc tubers, baskets of smoked fish, mounds of edible leaves, and the carcasses of several dead duikers. Soon we're being carried off toward the logging town of Pokola at such high speeds that at times the big truck seems to go airborne. I offer a silent prayer that, having survived a month in the forest, I won't be killed in a car crash.

A decade ago, Pokola was a tiny fishing village on the Sangha River. It's now a sprawling shantytown built of scrap mahogany. In its busy market, the Bayaka spend their pay outfitting themselves in bright sports clothes until they look, in Blake's words, "like Cameroonian soccer stars." Blake and I drink wine with the French logging managers inside their fenced-off compound. I pull the tick out of my nose. Before I know it, I'm back in New York, where I am treated for schistosomiasis, amoebic dysentery, and whipworms.

Blake's ninth and last "long walk" capped the first phase of his doctoral research and gave him the data to begin writing his thesis. Since our trip he has returned to the interior of Nouabalé-Ndoki several times to collar more elephants and collect data to support his argument that by disseminating the seeds of forest-fruit trees, elephants play a crucial role in the evolution of Central African forests.

But in the interim, civil war has broken out again, and Blake reports that since our trip all of the remaining concessions in the north of Congo have been leased to logging companies. A new sawmill is being built north of the park, and a logging road now runs straight into Makao. Another road cuts across the Bodingo peninsula close to the park's southern border. The place where we saw the gorillas, Blake reports, is already a lacework of logging trails. "The civil war was a disaster for the country," he says. "If there'd never been a civil war, the government might have been more open to conservation. Now development and reconstruction have become the country's highest priority.

"In many ways," he says, "what we saw is already gone."

Kidnapped in the Gap
by Robert Young Pelton

Robert Young Pelton probably is best known as the editor of Robert Young Pelton's The World's Most Dangerous Places, *a guidebook for people traveling to war zones and other trouble spots. Pelton in early 2003 traveled to the Panama-Colombia border, where he hoped to cross the rugged Darien Gap jungle. His account of the experience appeared in* National Geographic Adventure.

A week into my trek across the Darién Gap, I'm finally starting to enjoy myself. For two days we fought through lowland thickets of flesh-hooking *chungas* and other spiked, thorned, and angry plants, but now the trail has widened and climbed to cooler elevations. Reaching a clearing, my companions and I drop our packs and relax while Víctor Alcàzar, our 54-year-old guide and majordomo, prepares lunch. Singing a cheerful song in Spanish, he takes his machete and hacks some branches into Y-shaped supports, then starts a fire and hangs a pot of water to boil. Into it goes a tin of sardines in tomatoes, chicken bouillon cubes, breadfruit, and wild limes. In little time we're all enjoying a passable "seafood" bisque. As we loll about, even the fire ants leave us alone.

It's a peaceful interlude in the Darién Gap, the hundred-mile missing link in the otherwise uninterrupted Pan American Highway, which runs along the western spine of the Americas between Alaska and Patagonia. The Gap is a stubborn jungle draped over the thin waist between the two American continents, the exuberantly green barrier where Panama meets Colombia. It's a place where you can find abandoned Scottish settlements, isolated Indian villages, gun runners and drug gangs, left-wing guerrillas and right-wing death squads. It was a place I was drawn to.

As we eat, three Kuna Indians come up the trail from the village of Paya, moving with an odd but efficient bowlegged gait. They wear rubber boots and carry walking sticks, wicker packs, and plastic bags of odds and ends. We met them two days earlier in Paya; they're on their way to visit Arquìa, just over the border in Colombia. We offer them food, and they sit and chat, with Víctor translating. Arquìa is about 14 hours of hard walking away—a day hike for them and at least two days for us. We're heading there, too, after which we plan to build a raft and float down the Arquìa River to the busy Gulf of Urabà. There, we'll hail a boat bound for Turbo, at the far end of the Gap.

Done eating, our three visitors pick up their packs and wave goodbye. We tell them we'll see them in Arquìa.

Half an hour later, full of bisque and contentment, we move on, too. A few steps down the trail, the silence of our soft, green world is ripped apart by heavy gunfire.

Long bursts of AK-47s thunder in the jungle—the cascading cadence of many gunmen shooting aggressively on full auto. We freeze. I glance at my watch—11:44. The gunfire sounds like an ambush from a fixed position about half a mile up the trail. The three Kuna who stopped for lunch must have stumbled upon a group of armed men. Why are they firing on unarmed Indians? And if three defenseless Kuna have triggered this kind of violence, what will happen to three foreigners?

My mind races. *Armed men, ambushes, attacks. What's the right thing to do? Think.* I write books on this stuff. *Think faster.* Then I remember: *Stay still, stay calm, gather information, think things through.*

I look around. Víctor is sitting on his backpack, staring worriedly at the ground. My two fellow hikers, a Bay Area firefighter named Meg

Smaker and a student from Washington State, Mark Wedeven, both 22, are listening with curiosity but, oddly, without much alarm. Our Kuna porters have dropped their packs and are already retreating down the trail back toward Paya. Before I can say anything, they're gone.

This is serious shooting. The gunmen could be members of the FARC, left-wing Colombian Marxists who attack, kidnap, and kill foreigners. Or they could be ACCU, the right-wing Colombian paramilitaries who usually leave foreigners alone but have murdered FARC rebels and their sympathizers and have kidnapped prominent Colombians. One thing is certain: In the lawless Darién, it is not the police.

"Do you want to go back?" I ask Víctor.

"No," he says. "We should stay together."

I ask twice more and get the same answer.

The gunfire finally stops; it's been six minutes. Now we wait to see if the Kuna who passed us on the trail come back. Then we can learn more and make a decision.

As if on cue, one of the Indians comes up to us. He's terrified. Between gulps of our water, he sputters in Kuna to Víctor. Twenty men with guns attacked them. They killed his friend.

Moments later a second Kuna runs up. He has an ugly bruise on the left side of his head; he taps his chest to show where the bullets struck his friend.

"They killed him!" he says, Víctor frantically translating. "They killed him!"

I try to get him to explain.

"We stopped to get water," he says. "They ambushed us. They killed him."

Then they're off, speeding toward Paya. We wait, but we know the third Kuna will never show up. The Darién is suddenly living up to its reputation.

Our smartest choice would seemingly be to run away from the gunfire. But I have been in ambushes and with men who ambush. Fear is used to drive the enemy out to be captured or killed. It's likely that the shooters will pursue the Indians to prevent them from spreading word of the attack. If we flee we might be fired upon. But if we walk toward the shooting and give plenty of notice that we are unarmed foreigners, we might have a chance. I set up the scenario for Meg, Mark, and Víctor—stick together, talk loudly in English so we don't surprise the gunmen, and don't run, even if they start shooting. I get no argument. With a sense of foreboding, we pick up our packs. We're going to walk into an ambush.

The Darién has intrigued me since 1975, when I was 19. After long months working on a drill rig in Canada, I needed to escape. Flush with cash, I stuffed a few items in a backpack and took off, down through the States to Central America. I ran out of road in Panama, where, over cheap drinks in the capital, I learned about the Darién. Between the two local end points of the Pan American Highway—the pavement stops at Yaviza, in eastern Panama, and picks up again in Turbo, Colombia—lay an undefeated wilderness.

I was told it couldn't be hiked. Then I was told it *could* be hiked—but there were stories about guides who, once paid, simply left their clients stranded to be robbed. People disappeared in the Darién. People were killed.

At the time, it didn't seem worth the risk. After a few days of half-hearted preparation, I bought fins and goggles and went off to live on the tiny Caribbean island of San Andrés, a place of white sand, night-clubs, and beautiful women. I would rise late in the day, swim out to the reef, and dive among the coral and fish. Then I would swim back and lie on the beach, reading and rereading Hemingway's short stories.

In the end, I did not avoid trouble by spurning the Darién for San Andrés; the island turned out to be a dangerous drug-smuggling center. One day two goons and a man in a cheap fedora took me for an informational ride around the island, and the next morning I was on a plane to Miami. But from then on, I knew what I loved. As I grew older and more confident, I mounted expeditions into wild places, and then into devastated war zones to research books like *The World's Most Dangerous Places* and a companion television program. But the Darién held my fascination as that one part of the world where, out of fear and ignorance, I had not ventured. After almost three decades, I felt ready.

Since my first trip to Panama, two national parks had been established that nearly span the Gap—Panama's Darién National Park and Colombia's Los Katíos National Park, both of which are UNESCO World Heritage sites. They are akin more to hunting grounds for rebels and death squads, however, than to refuges for nature lovers.

The rebels belong to the FARC (Revolutionary Armed Forces of Colombia), which was organized in the mid-1960s to fight rich landowners and the government on behalf of downtrodden *campesinos*—peasant farmers. To pay for a guerrilla army that now numbers about 20,000, the organization extorts an estimated $500 million a year in protection money from the coca growers and processors who operate in FARC territory throughout the country. In the early 1990s, the guerrillas began using the national parks on both sides of the undefended Colombia-Panama border as staging and rest areas. From these bases, the FARC rebels descend on the rich agricultural lands surrounding the Gulf of Urabá and terrorize cattle barons and banana growers. They also kidnap and ransom foreign workers and the occasional unwary backpacker.

In a region of Colombia with little or no government or military presence, the only force that has fought back is an ultra-right-wing militia, the ACCU (United Self-Defense Forces of Córdoba and Urabá), a disciplined and feared private army that evolved from vigilante groups organized in the 1980s by drug traffickers and wealthy ranchers. Officially outlawed by the Colombian government and considered terrorists by the United States, the ACCU fighters are part of a nationwide affiliation of *autodefensa* paramilitaries that number roughly 12,000. Their tactics are simple and terrible: Gangs of armed men—the death squads—descend on villages and use guns, chain saws, machetes, and hammers to torture and execute anyone suspected of being a FARC informant or sympathizer. Just the rumor that the paras are coming sends entire villages fleeing into the jungle.

In the 40-year battle between Colombia's left and right, the paramilitaries have been responsible for most of the deaths of non-combatants. And the paras have never hesitated to pursue rebels across the boundary into Panama's Darién province, where the police post closest to the border is 20 miles away, in the town of Boca de Cupe. (Panama doesn't have an army; the country's constitution, which was revised after the 1989 U.S. invasion, forbids it.)

From various journalistic assignments, I knew the leaders of both the FARC and the ACCU. I e-mailed them, telling them I planned to hike the Darién, asking whether it was safe. Neither responded, but a Colombia-based photojournalist told me that no group fighting in the Darién had ever held a foreign journalist hostage.

I didn't want to hike the Darién alone: Jungles and solitude don't mix. I realized that I also wanted to see the Gap through others' eyes, maybe even replicate what the experience would have been like if I'd had it in my youth. Meg came to my attention in the winter of 2002, when she posted messages to a bulletin board on my Come Back Alive Web site. She sounded like a hard-core *Dangerous Places* reader—but one who had missed the point of the book, which is how to *avoid* trouble. Just nine months after September 11, she had hitchhiked solo in Afghanistan "to see for herself." Her first ride: a drug smuggler whose associate threatened Meg by holding a gun to her head. In Pakistan, four men beat her for traveling on her own. She was mugged in India, shot at in Myanmar. I admired her ambition to see the unfiltered reality of the world, but her complete disinterest in the dangers of travel astounded me.

Undeterred by her painful experiences, she e-mailed me for information about crossing the Gap. I advised against it: She spoke no Spanish and had little understanding of the groups she would likely encounter. When she persisted, I decided that instead of trying to dissuade her I would join her and finally take my long-delayed trek. We met at the airport in Panama City, where I discovered that she has the ideal appearance for attracting unwanted attention in the Third World: tall, blond, blue-eyed. She comes across as tough and aggressive, a proud firefighter whose profanity is of Marine Corps quality.

I met Mark while looking in vain for maps of the Gap at the Tommy Guardia National Geographic Institute. He has a slight build, delicate hands, and long eyelashes. Soft-spoken and darkly humorous, he was born in Bogotá to a Colombian woman and adopted at the age of two months by a middle-class couple in the Pacific Northwest. He was loved and sheltered, but now he was searching for someone or something that would reveal who he is and what he wants. After backpacking for a year in Central America, he had focused on the Darién.

I suggested that he join us. Meg had trained as an EMT; Mark knew Spanish and could help translate. Our team was set. We would depart the next day.

As I packed my gear, I sized up my own motivation. When I was Mark and Meg's age, I was skeptical of knowledge—eager to dive into the shallow end of any kind of pool with my eyes closed, confident that luck and bluster would see me through. But my expeditions into some of the world's wildest places provided few insights and little sense of accomplishment. Seeking a deeper understanding, I threw myself into learning about the history and politics of war zones and stumbled into my calling. But over time, I had lost my sense of adventure. My last trip, with the rebels of northern Liberia, felt like a routine TV shoot, just another stop on a 20-year tour documenting familiar horrors: starving refugees, shrieking bullets, and drug-addled teen soldiers who maim and kill for a cause they barely understand. At filming's end, it was off to a bar for a wrap party, then home.

I needed to find something, to reembrace a naive hunger for the unknown. To dive into the shallow end and come up laughing again. With Mark and Meg, I felt that I was back on the path that had first brought me to Panama.

Twelve hours on a bus puts us in Yaviza—the Panamanian end of the Pan American Highway. The town certainly has a terminal look to it: wooden houses haphazardly lining crude sidewalks, scabby dogs, locals sliding in and out of loud bars. The breeze is rancid with the smell of garbage and tropical rot. A domino game clatters down by the docks on the Tuira River.

We plan to motor upriver to the Kuna village of Paya to launch the overland leg of the Darién traverse, but that agenda gets scuttled when the police threaten to arrest our boatmen. The FARC control the entire border with Colombia, they say. The countryside and Kuna villages are hotbeds of *robo, secuestro, narcotráfico*—robbery, kidnapping, drug running. Intimidated, the boatmen take us instead to the riverside town of Capetí, where they introduce us to Víctor Alcázar. His English is spotty—it's been a while since he guided people—but he seems quite eager to attempt the Darién. When we mention the authorities, Víctor winks slyly. There will be no police outposts if we go cross-country to Paya.

We work out a deal with Víctor—$50 a day—and leave that afternoon for our first objective, a small village an hour away. On the trail, we settle into what will be our typical hiking routine: Víctor in front with me; then Mark, listening to the Doors on his Discman; Meg in the rear, marching grimly to Limp Bizkit at max volume. She proves to be deadly serious on the trail and doesn't like to talk. Víctor tells me he has 12 kids, no wives. When he was young, he was an electrical repairman. He traveled to Tijuana and tried to cross the border into the States to eventually get into Canada. But after three months, he gave up. He then went to Nicaragua and joined the Sandinistas. Víctor certainly has the gift of gab; he wants to run for office someday.

I ask him about the FARC, since he seems predisposed to the political left. "This area is controlled by the 57th Front," he says. "These people are not thugs, they are intellectuals." He admits, however, that the FARC kidnaps people for ransom and that sometimes the locals abduct people and sell them to the guerrillas.

"What kind of people do they kidnap?" I ask. "Rich people?"

"Sure."

"Gringos?"

"Maybe," he says with a laugh. There is an uneasy pause as we trudge into the jungle. It would not be the first time gullible gringos have been led into the waiting arms of kidnappers. And our guide seems a little too eager to circumvent the police.

It's just two miles to a small clearing by a river—the "village" that's our first stop. The population consists of five Indians and Emilio Rebas, a Colombian who came here 36 years ago. A giant, boarlike white-lipped peccary with a herniated testicle is the only entertainment until I set up my hammock. I end up pulling out one of the support beams of Rebas's house and land on my ass. It's the funniest thing the populace has seen in years.

Roosters start to crow at 4:44 a.m. At 6:30 the sun rises, along with the heat. We eat the remnants of night's dinner: Spam, rice, and lentils. It's miraculously tasty; Víctor is a good cook. The last of our *aquardiente*— fiery-tasting alcohol—disappears into Víctor's cup, and we get ready for a long slog.

Víctor does yeoman's duty as a guide, happily chattering in Spanish and broken English. *There is a plant that can cure gonorrhea; feel it. Here is a vine with water in it; try it. There is ginger; taste it.* There are traces of a path, but it's tough to spot the machete cuts that mark the way. Sometimes the track just vanishes. It's clear Víctor hasn't been here in a long time.

As we follow dry creek beds up and down steep hills, the insects start to have at us—ants, spiders, mosquitoes, wasps. The day gets hotter, and my urine gets darker. I can't drink enough water to bring it back to clear. I am burning with heat. My first day out carrying a heavy pack, and I'm sapped from dehydration and fatigue.

Finally, night falls. We've been walking 13 hours. My feet are blistered; my legs are cramping. When I reach the banks of a gloomy black river, I pause at the sound of voices—people on the other side are calling to us. A man swims across the river and emerges naked, cupping his genitals.

"Paras?" he asks. "*Paramilitare?*"

I'm confused. I ask if *he* is a para, but he just smiles and returns to the water. We cross, too, and follow the man to a village.

The bathers are neither paras nor FARC; they are Kuna. But Mark's and my military-style packs and boots convince them that *we* are paras, and their chief is not happy to see us.

"You cannot stay here," he yells as Víctor translates. "Absolutely not. You are frightening us."

We try to explain that we're backpackers who want to get to Colombia. The chief won't hear of it. I let Víctor handle the diplomacy.

After a few exchanges, the tension dissolves. The Kuna invite us to stay; the next day they will discuss our fate at a village meeting.

We are in Púcuro, a ramshackle collection of huts that houses around 400 people. Our host is Javier Cervado, a son of the chief, whose home is a one-room, thatched-roof affair. His wife cooks over three hardwood logs; the smoke keeps the thatch dry and the insects at bay. His children swing in a hammock and study us as a puppy staggers around the dirt floor.

Javier shows us a mildewed photo of very white, very midwestern-looking people from the New Tribes Mission, which has been sending evangelists around the world since 1942. Exactly ten years ago—in January 1993—FARC guerrillas kidnapped missionaries David Mankins, Mark Rich, and Rick Tenenoff from this village, bursting into their homes and pushing them into the jungle. The 57th Front demanded a multimillion-dollar ransom, and then there was silence. In September 2001, an imprisoned FARC guerrilla testified that the missionaries had been shot three years after their capture, when Colombian troops closed in for a rescue attempt.

There is a sense of wistfulness as Javier carefully puts away the photo of his dead friends. It is clear he misses them.

While Javier cleans a large iguana for tomorrow's dinner, his wife serves up fish and plantains. Afterward, she shows us *molas*—the colorful embroidery of the Kuna—and asks if we're interested in buying some pieces. The villagers come by to shyly stare at us. The children fuss over Meg's hair. Meg enjoys the attention and laughs with them, and then one of the girls gets up the courage to ask if she can braid it. So we sit in the evening light, listening to the choir at the church service across the way, as the children softly chatter and giggle and plait Meg's long, blond tresses.

The next morning we awaken stiff and tired. Víctor updates us: There is a FARC commander in the region who has asked the chief to tell us to wait until he gets here. It's a disturbing wrinkle. How, I ask, could the FARC have communicated so quickly with the Kuna? "They have communications," Víctor replies. "But don't worry, the commander is my friend." He says it will be good for our security if the FARC knows where we are. Experience tells me otherwise.

At 8 a.m. the sounding of a conch shell calls Púcuro to congress, and its citizens walk to a large building of grass and wood. The women sit on one side, the men on the other. In the middle the elders face one another on two benches. They hold thin, polished staffs of dark wood. There are speeches, very long speeches, and very, very long speeches. The older women, their noses pierced with gold rings, sit impassively; some of the younger ones wear bright beads and colorful skirts. Many women sew molas as they listen. The men are dressed neatly in trousers and cotton shirts.

It seems there is concern that if they let us pass, more will follow. Should strangers be allowed to show up uninvited? What will happen if the police find out they let us continue on to Paya? Víctor jumps in, impassioned.

"Is this not a peaceful village?" he asks, showing his potential as a politician. "Shouldn't foreigners be allowed to come and meet the Kuna? Shouldn't the Kuna benefit from tourism?"

After about three hours, not only do we have permission to leave, but we gain the chief's son and two of his nephews as escorts to Paya. It has been decided that we will pay a $125 hospitality fee, $20 for still pictures, and $50 for video footage. We call it a flat $200, since the Kuna don't have much in the way of change, and hand over crisp $100 bills—U.S. currency being legal tender in Panama. The money is deposited in a safe box with the rest of the village funds. Despite feeling fleeced, I admire the Kuna for their business savvy.

We wait for the FARC leader to make appearance, but by the next morning he still hasn't shown, so we set off for Paya. The route is well-trod, but there are numerous river crossings. Endless lines of leaf-cutter ants hustle up and down the path, clearing four-inch brown trails in the undergrowth. At one crossing our guides give chase to a large, rat-like capybara bobbing in the river. They are quite pleased when they catch the jungle rodent: dinner.

Mark, however, insists that they not kill the animal. At first the guides stare in disbelief, then in disgust. They let the animal go. Mark suddenly realizes the stupidity of his actions. "I have no right to tell those people what to do," he says. For the rest of the day he worries about what he calls his "ethnocentrism"—his attempt to impose his values on the people who have to survive in this jungle.

Mark is anxious about returning to Colombia. Not because of the dangers, but perhaps because of what he might learn about himself and the culture of his birth family. Growing up in a mainly white town, he was sometimes viewed as different because of his darker skin. Some people assumed he was Mexican. When I mention his similarity to Indians I have met in Colombia, he becomes agitated.

He is an intense young man who has studied Latin and Greek and thinks he might become a writer—except, he says, nothing ever happens to him. He has enjoyed his trip through Central America. He climbed volcanoes and surfed. He was robbed three times. Spent a month in the jungle with a medicine man. Swam to an uninhabited Caribbean cay, towing all his supplies, and lazed away the days reading—what else?—Hemingway's short stories.

Mark sees crossing the Gap as his coming-of-age ritual, like the lion hunt of a young Masai warrior or the Sun Dance of the Sioux. As reserved as he is, he has no difficulty telling me that I'm an elitist L.A. yuppie who wants to compress what he considers the adventure of a lifetime into a jaunt between taping sessions of my TV show.

Meg, too, has problems with me. Her initial inspiration for coming here was *Romancing the Stone,* the Michael Douglas-Kathleen Turner movie about a novelist who tries to rescue her kidnapped sister in

Colombia with a grizzled adventurer. She's disappointed that I'm not as macho as she expected; her ideal man is wrestler-turned-movie-star the Rock. Though she carried a duct-taped copy of *Dangerous Places* in Panama City, she mocked it, chiding me about its lack of in-depth info about the Gap.

Are they right? Have I become what I once ridiculed? A creator of pop-culture myths that have numbed these young people into thinking that adventure is risk-free?

In the late afternoon, we emerge from the jungle at Paya, a village of about 500 on a sharp bend of a river. The guides from Púcuro are paid, and they return home. The chief of Paya, a small, smiling Kuna named Ernesto Ayala, invites us to stay with him. He swings slowly in his hammock and makes small talk, scoffing when I mention the police descriptions of his village as a rebel hideout. "No FARC, no criminals, no kidnappers, no threats," he says in Kuna. "The police haven't been here in six years." As the sun goes down, six men play bamboo flutes and dance around the central pole of the chief's grass house. They crack up whenever their jam session meanders out of tune. Exhausted, I go outside and string up my hammock. As I drift off, the flutes echo over the river and chickens scratch in the dirt.

With the morning's light, I wander to the end of the village, where I meet Chief Ayala. He grins and introduces me to members of his extended family, who open up their tiny store for me. There is a small gas-powered fridge with sugared drinks, some cardboard boxes of juice, and a few tins of sardines. I buy a round of juice, and we discuss my trip. The path south is overgrown and leads to swamps controlled by the FARC, Chief Ayala says. He suggests hiking to Arquía—a long walk but much less physically challenging. From Arquía, we can reach the headwaters of the Arquía River and float down to the Gulf of Urabá.

I return to the group to discuss the plan, which is agreed upon. Then a long conch bellow summons the village to a meeting. Once more, we need approval to move on. In the great hall, 40 men discuss our fate; the chief denies us permission. Moments later, three men, surprisingly, stand to be introduced as the guides who will take us to Arquía for $20 each. Not surprisingly, they are the chief's relatives. The chief then decrees a hospitality fee of $250, which we negotiate down to $150. The men vote, we get our OK, and the parliament ends.

That night, the chief uses a string to gently garrote dinner—a prize chicken. While we are eating, a baby steps on a scorpion and fills the night with screams of pain. This is not quite Shangri-la.

After a predawn breakfast of fried eggs and plantains, we head off at 7:30 with our three Kuna guides leading. As we pass the last house in the village, an elderly woman hobbles out. She wags her finger and speaks in Kuna. I ask Víctor what she said. He shrugs. I persist. Víctor replies, "She said we will all be killed when we enter Colombia."

An hour later we run into two young FARC rebels—a man with a rusty AK-47 and a woman wearing something akin to a jungle Wonder Bra. There is always tension when you encounter armed people in a jungle, but the man seems unconcerned that three gringos are cruising into FARC territory. He asks Víctor if we have seen anyone on the trail, what time we left Paya, where we are going, what our business is. His pants and belt are military issue, but his shirt is a rag. He warns us there are paras in Arquía. We wave as they head off, and we continue toward the border. Víctor says he has known the man for two years; the rebels are *socios,* a FARC-approved couple.

The trail slowly climbs. We are now in pristine jungle. Birds screech high above; a large eagle follows our convoy overhead. By 3 p.m. we are at 1,800 feet, walking along a ridge; the green canopy stretches as far as I can see. Mark, a former long-distance runner with a year of backpacking behind him, enjoys the walking. Meg is in shape, but her heavy pack weighs her down and one of her toes is infected. I thought I was in shape, but I am still acclimatizing to the tropics. I'm covered with cuts, bites, and scratches. My feet are bruised and blistered, and I step gingerly.

We stop on the ridge at 4:30 p.m. for our first night of camping in the jungle. Toucans, parrots, and other birds begin their squawking and shrieking; howler monkeys join in. In the evening cool, we dine on Spam and rice as insects dine on us. Though we've been walking all day, we're not even halfway to Arquía.

The morning brings the realization that we are running out of water. It is the dry season, and any water to be had from rivers and streams is far below. We'll have to get creative. The Kuna look for groves of green bamboo, whose thick trunks can hold massive reservoirs of water—if they're not bone-dry or filled with black, septic swill. The first grove we find is arid. Finally, the guides locate another grove and chop into the hard monocots. Inside is—yes!—cold, perfect water in its own natural drinking container. We gulp to our satisfaction and refill our canteens.

By 9:30 a.m. we reach 2,270 feet. The guides point out a red-and-white radio tower in the distance—paras, who have many guns and are very violent, they say. We slip and slide down to around 2,000 feet, where a plateau makes for easier walking. At 10:10, we stop for an early lunch—Víctor's trailside bisque. I take a GPS reading and announce that we are officially in Colombia, the kidnapping capital of the world.

So we've agreed: we're heading into the ambush. Meg volunteers to walk up front. It's a brave gesture, but she doesn't know the trail. It is up to Víctor to find the path, with me shadowing him. We keep up a running patter about plants and culture; Meg and Mark, behind us, about sex, drugs, music. Time seems to slow down. Every sound and sight is magnified; every bend in the trail looks like an ambush site.

I can't stop myself from visualizing an explosion of gunfire aimed at us. How much distance, how much time, how much pain until I drop? To Meg and Mark, I am the expert on violence and warfare, and now everything I've learned about ambushes and firefights—from Afghanistan to Algeria, Chechnya to the Republic of the Congo—is being played out in my own life-and-death game. I admire Meg and Mark's courage, and I feel confident that we are doing the right thing, but I have made a decision that affects three other lives. If I'm wrong, we're dead.

After half an hour, conversation begins to flag. I urge Mark and Meg to keep talking. Then I notice a freshly harvested bamboo water container. "This looks like the place where the Kuna stopped to get. . . ."

I do not finish. A man with a large scar across his left cheek bursts out of the brush and thrusts a rifle in my face. He is yelling at me to do something, but I am fixated on the flash suppressor of his AK-47. My eyes travel up the barrel to the man's round, sweat-drenched face—eyes wide, pupils dilated, jaw clenched. I stare at the gaudy feather in his headband, which bears the slogan "ACCU Contra Guerrillas." My mind begins clicking again: We've been jumped by a paramilitary death squad. Other men in camo crawl out of hiding spots along the trail, their guns pointed unwaveringly at us.

Everyone is yelling. We yell not to shoot. A soldier yells at us to get down, motioning to the ground with his gun barrel. Another yells at us to drop our packs. Still others flick their gun barrels upward—hands in the air. We freeze: We can't do all three simultaneously. Víctor tries to take off our packs, but he's stopped by a gunman who pushes him into a clearing and makes him kneel, execution style. I charge over and stand between Víctor and the gunman, who then forces me to my knees. Mark and Meg drop their packs. Now we're all on our knees in the clearing. I begin to think I made the wrong call.

But then the yelling stops, and the tension levels off. I count five very agitated, unsmiling young men with marine-like brush cuts. They search us quickly and motion for us to sit and remain silent. They try their radio, using the call sign "Scorpion," but in the thicket they are unable to make contact.

The commander leans on a rotting tree stump and launches into a speech. He avoids eye contact, as if he's embarrassed: "We are members of the FARC, 57th Front," he says mechanically. "We do not have a war against the Americans or the people of Colombia. We are opposed to the state and are here to protect the campesinos."

This doesn't make sense. In addition to the slogan on the headband, the webbing on the men's vests has homemade vinyl letters that clearly spell out ACCU BEC—the Bloque Élmer Cárdenas, a 2,000-member paramilitary faction. Is this an elaborate hoax? Víctor, I notice, looks disbelieving.

We sit for three hours, until a larger group of armed men and women marches down the trail. They are led by someone introduced as Commandante Roberto, a compact man in his mid-20s dressed in black fatigues. He has a shaved head and the intensity of a serious fighter. His second in command, a nameless, thick-lipped man, records Roberto on a microcassette. I privately nickname him Intel.

Roberto and Intel want to know who we are, why we are here, who knows we are here. Then more questions, about Paya; it's obvious they've never been to the village. We mention the two young rebels we ran into on the trail, but we try to convince them that there is nothing in Paya—definitely no FARC. Intel decides that Víctor will guide them to the village.

Víctor pleads with us not to let them take him. "I do not like these people," he says. "They make me very scared."

We argue intensely with Roberto and Intel. Víctor is old, we say; he is stupid, he does not know the trail. But it's been decided: They will set off for Paya at 7 p.m., with Víctor guiding them. Then, almost light-heartedly, they tell us we can wait here for him, if we care to.

A soldier brings us a roasted animal that was tied to his belt—probably a rabbit, judging by the bits of singed fur clinging to the meat. Being fed is a positive sign. The gunmen stare at us while we eat. They are particularly interested in Meg. When she walks past, one grabs her buttocks. Now we have something else to worry about.

With no prompting, the leader of our guards tells an odd story: "There are many tigers here"—probably meaning jaguars. "One was on the trail. We shot at it, and it ran away." He laughs. "Tigers do not eat tigers." He adds suggestively, "You may have heard the shots." We feign ignorance, insisting we heard no gunfire. The situation becomes uneasy. We could be in jeopardy if our captors think we've witnessed a murder. For a moment I wish I had brought a sat phone. Then I laugh to myself. The worst thing I could do would be to call for help. We could be killed in a botched rescue attempt or shot by our captors, like the Púcuro missionaries.

At seven, more soldiers arrive. Despite our protests, the terrified Víctor is pushed off into the darkness, and we are left feeling hollow.

Dozens of fighters march us in the opposite direction. They giggle and whisper as we stumble along in the dark; we have walked into a much bigger group than I originally thought. We are led off the trail and told to lie on a black tarp in a clearing. The fighters say we will leave for Arquía first thing in the morning. But armed guards stand over us all night, whispering sharply to groups of fighters that come and go, their gun barrels silhouetted in the moonlight.

After a fitful sleep, we are roused and led past the scattered possessions of the three ambushed Kuna—food, bits of paper and plastic, wicker packs. I see the shirt and pants of the missing Kuna trampled into the mud, and my heart sinks. Maybe we're about to be shot, our possessions rifled.

Less than 20 yards from this grim scene we are led off the path and passed on to five other soldiers. Then the larger group moves out in the section of Panama. The leader of the new team is Carlo, a 20-year-old; his adjutant is the equally young Patricia. "There are many groups of armed men in the jungle," says Carlo. "For your own security we will wait for more of our men before we move on."

And so we pass the next two days under armed guard in a makeshift encampment. Our captors are still spinning stories about being the FARC. At first I was certain they were ACCU paras; now I don't know what to think. They are young and unassuming and wear uniforms of black rubber boots, black T-shirts, green bandannas, U.S.-style woodland camo, and utility vests stuffed with 30-round clips of ammunition for their AK-47s. In small green vinyl backpacks they each carry a black poncho, a hammock, gun-cleaning equipment, a toothbrush, and a few other personal items. They come from poor families in the area, many from farms. They fight for six months on, six months off. For that, they get paid about $150 a month, plus meals. Their motivation for signing up seems the same as most soldiers': It's one of the few jobs around.

The junior members of the team—three boys about 17—pull guard duty on a rotating basis. They sit quietly in the forest, just off the path on either end of our camp. Patricia and one of the boys handle the cooking—rice and tinned tuna, flavored with garlic or onion, served on broad leaves. Our captors eat with plastic identity cards; Mark, Meg, and I share a spoon. Water involves a long walk down to a stream. Over all wafts the sickly odor of something large and decaying, a pungent reminder of what can happen in the Darién.

Carlo is never far from his pistol, a nine-millimeter Ruger P38. He likes to clean it, unload it, reload it. Carlo is shy at first, but as the hours pass he opens up. He's from a nearby community, the youngest of eight. "They came to my village," he says. "I was away. Something terrible happened." Who came? What happened? But Carlo talks around the incident as if it is obvious why he started fighting in the jungle when he was 16. He seems to want to avenge some unspeakable horror visited on his family, but when I ask him why he is a soldier, he replies, "I am fighting for human rights."

Patricia spends a lot of time lolling on her tarp. Sometimes Carlo or one of the other men comes over, pushes up her shirt, and rubs her stomach. She has short hair, dark eyes, and the soft body of a mother; her children are four and seven, she says. On her left upper arm is a tattoo of a teddy bear. Her lover is away, but she and Carlo seem to be pals. They sleep together at night and giggle.

I encourage Mark and Meg to pay attention to what's going on around them, to interact with our captors. Instead, they each retreat to their hammocks and Discmans—Mark calls this his "happy place." He listens to his sixties rock as he jots in a notebook; Meg reads *Bitch*, a collection of druggy profiles of self-destructive women.

Although Meg won't admit it, she suffers greatly from night terrors. She tosses and turns and moans. Her work as an EMT and firefighter has exposed her to car crashes, suicides, and worse. "Children die differently than adults," she says. "They can be talking to you, then turn their heads, and they're gone." At one point, she announces melodramatically, "I killed a six-year-old." She means her EMT team was called to an automobile accident involving a mother and daughter, and the child died in Meg's arms. I ask why she tells people she killed the child when undoubtedly she did all she could.

"People are not supposed to die when I am in charge," she replies.

As I track our captors' routine, I decide that the best time to escape will be late afternoon, when the effects of heat and lunch make them doze off and darkness will fall in less than two hours. They don't have flashlights.

I learn the gunmen's names, their radio call signs. En route to this camp, I tried to track altitude, time, distance walked, and landmarks. Occasionally, I dropped a rolled-up piece of paper with my name, the date, and the time. Around camp I carve my initials and the date into trees. I hoard water and beef jerky. I keep my flashlight, compass, and fire starter on me at all times so I'm always ready to make a dash for freedom.

I explore our limits, making long trips to relieve myself to see if anyone comes after me. When I'm alone, I try to get a GPS reading. I get the soldiers used to my handling their weapons. I pick up loaded guns, admire them, then hand them back. I debate what I will do if faced with execution. Could I kill all five captors before they can shoot back? I pester Carlo and Patricia—when will we be allowed to continue? Where is Víctor? Where are we? I wonder if anyone knows we are missing. Mark has been gone for a year and is normally out of touch; Meg says she seldom tells her parents where she goes so they won't worry. But I sent a detailed e-mail home and I was supposed to be back five days ago.

This is not what I do; my job isn't backpacking in the developing world. I earn a living documenting the horror of places gone mad with fear and war. The reason I came here was to get away from all the turmoil. I wanted to find value in a simple hike, an untouched jungle, a physical challenge against calculated odds. Like Mark and Meg, I wanted an experience with life-changing impact and clear meaning. And yet here I am, again, surrounded by armed killers, a minor but privileged player in yet another of the planet's conflicts.

A faint but ominous sound alarms us on the fourth night. It's an odd combination of clacking bones, the low-pitched rumble of grunts and breathing, and the rustling of leaves by dozens of feet. Fear charges the air. I roll out of my hammock and tell Meg and Mark to get down. Carlo and Patricia spring out of their bed and crouch low, weapons in hand. The sound gets louder. Carlo whispers to the kids guarding the trail: "What is it?"

There are sharp bursts of static as Carlo radios his superiors, trying to find out who's coming toward our camp.

The noise grows louder by the second; my confused brain can't connect an image to it. I imagine an army of ogres breathing noisily as they walk carelessly through the jungle, carrying spears that knock against their packs. It must be an entire column of men. When they are almost upon us, Carlo and the others start firing. When the salvo stops, there are grunts and squeals and then silence. The soldiers cautiously check for survivors among the terrifying horde: a big herd of white-lipped peccaries with their clacking, saberlike fangs. We all laugh at our fear.

Late the next afternoon, Carlo gets a radio call. Afterward, we are told to pack. Less than two miles down the trail, we're left at another camp manned by five soldiers. This group seems more relaxed. We string up our hammocks and sit around the fire and talk. It's almost like coming upon a group of hikers and sharing a campsite. The men here are fascinated by Meg's pierced tongue. The soldiers have a hard time believing that back home Meg is a firefighter, a *bombera*. They get a kick out of Limp Bizkit and page through her copy of *Shutterbabe*, the memoir of a female photojournalist who traveled alone to the world's war zones in the 1980s and 1990s.

We're packed and walking by nine the next morning. Our spirits are high: I take a GPS reading and confirm that we're moving toward Arquía. A few hours later we reach a new camp, where eight Kuna sit nervously off to one side with yet another team of five fighters. This group includes Andrea, a heavily armed 16-year-old with an infectious giggle and a death's-head pendant. She has lost both her parents and her partner, whom she's memorialized with a swastika-type tattoo on her left hand. She grills me about Mark. She thinks he is very handsome, very clean, and very smart.

Our captors now number 15. I can't figure out why the Kuna are here, but we are told they will guide us to Arquía. We start hiking through scenery that's stunning in its tropical verdancy—forests of *heliconia,* swaths of red-and-yellow flowers that remind me of dragons, and clear jungle streams bridged by logs. At one spot Mark pauses to take in the beauty of his lost homeland. "You know, Robert," he says, "I love Colombia."

Just before dusk, we are led down and up two steep ravines to a jungle hideout. With our tiny flashlights probing the early dark, we find a river; the sound of burbling water is everywhere. As we settle in on bare rock at the top of a waterfall, I light tiny candles around our site. On a nearby ledge, Andrea and Mark talk softly. Later, Mark calls out. "Robert, blow out the candles."

The next day our captors do laundry, eat, and splash in the waterfalls. Club FARC, we name this R&R spot. The mood is light; men and women sneak off to bathe and play in private. Weapons are left strewn around, and soldiers doze. It would be a perfect time to escape, but to where? And why? We are nearing Arquía. I lie back and listen to the rush of water and watch the blue smoke from the fires drift up through the leaves.

The mood is dashed that afternoon as we make the hellish climb out of the ravine. We pass more than 30 grim fighters heading to the river camp—older men with heavy machine guns. Unlike the kids who shuttled us from camp to camp, these men don't smile at us; they grunt and sweat as they work their way down the slope. I have the uneasy feeling they are the soldiers who marched off to Paya.

Up top are more soldiers, including Roberto and Intel. They are not pleased to see us, and we're not pleased to see them unaccompanied by Víctor. Mark asks about the expedition to Paya. Roberto wags a finger: "Paya was very bad." He insists that Víctor is waiting in Turbo, but we don't believe him. Our hope of seeing our guide again is fading.

In a chilling reenactment of our first meeting, Roberto curtly tells us to dump out our packs. The soldiers search first Mark's, then mine, including our film and cameras. I pull a three-card monte while they inspect Mark's gear and pocket the storage disks from my cameras. Each confiscated item is noted by Roberto in a book. "We are not thieves," he says, promising that our gear will be returned.

Then it's Meg's turn. She doesn't want to give up her expensive camera and starts to yell and curse. Roberto and Intel tell her she cannot go to Arquía unless she hands over her film and camera. She berates them nonstop.

"*Mujer brava,*" murmurs one of the soldiers. Brave woman.

Roberto gives me a pleading look. Mark and I shrug and explain that this is how American women act; we're enjoying Meg's gutsy tirade. Still, we try to persuade her to comply, to remember that none of us—including the Kuna—can leave until she does so. Meg rants on, Mark refusing to translate her profanity-laced remarks, as Roberto and Intel endure the harangue. Finally, she reaches into her bag, but instead of surrendering her costly camera, she hands over a disposable one.

At midnight we reach Arquía, where we're marched to a soccer field and handed over to a stern commander in a bush hat. He tells us to sit and seems quite concerned that we might escape. Something is up; I don't like the vibe. Mark and Meg feel it as well.

Dehydrated and cold, we try to sleep while guards loom over us. At 4 a.m. we're prodded into consciousness and taken across a river and into the forest. As morning breaks, we discover we're in a Kuna grave-yard. Obviously, our captors do not want us to be seen by the villagers.

At mid-morning, a new soldier arrives. He speaks with our guards, then signals for Mark alone to follow him. I'm immediately alarmed, though the gunman leads Mark from the front, not the rear. An hour goes by. There is no gunshot, and no sign of anxiety among our guards. The soldier returns for Meg and me.

Again he leads from the front, which means he is unconcerned about our actions. I test him by asking if I can wash my hands in the river. He is surprised but doesn't stop me. The average accurate range for an AK-47 fired by a surprised gunman is about 50 yards; I see how much distance I can put between us, which again doesn't seem to worry him.

The fighter takes us along the riverbank to where some 40 men and women are gathered. There are machine guns and horses with high-horned saddles, soldiers cooking and doing laundry. Mark is sitting in a circle of older men, smoking a cigarette and chatting. When we sit down, he says to me quickly, "Hey, man, they're paras, everything's cool. We've been pardoned. They're not going to shoot us."

The soldiers apparently asked Mark what he thought of the FARC and the paras. "I talked and talked," he says. "Probably more than I should have." Then the man who seemed to be the leader took off his jacket to reveal a T-shirt decorated with a skull and crossbones and the letters ACCU EEC. The soldiers told Mark that they'd had to pretend they were FARC. They didn't know if we were missionaries, sympathizers, or arms dealers.

We are offered juice, Gatorade, and food brought from town. The game is over; the paras laugh and laugh, which annoys me. Maybe they're relieved that they are no longer responsible for our security or have to wear their T-shirts inside out or mumble FARC doctrine. I expect them to release us, but they have other plans. Before we can go, we must meet the big boss, "the German." So off we ride to a burned-out *finca*, or ranch, where we wait another two days.

Despite his name, the German—Commandante Alemán—turns out to be a large Colombian. He strides into the ranch house in the company of a very large, bald man. The commandante is a bit taken aback that things have not been set up for him. A drawer is upended to serve as a chair, a box overturned to become a table. He explains proudly that his nom de guerre was conferred on him for his Teutonic sense of organization and precision. Big baldy is another Colombian, a professor of philosophy. I ask where he teaches; the answer is evasive—unnamed institutions in Europe and Latin America. His function, he explains, is to teach human rights to the ACCU. It seems the death squads look to the professor for guidance on the subtle moral issues of their cause.

Alemán produces a plastic bag that contains our possessions, including my cameras and notebook. But we're not yet free—now he wants to discuss the autodefensas. "We are not paramilitaries," he says. "We fight the government. We fight the communists. We are negotiating a peaceful settlement, but we will not put down our arms until we're guaranteed security."

So why were we kidnapped and held for ten days? I ask.

"The situation was delicate," he says. "The guerrillas live in the Darién. They buy supplies in Panama City and truck them south. Then they drop them off along the highway, and the Kuna carry the supplies into the jungle. We were on a big operation to block the frontier zones. When we found you, we were surprised. But we guarantee the safety of Americans, so we decided to keep you until our group came back safely from Panama.

"We have been communicating with the authorities," he continues. "They have been informed you are safe." He pauses. "You understand this was a little bad for us. The government has been asking if we kidnapped you. The press has talked with President Uribe [Alvaro Uribe Velez, of Colombia]. But now you can continue with your work."

I tell him that my "work" was to cross the Darién without getting kidnapped or killed.

The commandante laughs. "The Darién is beautiful. Except, of course, for the war."

The next 24 hours are a blur. A priest arrives to take us to freedom. We spend the night with him and are then handed off to Colombian officials. A car, boat, and plane ride later, we're in Bogotá. Along the way, we endure a press conference and learn that our families and several groups have been working for our release.

When we meet the Panamanian investigators who have flown to Bogotá to take our statements, we are confronted by the horror of what unfolded in the Darién. While we were being held captive, Roberto and his men were stumbling through the jungle under the inept guidance of Víctor. After two days the paras arrived in Paya, no doubt exhausted and frustrated. According to Casildo Ayala, the son of the chief who had invited us into his home, Roberto and company had interrupted a birthday party. The men of the village were drunk on banana liquor.

The soldiers presented themselves as members of the FARC. At first they were welcomed. But some of the Kuna recognized their ACCU BEC markings and spread the word: These were not FARC fighters, they were a death squad.

The paras went on a rampage. They stole food, shot the dogs, and then grabbed Chief Ayala, the deputy chief, the village's spiritual leader, and Gilberto Vásquez, the mayor of Púcuro, who was attending the celebration, and marched them into the jungle. Outside of Paya, they ran into Ayala's son, Casildo, who was returning from a trip to Púcuro. Then something evil happened.

Maybe the paras were furious over the Kunas' lack of cooperation. After all, the paras had persuaded the Kuna in Arquía to work with them; why not the Kuna in Paya? Or maybe Roberto and his men had marched too long for too little, and somebody was going to pay. Whatever the reason, they attacked the Kuna. According to Casildo, they killed his father first, slashing Chief Ayala's throat and shooting him. Then they attacked Casildo's uncle—the deputy chief—and the two other Indians with machetes and guns. Casildo was stabbed in the stomach and had his throat slashed; he survived by playing dead. Somewhere before Púcuro, Víctor escaped and managed to warn the residents. When the paras arrived the village was deserted. The Colombians stole everything of value and burned five huts. As for Víctor, the Panamanian police tell us, he was arrested in connection with the killings in Paya. (He was held for 48 days, then the charges were dropped.) It turns out Víctor has a rap sheet stretching back to 1971—forgery, robbery, assault. We understand why he was so eager to avoid the police.

We *don't* understand the murder of the Kuna. There were no FARC rebels in the villages—just a handful of gentle people isolated by others' fear and ignorance. The fear that kept the police from venturing into the Darién to protect them; the ignorance that provoked the paras to attack.

We are all shocked. Mark and Meg insist we are responsible for the deaths, since Víctor guided the paras to Paya. I remind them that a full-blown incursion was already under way when we entered the Gap; the paras would have found the Indians with or without Víctor. If anything, he may have saved lives by sounding the alarm in Púcuro. My attitude angers Meg and Mark. Suddenly, their grand adventure has become a nightmare.

When we return home, Mark and Meg vanish for a week while they try to come to terms with the incursion and their role in it. I work with the authorities to investigate the Kunas' deaths, emphasizing that we can link the ACCU leadership with the murders. I e-mail ACCU leader Carlos Castaño, asking him why his men did this, but get no reply. Within a month, Panamanian President Mireya Moscoso appropriates $6 million to buy helicopters to patrol the Darién. Additional funds are secured to build 15 more police posts in the Gap. The U.S. offers to help Panama fight incursions.

Most newspaper accounts tally the dead at four. But out in the jungles of the Darién is the body of a forgotten fifth victim, the ambushed Kuna. The man who haunts me.

from A Sword for Mother Nature
by Terry Grosz

Surviving in the wilderness sometimes requires a change in diet. Former game warden Terry Grosz tells the story of a survival instructor who drove home the point with gusto.

The California Department of Fish and Game, where I was employed as a warden for four and a half years in two duty stations in the 1960s, was always big on keeping its officers current by presenting various types of training on a regular basis. To their credit, the department leaders realized that ignoring this need might subject the state and its workers to adverse legal consequences. As a result, it was not uncommon for game wardens to be subjected on a monthly basis to some kind of training designed to enhance our skills, reduce the prospect of liability, and increase our chances of survival. I remember being trained in crowd control, first aid, the operation of snowmachines, firearms proficiency, fire safety, safety around aircraft, pursuit driving, watercraft safety, search and seizure, and rules of evidence, among other things. The opportunities to learn seemed endless in those days.

For the most part the training was good quality and well intended. But the old-timers always grumbled long and loudly about being taken off the job to get more "dadburned" training. They felt that this new-fangled regimen was a waste of their time, and they attended such "tomfoolery" only because they had to. A great many of our officers were World War II and Korean War veterans who had seen just about everything and just wanted to get on with their lives without what they saw as the constant interruptions of training assignments. When they had come to work for Fish and Game in the late 1940s and early 1950s, there had been little or no training given or required. In fact, most of them had had to furnish their own cars and weapons. It seemed that when they had become wardens, they had simply been given a badge, a code book, and a citation book and told to "go get them." I guess I could see why they grumbled so much. They probably longed for the freedom of the "good old days," just as I do today. After all, they had performed the tasks of the profession without any training, so why should they have to go through it this late in the game? However, I ate the damn stuff up because I was a rookie and dumber than a post. Realizing its possible value to my success as an officer, I was happy to get as much help in the form of training as I could. Plus, it gave me a chance to mingle with older squad members, listen to their wildlife law enforcement war stories, and in the process glean a few tips of the trade from those more sage and seasoned than I. Those training assignments also had a hidden value because they brought a lot of us together so that officers got to mingle and renew old friendships and catch up on each other's news. So like it or not, training opportunities were mostly beneficial to us hardheads.

One afternoon I opened my official mail and found a letter assigning my regional law enforcement squad to another training assignment. This time we would be located in the Nevada City area in the western foothills of the Sierra Nevada Mountains. The squad was to gather at a bible camp, whose name I have long forgotten, on a Tuesday evening and spend the following two days being trained in field survival and firearms proficiency. It sounded good to me, especially the part about firearms. In those days I was a crack shot with my .44 magnum and always enjoyed the afternoons I spent shooting competitively with my squad mates. I figured I could always stand to learn more about how to survive as a law enforcement officer, and I figured this survival class might be a training opportunity in street survival. Man, was I off base. . . .

As I hammered up along the mountain roads on my way to the bible camp that Tuesday afternoon, I let my mind wander through the pages of California gold rush history passing before my eyes. Small piles of rock along a streambed told of the miners hard at work to get at the paydirt and gravel beneath the large rocks but above the bedrock. Small pine and incense cedar trees, all of the same age, told me a mining town was nearby that in the mining days had cut down all the trees for miles around for mine timbers and firewood. Because this deforestation had occurred about 120 years earlier, the forest was still growing and the trees were all about the same height. Then the bright orange and softer reds of several hillsides with even smaller pine trees reclaiming a toehold on the almost sterile soil told of the huge "monitors" with their powerful streams of water directed at the hillsides during the gold rush heyday, eating up huge chunks of land and destroying the waterways and fisheries below in the miners' frantic quest for the yellow metal. I passed many small remnants of mining camps as I continued through the gold country and its many larger, sleepy towns with rich historical names such as Downieville, Rough and Ready, Poker Flat, Dutch John, and Hang Town, adding spice to an already exciting trip.

Stopping at the only stoplight in the town of Downieville, I let my eyes wander over the storefronts of old buildings on both sides of the street, stone buildings from long ago with eight-foot-high windows and long iron shutters to protect them against the spread of fire, the nemesis of many a town a hundred-plus years ago. I knew that if I went inside I would be greeted with the view of dark-stained wooden floors that rolled unevenly across the building, high pressed-tin ceilings, and a smell that still spoke of stale cigar smoke deeply ingrained in the wood. A dreamer like me could still sense the strains of excitement and disappointment involving the signs of "color" discovered on the claims so many years ago. Or the arrival of the latest mud-wagon stage bearing mail from loved ones in faraway places. Or the arrival of freight wagons and cursing teamsters bringing flour, fresh onions, potatoes, canned sardines, or barrels of whiskey.

With the changing of the light, I mentally rolled back to my modern-day world and began to follow the letter's directions to the nearby bible camp. When I arrived at the place that would be my home for the next day or so, I stepped out of my patrol truck, stretched my tired frame, and slowly looked around. It was like most camps I had visited, either as a kid or as a state employee. This one was surrounded by a forest of ponderosa pine trees a hundred or so feet high, with many single-level wooden bunk-houses scattered about. A small lake and a .22-caliber shooting range lay off to the west. In the center of the wooden sprawl was a house of worship and another large building I took to be the mess hall. A hearty "Terry, over here!" from Clyde Shehorn, the Blairsden warden, brought me back to the work at hand. After a firm handshake and a quick, genuine smile from beneath an 1850s walrus mustache from one of the finest human beings and wildlife professionals in the country, I got down to the business of registering and locating an unoccupied bunk on which to throw my sleeping bag. I spent the rest of the afternoon and evening with old friends, many bottles of good whiskey, and numerous tales and jokes from times past. As the evening got long in the tooth, the group began to drift away to the bunks and the noisy talk and laughter were replaced with the soft, velvet dark typical of a night in the Sierra Nevada Mountains.

The next morning found me and the rest of my squad standing in line in the mess hall waiting for a typical tight-budget bible camp breakfast: two eggs, two hard-as-a-bullet strips of bacon so thin I could see through them, and two pieces of burned toast. That was it except for coffee, milk, and a small glass of watery orange juice. I found that each bite had a tendency to vaporize before it even hit my stomach. No wonder Jesus appeared so thin in all the pictures and icons, I thought. Since there were no offers of seconds, I retreated to my truck, a good game warden's ever-ready larder, and partook of a feast of sardines, crackers, cheese, apples, and two cans of apple juice. Looking around the parking lot, I noticed several others visiting their mobile larders for the goodies they too had stocked for just such emergencies. Grinning at my compatriots, I slid two large chunks of homemade venison jerky into my uniform shirt pocket and was set for what the day was to bring. You laugh! At six foot four and topping the scales somewhere around 320, I would have been a mere shadow of myself after a few days on that bible camp fare. Since Jesus wasn't there with his loaves and fishes, I did unto myself before others did me in. . . .

When we gathered back at the mess hall, the captain told all his officers to meet at the small rifle range by the lake. He also informed us that the district's wildlife biologists would be going through this training with us. That news created quite a stir, to say the least. In those days in California, plain and simply, the game wardens hated the wildlife biologists and the wildlife biologists hated the game wardens. The game wardens felt that the biologists gave away the shop with their liberal bag limits, doe hunts, and long seasons, and the biologists felt that the game wardens were a bunch of whiskey-drinking, skirt-chasing, uneducated louts who didn't know a good game management plan from a bag of popcorn. So that joint participation announcement set the stage for the commencement of grumbling from many of the more senior lads. In addition, the captain announced that the training to take place that morning was wilderness survival training, not the "street" survival we had thought would occur. Boy, that set the lads a-buzzin' and chirping big time! There wasn't a game warden in the room who considered himself (we didn't have women in the force in those days) anything less than a Jim Bridger, Kit Carson, Hugh Glass, and Joe Meek all rolled up into one bundle of fighting, surviving fury. When the open grumbling and bellyaching hit triple forte, the captain waved his hand over the heated assemblage, requesting quiet. "Gentlemen, the training is going to be given by one of the Strategic Air

Command's finest survival training instructors. I think once you hear him and see what he has to offer, you will see that every one of you will benefit from this information and will find that it may help you survive an unplanned wilderness stay or accident someday."

The grumbling was still there but what could one expect from such a bunch of know-it-alls? I knew what was going through everyone's mind (except those doorknobs like me) regarding a survival instructor trying to teach us something we thought we did on a daily basis. To make matters worse, we had to sit beside those hated biologists, who at best had only half a brain and were hippie wimps in bad need of a shave, a bath, and a decent pair of shoes!

Needless to say, Captain Leamon had an unhappy crew gathered behind him like a gaggle of wing-clipped geese as he led the way out to the bleachers by the shooting range. Not wanting to sit near the hated biologists, almost all of us wardens took seats in the top of the bleachers and let the biologists sit in the bottom rows. Soon about forty wardens and biologists had filled the small bleacher area and were waiting for the arrival of the vaunted instructor. I could already sense that some of the older wardens, if they got their head and the bit in their teeth, would give this Air Force guy a real run for his money.

We didn't have long to wait. Without any fanfare, a mountain of a man hobbled out in his Air Force work uniform and took a position directly in front of the center of the bleachers. He stood there without a word, studying us as we stared at him. He had to be at least six foot nine, even slouching, and weighed at least 385 if he was an ounce. The stripes on his sleeves identified him as the highest-class sergeant in the Air Force, and he appeared to have served about three hundred years in the military given the number of length-of-service stripes! He carried a cocked and locked Colt .45 ACP on his right side and a rather large Bowie knife on his other hip. His pants were tucked into a highly polished pair of black jump boots, and he wore no hat. His face showed many prominent scars, including one showing that his nose had been sliced almost in half. He continued to stare at us with a pair of flat, coal-black, gunfighterlike eyes, shaded by the furriest set of eyebrows I had ever seen. No two ways about it, this man had our undivided attention, and I do mean every man jack of us in those bleachers that fine, hot day!

"Good morning, gentlemen," came a deep, resonant bass voice. A heavy smoker, I thought until I looked more closely at his throat and saw what appeared to be an old knife wound running from one side to the other below his Adam's apple. Damn, I thought; this lad has been there and lucky to get back, from the look of all those wounds and scars.

There were a few halfhearted "good mornings" from the crowd, but most just stared at this larger-than-life apparition. All of a sudden we weren't as tough as we had somehow thought. . . .

The voice boomed again: "Gentlemen, I am Chief Master Sergeant Renaldo Hernandez from Stead Air Force Base, which for those of you lost in a geographic funk is located just outside Reno, Nevada."

Some of you may say, "There isn't any Stead Air Force Base just outside Reno." You would be correct because it was shut down in a round of base closings years ago, sometime in the '60s, I believe. However, the base at that time had one claim to fame: its Strategic Air Command (SAC) survival training center and prisoner-of-war (POW) camp. The SAC would train its air crews in methods of survival in case they had to bail out or were forced down over hostile territory. Then, after weeks of training, the SAC would dump the lads out over the semiarid eastern slope of the Sierra Nevada Mountains and make them try out their skills as they attempted to live for two weeks off the bounty of Mother Nature. Meanwhile, Stead aircraft and ground patrols would comb the backcountry, trying to "capture" the air crews. If captured, they were interned in the then supersecret POW camp at Stead Air Force Base, where they would be treated no differently than if they had been captured by, say, the Russians. In short, this training program was as close to the real McCoy as they could make it, even down to the beatings and brainwashings that routinely took place. The purpose was to avoid a repeat of the huge numbers of men who had broken under POW treatment in Korea. Those who were caught repeated the survival training and escape process all over again. Those who survived moved on within the SAC training system.

The survival instructor continued, "I have been in the Air Force for over thirty-five years. I have tried to retire, but the Air Force will not let me out until they find a replacement for me. At the rate they are going, I will be here for another five years or until I die." Without taking his coal-black eyes off us, he took an ugly, twisted black cigar out of his shirt pocket, unwrapped it, and looked long and hard at it. There wasn't a sound from his awestruck audience, and every eye in the place was on that ugly cigar. I recognized it immediately as one of those very strong Toscanni devils that only *real* men and Italian fishermen smoke. In fact, I smoked that same kind of cigar during the summer and fall in the Sacramento Valley because its smoke would kill mosquitoes at twenty feet! They are one of the deadliest cigars I ever came across, and not many folks smoke them because they are so damned strong.

Without a word, the instructor popped the entire cigar into his mouth and began to slowly and methodically chew it like a regular mouthful of mild chewing tobacco, all the while eyeballing us for any reaction. Not a soul moved, including the battle-hardened veterans. This is one tough son of a gun, I thought as I observed some of my comrades looking like they might gag at this display. I knew I would listen to anyone tough enough to eat a Toscanni cigar and not die on the spot. There was no way I could do what he was doing without puking up everything inside my abdominal cavity. And in those days I chewed as well. I'm sure my compatriots were thinking the same thing.

"Let me give you a little background on what I do for a living, gentlemen," came the deep voice. "I train many of the nation's SAC fighter and bomber pilots and crews in the art of survival. Some of those chaps will get shot down in foreign lands, and not all will make it home. That is to be expected. Some will be killed in the crash or during the moments when they are being shot down. Some will die at the end of the parachute fall or in the hands of the enemy. Others will die of starvation or end up giving themselves up because they didn't listen to me. Others will survive because they paid attention and did as I told

them. That is why I am here with you today—not because you will be
shot down over some foreign land but because you make a living in
the back-country and may find yourself in need of survival skills at
some point in time. You may fall from a horse or injure yourself using
a snowmachine and have to survive for a while before help arrives. You
may get stuck in the backcountry, trapped in a winter storm, or busted
up traversing a piece of rough country on foot patrol and need to hold
on and hole up until help arrives." By now, anyone who wasn't paying
rapt attention was a damned fool. He hadn't missed a scenario that
every one of us had been in at one time or another, and every man was
now there for himself. "So today I will teach you some of the basic survival skills and hope you will listen as my troops do. Whether you do
or not is your call. However, I understand that the first rule of law
enforcement is to come home every night." He let those words sink in
and then said, "Listen to me and follow my teachings and you will
come home every night."

Pausing, and looking off to one side, he let out a stream of tobacco
juice that totally covered an unfortunate stinkbug that just happened
to be crawling across the concrete pad where he was standing. It didn't
take long for the nicotine to do its job, and the beetle rolled over,
waved its legs in the air for a few moments, and then died. Forty sets
of eyes watched that little drama, and no one moved; in fact, most of
us found ourselves hardly daring to breathe for fear of being singled
out by this giant. The instructor reached over, picked up the dead
beetle, placed it beside his feet, and then began his instruction as if
nothing out of the ordinary had happened. However, forty sets of eyes
were still on that damn bug, wondering why it was next to those size
15 feet holding up the man mountain before us.

"Gentlemen, I was a crew member on a B-25 in the South Pacific
during World War II." I couldn't believe it. A B-25 is a twin-engine
medium bomber, not much bigger than the man in front of me. How
the hell he had gotten inside that plane was a marvel to me! "My plane
was shot down, and I was the only survivor, breaking both of my legs
when I landed in the treetops of New Guinea after parachuting out. I

remained in the jungle for two weeks in that condition, slowly crawling inch by bloody inch toward the Australian lines, before I was rescued. Know what saved me?" None of us moved because obviously we didn't have the foggiest idea what had saved him in some fetid jungle more than twenty years earlier. "A stinking Asian buffalo killed by an artillery shell that had been dead for about two weeks before I got there. Yes, I ate the damn rotten thing, maggots and all, and survived, and you can do the same thing if you just do what has to be done." He paused to let those words sink in and then said, almost as an afterthought, "You know, that meat was so rotten from the hot jungle sun that it was green in color and had the consistency of Jell-O about to set. I was glad because my face had gotten messed up by the flak that had hit the plane, and it made it easier to eat with what I had left of a broken jaw. In fact, gentlemen, I just sucked it off the bones and was damned glad to have it."

By now several of the hated biologists with lighter-than-air stomachs had dismissed themselves and were walking away at a rather brisk pace. The rotten-water-buffalo story had plain and simply done them in. The instructor watched them walk away and shook his huge, furry head. All the game wardens, tough as they were, just grinned and watched in glee.

"In case some of you don't believe what I have to say, take a look at these." He pulled his pant legs from his boots and lifted them up to about the knees. I don't think I ever saw a worse set of legs in my life. They were of many ugly colors, purple predominating, with immense holes where huge chunks of flesh appeared to have rotted off. Then there were the terrible scars from the damage to his legs as he had crawled to safety from behind the Japanese lines, and from the subsequent operations to repair what was left. Another biologist in the front row, seeing the legs close up, just got up and without a word left the bleacher area, and shortly afterward the bible camp. Damn, it was tough just surviving the man's presentation, I thought. I wondered what his survival lectures were going to be like. Another hour of this chap and I would be the only man left!

"Now, gentlemen, let's get down to the business at hand." For the next several hours the survival instructor talked about how to set snares with fish line to catch rabbits and other small creatures. How to build woven willow fish traps and, with the aid of a rock dam, run fish into them so one could have something to eat, even if it had to be eaten raw. How to identify certain plants—which ones to eat and which had medicinal qualities. What those medicinal properties were. How to alert those hunting you from the air if they were friendly and how to survive in everything from snow caves to the front seat of our vehicles during snowstorms. He instructed us in how to build fires without matches using flint, steel, wooden sticks, and pieces of glass and the sun. He also told us how to care for minor and major wounds and how to forestall dangers such as infection.

As he droned on, the warm midmorning sun began to take its toll, and many in the audience began to drift off. After all, most of us hadn't slept worth a damn in those small wooden bunks the night before. In fact, most of us were fairly tall, and our feet had hung out over the ends of the bunks most of the night. The survival instructor seemed to sense that he was losing his audience, but he was unable to bring some of us back from la-la land. He droned on, and those of us who could tried to stay with him.

Then Warden Bill Frazier, a friend of mine, noticed a small blue-bellied lizard running along the shooting-range backstop about ten feet behind the instructor. Bill poked me in the ribs to get my attention and showed me the lizard. It was catching flies, so like a dingbat I watched the lizard instead of listening to the instructor. Fascinated with the lizard's antics, I pointed it out to another warden beside me, and soon about a dozen of us were leaning to one side, looking around the instructor, watching the lizard procure a breakfast that had to be better than ours and ignoring the steady droning of the survival instructor.

The instructor, mindful that he was losing his audience to the warmth of the sun and the lizard's own survival tactics, turned and looked hard at his competition. He turned back toward us for a moment, then reached up behind his neck and in a whirling flash pulled a dirk from a neck holster, spun, and in the blink of an eye and one blurred throwing motion pinned the lizard to the wooden backstop with the knife! He had moved so quickly and unexpectedly that it caught everyone unawares. About half of us jumped at the quick movement, and the rest just sat there slack-jawed as we watched the lizard wriggling on the tip of the knife.

Without a word, the survival instructor walked to the lizard and withdrew his knife from the backstop with the lizard squirming on the tip of the blade as we watched, now alert, wide-eyed, and transfixed. Without a word the sergeant withdrew the dirk from the lizard, wiped the blade between his fingers, and put it back into the holster behind his neck and under his shirt collar. Holding the dying lizard in his left hand, he reached with his other hand into his right-hand pants pocket, withdrew a small pocketknife, and opened it, droning on all the while about keeping our knives very sharp because we might be out in the bush for a long time and a very sharp knife would give us a better chance to survive.

A flash of sunlight glinted off the blade as he held the lizard up high by its head for all to see. Then, taking the tip of the small knife, he started at the lizard's vent and with one quick upward thrust opened the critter from stem to stern. Then, with the tip of this obviously very sharp knife, he flicked out the intestines, held the lizard up again, and then opened his mouth and dropped the whole animal down his throat. He didn't chew once, just swallowed the whole damn critter in less time than it takes to talk about it.

Jesus, about a third of the folks still in the stands bailed out and headed for somewhere other than here. It was plain that a lot of those lads would rather die than try to survive on what Mother Nature had to offer from the bottom of her larder. I will admit that I would rather have a hamburger than a lizard, but to each his own. Without missing a beat and ignoring the loss of part of his audience as if they had never existed, the survival instructor told us that the lizard tickled going down, but in a few moments the acids of his stomach would kick in and the movement would cease.

By now there were about twenty-five of us left, all wide awake and intently listening to this lizard-eating giant. He went on to inform us that most of the things out there in the wild were eatable and a good source of protein, and if we wanted to survive, we would eat what was set before us by Mother Nature and keep going. Then he picked up the tobacco-spit-covered stinkbug he had killed earlier, cleaned the dirt off, and gently but deliberately placed the dead bug directly between his molars. *Crunch* went the bug, and I could hear it plainly clear up where I sat. "You place large beetles on your molars because they still may have a bite left in them," he said in a matter-of-fact tone. With a noticeable swallow, down it went to the lizard's happy hunting ground. Damn, I thought, no wonder this guy is so large; he eats everything in his range of view. Off the bleachers went another three guys. That iron man looked at his shrinking assemblage with a hint of disgust. Oh Lord, let me tell you, there wasn't a man jack among us who was not now totally glued to what the instructor was saying and doing.

The instructor took a three-pound coffee can out of his rucksack and walked back to stand before the group. He tipped it slightly so we could look inside and showed us about two pounds of maggots, alive and wiggling in the bottom of the can. By now every one of us in the stands had a bad case of the "big eye"! He held a large lit candle to the bottom of the can until we could hear the maggots popping like popcorn. After a few moments of "cooking," the instructor turned to us and said that maggots were a super source of protein because they concentrated the energy from their food source, and that if we were in the backwoods in a bad sort of way, they were the way to go. He walked along the front row of the bleachers, holding out the can and asking everyone to reach in, grab a handful, and try. Everyone demurred until he got to a biologist and old-time government trapper named Jack Foster, who was sitting on the end of the bench. Good old Jack, without a moment's hesitation, reached into the can, took out a handful of maggots, and popped the lot into his gaping maw. The maggots squirted through Jack's stubby fingers and fell down the front of his shirt and onto the ground. However, a large number made it into his open mouth. The rest of the biologists, except Jack, fled the bleachers, leaving all the game wardens perched on the top with their "big eye" and, I'm sure, a few rolling stomachs. The instructor asked how the maggots tasted. Jack said, "Not bad. In fact, quite pleasant." The survival instructor offered the can to Jack again, and without a moment's hesitation he put his hand back in, took out another handful of maggots, and stuffed them into his mouth. It was as if a bomb had gone off under the wardens as they bailed out of the bleachers. The man who had been sitting next to me broadcast-puked perfectly into Warden Bud Reynolds's holster as Bud left the performance as well. I sat there in disbelief. Old Jack Foster was a tough man and had been known as such by my family for over fifty years. I conceded that he was one biologist who was one hell of a lot tougher than any game warden I knew, myself included! I looked around and saw that there were just four of us wardens left in the bleachers, including my captain, who was a beautiful shade of yellow.

"Sergeant," he said, "maybe we'd better pick this up tomorrow after the men have a night to settle down."

The sergeant just chuckled. "Maybe that was just a little too graphic for the class of students here today, but I enjoyed it just the same," he said with a large grin as his paw of a hand went into the can for a handful of maggots, which he promptly shoveled into his maw of a mouth. Brushing loose maggots off the front of his shirt, he grinned and chewed with obvious relish. That cleared out the captain and the rest of us in short order! Jack and I were the last to leave, with Jack grumbling about how the maggots gave him a stinking breath.

We spent the rest of the afternoon qualifying on the pistol range, and just about everyone shot ten to twenty points under their previous best scores. Guess what? It got even better the very next day.

The next morning I rose early and beat it over to the mess hall, figuring that if I got there early enough I might be able to con the cooks into giving me an extra share of grits. I found four other wardens heading for the chow line with the same thought in mind. Four female camp counselors slid into the chow line just ahead of me, and I quietly joined the queue behind them. Then I heard heavy footsteps behind me, and it was as if the lights in the building had gone out. Turning, I saw the sergeant major standing directly behind me with a pleasant smile on his face. I stuck out my hand and said, "Good morning, Sergeant." He took my hand, which is a damn good-sized one itself, and buried it in his powerful paw as he returned my greeting. The thing I remember about that handshake, other than the sheer power of his grip, was that his fingers were above my wrist during the shake!

The chow line began to move, and we moved with it without a lot of fanfare. We got the usual piss-anty amount of food, and all I could think of was another trip to my pickup for survival rations of sardines, crackers, and cheese. We early arrivals picked out a large table, sat down, introduced ourselves all around, and began to eat. I had just put some jam on my toast from a collection of condiments in the middle of the table when I noticed out of the corner of my eye that the survival instructor appeared to be looking intently at me. Looking up, I saw that he was actually looking at the condiments in the middle of the table. I looked to see what caught his eye but saw only several kinds of jams, a sugar bowl, mustard, salt, pepper, and ketchup. Nothing out of the ordinary, but the sergeant sure thought so. After a moment everyone at the table stopped eating and began to look at the condiments and watch the sergeant as well. Finally the sergeant slowly moved his food tray from in front of him and began to slowly move his beefy right hand toward the jam. By now the entire table was frozen as we watched the drama being played out. A very large blue-bottle fly was happily enjoying a breakfast from the lip of the jam jar until, with a lightning move that bespoke a mongoose rather than a man his size, the sergeant's hand flew forward and neatly snapped it up, touching nothing but the fly. None of us said a word or even moved as we watched the sergeant bring his hand up to his ear and listen to see if he had the fly. A big grin on his scarred face told the observers that he had his quarry.

Slowly, to the accompaniment of our noticeably loudly beating hearts, he stuck his index finger and thumb into his paw, careful not to lose his prey, and extracted one very live blowfly. Without looking at his audience, he carefully removed the wings, tossed his head back, and gulped the fly down like there was no tomorrow. The four female counselors screamed in unison and fled the table in a heartbeat. My four game warden buddies, with a little more reserve than the ladies, stood up and walked away in disgust, leaving me quietly alone with the sergeant. I probably would have gone with them except that I was in shock. The sergeant said, "I take off their wings because if you don't, they tickle on the way down. Besides, the wings hold no food value."

Then the sergeant stood up and, with a huge grin on his face, scooped up the abandoned breakfast trays from the eight diners who had fled and scraped their contents onto his plate. With a flourish, he sat his massive frame back down at the table and, seeing me just staring at him, said with a big grin, "I get more food that way." Without another word, we finished our breakfasts.

After input from many of the squad, the captain decided that we game wardens had had enough survival training and canceled the rest of the day's training in that arena. I was disappointed. Having studied under various wildlife instructors in college, I was used to blood, guts, parasites, and the like. I wouldn't have enjoyed eating some of the things the instructor had eaten, but I understood his reasoning and didn't have a problem once I got it past my nose.

Many years have passed since that survival class, and in that period I have eaten shark, raccoon, beaver, muskrat, bobcat, mountain lion, crab and crawdad guts, tripe, coyote, eyes from sheep while a guest in Indonesia, monkey, spider, alligator, and much more. None of it killed me, and I came to realize that such foods were nothing more than another good life experience. However, I always kept my patrol vehicles well stocked after that survival training experience so I never had to resort to eating anything that didn't come out of a can, a bag, or a cast-iron skillet over a roaring fire.

I imagine the survival instructor is retired or dead now, and the survival concept once preached at Stead Air Force Base is long gone or even more advanced. I truly hope that before he died the sergeant had a chance to launch into a platter of home-fried chicken; heavily sea-soned mashed potatoes mixed with sour cream, cream cheese, and a cube of butter and smothered with good chicken gravy; a platter of fresh-cooked peas; biscuits so light you had to eat them to keep them from drifting off into the air; and a fresh blueberry pie with a crust like my bride routinely makes. If he had that kind of feast before him, he wouldn't have to trap flies off jam jars. Then again . . .

These Pants Saved My Life
by Natasha Singer

No one who owns a pair of Carhartt work pants should be surprised to hear that they've saved lives. Natasha Singer attended an annual party in Talkeetna, Alaska, where locals swap tales about the super-tough clothes' heroics. Her report appeared in Outside.

I f you are the Carhartt sales representative in Alaska, you hear so many stories about how your durable, mud-brown work wear has saved people's flabby backsides from wolf fangs and grizzly-bear bites that, after a while, you stop recalling the individual anecdotes. Except during the annual Carhartt Ball in Talkeetna, a winter festival at which fans gather to celebrate another year of survival on The Last Frontier.

"One time," says Doug Tweedie, Carhartt's man in Alaska for the last 25 years, "there was this walrus attacked a guy tying his boat up to a dock somewhere in the Aleutian chain who said what saved him were the black extreme-heavy-duty Carhartts the walrus's chompers couldn't bite through." Tweedie tells me this as he busily checks the microphone onstage at the Denali Fairview Inn during a lull in the festivities. "Another time there was this couple pulled over by the side of the Alcan Highway; a grizzly bear mauled the husband, who had gotten out of the car, but our coveralls deflected the claws and saved his hide."

The Carhartt Ball is not your traditional black-tie-and-strapless-gown gala with a sit-down four-course dinner. It started in 1996 after Talkeetna's garbage-removal and snowplow magnate, Bill Stearns, came up with the idea of a Carhartt shindig as an antidote to cabin fever. Although Carhartt rarely advertises, Tweedie agreed to drive up from Anchorage to sponsor the first ball and hand out prizes in the storytelling competition, where winners take home the eponymous outerwear. Six years later, the annual event has become an occasion for area hunters, fishermen, carpenters, trappers, mountaineers, white-water rafters, and back-to-the-land curmudgeons to don their multi-colored patched chore coats, kneeless pants, and worn overalls reduced to strings, and snowmobile into the two-block-long town in the foothills of Mount McKinley to entertain one another with accounts of death-defying animal attacks and engine failures.

On December 29, festivities start early at the local VFW hall (a 60-by-80-foot log cabin), where a catwalk is set up and Talkeetnans make like Gisele Bündchen and strut down it, modeling Carhartt's upcoming spring line. Then the party moves to the Fairview Inn, where everyone crowds around the horseshoe bar wearing spanking-new carpenter pants saved just for the occasion, as well as cruddy "roadkill Carhartts"—articles of clothing that have blown off the backs of pickup trucks, gotten run over, and been rescued by passersby. With the per-fectly groomed hair of a national newscaster, 51-year-old Tweedie stands out among the guests in a bespoke brown Carhartt tuxedo with black lapels. He is, after all, the master of ceremonies. So that I will blend in, Tweedie has lent me a purple jacket (brighter hues were recently intro-duced in the Carhartt line, to appeal to rap stars and women) festooned with battery-operated blinking lights and a gigantic hieroglyph on the back that spells out c-a-r-h-a-r-t-t in sequins and glitter.

Alaskans buy an estimated four times more Carhartt work duds per capita than their compatriots in the Lower 48, and their loyalty is not due to just the harsh weather. Up here, hair-curling adventures featuring these sturdy $40 pants and $70 jackets are what distinguish weather-beaten sourdoughs from virgin flatlanders. The company was founded in Michigan in 1889 by traveling salesman Hamilton Carhartt, who started the trend by fashioning railroad uniforms out of surplus army tent material. Today, his great-grandson Mark Valade presides over the family-owned, Dearborn-based business, which reportedly grossed $324 million in 2000. Still, what is it about this brand that has made the Carhartt survival story a phenomenon so peculiar to Alaska, a kind of currency swapped in bars late at night, over breakfast in diners, and at the state fair? As the epicenter of what could be called the Rescue-Pants Epic, Talkeetna's Carhartt Ball seems a good occasion to investigate why this extra-thick, water-repellent, 100 percent ring-spun duck cloth has become the stuff of frontier fable.

"In Alaska, you're always getting into extreme situations where everything fails but your Carhartts," Tweedie theorizes. "Then when you get out of the situation, you tell everyone about it." And they tell everyone else. All around us at the Fairview Inn, drinking from beer steins at wooden tables, standing by the house-rules sign warning "All firearms must be checked with the bartender," villagers are one-upping each other with Carhartt war stories.

"People call every week, with animal stories, chainsaw stories, accident stories—stranded off the road in 70 below zero, skidding hundreds of feet on icy roads on tipped-over motorcycles. I've stopped writing them down," Tweedie says. Then he perks up at the thought of a humdinger. "Do you know the one about the Fairbanks policeman who was saved when an assailant's bullet ricocheted off the brass zipper of his Carhartt jacket?"

As an infamous plaque, no longer on display, put it, the winter population of Talkeetna was once "378 people and one grouch." These days it's pushing 800. If you count the tourists, the spring-summer population runs into the tens of thousands, with climbers, campers, and sightseers passing through en route to Denali National Park and Preserve. Carhartts are so prevalent here, and the villagers so vociferously loyal to them, that visitors sometimes catch Carhartt fever.

"I've had Californians and Japanese tourists, total strangers, try to buy my Carhartts right off me. Yuppies!" scoffs Ted Kundtz, a Talkeetna jack-of-all-trades, when I meet him one morning before the ball for breakfast at the town's Latitude 62° Lodge. "They called the years of wear and tear I put in them 'authentic character.'" What seems to irritate him is not that the interlopers hoped to wheedle him out of his sorry-ass jacket, but that they wanted to appropriate the adventures that came with it.

Kundtz, a no-nonsense 60-year-old with a stubbly gray beard, sits over his eggs and reindeer sausage in padded black Carhartt bibs stained with yesterday's cheeseburger juice, last night's spaghetti sauce, aviation gas, engine grease, moose turds, moose innards, and moose blood. He has just pulled an all-nighter at mile 110 of the nearby Parks Highway, helping adult students learn to carve up abandoned game for a community-ed course called Roadkill 101.

"The difference between formal and informal in Talkeetna is clean Carhartts and dirty ones," he says. "The washed ones, you wear to church. Ones as cruddy as these"—he points at various blotches on his chest and pant legs—"you clean. Preferably in someone else's washing machine."

In his varied career, Kundtz tells me, he has been a pilot, a tester of Berkley fly rods, a ski instructor, a forensic photographer, and a Green Beret. A life such as his is full of Carhartt flashbacks. On one particularly memorable night several years ago, as he drove home from Talkeetna, with the mercury hovering at minus 25 degrees, Kundtz's 700-pound snowmobile skidded off a trail by the side of the road, tumbled down a slope, and flipped on top of him. He credits the thick insulation of his jumpsuit for keeping him alive and warm during the slow, cumbersome process of digging a snow-tunnel escape route. Kundtz's story exhibits typical Alaskan sangfroid and quick-wittedness in an emergency, as well as frugality; he still has the clothes he wore that night.

"I just heard about some new high-tech, battery-operated parka," he says. "But for me, out in the remote after the batteries ran out, where would I plug it in to recharge it? A birch tree? If you live here, Carhartts are bound to save your life one time or another. Once they do save your life, you're obviously not going to throw them away. That would be like scattering diamonds on the floor."

As we head out to the restaurant parking lot, Kundtz points to his truck. In the bed is his dead Australian shepherd, Jillaroo, wrapped in . . . a beloved Carhartt. "I'm about to bury the dog in my oldest Carhartt jacket and build a spirit house over her," he says, before driving off. Even in the afterlife, Carhartts are too precious to discard.

"Where is our Carhartt machete holster, honey?" computer consultant Tom Kluberton asks his girlfriend, Hobbs Butler. At the moment, Butler, a fresh-faced, red-haired 32-year-old, is too busy to help. She's occupied talking about the homemade brown Carhartt tool belt—recycled out of worn-out pants—that she is modeling for me over a pair of newish Carhartt blue jeans.

"Other people wear through the knees first; I wear through the seat," she tells me. "Then I save the waistband and the back pockets. Turn them around and you get a great tool belt you can hang a hammer on and keep nails in."

I've dropped in on Kluberton and Butler at their 1940s hunting lodge, over near Talkeetna's railroad tracks, because I heard in town that they were a repository of rescue-pants epics—not only because they have spent most of the last decade outside, rebuilding their house from the foundation up, but also because they own 12 antic sled dogs.

"Day to day, these pants will last a lifetime in someplace like Oklahoma," Kluberton says. "Up here, getting pawed, clawed, and chewed by sled dogs all day long, or being dragged along behind them through thorny devil's claw when you fall off the sled, you might get a year's wear out of them." He looks down at his raggedy, paint-stained trousers, which are five months old but could pass for antique. Kluberton, 50, is tall and loping, with a boyish face and a thick mane of graying hair. He gives me a fast-paced tour of the grounds, breezing past a retaining wall constructed by "the Sherpa that our Everest-guide neighbor, Todd Burleson, sent over to help.

"Twice now, I've had a chainsaw swing up and catch me on the leg," Kluberton continues. "That's why you wear the double-knee pants—so the chainsaw cuts off a good, long slice of your Carhartts, instead of a good, long slice of your leg. Even so, you hate to lose a pair of Carhartts. What I do is get high-temperature automotive silicon gasket sealer and glue the pants back together." When I point out that silicon gasket sealer is neon orange, he offers a more color-coordinated alternative: "You can also use duct tape as a temporary fix."

Kluberton shows me other pairs of archival trousers he has not repaired, because they serve as badges of honor. Like the pair with the black-rimmed burnt-out crotch—the pants that illustrate a kind of infallibility principle.

"What happened was, while I was driving out of the Costco parking lot in Anchorage, I was futzing with this new minitorch—the kind that will flame a cigar from 11 inches away—which I bought to melt the ice that builds up overnight in my ignition. I dropped the torch in my lap, and kept driving until I noticed I was feeling a bit warm. I looked down to find my crotch on fire." Kluberton holds up the gutted pants as evidence.

"The family jewels were at risk," he says. "If I'd been wearing any other kind of pants, I'd have been dead or dying, in trouble, flambé even. Instead, I pulled over to the side of the road, put myself out, and turned the lighter off. OK, they're crotchless, but they're still good Carhartts. You can wear them as long as you've got boxers on underneath."

Kluberton goes into a bedroom to change into "the pants that survived auto-da-fé" to prove it. He is right. His crotchless Carhartts don't look so bad—if you like chaps.

Fisherman John Ferrell has a story that gives new meaning to the term "fashion emergency." A 50-year-old charter-fishing-boat captain from Anchor Point, Ferrell made national headlines several years ago after his 37-foot aluminum boat, the Irene, capsized dramatically in Cook Inlet, south of Anchorage. I track him down by phone from Talkeetna one evening after several folks tell me he is the ultimate protagonist in the definitive Carhartt narrative.

Ferrell had taken a party out fishing when the shaft connecting the Irene's engine and its transmission broke off, piercing the boat's hull and flipping it in turbulent 40-degree water. His six passengers and deckhand all clambered onto a four-person life raft. This left no space for the captain, who had to hang on to the hull of his overturned craft. The first Coast Guard helicopter on the scene pelted Ferrell with 110-knot rotor winds as it extracted the tourists from the life raft and flew away, leaving him to await the second rescue team.

"I should have died, because I was out there for more than an hour, and generally you're a goner in 10 to 15 minutes," Ferrell recalls nonchalantly. "But I was wearing my double-knee Carhartts, which were so insulated the wind did not penetrate and I didn't get hypothermia. Sure, my arms gave out and turned to Silly Putty, but the Carhartts protected my bottom half, allowing me to keep afloat by moving my legs."

To hear him tell it—and he tells it often, since it's his best story—his boat anecdote is less about almost drowning than about clothing as miraculous as the Shroud of Turin. But behind the clothing trope, the Carhartt survival yarn is a type of Freudian talking cure: a way to get over the aftershock by retelling your life-threatening experiences to others.

"Bottom line, those pants saved my life," Ferrell says proudly. "I'm the Carhartt poster boy."

The Carhartt ball takes place on my last night in Talkeetna. And, with all due respect to John Ferrell and his pants, there are a lot of poster boys in attendance. Not to mention poster girls. Emcee Doug Tweedie makes a halfhearted attempt to be heard over the raucous crowd standing three deep at the Fairview Inn bar as he introduces the handful of contenders for the survival-story contest, while in typical anarchic Alaska fashion, the majority of survivors are loudly swapping their bios offstage. Up at the microphone, nurse Colleen Hogan describes the time she saved a car-crash victim by covering him with a warm jacket. Offering a business survival story, jam and jelly maker Laura MacDonald recounts how she once lugged 50 gallons of blueberries home in a spare jumpsuit.

The contestants are so few that all of them take home Carhartt prizes of hats and T-shirts, and their anticlimactic tales turn out to be so downright mild that I wade into the Fairview's back room, where real cliffhangers are being traded under a mounted bull buffalo. I hear some archetypal stories of Alaskan ingenuity—like the one about Donnie Elbert, the mechanic who used his overalls as a frostproof tent one night after his plane crashed in the tundra; and then there's Carl Ober, the quick-thinking river guide who saved his own life, after flipping out of his 35-horsepower boat, by tying his waxed Carhartt pants into a knot and inflating them into an emergency life vest, all while careening down the Talkeetna River.

I head across the room, where teamster Randy Brooks hoists his right leg up on a table and rolls up his pants. He has an ugly eight-inch scar on his right shin. This happened when a birch tree he was cutting for firewood fell, pinning him beneath it and bending his leg at a right angle until the fibula was shattered and the tibia broke through his flesh. Brooks says the reason he's still walking is that the thick insulation of his Carhartts kept him warm, which stopped him from going into shock during the two hours it took his two sons to dig him out from beneath the tree, call for help on a nearby radio phone, and put him in an ambulance.

"This is a true story, backed up by bills and hospital records," Brooks says, as his wife, Edie, nods. "I would have been carving a peg leg for myself out of that birch tree had I not had my Carhartts on. And I still got them. I wear them all the time."

As Brooks rhapsodizes about how his pants saved his leg, I realize that whatever permutation of Carhartt yarn you hear, it represents more than an I-lived-through-this epic or a psychological coping mechanism. It's an initiation rite, an application for citizenship. If you haven't lived through such a tale, it means either you just arrived in Alaska or you have no business being here in the first place.

And so, one last story. Even if you're born and bred Alaskan, Carhartts do more than save your hide; they can also save your love life. In 1997, Anjanette Knapp, a 26-year-old ecologist from Sheep

Mountain, was trying to impress her musher boyfriend Zack Steer, 25, when she agreed to dogsled with him through a trailless stretch of backwoods in the Chugach Mountains. It was a bold move; Knapp was new to mushing. Steer would pilot the lead sled and she would follow him on her own sled. He instructed her to not let go of the dogs, no matter what.

Soon after they started, Knapp accidentally slipped off her sled into deep snow and tumbled. Steer, far ahead and oblivious to his girl-friend's predicament, sped along as she was dragged facedown, losing her boot and sock but never leaving the sled because the leg of her Carhartt trousers snagged on the brake pedal. Finally, the dogs, real-izing something was amiss, reined themselves in and brought the hell ride to a halt. Needless to say, Steer was impressed by Knapp's endurance. Soon after, he ran the Iditarod with an engagement ring tied to his lead dog's collar and proposed to Knapp at the finish line.

Those pants proved not only that Knapp truly belonged in Alaska, but that she also belonged to her beloved. Reader, she married him.

A Thin White Line

by Ted Kerasote

An avalanche on British Columbia's Tumbledown Mountain engulfed thirteen skiers and snowboarders on the morning of January 20, 2003. Seven people died. Ted Kerasote wrote this story about the disaster for Outside.

There was absolutely no doubt about it—can I go, can I not go. It was a clean decision. The snow was superstrong, superpositive. Fantastic."

In his lilting Swiss-German accent, Ruedi Beglinger, the founder and owner of Selkirk Mountain Experience (SME), a popular hut-skiing operation in Revelstoke, British Columbia, begins to describe the conditions five days earlier, on January 20—the day a large Class 3 avalanche killed seven of the 20 people he was guiding on a peak named La Traviata. "If I would have come home that evening with nothing having happened," he continues, speaking quietly inside the third-floor office of his Revelstoke home, "I would say that today was the best day ever. Absolutely amazing snow. You can jump into that stuff with no worrying. Like a hardwood floor. But that's not how it was."

As fate would have it, the Revelstoke slide was just the start of a particularly brutal two-week period in British Columbia. On February 1, 12 days after the Selkirk avalanche and less than 20 miles away, another powerful slide claimed the lives of seven Calgary high school students on a school-sponsored cross-country excursion. Combined, the two accidents represented the deadliest fortnight in the history of North American alpine touring, prompting deep questions about ethics, risk, and the business of skiing the backcountry.

Despite the eerie similarities, these disasters involved very different circumstances. In the second incident, an inexperienced and young group passing through a high-traffic area was blindsided by a more-or-less random event. In the January 20 avalanche, however, expert skiers who had signed on expressly to seek downhill thrills on exposed terrain were led by a guide with a flawless safety record. Both avalanches left devastated families, friends, and survivors in their wake. But the fate that befell Beglinger's SME group seemed less purely accidental, and more subtly problematic, because it involved the judgment and decisions of a renowned backcountry guide—a man known for aggressively providing his clients with access to some of the most demanding landscapes on earth.

A 48-year-old from Glarus, Switzerland, Beglinger grew up skiing in the Alps, and in 1977 completed his Union Internationale des Associations de Guides de Montagne certification—the gold standard for mountaineering and skiing guides. Spare and of medium height, he is nearly inexhaustible in the mountains, spending 200 days a year in the backcountry, breaking more than a million vertical feet of trail for some 400 skiers a year. Beglinger's customers must be prepared to push themselves mentally as well as physically—a day of skiing with SME usually involves seven hours, and the pitch of some powder runs approaches 50 degrees.

Furthermore, unlike heli-skiers and cat-skiers, SME clients climb every inch of vertical they descend. "It's a chance to come out of your regular life and really go for it," one skier told me. "Ruedi's a real hard driver," said another SME veteran. "He's out to squeeze the last drop of skiing from the mountains."

Such full-tilt charging at the winter backcountry, as well as Beglinger's old-school European approach—in which the guide's word is law, and you're ready by 8 a.m. or you're left at the lodge—aren't for everyone. Some clients have called him "militaristic." Others have even declared his style of probing the steep and the deep for more exquisite powder lines "a time bomb waiting to go off."

The criticism hasn't altered Beglinger's style; it has, however, made him more willing to explain to weak skiers that his emphasis on speed, precision, and efficiency isn't some autocratic power trip, but a crucial element in his approach to safety. "My style was learned in the Alps," he says, "and is the one given by all big mountains."

SME'S brochure doesn't mince words about the ability levels required of customers. Skiers must be able to negotiate "rugged terrain" that is "very remote and wild"; safely link 20 turns down the fall line in deep snow and on slopes equal in steepness to black-diamond runs at international resorts; and climb at least a vertical mile each day of the trip. SME staff also conduct phone interviews to make sure skiers comprehend what's involved. Up to two months prior to the trips, which last from four days to a week, guests are told, "If you're not comfortable with any of this, you can back out and we'll give you your money [about US$1,000] back."

Until January 20, SME had never had a serious injury or fatality in 18 years of operation. Yet in the days immediately following the accident, the questions multiplied: Why were Ruedi Beglinger and his group skiing when the official avalanche forecast was "considerable"? Why were there 21 people in two groups on a single slope, with one group skiing above the other? Who—if anyone—was to blame?

"My guests are my friends, and I take care of my guests," Beglinger tells me, on the verge of tears. "But on the 20th of January, at 10:45 a.m., I failed. And I failed not because I made a mistake. I think I failed because nature wanted to hit us."

The group that set off on on January 20 was a strong one. In addition to Beglinger and 38-year-old assistant guide Ken Wylie, it included five

SME staff. One of the staff members was snowboarding legend Craig Kelly, 36, who was training to become a certified mountain guide. There were 14 clients—three were returnees, and two others were part-time skiing and mountaineering instructors. Six of the clients were friends from Truckee, California; one of them, Rick Martin, a 51-year-old electrician, later noted that "most of us had 20 years of experience in the backcountry." As always, SME had conducted transceiver and rescue drills with all the clients before embarking into the backcountry.

It was the group's third day at the lodge. The skiers left at 8 a.m., with the temperature climbing into the low twenties as they glided along in single file. The pace was stiff, the mood buoyant. Beglinger led the skiers northwest toward 8,400-foot La Traviata and its 30-degree west couloir. Their original destination had been a peak called Fronalp, but the mountain was socked in. Conditions on La Traviata—with only high, broken clouds above—looked more favorable. The skiers had traveled in fog the previous day, and Beglinger wanted them to have a view.

Each avalanche season has its own unique meteorological history and risk profile, as weather and temperature build layers in the snowpack. In November, rain throughout the Selkirks had left an icy crust upon which moderate December snowfall did not bond. In early January, a warm spell triggered multiple avalanches that slid down that crust, but cold temperatures soon returned, and SME's snow-pit, compression, and shear tests during the following two weeks indicated that conditions were stabilizing as the snowpack began bonding to the underlying ice. On January 17, Beglinger dug a test pit on a 45-degree, west-facing slope called the Goat Face, not far from the chalet, and he could no longer find the dangerous November layer. Moreover, for the past two weeks the Canadian Avalanche Association had pegged the risk of avalanche around the Durrand Glacier at "considerable"—a midlevel rating, and one that generally doesn't deter guides from taking groups out.

About two hours after departing the lodge, the group reached the bottom of La Traviata and entered the west couloir. Beglinger put in four switchbacks to the top, where the slope eased off to a bench below the summit ridge. Probing along the way, he found excellent conditions.

"Not one hollowness," he said later, "not one little bit of a crust that I picked up. It was beautiful. As good as it gets." Rick Martin, third in line behind Beglinger, also remembers seeing nothing on the way up that made him nervous. "There were signs of old activity, but none of the classic signs of avalanches," he says. "No cracks. No whumping. I saw no windloading. I considered it pretty ordinary."

The skiers were traveling in two groups: 12 of them following dutifully behind Beglinger near the top, and seven others, led by Ken Wylie, just beginning the first traverse.

Following in Beglinger's tracks, Martin exited the gully onto a gently sloping bench and moved right, away from the slope beneath him. He joined Beglinger and a client named Age Fluitman, who had paused on an almost-flat spot below the ridge to let the rest of the group catch up. Not too far below, but still on steep ground, were Jean Luc Schwendener, a 40-year-old chef from Canmore, Alberta; Evan Weselake, a 28-year-old corporate trainer from Calgary; Craig Kelly; Naomi Heffler, 25, a canoeing guide also from Calgary; and Dave Finnerty, a 30-year-old SME trainee from New Westminster, B.C., bringing up the rear.

When Weselake had nearly reached the top of the couloir, he stopped and looked back to observe the lower group's progress. He saw Wylie, the guide, about halfway across the bottom of the slope, with the others trailing, and then he returned his concentration upward.

There was no warning for what came next. Beglinger, standing on his perch above the couloir, felt a sudden huge settlement almost directly beneath him, not anything like the normal whump experienced by countless backcountry skiers. Then he heard a percussive explosion. "Unbelievably loud," he says.

Just moments later, Weselake saw a crack open in the snow uphill from Schwendener. Then a second fracture line ripped between them, and the world began to move.

Weselake yelled, "Avalanche!" and was reaching down to release his telemark bindings when the moving slab pushed him over. Schwendener, Kelly, Heffler, and Finnerty were also caught and began moving down the slope. Weselake tossed his poles aside, lay on his back, and tried to swim as everyone and everything around him disappeared in a maelstrom of snow.

Below, third in line in the lower group, was John Seibert, a 54-year-old geophysicist from Wasilla, Alaska, who was on his eighth trip with SME and had skied this very slope a year before. He heard what he later described as a "shotgun blast" and, a millisecond later, a "whump." As the slope began to move, Seibert tried to turn and ski off it to safety, but the slide knocked him on his butt. "I backstroked from here to eternity," he said, "and in my peripheral vision I saw the slab breaking up into blocks. It was like being in big whitewater. I never lost sight of the sky. It didn't slow down. I thought I was going to get my hands in front of my face to make an air pocket. But it stopped instantly. The snow was level with my neck, and my head and my left hand were sticking out."

The three skiers at the end of Seibert's group, all of them SME employees, had managed to turn in the track and were trying to ski toward the side of the gully when they were overwhelmed by the slide and buried. Also engulfed were Wylie and three clients: Vern Lunsford, 49, an aerospace engineer from Littleton, Colorado; Dennis Yates, 50, a ski instructor from Los Angeles; and Kathleen Kessler, 39, a realtor from Truckee.

Now completely submerged, Weselake felt the slide abruptly come to a standstill as the leading edge of the avalanche halted in a depression at the bottom of the slope. Blocks of snow were wedged around his head, and he could see dim light and take rapid, shallow breaths. But he was locked tight in the debris, unable to move anything except his right ski tip. He tried not to panic. He remembers thinking, "Relax your body, slow down your breathing, and just wiggle your ski."

From his vantage point above, Beglinger watched the avalanche roar to life. After the explosive noise, he recalls, "It was quiet for maybe a tenth

of a second, and then it was like a rocket went down the slope—
woosh-shoo!—accelerating as it went. The ground started to vibrate, and
I realized that the energy was going behind me to the west."

The first slide set off a second, smaller avalanche—still to the right
of the ascent track. But then a third, huge split opened up high in the
chute above Ken Wylie's group, and the entire couloir washed down
the mountain.

Beglinger whirled around and ran over to get a better view down the
couloir, yelling into his radio as he went, "Durrand Glacier Chalet
from Ruedi! We have a terrible accident! I need all help there is!"

He looked past the crown of the avalanche and saw a nightmare.
Twenty-one skiers had started out that morning from the chalet; 13
were now buried below.

"It's huge!" Beglinger shouted into his radio. "Everybody's down!
We need all help there is. Nobody on standby, everybody coming up
here. Selkirk Tangiers, CMH, Department of Highways, avalanche-dog
masters, paramedics, and everything you can find—bring it up!"

The cook at the Durrand Glacier Chalet fielded the call and
handed it over to Beglinger's wife, Nicoline. The call was also picked
up by Ingrid Boaz, a part-time SME employee in Revelstoke, where
radio communication is constantly monitored. She radioed Selkirk
Mountain Helicopters and reached Paul Maloney, one of the pilots,
who happened to be in the air about 28 miles away. Maloney sped
toward the chalet, where he picked up two guests, extra shovels, and
a trauma kit.

On La Traviata, Beglinger jumped over the crown and glissaded down
the icy bed surface of the avalanche. "I was talking on the radio," he
says, "and with the other hand I took out my beacon, put it on receive,
and as I came to a stop, I threw the radio inside my jacket, picked up
the first person, flagged him with a probe, went over, picked up the
second person, put a pole in, the third person, put a pole in, and that
was like two minutes from when the avalanche cracked loose."

With all the SME staff except for Beglinger buried by the
avalanche, it fell to the clients to aid in the rescue effort. Charles

Bieler, a 27-year-old skier from New York City, reached Seibert, who was trapped but uninjured.

"Are you OK?" Bieler asked. "Can you breathe?" After Seibert indicated he was all right, Bieler told him, "We've got a lot of people buried—we'll get to you as soon as we can." Another client—Seibert can't remember who—reached down and turned Seibert's avalanche beacon to receive, so it wouldn't confuse the search, and handed Seibert the shovel from his pack, which he used to dig himself out. He stood up and saw a sea of debris, packs, skis, and eight members of the group searching, probing, and digging. He joined the rescuers and began pitching in.

Evan Weselake, locked in blocks of hard snow, was still wiggling his ski tip, which was protruding above the surface. One of the clients, Bruce Stewart, 40, a skier from Truckee, noticed it and dug him out. Weselake paused long enough to put on heavier gloves and then began searching with his transceiver, finding a signal only 2.6 meters away from the hole he'd just climbed out of and 1.2 meters below the surface. "Those numbers will be burnt into my memory forever," he told me. "It was Jean Luc." He yelled for a shovel and Beglinger appeared. The two of them frantically began to dig, but when they finally reached Schwendener, he was dead.

Meanwhile, Rick Martin had ripped off his climbing skins and skied down the bed surface of the avalanche. He located a victim and began to dig, eventually uncovering Naomi Heffler's face and chest. Heidi Biber, a 42-year-old nurse from Truckee, performed CPR—to no avail.

After several rescuers succeeded in digging down to Dave Finnerty, they lowered Biber into the hole by her ankles. She again attempted CPR, but Finnerty did not regain consciousness. When the bodies of Vern Lunsford, Dennis Yates, and Kathy Kessler were uncovered, efforts to revive them were also unsuccessful. Craig Kelly, lying lifeless almost nine feet below the surface, was the last victim removed.

In the end, six of the skiers who had been buried were saved, including the three SME employees from the lower group. Ken Wylie also survived—barely. After finding his signal, rescuers first uncovered

Wylie's hand, then cleared away the snow around his head. His cheeks were still pink, and Seibert felt his carotid artery and detected a pulse. Beglinger, who was trying to reach another victim, remembers that a great shout went up behind him: "We got Ken!"

"I cleared his airway," Seibert said. "I don't recall if I gave him a breath or two. We were talking to him, saying, 'Wake up!'"

But then Wylie's head rolled back. Joe Pojar, one of the SME staffers, jumped into the hole and slapped his face hard. "Ken!" he yelled. "Hear me! Let's go home!" Wylie opened his eyes and started to breathe.

Roughly 40 minutes after Beglinger radioed for help, Paul Maloney, the Selkirk Mountain Helicopters pilot, flew his chopper under the lowering fog and landed at the base of La Traviata. Moving fast, he flagged a landing zone for three more helicopters, two from SMH and one from Selkirk Tangiers Helicopter Skiing.

Wylie was flown to a hospital in Revelstoke. At the avalanche site, Beglinger stood in the debris field, despair over the general disaster only now beginning to descend on him. One failure was particularly haunting: his attempt to save Vern Lunsford. "He was only 1.2 meters down," says Beglinger, "and I felt I would find him alive. I was hoping because the snow was soft. Then I hit a great block of ice. He wasn't alive when I reached him."

The survivors, exhausted, in shock, some beginning to break down, were flown back to the chalet. There they would try to console one another while taking turns on a satellite phone to call their families. Most of the next of kin were notified by police in Canada and the U.S., but Heidi Biber personally made the hard call to Scott Kessler in Truckee. In tears, she told him there had been a devastating avalanche, and that his wife, Kathleen, had been killed.

Before any of the survivors had even returned to Revelstoke, where a makeshift morgue had been set up, wire-service reports—patched together from talking to the B.C. Ambulance Service and the helicopter operators—began to filter out. The earliest of them declared eight Americans dead, then seven, then the correct figures: three Americans and four Canadians. E-mails shot back and forth within the skiing community, and within 24 hours at least 30 print and broadcast journalists, photographers, and TV cameramen had swarmed over the small Wintergreen Inn, the main base camp for SME clients.

Most of the survivors wouldn't speak publicly about the incident, but John Seibert, acting as spokesman for the group, appeared at a press conference at the Royal Canadian Mounted Police office on January 21. While his companions attended a grief-counseling session at the inn before quietly slipping away, Seibert told reporters and the police that the avalanche was "a fluke of nature." The same day, in what seemed like a clear attempt to quell the rising storm of media speculation—What happened up there? Was someone at fault?—the RCMP released a statement that said, "There is nothing in the initial investigation at this time to lead investigators to believe that this is anything other than a tragic accident."

Like many people in Revelstoke's snow-science and law-enforcement communities, Clair Israelson looks puffy-eyed and tired three days after the accident. As the managing director of the Canadian Avalanche Association, Israelson, 53, has been helping the B.C. coroner's office with the investigation into the SME incident and, a few days later, the avalanche on February 1. Official reports won't be out until the end of May, and, with the newspaper and TV reporters temporarily gone, Israelson gets a rare moment to sit back in his map-and file-cluttered office to explain his job's complexities.

"I believe we can forecast avalanche danger and snow stability at a mountain-range scale with a reasonable degree of confidence," he says. "What we can't do is forecast for every slope on every mountain in that range with a high degree of confidence. And so the art of guiding is moving safely through dangerous places."

Of course, this is what guides do every day of the winter in British Columbia, the risk of "considerable" avalanche danger notwithstanding. As Israelson points out, considerable is only halfway up the five-level International Avalanche Danger Scale, which begins at low and moderate and ends at high and extreme. If people stayed home when the avalanche danger was considerable, no one would go skiing.

Guides base their decisions to go or stay on an aggregate of factors, including recent weather history, their own experience with the terrain, on-site testing, and daily regionwide data gleaned from the Information Exchange—a report compiled by guides, heli-operators, highway departments, and national parks logging every observed avalanche in western Canada. The January 20 Information Exchange showed a particularly quiet day in the region: only eight avalanches triggered by explosives, and two small ones triggered by skiers. On an active day, there would be pages of avalanches reported.

So if the slope was stable, why did it go? "The problem is that unstable conditions can sit way out on the end of the bell curve, a couple of standard deviations away from the mean," says Israelson. "They're there; we know it. But despite our best science, we haven't found the means to forecast them."

In Beglinger's case, when he reached some shallow snow—maybe 20 inches deep—on the ten-degree upper slope of the ridge, it settled over the old November rain crust. That settlement started the initial avalanche and set up a domino effect, sending energy toward the skiers and triggering the massive third slide, which buried them.

The day after the accident, Larry Stanier, an independent avalanche expert from Canmore, Alberta, hired by the B.C. coroner, traveled to the site. He measured the slope angle at the crown: 33 degrees, not something experienced backcountry skiers would think particularly steep. He also did several compression tests, which evaluate weak layers in the snowpack that might be prone to being triggered by a skier. He tells me that he got a "very hard" result, which means that the slope wasn't likely to slide from skier traffic.

"Ruedi ascended in the strong snowpack, and he wasn't in the fall line above the skiers who were killed," Stanier says, "but he managed to find the needle in the haystack."

Stanier's position corroborates the eyewitness accounts of Keith

Lindsay, Evan Weselake, and John Seibert. Nonetheless, the configuration of skiers on La Traviata put 13 people in harm's way simultaneously, and, as the quick-to-condemn pundits of Internet ski chat rooms were alleging within hours of the accident, this equaled a "major fuckup."

The logistical realities of guiding large commercial groups tell a different story. It isn't atypical in the heli-skiing industry to have a dozen or more skiers at the bottom of a run when the next group begins down. As Alison Dakin, one of the owners of Revelstoke-based Golden Alpine Holidays, which began backcountry powder tours in 1986, says, "Unless you have a concern about a slope, you won't spread your clients out. It takes a lot of time, you can't keep your day going, and your clients get cold."

The operative words here are "unless you have a concern." Backcountry skiers pay people like Beglinger and Dakin to make those calls. And when things do go very wrong, as they did on January 20, should the guides be held criminally negligent?

A 1996 British Columbia Supreme Court case helped establish some legal precedent. In 1991, nine skiers were killed in an avalanche on a run called Bay Street, in the Bugaboos—still the largest single-day ski accident in the history of the province. A victim's widow sued the operator, Canadian Mountain Holidays, and the guide (the only skier struck by the avalanche who survived), claiming that the guide had not dug a snow pit before attempting the run. She also maintained that it should have been obvious to any competent guide that there was a potential for deep-slab instability in the snowpack, since the slide ran down a deep, weak layer.

After extensive testimony from a variety of snow-science experts, a Supreme Court judge concluded that it was the assessment of all the CMH guides on the day in question that there were no concerns about deep-slab instability. Since this was the consensus, and it was extrapolated from a season of observing the snowpack, it wasn't deemed reckless, dangerous, or even a marked departure from standard operating procedure to not dig a pit before attempting the run. Even though the slope did slide, the judge observed, "Liability. . .will only arise where a defendant has transgressed the standards to be expected of a reasonable man, not where he has acted with due care but nevertheless made what turned out to be a wrong decision."

One of backcountry skiing's well-kept secrets is that skiers get caught in avalanches with fair regularity, though they are often small and rarely fatal. Because the hazards can never be eradicated, SME, like other operators, maintains rigorous standards to protect its patrons and its employees. The company's waiver—which all clients sign in the presence of a staff person—is laboriously explicit about the hazards of wilderness skiing, including the fact that guides "may fail to predict whether the alpine terrain is safe for skiing or whether an avalanche may occur." The waiver was crafted by Robert Kennedy, an attorney who represents all the ski areas in British Columbia and who has successfully defended at least a dozen previous claims brought against other operators. It continues to be the primary document establishing that paying customers understand and accept the risks they are about to encounter.

At press time, there was no indication that any of the victims' families were filing suit. In fact, the response, both from other outfitters and from grieving survivors, has largely been supportive rather than derisive or litigious.

"I respect Ruedi's judgment and how he transfers it to his guiding style," says Jim Bay, 50, who owns Mountain Light Tours, another backcountry operation in Revelstoke. "He has an admirable safety record if you look at how many skier days he's put through his operation since its inception. Over the years he's done a remarkable thing up there, and it would be a real shame if this incident colors it in a negative way."

As for potential lawsuits, Kennedy says, "I haven't heard a whisper of a notion that there may be a claim arising out of this. Just the opposite. There's been an outpouring of sympathy for Ruedi from the next of kin."

"I don't think it's anyone's fault," says Kathleen Kessler's husband, Scott. "Spreading blame will do no good. Risk is part of being in the backcountry, part of doing something that you love. At Kathleen's memorial service, I spoke, and I said, 'Hey, all you folks who went out and did something this morning? That's what Kathy would have wanted.'"

Before Beglinger leaves for his first funeral—Vernon Lunsford's, in Denver—we have dinner at his home in Revelstoke. Nicoline makes raclette, served with thick brown bread, pickles, sweet onions, and wine. The atmosphere reminds me of their Durrand Glacier chalet, the smells rich, the table elegant, his two young daughters, Charlotte and Florina, politely passing the dishes, Nicoline lovely and gracious.

This is part of what clients pay for when they sign up at SME: not only great powder, but also the chance to experience—if only for a week—the alpine dream created by this Swiss family. John Seibert has told me, "I'm positive I'll go back and ski at SME again." Rick Martin was also unequivocal that he would return—not only to SME and the Selkirks, but to skiing challenging lines.

They are not alone. The backcountry skiing community has grown tremendously as ski areas have become more crowded and expensive. Black Diamond Equipment Inc., based in Salt Lake City, has seen the sales of its alpine touring gear increase 20 percent a year for the last five years. Those rising numbers correlate with problems occurring off-piste: In the U.S., during the two seasons from 2000-2002, ten backcountry skiers were killed in avalanches. During the previous six years, avalanche deaths among backcountry skiers had averaged only one per year.

In British Columbia, the popularity of the backcountry has helped turn guided skiing into big business. According to a survey of the British Columbia Heli and Snowcat Skiing Operators Association, 28,000 skiers took a backcountry trip during the 2000-01 season in B.C., pumping an estimated US$68 million into the province's economy—most of it from visiting Americans and Europeans. Heli-accessed huts create an additional tourist engine not reflected in the BCHSSOA study.

And the risk? Of the 28,000 heli- and snowcat skiers in B.C. during the 2000-01 season, three died in avalanches. Among heli-accessed operations, until this January nobody had been killed in 17 years. Disasters like those on January 20 and February 1 give the perception of high risk, but statistically speaking, it's not supported by the numbers. "It's horrible," says Beglinger when we talk later, referring to the February 1 slide, "but they just got nuked from above."

Before I depart, I ask Beglinger if anything will change now, after his accident. "Maybe we cut the groups back from 12 people to eight," he says. "Less pressure. We will have to charge more, but I think even charging more, people will still come."

"I know what happened," he continues while walking me down to the end of his long driveway. "It would be a different ballgame if I couldn't figure it out. I would be scared of guiding if there had been a bad layer I did not see and I just jumped onto it. But that was not the case. I had a conservative approach of the gully. I chose a self-supporting gully instead of a headwall. I choose the terrain feature which is in my favor instead of something exposed, and I did not trigger that gully. We had a settlement away from this. It fired into a different slope, and wrapped around the mountain and multiplied many times."

We stand with the snow falling on us; the forest smells moist and sweet. He can't talk anymore. He seems spent, and much lies ahead. Jean Luc Schwendener's family will be arriving in an hour. Ken Wylie wants to debrief an hour after that. Tomorrow, Beglinger will be on a plane, bound for memorial services.

Before I leave, he offers a hopeful goodbye: "Until better times and happier skis." He shakes my hand, turns, and climbs the drive, head bent, scuffing at the snow with his boots, his despair just peeking through the surface, but under control. It's a large part of who he is—who he has to be, to move people through the shifting dangers of the alpine world. It is the side of him so many have seen and probably many more will view. But it's not Rick Martin's memory of him. Boarding the helicopter for the flight to the chalet after the rescue, the Truckee skier looked back and saw the seven bodies of his companions lying on the debris. Beglinger was sitting among them, weeping.

Avalanche: A Survivor's Story
by Evan Weselake,
as told to Mike Grudowski

Evan Weselake survived the avalanche on Tumbledown

Mountain's Durrand Glacier (see page 183), and told his

story to journalist Mike Grudowski. Their account appeared

in Men's Journal.

Whenever I'm not busy, my mind immediately goes back to the avalanche. Often, I purposely do things so my mind won't go back there. For the first couple of days, I didn't have a choice. That's where I lived, in that day, over and over again.

I had taken avalanche-awareness courses and a course in route finding. This was my third trip to ski with Ruedi Beglinger; the first was a mountaineering leadership course, the second was "Let's go have some fun," and then this last one . . . all on Durrand Glacier.

I had originally planned to go on this trip with a friend, Brendan. He had an accident two weeks earlier and separated his shoulder, so Naomi Heffler took his place at the last minute. She was 25 and had just graduated from the chemical-engineering program at the University of Calgary. She was a river guide in northern Saskatchewan for four or five years. She was a dear friend of mine. We met at a telemark race about four years ago, and we'd gone skiing together ever since. In the past five years, I've gone backcountry skiing 60-plus days a year. Someone told me that if you added it all up, between the skiers in our group there was more than 300 years of backcountry experience on that mountain that day.

We arrived in Revelstoke on Friday and stayed at a bed-and-breakfast. Except for Ruedi and Naomi, I didn't know any of the other people. My initial sense was, Here's some people who have spent years—in some cases decades—more than I have pursuing these same activities. Everybody was excited to be there. It's quite an honor to spend a week with people like that.

Weigh-in for the helicopter was at 5:45 Saturday morning, to get things going early. You get in that helicopter and fly up to a lodge owned by the outfitter. Just the view of that space is exhilarating. Even though Canada was having a lean snow year, I knew I was guaranteed one week of absolutely amazing skiing. That's what I was telling people for weeks before I went.

Up at the lodge, Ruedi officially welcomed everyone and talked about some of the chalet's guidelines for keeping people safe—what to do if you're caught in a slide, stuff like that. Saturday afternoon, there was a clear blue sky, and we did a long descent from Goat Peak and another beautiful descent from Elm Peak. We skied 4,000 vertical feet in all.

Each morning, you're up at about six and out on the snow ready to start hiking by 7:45 or eight o'clock. Sunday, we went up through a series of ridgelines toward Centrale Peak and Forbidden Glacier, then did a long descent, with visibility fading in and out. There was valley fog moving through; sometimes we were above it, sometimes below it, sometimes right in it and skiing by Braille. That was most of Sunday: cursing the fog and then loving the snow. There was pretty much a foot of ski penetration on the way up, and anywhere from boot-deep to thigh-deep on every descent.

Monday—I don't know where to start, because I know where my head goes first and it isn't the beginning of the day. We skied down from the lodge, maybe 500 feet. Then everybody put on their skins and began walking up, through massive spruces and evergreens, across an old slide path up to this little saddle above Tumbledown Lake, where we had a snack. Ruedi pointed up to the top of Tumbledown Mountain, indicating that that was where we were going. We started a long right-hand traverse, across the base of this massive concave slope. We were thinking, "Oh, my God, we get to ski this?"

Typically, you split into two groups at the beginning of the day. Approximately half ski with Ruedi, and half ski with, in this case, Ken Wylie, the other head guide. The people who ski with Ruedi are the stronger, the faster, the A-group, for lack of a better description. Often, that's determined by the skiers themselves. On Monday, there were 13 in the lead group and eight in the secondary group. You're always climbing single file; it's easier to walk in someone else's tracks than to break your own trail. I was close to the back of Ruedi's group. Five feet in front of me was Jean Luc Schwendener, a Swiss chef living in Canmore, Alberta. Behind me was Craig Kelly. Behind him was Naomi, and right behind her was Dave Finnerty, who worked at the chalet. Over the course of about two and a half hours, we went about two thirds of the way up, making switchbacks up the slope.

Above Jean Luc, I saw the snow crack open. I thought, "Hey, a little bit of snow is moving," because it's quite common for a small piece of snow—six inches, or 12 inches—to slide off onto your traverse track. The second thing I saw was the snow in between Jean Luc and me crack open. And that got bigger and bigger, and I realized that the snow wasn't moving past my feet; my body was moving with the snow. And all of that—seeing the snow crack above Jean Luc, seeing the snow crack between us, seeing the world move past my vision—took about a second.

In those situations, your mind goes into overdrive. I yelled, "Avalanche!" and I don't think I could yell it that loud again. I was going down sideways; downhill was to my right. You start trying to turn your skis downhill, but you don't get that far. My first thought: Take off the skis. I reached down to the heel-throw, and I felt the snow pushing on my back. So I gave up on that idea, because I wanted to be on top of the snow. Somewhere in there I tossed my poles—I don't remember when.

You're supposed to get big, and you're supposed to swim. Something that's big doesn't get buried as deep; a ball will be buried deeper than a starfish. So you stick your arms out, you stick your legs out, you make yourself big. You're swimming like it's Class V rapids, except it's worse. It's fighting for the surface. It's clawing at everything going past you in order to move up, to try and stay up, to not get pushed down.

I'm guessing that from when the snow cracked open until I stopped moving was maybe 30 seconds. But I did about an hour's worth of thinking. Where was Ken? Where was Naomi? Where was Ruedi? How many people would get caught in this? Jean Luc was right above me—was he gonna hit me? If I kept my skis on, would it break my leg?

I get the shakes talking about this.

At one point in that turbulence of snow, I felt weightless. Maybe that's the nature of an avalanche, maybe that's the slope getting steeper and me going off of it a little, I don't know. But I thought, "Oh, shit, this is gonna hurt." Not only did I not know when I was going to land but there was tons of snow surrounding me, and it was going to come down with me. You're stuck on a path that's running the fine line toward your death, and there's nothing you can do about it.

You know instantly that it's gonna be really bad.

People say that an avalanche comes to a progressive and eventual halt after it slows down. In my case, it stopped instantaneously. I was encased in snow.

I was more or less on my left side, facing downslope, both legs out. When the snow slows down, you attempt to protect an air pocket around your face, but I didn't have time to do that with both hands, because it stopped so fast. And once it stopped, the snow was solid. I couldn't take a deep breath. I could breathe shallowly, and I remember thinking, "Why am I panting?" But I'd been working pretty hard. Damn hard. My left leg was contorted; I had no feeling in my left foot.

I did a self-check to relax myself, running through each muscle and letting it go to save oxygen and energy.

I could see some light. That told me I was close to the surface and would likely have clear air. I could move my right ski tip. So I lay in the snow, trying to relax, wiggling my right ski tip, thinking, "Someone on the surface will see it." It was like this little flag. You don't yell, because it's a waste of oxygen. A person under the snow will hear everything going on on top, but people on top will not hear you underneath. I'm lying there thinking, "My left hand is getting really cold, and I can't feel my left foot, but that's okay, because I can breathe." I'm afraid of how few people might be up there. I'm thinking, "How bad is this gonna be when I get out of the snow? Where's Naomi?"

It was a long time. Ten minutes is my guess; I don't know.

I heard footsteps on the snow. I heard someone say, "I'm here." And I said, "Thank you!" And Bruce [Stewart, from Truckee, California], I know now, began removing the snow from around me. Relatively speaking, it didn't take very long to dig me out, maybe ten or 15 minutes. At one point, Bruce had taken off my skis, and every part of me was free except my left forearm. I like to think I'm a strong guy, but I could not pull my left forearm out of the snow. I think I asked Bruce, "How bad is it?" He said, "I don't know. A lot of people are buried. More than half." I said, "Well, let's get me out of here, cause I can help." I understand now what it means when people say you do what you have to do. There was work to be done, so I got free of the snow, took three breaths, changed my beacon to "receive," put my shovel together, pulled out my probes, and started searching. By this point, the first two helicopters had already arrived.

I didn't get very far. My beacon said 2.6—someone was 2.6 meters away. And I followed that to where the beacon told me someone was 1.2 meters below the snow. Two-point-six and one-point-two: Those numbers will be burned in my mind forever. So you probe. I stuck my probe in the snow, and it disappeared two meters down: Nope. And you start probing in a ring moving outward, and you probe two meters down, you probe two meters down, you probe two meters down, you probe—*thoonk!* And you know what it feels like when you probe a body, versus a rock, versus empty snow. You can feel the difference. I yelled, "Shovel!" and Ruedi appeared out of nowhere, and the two of us dug, quite manically. I suspected it would be Jean Luc, because he'd been close to me when the slide started.

It took a long time; the snow was really hard. I could have stuck my shovel into the hole horizontally and stood on it without it penetrating the snow. We found Jean Luc's backpack and then dug around his head, and Ruedi yelled, "Help! Nonresponsive!" Ruedi was upside down in the hole, 1.2 meters down, giving Jean Luc artificial respiration, while I was digging out his back and his chest cavity so the air had somewhere to go. We did that for another five, ten minutes, and he was still nonresponsive. Ruedi said, "That's it. Dig him free." I kept digging, alternating between digging and giving him artificial respiration, even though I knew it was too late.

Maybe another 20 minutes had passed. The whole time, I was wondering, "Where's Naomi?" At one point, I looked out and saw people on the snow. Some were looking with transceivers and some were probing and some were doing artificial respiration. I couldn't see Naomi. I also heard someone yelling at Ken. "Come on. Ken, come on! Wake up! We're here! Slap him!" As if maybe he was on the edge. Turns out he was. He was the only deep burial who was resuscitated.

Once Jean Luc was free, I climbed out of that hole, knelt down on the snow, and took a few breaths. I wanted to throw up right there. But that would have confused any avalanche dogs that came. So I choked it back and thought, "Go back to work. Find something to do. It's the only way to not be sick." One person still had not been found, and that was Craig Kelly. Once his location was identified, six or eight of us were digging, and rotating digging; we'd get tired and we'd come out, and someone else would dive in there and dig.

While looking for Craig, I had moments when I was standing outside the hole, resting. I remember turning to Charles Bieler [from New York City] and saying to him, "Where's Naomi?" And he told me. "She's over there. We couldn't revive her."

I walked toward her, and when I got to a point where I recognized her jacket, I had to stop and kind of compose myself. I took a couple of seconds, then walked up a little closer. I said goodbye. I said, "I'm sorry." And I went to find Ruedi. "Find something to do, because otherwise you're going to be sick."

I asked Ruedi what I could do, and he asked me to collect beacons from those who had died. What's it like to walk up to seven people lying dead on the snow and take their avalanche transceivers? It's really hard. Each person I went to, I pictured something. I went up to Dennis [Yates] and I thought, "Last night, I was teaching him yoga stretches." There was Kathy [Kessler]; she had offered to teach me how to polka. And Craig . . . man! Before the accident, I didn't even know he was Craig Kelly. He was just a guy on a snowboard named Craig. How humble!

And Naomi. I lost track of how many times I apologized to her. I guess I kind of arranged her clothes, to make her a little more . . . dignified. I told her, "I miss you, and I love you, and I'm here, and I'm sorry I couldn't be there." Whenever I thought about Naomi, during the slide, or while I was trapped in the snow, it didn't once occur to me that she wouldn't make it. Every time I thought of her, I thought of seeing her on top of the snow, and giving her a big hug and saying, "Thank God you're alive."

I am one of the reasons she was there. That's gonna take a while.

Closure is such a tough word to apply to this. On one hand, I think, "Seven beautiful people lost their lives with no warning, with no time to prepare, no time to say goodbye." I'm mad there was an accident. But I'm glad it was an accident in a place that they chose.

I still don't understand what caused the avalanche. I hope to. I'd like to see what they learn.

In retrospect, every member of our group, frankly everyone from the lodge that week, was a savior. It was a bizarre cycle, in which I found myself supporting someone in their grief and moments later seeking that same support myself. People drew on reserves of character and strength to do things that none would ever wish on another. I would call these people heroic, except I'm not comfortable applying that term to myself. It seems somehow wrong to be a hero at such a cost.

The Journalist and the Terrorist
by Robert Sam Anson

North Vietnamese troops captured and nearly executed Robert Sam Anson in 1970, while he was covering the Vietnam War for Time. *Anson went to Pakistan in 2002 to retrace the steps of murdered Wall Street Journal reporter Daniel Pearl. This story appeared in* Vanity Fair.

The reporter who comes to Karachi, Pakistan, is given certain cautions.

Do not take a taxi from the airport; arrange for the hotel to send a car and confirm the driver's identity before getting in.

Do not stay in a room that faces the street.

Do not interview sources over the phone.

Do not discuss subjects such as Islam or the Pakistani nuclear program in the presence of hotel staff.

Do not leave notes or tape recordings in your room.

Do not discard work papers in the waste-basket; flush them down the toilet.

Do not use public transportation or accept rides from strangers.

Do not go into markets, movie theaters, parks, or crowds.

Do not go anywhere without telling a trustworthy someone the destination and expected time of return.

And, above all, do not go alone. Ever.

The Marriott in Karachi satisfies lodging guidelines. Metal detectors flank the entrances, guards with sawed-off shotguns patrol the premises, and the shopping arcade leads directly to the U.S. Consulate—which seemed a plus until a car bomb killed 12 people there on June 14. My room, per instruction, is on the Marriott's backside, and offers a fine view of the nearby Sheraton, where a bus containing 11 French nationals was blown up by a suicide bomber in May. It is also where, according to a U.S. official, F.B.I. agents recovered a videotape showing an American journalist having his head cut off. His name was Daniel Pearl, he was 38 years old, a father-to-be, and South Asia-bureau chief for *The Wall Street Journal*. He got the same security briefing I did.

By now, the horror that befell Danny Pearl is deeply engraved. A handsome young man, loved by everyone—"Sweetest guy in the world," friends call him—goes to a rendezvous he believes will lead him to a scoop. Instead, terrorists are waiting to snatch him from the street. They issue photographs of Danny in chains, a pistol held to his head, and charge that he is a spy and will be executed unless demands are met. Danny's French wife, Mariane—six months pregnant with their first child—appears on television to appeal for his life. But there is only silence. Then, just when things are at their darkest, the terrorist ringleader, a former British public-school boy named Ahmed Omar Saeed Sheikh, is arrested and says Danny is alive. Hopes soar as Pakistan's president, General Pervez Musharraf predicts his imminent freedom. But all that is released is the videotape. "My father's Jewish, my mother's Jewish, I'm Jewish," it records Daniel Pearl saying. Then he is butchered.

We've been told that Danny was not only a great reporter, with an eye for the offbeat and the absurd, but a cautious one—not the sort who'd look for trouble. We've heard how he grew up in suburban Los Angeles, went to Stanford, and landed at the *Journal*, which sent him to Atlanta, Washington, London, Paris, and, finally, Bombay, a posting he accepted after confirming that there were venues where Mariane could exercise her passion for salsa dancing. We've had described how he was skeptical in the best sense of the word, questioning things taken for granted, unearthing stories others overlooked.

He was working that way on his last story, an investigation of the connections between the "shoe-bomber," Richard C. Reid, and a virulently anti-Semitic Muslim militant, Mubarak Ali Shah Gilani, tracing an unbeaten path that led to who knows where.

The who, what, when, and where have been laid out. Everything except the why. Why did Danny Pearl die? Because he was a Jew? A journalist? An American? Or was he simply in the wrong place at the wrong time?

The why is always the hardest question for a journalist to answer, and it's what brought Danny Pearl to Pakistan. "I want to know why they hate us so much," he said. Why he died trying to find out brought me.

My qualification is having been in a similar circumstance a long time ago—August 1970, in Cambodia, to be precise. I was 25 years old then, covering the war for *Time* and feeling invulnerable, a frequent, sometimes fatal journalist's malady. The short of it is that I drove alone to somewhere I shouldn't have, and wound up in a hole with the barrel of an AK-47 pressed to my forehead. I was presumed dead for several weeks, and the conviction of my fellows back in Phnom Penh—just as it is among many today about Danny Pearl—was that I'd asked for it. The difference is, I came back.

There is a lot else about Danny and the people who picked him up that is dissimilar, but every reporter has got to start somewhere. And the place Danny Pearl began, shortly after 9/11, was with a phone call to a number in Manhattan.

On the line that morning was Mansoor Ijaz, founder and chairman of Crescent Investment Management, L.L.C., and a U.S.-born-and-bred Pakistani-American with unusual friends and interests. His business partner is Lieutenant General James Abrahamson, former director of Ronald Reagan's Star Wars program; the vice-chairman of his board, R.

James Woolsey, director of the Central Intelligence Agency under Bill Clinton. For a time Ijaz was also chums with Clinton and his national-security adviser Samuel Berger. This came in handy in April 1997, when, as a private citizen, Ijaz negotiated Sudan's counterterrorism offer to the U.S., and again in August 2000, when Ijaz had Pakistan and India on the seeming verge of cooling the Kashmir cauldron. The deal broke down, as did the relationship with the White House. But soon enough Ijaz was back, as tight with George W. and Condie as he'd been with Bill and Sandy.

Danny called on a tip from Indian intelligence, which said Ijaz was wired with leading jihadis. Figuring that a prominent Pakistani-American who came recommended by Indian spooks to get to Muslim militants must have been a gold mine for Danny, I did the same nine months later.

Ijaz confirmed my figuring.

"He said he wanted to try to understand the psychology behind the jihadi groups," Ijaz recalls. "He wanted to try to get into the mind of the people running the show. . . . He wanted me to introduce him to people who could open doors for him."

Danny's religion also came up.

"I said to him at one point, 'I presume from your name that you are Jewish. Is that correct?' He said, 'Yes.' I said, 'Well, you have to understand that this is going to be a huge stumbling block for you. Because [the militants] are going to pick up on that very quickly, and *The Wall Street Journal* is not viewed as the voice of the Muslim people.' "

Danny, who'd reported from Iran and Sudan without difficulty, did not seem concerned, and Ijaz made introductions to three sources: Shaheen Sehbai, editor of *The News*, Pakistan's largest English-language daily; a jihadi activist he declines to name; and—most fatefully—Khalid Khawaja, a Muslim militant and a onetime agent with Pakistan's Inter-Services Intelligence agency (ISI) who counts among his very best friends Osama bin Laden.

In late September 2001, Danny flew to Karachi, a sprawling port city of 15 million that is Pakistan's commercial center. Mariane, who is a freelance journalist and frequently accompanied him on interviews, went, too.

"We didn't choose a profession," said Mariane, a strong-minded Buddhist who has been likened to Yoko Ono. "We didn't choose it for ego purposes but we chose it because we wanted to change the world."

They checked into the Pearl Continental, where reservations had been made for them by Ikram Sehgal, proprietor of Pakistan's largest security company. Danny had called him before departing from Bombay to see if it was safe to bring Mariane, who they'd recently learned was pregnant. Sehgal delivered a sobering lecture about security precautions, and offered to provide them with an armed guard free of charge. Danny accepted.

I empathized. Compared with Karachi, Cambodia seemed a walk in the park.

For a time in the early 1990s, violence in Karachi was so endemic that the army took over for the cops. When the troops pulled out, killings started averaging eight per day—and those were merely the ones involving political and criminal gangs. No one bothered to count the shootings, bombings, garrotings, and throat slittings between ethnic and religious groups, much less the toll racked up in quotidian armed robberies, home invasions, and just-for-the-hell-of-it sniper slayings.

Americans were special targets. In March 1995 two U.S. consular personnel on their way to work were mowed down by automatic weapons in an ambush at a busy intersection. Two years later, in November 1997, four employees of an American oil company were shot dead in a carbon-copy replay a few blocks from the Sheraton.

Karachi was somewhat quieter when the Pearls arrived—at least, a local magazine was no longer publishing a foldout, color-coded guide to where one was likeliest to be bumped off. Americans hadn't been murdered in a while (Shia Muslim physicians were the victims du jour), but the U.S. Consulate was taking no chances. Its staff members were ferried around in armor-plated Chevy Suburbans driven by U.S. Marines.

Journalists acquainting themselves with Pakistan usually come to Karachi last or don't come, period. I'd resolved to be among the latter category, after Benazir Bhutto advised that Karachi was "so dangerous." I changed my mind after several weeks testing calmer Pakistani waters and convincing myself that former prime ministers don't know anything—typical journalist thinking, when a story's good. Danny, however, came here first. He was after Muslim militants, and Karachi is their Rome. Besides, an old friend from the *Journal* was soon to arrive. Her name was Asra Nomani.

Asra, who'd been at the *Journal* since 1988, was a Dow Jones original. For starters, she was an Indian-born Muslim from Morgantown, West Virginia, where her father helped found the first mosque. And corporate America, Asra wasn't: in January 2000 she took a leave to write a book about Tantra.

She'd been conducting her research from India. Shortly after 9/11, however, Salon.com appointed her its Central Asia correspondent and she later took a house in Karachi, a fact that almost certainly did not go unnoticed by Pakistan's ISI, which keeps tabs on foreign journalists, particularly those from India, who are presumed, ipso facto, spies.

Initially, the Pearls' time in Karachi was unremarkable. They lunched with *News* editor Shaheen Sehbai, who found Danny "very keen to do work" but with "no clue how to go about it," and called on Ikram Sehgal, who arranged several appointments to get Danny grounded. "I liked him," says Sehgal. "He was very inquisitive and intense, you know."

It showed. Hardly had Danny cleared customs than he was quoting Sehgal in a *Journal* assessment of Musharraf's future (bleak, Sehgal judged). Within weeks, Danny had dispensed with his gun-toting chaperon—"this shadow," he said—and was in the capital, Islamabad, 700 miles to the north, for a several-hour session with Khalid Khawaja.

Khawaja was always good for a provocative quote, which made him a journalist favorite. "America is a very vulnerable country," he'd told CBS in July 2001. "Your White House is the most vulnerable target. It's very simple to just get it." After the U.S. began bombing Afghanistan

on October 7, 2001, Asra got a zinger, too: "No American is safe now.
. . . This is a lifelong war."

Some dismissed Khawaja as a P.R. man. But when it came to Muslim
militancy, he was the real deal, having acquired his credentials during
the war against the Soviets in Afghanistan, where, as an air-force
squadron leader, Khawaja was serving with the ISI, which was distributing C.I.A.-purchased munitions to mujahideen. The more radically
Islamist the fighter, the more weapons he got, including Osama bin
Laden, who formed an instant bond with Khawaja. It deepened when
Khawaja was forced out of the ISI in 1988 after criticizing military
strongman Zia ul-Haq for not doing enough to Islamize Pakistan—
equivalent to questioning the piety of the Pope.

But despite his talk of bin Laden's being "a man like an angel,"
Khawaja was sufficiently broad-minded in his allegiances that he got
the Taliban to agree to receive Ijaz and ex-C.I.A. director Woolsey.

Khawaja, in short, was a source to kill for, and Danny charmed him.
Describing the reporter to Ijaz as "competent, straightforward," and
not given to asking "inappropriate questions," Khawaja agreed to steer
Danny to leading jihadis and to be a sounding board during his time
in country.

Danny made another valuable acquaintance in Hamid Mir, editor
of Islamabad's Urdu-language *Daily Ausaf* and self-proclaimed "official biographer" of Osama bin Laden. In their last chat, in early
November, bin Laden had boasted of possessing chemical and
nuclear weapons. But, according to Mir, the real reason for his summons was remarks he'd made on a U.S. TV show, saying that bin Laden
couldn't back his beliefs with Islamic teachings. "I watched you on
Larry King," Osama said. "I want to tell you my position."

When I call on Mir he extracts Danny's business card from his wallet
with a flourish. "This is his memory," he says. "I was aware he's a Jew
and that he works for *The Wall Street Journal* . . . but I can say that he
was a very good friend of mine."

He fondles the card, which is worn from showings. "Some people accused him that he was a spy, because the kind of assignment he was doing and his way of meeting with people and going after the story. . . . I came on CNN and I said, 'No, he was a journalist . . . like me. We journalists take these kinds of risks.' "

Mir, a Taliban enthusiast, was wary of Danny until they attended an anti-American street demonstration in November. Several hundred were on hand, chanting denunciations of the U.S. and fealty to bin Laden, Danny in the midst of them.

"People were burning the flag of the United States of America . . . and I was real careful that I should not become a victim of that fire," says Mir. "But he was standing right under the flag. I said, 'Danny, you should be careful!' He said, 'I want to see in their eyes why they hate us.' I said, 'At least there is one American journalist who wants to find out the reasons.' "

For all Danny's great contacts, his stories weren't leaping off the *Journal*'s front page. While he was writing about trading in Afghan currency, other correspondents were packing up to cover the war next door. But by late November, seven journalists had been killed there. "It's too dangerous," Danny said at a meal with other reporters before Thanksgiving. "I just got married, my wife is pregnant, I'm just not going to do it."

Quietly, though, Danny was onto something much more compelling than the daily bombing reports: he'd found links between the ISI and a "humanitarian" organization accused of leaking nuclear secrets to bin Laden.

The group—Ummah Tameer-e-Nau (U.T.N.)—was headed by Dr. Bashiruddin Mahmood, former chief of Pakistan's nuclear-power program and a key player in the development of its atomic bomb. Mahmood—who'd been forced out of his job in 1998 after U.S. intelligence learned of his affection for Muslim extremists—acknowledged making trips to Afghanistan as well as meeting Taliban supreme leader Mullah Mohammad Omar. But he claimed that all they'd discussed was the building of a flour mill in Afghanistan. As for bin Laden, Mahmood said he knew him only as someone who "was helping in different places, renovating schools, opening orphan houses, and [helping with] rehabilitation of widows."

That's not how the C.I.A. saw it. According to the agency, Mahmood and another nuclear scientist, Chaudry Abdul Majid, met with bin Laden in Kabul a few weeks before 9/11—and not to talk about whole-wheat bread. U.S. pressure got the scientists detained in late October, and they admitted having provided bin Laden with detailed information about weapons of mass destruction. But, for what was termed "the best interests of the nation," they were released in mid-December.

All this had been reported. What no one had tumbled to, except for Danny and *Journal* correspondent Steve LeVine, were U.T.N.'s connections to top levels of Pakistan's ISI and its military. General Hamid Gul—a former ISI director with pronounced anti-American, radically Islamist views—identified himself as U.T.N.'s "honorary patron" and said that he had seen Mahmood during his trip to brief bin Laden. Danny and LeVine also discovered that U.T.N. listed as a director an active-duty brigadier general, and ran down a former ISI colonel who claimed that the agency was not only aware of Mahmood's meeting with bin Laden months before his detention but had encouraged his Afghan trips.

"It could be a big scoop—like your scoop," Danny told Mir. But the *Journal* played the story on page 8 on Christmas Eve and it passed without impact.

A few days later Danny was back in the paper with another exclusive, date-lined Bahawalpur, headquarters of Jaish-e-Mohammed (one of the most violent jihadi groups, as well as one of the best connected to the ISI). Jaish had been banned by Musharraf, its bank accounts frozen, and its founder, Maulana Masood Azhar, placed under house arrest. However, Danny later reported that the Jaish office in Bahawalpur was still up and running, as was the Jaish account at the local bank.

If Danny hadn't been on the ISI's radarscope before, he was now. But Danny wasn't letting up; he now had his sights set on the "shoe-bomber," Richard C. Reid.

Interest in the British ex-con turned Muslim radical had tailed off since December 22, when he had tried to blow up an American Airlines Paris-to-Miami flight by touching a match to an explosive in his tennis sneakers. But there remained some dangling ends, none more intriguing than who was giving Reid orders.

A story in the January 6 edition of *The Boston Globe* got Danny on the case. It reported that U.S. officials believed Reid to be a follower of Sheikh Mubarak Ali Shah Gilani, a leader of an obscure Muslim militant group named Jamaat ul-Fuqra ("The Impoverished"). Described by the State Department's 1995 report on terrorism as dedicated "to purifying Islam through violence," ul-Fuqra recruited devotees from as far away as the Netherlands and had sent jihadis into battle in Kashmir, Chechnya, Bosnia, and Israel. Since the early 1980s, ul-Fuqra had also operated in the U.S., where, under the name Muslims of America, its largely black membership lived on rural communes in 19 states, where they were linked to a variety of activities, including—according to authorities—money-laundering, arson, murder, and the 1993 attack on the World Trade Center. Gilani—who was said to have had four wives, two of them African-American—was, for a time, based himself in the States, but now he was mostly to be found in a walled compound in Lahore, Pakistan, where a Pakistani official said that one of his visitors was Richard C. Reid.

The *Globe* quoted a Gilani "spokesman" and "friend" as denying any relationship between the sheikh and Reid, and warning that further such accusations were not advisable. "If you push him . . . he has no option but to declare jihad on America," said Khalid Khawaja. "It will blow like a volcano."

Danny had stayed in regular touch with friend Khawaja and, after seeing the *Globe* piece, asked if he could put him together with Gilani. Out of the question, Khawaja said: Gilani hadn't granted an interview in nearly a decade, and he certainly wasn't going to give one now to an American reporter. "Don't try," he warned. "You will not be able to do it."

Undeterred, Danny asked his "fixer," an Islamabad reporter named Asif Faruqi, for a way in.

Faruqi asked around, and a journalist friend told him about a man named "Arif," who knew another man named "Chaudry Bashir," who could lead them to Gilani. Turned out, Faruqi's friend was mistaken. "Arif's real name was Hashim Qadeer, and he was a jihadi wanted by the police. As for "Chaudry Bashir," his real name was Ahmed Omar Saeed Sheikh.

Like every reporter in Pakistan, I wanted to meet the fabled Sheikh, who'd been described as well educated, charming, arrogant, and a sociopath. But Sheikh wasn't granting interviews just then; he was in solitary confinement in the Karachi Central Jail, a colonial institution that would do well in a remake of *Midnight Express*. I had to settle for learning about Sheikh, and once I had, it was no mystery why Danny had trusted him. I would have in a heartbeat.

He was born December 23, 1973, in Wanstead, an East London suburb. His parents had immigrated to the U.K. from a village outside Lahore five years before, and Sheikh was the eldest of their three children. His sister would study medicine at Oxford, his brother law at Cambridge. Sheikh's father, Saeed Ahmed Sheikh, was a successful businessman who generated enough income to send Sheikh to the $12,000-a-year Forest School, where one of his classmates was Nasser Hussain, currently captain of the British cricket team.

In 1987 Saeed Ahmed Sheikh moved the family to Pakistan, and Sheikh, then 13 and on his way to being a burly-chested six feet two inches, was enrolled in Aitchison College, the subcontinent's Eton.

He was a standout in his studies and popular with his classmates. The only problem was that once a month or so there'd be a scrap between an old boy and a new, with Sheikh in the middle, punching for the underdog.

Teachers admired his spunk and protected him from serious discipline. But one day late in his second year, the bully Sheikh took on happened to be the son of a most influential personage. Sheikh broke the boy's nose, then presented himself to the headmaster. "Sir," he said, "the chap was very disagreeable. I tried to control myself as much as possible and I have given him the thrashing of his life."

This time, there was no saving Sheikh from expulsion. "He was a wonderful soul," a teacher laments. "A gentleman of the highest order."

Shipped back to the Forest School, Sheikh passed his A levels in 1991 and was admitted to the London School of Economics. He read math and statistics; made $1,500 a day peddling securities to his father's customers; and, in 1992, the same year he received a certificate of commendation for leaping to the rescue of a woman who'd fallen onto the tracks of the Underground, was a member of the British arm-wrestling team that competed in the world championships in Geneva. "A nice bloke," his economics tutor, George Paynter, remembered him.

The first of several turning points came in November 1992, when, during the Islamic Society's "Bosnia Week," Sheikh saw *Destruction of a Nation*, a graphic, 45-minute documentary on Serb atrocities committed against Muslims. "[It] shook my heart," he wrote.

During the next Easter holiday, Sheikh joined a "Caravan of Mercy," taking relief supplies to Bosnia. But in Split, Croatia, he became seriously ill from the cold and was forced to remain behind. While he recuperated, bodies were carted in, one of a 13-year-old Muslim girl who'd been raped and murdered by Serbs. Years later, Sheikh would tremble at the memory.

On his return to London, Sheikh immersed himself in military theory, dropped out of the London School of Economics, and went to Pakistan with an elaborate plan for guerrilla operations in Kashmir, including—novel twist—kidnappings. A four-star general who examined his scheme was not impressed, but the jihadis were. Spotted as a comer, he was dispatched for four months of advanced schooling in the arts of ambush, explosives, surveillance, and disguise.

Again his skills were noticed, and in June 1994 he was invited to join a kidnapping plot in India, where his role would be sweet-talking foreign tourists into captivity. The hostages would then be traded for Maulana Masood Azhar, a Harkut ul-Ansar leader, and others who had been taken prisoner in India.

There were miscues from the start. Sheikh didn't think much of his bosses, and they, in turn, didn't appreciate his kibitzing. They liked even less the six-foot-three-inch Israeli tourist Sheikh brought back to their hideout as a proposed first hostage. "You fool," one of them hissed. "You'll get us all killed. Take him back to his hotel at once and come back in the morning."

Posing as a Hindu named "Rohit," Sheikh by and by rounded up three Britishers and an American, and dropped off a ransom note with a "rather nice" receptionist at the BBC. "Tonight she'll be telling the whole world that this big, monstrous, terrorist-looking chap came to her in person," he wrote in his diary. "Tomorrow, I'll ring her up and say, 'Actually, my dear, I'm not like that at all.' "

He seemed equally blithe about his captives, challenging them to games of chess (at which Sheikh was expert) and assuring that he would kidnap only people whom he considered intelligent and wanted to spend time with.

At other moments, Sheikh joked about their prospective beheadings and rattled on about Jews' running the British Cabinet and the truths to be had from reading *Mein Kampf.* He also rhapsodized about the pleasures of martyrdom, saying that holy warriors ejaculated at the moment of death, knowing that they had entered heaven.

The bizarre idyll climaxed in late October 1994, when Indian provincial police raided the kidnappers' hideouts. In the ensuing gun battles, two officers and one of the kidnappers were killed, and Sheikh shot in the shoulder.

The ISI paid for a lawyer, but it didn't do any good for Sheikh, who was held without trial for the next five years in a maximum-security prison, where, he said, he had been beaten and urinated on. But it didn't prevent Sheikh from smuggling out a note to a favorite Aitchison teacher:

I hope this letter finds you soaring the heights of happiness.

Living in the cold, hard world of criminals and the brutal echelons of state power, a world of self-interest and devious calculations . . . I often wander down memory lane, seeing with more experienced (hopefully wiser) eyes all those people who gave me love—glowing, unselfish love. Yes, sir, you encouraged me so many times and you stood up for me when I was a hot-headed youngster. I feel indebted to you, and more than a little wistful.

Sir, if possible, please do jot a quick note telling me how you and your family have fared over the last few years. . . . My parents are in London, busy with the old garment business. Naturally, my case came as quite a shock to them, but Allah has given them the strength to cope. They understand that this is the path I've chosen. They have been tremendously supportive.

Sir, if you could put in the occasional prayer for me that would be wonderful. I'll sign off now. Who knows, perhaps I'll pop round to see you soon.

Yours with affectionate respect . . .

In a PS, Sheikh added, "If there are some spare copies of the last few *Aitchisonians* [the school magazine], I'd be thrilled to have them."

It didn't look as if Sheikh was going to be "popping round" anywhere but his cell for the foreseeable future. But in late December 1999, Azhar's terrorist outfit—now renamed Harkat ul-Mujahadeen—seized an Indian airliner with 155 passengers and crew aboard; slit the throat of a honeymooning Indian businessman; and demanded the release of Azhar, Sheikh, and another jihadi. After the plane sat six days on the Kandahar tarmac under the watchful eyes of the Taliban, the Indians gave in.

Azhar went to Karachi and, before 10,000 howling supporters, called for the destruction of the U.S. and India. Then, after a few weeks touring under the protection of the ISI, he announced the formation of Jaish-e-Mohammed, the terrorist group Danny would find thriving in Bahawalpur.

Sheikh, for his part, stayed at a Kandahar guesthouse for several days, conferring with Taliban leader Mullah Muhammad Omar and—reports had it—Osama bin Laden, who was said to refer to him as "my special son." When he crossed the Pakistan frontier in early January 2000, an ISI colonel was waiting to conduct him to a safe house in Islamabad. From there he proceeded to London, where he reunited with family.

Relaxing with friends on his return to Lahore, Sheikh showed off his wound ("This is the benefit of speaking good English," he joked), talked about his forthcoming marriage ("My wife has an M.A.," he bragged about his bride-to-be), and confessed to pangs about killing. Poison was his instrument of choice (he demonstrated how he secreted it in his wallet), though, according to a U.S. official, he slit a throat once to make his jihadi bones. As for the moral qualms, Sheikh said he resolved those by recalling images of Kashmir and Bosnia.

He went next to Afghanistan, and reportedly helped devise a secure, encrypted Web-based communications system for al-Qaeda. His future in the network seemed limitless; there was even talk of one day succeeding bin Laden.

But Sheikh kept running afoul of superiors. Azhar was said to have sidelined him from Jaish after getting fed up with his bragging about Indian exploits. Following further spats with two other terrorist groups, Sheikh joined up with Aftab Ansari, an Indian-born gangster.

By August 2001, Sheikh's activities had come to the attention of British intelligence, who asked their Indian counterparts to help apprehend him.

Then came 9/11. Tracing the hijackers' funding, investigators discovered that in the weeks before the Trade Center attack someone using the alias Mustafa Muhammad Ahmad had wired more than $100,000 to hijacking ringleader Mohammed Atta. On October 6, CNN reported that the U.S. had decided that Mustafa Muhammad Ahmad and Sheikh were one and the same. Not much later the U.S. asked Pakistan to extradite him for the 1994 kidnapping.

With recruits picked up from other jihadi groups, Sheikh and Ansari, meanwhile, were mounting their first big operation, the October 1 suicide truck-bomb attack on the Kashmir assembly, which left 38 dead. On December 13 they struck again, with a shooting and grenade assault on the Parliament building in New Delhi. That incident—which India charged was staged at the direction of the ISI—claimed 14 lives and prompted India to mass half a million troops on the Pakistan border. Sheikh was in the midst of planning yet another operation—a drive-by shoot-up of the American Center in Calcutta on January 22, in which five guards were killed—when Danny Pearl dropped into his lap.

"We had nothing personal against Daniel," Sheikh would later say. "Because of his hyperactivity, he caught our interest."

Danny had been here, there, and everywhere, an American Jewish reporter who lived in India, asking inconvenient questions. But his quest for a big score finally seemed within reach. Come to Room 411 of the Akbar International Hotel in Rawalpindi on January 11, he was told; "Bashir" would be waiting.

They talked for three hours. "It was a great meeting," said Sheikh, who shaved his beard and donned sunglasses for the occasion. "We ordered cold coffee and club sandwiches and had great chitchat."

But chitchat is all it was. Not wanting to seem too eager, Sheikh stressed that Gilani was a busy man; he'd have to weigh the question carefully. "I never asked Daniel to do anything," Sheikh later told his interrogators. "It was always him insisting." At the end of the meeting, Danny said he'd send along some examples of his work, and "Bashir" promised to keep him updated via E-mail.

Danny and Mariane then departed for Peshawar—Dodge City, except with Kalashnikovs instead of six-guns. But, according to Rahimullah Yusufzai, the local stringer for the BBC and *Time*, the only thing that bothered Danny was the difficulty in gathering information.

"He said he would be keen to meet anybody from Taliban or

al-Qaeda," Yusufzai recalls. "I said, 'They may be here, but [it] is impossible for you to meet them or me to meet them. They are all wanted and they would like to stay quiet. Especially they won't be meeting an American journalist.'

"I told him, 'If you try too hard, it could be risky.' But he was very focused. He was so persistent in meeting everybody who could have helped him in the story. He was after something and he wanted it."

A *Journal* reporter's need for a replacement computer gave Danny more reason than ever to get it.

The reporter, Moscow correspondent Alan Cullison, had had his smashed in late November, when his car rolled over while crossing the Hindu Kush. On his arrival in Kabul, a shopkeeper offered to sell him a used IBM desktop and a Compaq laptop for $4,000. Too steep, New York said; bargain him down. Cullison did, and paid $1,100 for two machines that—in a billion-to-one shot—turned out to have been recovered from the bombed headquarters of Mohammed Atef, Osama bin Laden's abruptly deceased military strategist.

Cullison couldn't get past the Compaq's encryption scheme, but on the IBM's hard drive he found a treasure trove of al-Qaeda materials— at least 1,750 files, recording four years' worth of terrorist doings.

Fearing lives might be at stake, the *Journal* turned over the material to the Defense Department and the C.I.A. for review. The spooks did their screening, and the first *Journal* report about the documents from the IBM machine appeared December 31. But the Compaq laptop was much harder to crack, and it wasn't until January 16 that the *Journal* was able to publish the results. For Danny, it was worth the wait. On the hard drive was the itinerary of a target-scouting expedition by a terrorist referred to as "brother Abdul Ra'uff." It matched to a T the pre-9/11 travels of Richard C. Reid.

There was more good news the same day, with the arrival of an E-mail from "Bashir," using an address that showed Sheikh's sense of humor: Nobadmashi@yahoo.com—Urdu for "no rascality."

He reported that he'd forwarded Danny's articles to Gilani and apologized for not having contacted him sooner. "I was preoccupied with looking after my wife who has been ill," Sheikh said. "[She] is back from the hospital and the whole experience was a real eye-opener. Poor people who fall ill here and have to go to hospital have a really miserable and harassing time. Please pray for her health."

Having tugged at Danny's heartstrings with a phony story about his wife, Sheikh set the hook deeper three days later with an E-mail saying that Gilani was looking forward to a get-together. However, he was currently in Karachi and wouldn't be returning for "a number of days." "Bashir" gave Danny a choice: wait for Gilani's return, or send E-mail questions, which he'd relay to Gilani's secretary. "If Karachi is your program," Sheikh said, "you are welcome to meet him there."

Danny chose the Karachi meeting, as Sheikh—who understood reporters—must have known he would. Before catching the Pakistan International Airlines flight south, Danny E-mailed him his plans, along with something that Sheikh didn't know: on January 24, he and Mariane would be leaving for Dubai and from there transiting to Bombay.

Friends had been urging Danny to take a break, and though another tour of Pakistan was planned, it wouldn't be for an indefinite while. If Danny was going to get Gilani, he had to get him now.

There was another story he wanted to try to cram in: a piece on Karachi underworld boss Dawood Ibrahim, an Indian-born Muslim terrorist who enjoyed the patronage and protection of the ISI. In mid-January, while waiting for "Bashir" 's next missive, Danny called Ikram Sehgal for leads.

"I hadn't heard from him in weeks," Sehgal recalls, sipping tea in his cluttered office. "I think Danny got more and more confident. This was the biggest thing that hit him. He was suddenly having access and chasing down an area where he had no expertise." He stirs the heat from his cup. "I mean, Danny just didn't have it.

"He asked if I had any contacts with the local Mafia. I said, 'Danny, the Mafia head here doesn't function the way you think Mafias do. This is not something out of *The Godfather*. I know the direction you're going in. Don't do this! Forget it! If you want to know something, come over and we'll talk, not on the telephone.' "

Sehgal's phone rings, as it has constantly since March 17, when militants attacked a church in Islamabad, killing U.S. Embassy employee Barbara Green and her 17-year-old daughter, Kristen Wormsley. Sehgal is now providing protection for every Christian church in the country gratis.

"I found him a little naïve," Sehgal goes on. "I would tell him, 'Danny, stick by the rules. Anybody you want to meet, meet him in a public place. Don't get into cars. Anyone could pick you up.' He would always say, 'Yes, you're right, Ikram, I ought to do that.' But you always had the feeling that what he was saying was perfunctory."

"Bashir" checked in again on Sunday, January 20, saying that Gilani would be available that coming Tuesday or Wednesday. Sheikh said he'd forward the phone number of a Gilani *mureed* (follower), who would escort him to the meeting.

"It is sad that you are leaving Pakistan so soon," Sheikh wrote. "I hope you have enjoyed your stay."

The next day, Danny and Mariane learned that their baby would be a boy. They decided to call him Adam, a name that resonates with both Muslim and Jew.

Wednesday, January 23, was going to be busy for Danny. Asra was hosting a farewell dinner party for him that night; he wanted to check out a cyber café to see if it was where a message was sent to Richard Reid instructing him to board the next Paris-Miami flight; he had an appointment to see Randall Bennett, the U.S. Consulate's regional security officer, at 2:30, and another to see Jamil Yusuf, head of Karachi's Citizens Police Liaison Committee, at 5:45. And then there was Gilani. "Bashir" by now had told him that "Imtiaz Siddiqi" was the *mureed* who'd lead him to Gilani. But Danny had yet to hear from him. Nor did he know that Siddiqi's real name was Mansur Hasnain and that he'd been one of the Indian Airlines hijackers who'd freed Sheikh in 1999.

Danny phoned his fixer in Islamabad.

"Give me a quick reply," he said. "Is it safe to see Gilani?"

Asif assured him it was; Gilani was a public figure.

Danny set off on his rounds. Mariane, who was to have come along, wasn't feeling well and stayed at Asra's.

He had a good session with Bennett at the consulate, but the cyber café was a bust; it didn't have the technology to trace who'd sent the E-mail to Reid. On the way to Yusuf's office, Danny called the Dow Jones bureau to ask the resident correspondent, Saaed Azhari, to set up a final appointment for him the next morning. Azhari, who couldn't fathom why Danny chanced taking cabs everywhere, rather than using a hired car and regular driver, like other correspondents, said there was something Danny ought to know: Ghulam Hasnain, the Karachi *Time* stringer, had gone missing the day before. Guessing was, the ISI had picked him up because of an expose he had written on Dawood Ibrahim for a Pakistani monthly.

Danny seemed unworried, and a few minutes later he was at the Citizens Police Liaison Committee building, talking to Yusuf, a former businessman who'd become a renowned crime-fighter.

On the afternoon I catch up to him, Yusuf—who played a key role in catching Danny's killers—is bemoaning his trouble in getting warrants for cyber searches. "Judges do not understand Yahoo is not a human being," he says, shaking his head. He then describes his last meeting with a reporter of whom he was very fond.

"He asked me about Gilani, and I said, 'I never heard of him. I don't think a lot of people have heard of him in this country.' Then he told me about this Richard Reid thing. I joked with him: I said, 'Danny, do something else. The guy is caught. He is with the F.B.I. Why waste time?'

"[When] he was sitting here, he got two phone calls. He said, 'Yes,' he is coming there at seven o'clock, somewhere close by. I did not know what was happening. He did not tell me who he was going to meet. . . .

"I advised him, 'You cannot go and meet strangers.' It's just like me going into New York and trying to meet the Mafia, then complaining to the world I got abducted. You don't do those things.

"He was a very docile person, quiet, humble. Not a person who would go out and take risks in reporting. That is what surprised me. . . . [How] he came and sat here for an hour and then went to that stupid appointment of his without telling us."

Yusuf looks out the window down to where the security car he has had to hire to trail him is waiting.

"Kidnapping a journalist is the easiest thing you can do," he says. "They are hungry for information. . . . Anybody could do it."

Danny's caller was the *mureed* he knew as Siddiqi, saying to meet him at the Village Garden Restaurant, next to the Metropole Hotel, a mile or so away. In the cab on the way over, Danny phoned Mariane, telling here where he was going and to start the party without him. He'd be back around eight.

The hour came and went without any sign of Danny, but initially his absence wasn't cause for concern. Pakistanis are famously sociable—Gilani may have insisted on serving dinner, and the talk may have run on, as interviews with Muslim militants tended to. But midnight passed with no word from Danny, who also wasn't answering his cell phone.

Now truly worried, Asra phoned Danny's boss, foreign editor John Bussey, at the *Journal*'s headquarters in South Brunswick, New Jersey, where it was late afternoon. Bussey told her that he'd alert the State Department.

Asra phoned Khawaja, thinking he would know whether Danny actually had a meeting. But Khawaja said he'd never heard of any meeting with Gilani.

The police arrived shortly thereafter, and Asra phoned Khawaja again, this time with an officer on the line. He asked that Khawaja put them in touch with Gilani as soon as possible. Then Asra read off "Bashir" 's and "Siddiqi" 's cell-phone numbers. Khawaja didn't recognize either of them.

By the time the flight to Dubai left the next afternoon, the story of Danny Pearl's disappearance was moving over the wires. No one was using the word "kidnapping" yet, but that was the suspicion. It was confirmed early Sunday morning, local time, by E-mails to *The New York Times*, *The Washington Post*, the *Los Angeles Times*, and two Pakistani news organizations. Attached were four photographs of Danny in captivity, one showing a 9-mm. pistol pointed at his head and a message in English and Urdu announcing the capture of "CIA officer Daniel Pearl who was posing as a journalist for the *Wall Street Journal.*"

The note demanded that the U.S. hand over F-16 aircraft, whose delivery to Pakistan had been frozen by 1990 nuclear sanctions; that Pakistanis detained for questioning by the F.B.I. over the 9/11 attacks be given access to lawyers and allowed to see their families; that Pakistani nationals held at Guantanamo Bay, Cuba, be returned to their homeland to stand trial; and that the Taliban's ambassador to Pakistan, now held in Afghanistan, be returned to Pakistan.

Of Danny, the note said, "Unfortunately, he is at present being kept in very inhuman circumstances quite similar in fact to the way that Pakistanis and nationals of other sovereign countries are being kept in Cuba by the American Army. If the Americans keep our countrymen in better conditions we will better the conditions of Mr. Pearl and the other Americans that we capture."

Sent on the account of kidnapperguy@hotmail.com, the message was signed, "The National Movement for the Restoration of Pakistani Sovereignty."

Police had never heard of the group, but the name sounded a gong at the Islamabad bureau of the BBC, which in late October had received a package from the "National Youth Movement for the Sovereignty of Pakistan." Inside were an unplayable videocassette and a computer printout announcing the capture of an alleged C.I.A. operative, "one Joshua Weinstein, alias Martin Johnson, an American national and a resident of California." Also enclosed was a photograph of a male Caucasian in his 30s. Flanked by two robed and hooded men aiming AK-47s at his head, he was holding up a Pakistani newspaper showing the date of his abduction—just as Danny would months later.

U.S. Embassy officials said at the time that no one named Joshua Weinstein or Martin Johnson had either come to Pakistan or been reported missing, and that the letter was a hoax. When local police agencies and other Western embassies said the same, the BBC let it drop. But the release of the virtually identical Pearl materials got the

BBC checking again with American diplomats. Was the first "kidnapping" truly a hoax? Why so many similarities between the October episode and Pearl's abduction? The response was a studied silence.

Police, meanwhile, were focusing their suspicions on Harkat ul-Mujahedeen, the terrorist group that had hijacked the airliner to free Sheikh and Azhar. With a number of its members killed by U.S. air strikes, Harkat ul-Mujahedeen had the motive, as well as the M.O., its predecessor group, Harkat ul-Ansar, being thought responsible for the kidnapping and presumed murder of a group of backpackers in India in 1995.

Trouble was, this didn't have the feel of a jihadi operation. Where were the *allahu ahkbars* in the note? The riffs about Palestine and infidels and Western demons? There wasn't even a mention of "Zionist conspiracy." Instead, the demands read like an A.C.L.U. press release. The English was too good, too. Usage, spelling, and grammar were virtually perfect, and the few errors seemed deliberate, as if the writer was trying to hide his education. Jihadis didn't have to feign lack of schooling; most were illiterate.

One investigator, inspired, typed "foreign," "kidnapper," and "suspect" onto Google.com and clicked search. The first listing that popped up was "Omar Saeed Sheikh." No one believed it; couldn't be that easy.

Within days, the elite Criminal Investigation Division determined the true identity of "Arif" and raided his house—where they found relatives in the midst of a Muslim prayer service for the dead. "Arif" had been killed fighting the Americans in Afghanistan, they claimed. No one believed that either, and a nationwide manhunt got under way.

The *Journal*, meanwhile, was moving on several fronts. Managing editor Paul Steiger issued a statement that Danny was not now nor ever had been an employee of any agency of the U.S. government, and the C.I.A. broke long-standing policy to say the same. Foreign editor Bussey and correspondent Steve LeVine flew in to shepherd Mariane, whose Buddhist group was chanting a mantra for Danny. A media strategy was devised. Mariane made herself available for interviews, but only to outlets that had Pakistan reach, such as CNN and the BBC. Questions about what story Danny was working on were deflected, lest the truth cause him harm. Finally, a confidential appeal was made to major U.S. media organizations to not disclose that Danny's parents were Israeli. All agreed.

But on January 30, Danny's Jewishness leaked. In a story in *The News*, Kamran Khan, the paper's chief investigative reporter, wrote that "some Pakistani security officials—not familiar with the worth of solid investigative reporting in the international media—are privately searching for answers as to why a Jewish American reporter was exceeding 'his limits' to investigate [a] Pakistani religious group."

"An India based Jewish reporter serving a largely Jewish media organisation should have known the hazards of exposing himself to radical Islamic groups, particularly those who recently got crushed under American military might," Khan quoted "a senior Pakistani official" as saying.

Having let the religious cat out of the bag, Khan—who doubles as a special correspondent for *The Washington Post*—revealed Danny's relationship with Asra Nomani, whom he claimed—falsely—Danny had imported from India to be "his full time assistant."

"Officials are also guessing, rather loudly, as to why Pearl decided to bring in an Indian journalist," Khan wrote. "[They are] also intrigued as to why an American newspaper reporter based in [Bombay] would also establish a full time residence in Karachi by renting a residence."

Khan's revelations stunned colleagues. But there was no wondering about the source of his information: he was well known for his contacts at the highest levels of the ISI.

The same morning Khan's story appeared, the kidnappers released a second note, changing Danny's supposed spying affiliation from the C.I.A. to the Mossad, the Israeli intelligence service.

The language that followed differed radically from the first note:

> U cannot fool us and find us. We are inside seas, oceans, hills, grave yards, everywhere.

We give u 1 more day if America will not meet our demands we will kill Daniel. Then this cycle will continue and no American journalist could enter Pakistan.

Allah is with us and will protect us.

We had given our demands and if u will not then "we" will act and the Amrikans will get teir part what they deserve. Don't think this will be the end, it is the beggining and it is a real war on Amrikans. Amrikans will get the taste of death and destructions what we had got in Afg and Pak. Inshallah

This did not sound like Sheikh—and it wasn't. A note later found on his computer read, "We have investigated and found that Daniel Pearl does not work for the CIA. Therefore, we are releasing him unconditionally."

Having lured Danny, Sheikh had ceased calling the shots; Danny's fate was now in the hands of more murderous others.

Investigators, however, were still concentrating on Gilani, who turned himself in on January 30, protesting his innocence and ticking off the names of more than a dozen senior and retired officials who would vouch for his services to state security.

After interrogating Khawaja—who backed Gilani's story—police began having second thoughts. Ul-Fuqra had never been involved with violence in Pakistan and indeed had become so inactive of late the State Department had dropped it from the terrorist list. Someone had set Gilani up. But who?

In Karachi, a newly arrived contingent of F.B.I men were tracing the source of the kidnappers' E-mails, while Yusuf's Citizens Police Liaison Committee was manually sorting the connections among 23,500 telephone calls. The effort paid off, with the identification of Fahad Naseem, an employee of a cyber café, as the sender of the E-mails and the linking of his phone calls to two other conspirators.

The police moved just after dark, heading off in unmarked vans to grab Fahad. If Pakistani interrogation methods had their usual brutal efficacy, Fahad would quickly lead them to the second kidnapper, who—likewise persuaded—would lead them to the third, who would rapidly decide that giving up the boss was in his best interest. When they got him, they'd have Danny. It all had to be pulled off by morning prayers at the mosque. After that, everyone in town would know.

Stops one, two, and three yielded the desired results. But they were stymied at four. They had the ringleader's name, his phone number, his uncle's Karachi address—before sunup, they even had his uncle, cousin, and aunt in custody. The aunt placed a call to his cell phone, begging him to surrender. Then the lead officer came on the line. "The game's up, Sheikh," he said. The answer was a click.

For days, nothing more happened. Sheikh appeared to have vanished, and there were no further messages from the kidnappers. Fake messages, though, were cascading in, including one which said that Danny's body could be found in a Karachi cemetery. Three-hundred-plus cemeteries were scoured; no body. But a fresh corpse was found in a vacant lot near the airport. Though the face had been rendered unrecognizable by a bullet, to Randall Bennett, who'd been summoned to the morgue, the victim seemed the right age, skin color, and body type. But something was odd about the mouth; ever so slightly, it seemed puffy.

"Roll back his lips," Bennett asked. He let out a breath at the sight of metal. Danny had smiled often during their meeting; Bennett knew he didn't wear braces.

On his way to visit George W. Bush, General Musharraf—who was now blaming India for the abduction—assured the world that all would be well. The case had been cracked; Danny's release was expected any minute.

February 14, Sheikh made a liar out of him.

According to the police, he'd been captured in a daring raid in Lahore two days before. The truth was that he'd been turned over by Brigadier Ejaz Shah, home secretary of Punjab and formerly a hardline officer of the ISI. Sheikh had turned himself over to Shah February 5, and for a week it had been hidden from the police. "Whatever I have done, right or wrong, I have my reasons, and I confess," Sheikh said when he was brought before a magistrate. "As far as I understand, Daniel Pearl is dead."

Police interrogated him for a week, a silent ISI man always present, but got little else. "You are my Pakistani and Muslim brothers," he said. "You can't be as cruel as Hindu policemen were with me in India."

Then, one day, the lead investigator—the officer who'd said, "Your game is up, Sheikh"—visited his cell. They discussed the Koran, and the investigator said, "Show me in the Koran where it says you can lie."

"Give me half an hour," said Sheikh. He said his prayers and made his ablutions, and then he told them nearly everything.

He'd learned that Danny had been killed, he said, when he called "Siddiqi" from Lahore, February 5, and ordered, "Shift the patient to the doctor"—a prearranged code for Danny to be released. "Siddiqi" replied, "Dad has expired. We have done the scan and completed the X rays and postmortem"—meaning that Danny had been videotaped and buried. As he understood it, Sheikh said, Danny had been shot while trying to escape. Where the videotape was or what was on it, he said he didn't know.

The sole subject he refused to discuss was the week he had spent with his ISI handlers.

"I know people in the government and they know me and my work" was all he'd say.

A week later the videotape was recovered in a classic sting. A man (authorities won't reveal his identity) called a Karachi journalist (nor his) and said he had a tape of what had happened to Danny Pearl, and would sell it to the movies for $100,000. The journalist told the U.S. Consulate, which instructed him to tell the man to bring it to the lobby of the Karachi Sheraton at four o'clock, where a movie producer would meet him. An F.B.I. agent played the role to perfection.

They watched the tape on Bennett's living-room VCR—over and over, to make sure of its authenticity. But that was Danny, all right, shirt off, unconscious, on his back. A three-inch wound could be seen in his left side. A hand and part of a forearm came into the frame, holding a large butcher knife. The person wielding it seemed expert.

• • •

The rest you probably know by now. Mariane appeared on *Larry King* and signed a book deal and had her baby. People wept at memorial services for Danny in New York, Washington, Los Angeles, London, and Jerusalem. As of this writing, Sheikh and three co-defendants were still on trial. Everyone in Pakistan expects all of them to be convicted and sentenced to die by hanging.

You no doubt are aware, too, that Danny's dismembered body was found in a shallow grave in the garden of a nursery outside Karachi in mid-May. The terrorists who led police to it said that Danny was picked up by a taxi outside the Village Garden, taken to a nearby location, put into a van there, and driven around Karachi for hours. He was very calm, they said, and did not resist. When at last they came to their final destination, he asked, "Where is the man I wanted to meet?"

His killing moved people who are normally very tough about such things. The lead investigator wept when he told Mariane Danny was dead, and for the first time in years working hazard posts, Randy Bennett let the grotesque get to him. He was coming back to the consulate after endlessly watching the videotape, and a Pakistani was standing in the street covered in the blood of a goat whose throat he'd just slit. Bennett saw a large butcher knife in his hand, then the man shot him an "I hate Americans" look. He slammed on the brakes, got out, and went up to him jaw to jaw. "You got a problem with me?" he said.

I never did answer the "why" of everything. Sheikh said that the reason was to strike a blow at Musharraf, while Musharraf himself said it was because Danny was "overly inquisitive." And more than a few knowledgeable Pakistanis think the ISI was involved. When asked by *Vanity Fair* whether it shares that view, *The Wall Street Journal* issued a two-word written answer: "No comment."

One "why" I was able to answer: Why did Danny risk everything for a story?

I didn't need to go to Karachi to find out; I could remember.

Terror in Paradise
by David Case

The bombing of the Sari Club in Bali on the night of October 12, 2002 killed more than 200 people. David Case's story about the aftermath of the disaster appeared in Men's Journal.

In long white sarongs and frocks, Hindu elders hide from the afternoon sun under ornate silk parasols. They chant in deep, harmonious tones that rise slowly, pause, and then fall. On one side of the street behind them are the ruins of the Sari Club; on the other, the charred carcass of Paddy's Irish Pub. It is October 18. Only six days earlier, about 200 people perished here. More than 300 others, mostly foreign tourists, were injured. A sign nearby advertises a "foam party," showing men and women frolicking up to their bellies in soapsuds in an open-air nightclub; another offers water sports ("parasailing, jet ski, big banana boat, windsurfing"); and another features snapshots of freshly minted tattoos on naked torsos.

Thousands of people, nearly the entire community of Kuta, line Legian Street for the ceremony, sitting cross-legged, talking softly with friends, holding irises and roses, candles and incense. Mostly they are

Hindu, the women wearing bright skirts and sheer-lace tops, the men in silk and cotton sarongs, pressed shirts, and white head sashes. The Muslims in the crowd wear more-somber tones, and dark skullcaps or white head scarves. There are also a few Christian nuns and some Westerners in T-shirts and shorts. Men and women walk through the crowd, throwing holy water from golden urns onto the worshipers, taking care to hit everyone.

The Balinese believe that events such as the bombing in Kuta knock the spirit world out of balance. The *Bali Post* is reporting that the island's powerful shamans, known as Balians, are having nightmares about desperate spirits searching for lost limbs. But the Balians cannot help: The spirits all speak in foreign tongues. As believers in karma, many Balinese also accept the bombing as punishment for something the community has done wrong, either in this life or in a previous one. The island's Hindu pundits have wondered out loud if perhaps the gods are punishing them for taking tourism too far, for selling their sacraments to outsiders on package tours. The ceremony today will help appease the desperate spirits and atone for the community's misdeeds.

For the rest of the afternoon and into the evening, people wait patiently to make an offering. When their turn comes, they file in front of the mountain of flowers between what's left of Paddy's and the Sari Club. The sweet smell of the flowers is overpowering. Behind a police line, crushed and burned-out cars are scattered about the street. Soldiers with machine guns slouch in the shadows.

The Balinese place their flowers on the pile, light their incense, add their candles to the hundreds that already glow in their faces, and kneel carefully on the shards that still litter the street. They press their hands together at their foreheads and pray, offering their wishes to the spirits left behind.

Around 9 p.m. on October 12, Anthony Stewart leads 19 of his teammates from Perth's Kingsley Cats, an amateur Australian-rules football club, through the narrow lanes of Kuta toward the Sari Club, the town's most popular bar. Having landed in Bali this afternoon, the Kingsley boys are juiced. Wearing short-sleeve shirts, surfer shorts, and flip-flops and holding Bintang beer bottles by the neck, they sweat in the tropical heat but hardly notice. They've been drinking all day—on the way to the Perth airport, they left enough empties in their limos to fill two garbage bags—and now they're dodging motorbikes and weaving on and off the sidewalks and under the awnings of open-air stores. Some of them are wearing the medallions they won in a Grand Finals playoff match a few weeks earlier.

"Stewy" is particularly elated. The Bali trip was his idea. He and Jason Stokes, his usual partner in mischief, organized beer fests and a seventies night to raise $3,000 to pay for group activities. Now the boys are in for a week of revelry in paradise. Some plan to surf at Uluwatu, where perfect waves crash at the feet of bikini-clad Brazilians. Others will dive the world-class reefs or head inland to climb one of Bali's volcanoes. But mostly the boys will bond, as friends and as a team. They'll stay together at the Bounty Hotel, attend a cockfight, and go bungee jumping, and every night they will have dinner together before making their way to the Sari Club. Back home in Australia, the Sari is known as one of the world's best international pickup joints. As Laurie Kerr, a Kingsley coach, put it: "If you were a girl and you didn't want to go and have a drink and a chat and maybe a dance with a bloke, you wouldn't go to the Sari Club."

At six feet four and 200 pounds, Stewy is a perilous force on the field. But he plays football mainly for the camaraderie. Having lost his identical twin, Rodney, in a car crash four years ago, he values his mates and can be counted on to bring levity to any situation. He and "Stokesy" are together so often that some of their teammates regard one as the shadow of the other. Their girlfriends even share the same name, Becky. In a team photo, among a score of serious fellows dressed in blue-and-red prisoner stripes, Stewy is the one with the boyish grin, flexing his biceps. Once, when a policeman arrested a mate for dropping a wrapper on the ground, Stewy launched a souvlaki at the officer. "He's not going in the cruiser alone," he argued. At 29, he's traveled the world, from England and Germany to Kuwait and Afghanistan, and the younger boys who've never left Western Australia look to him for guidance.

Although Stewy is the team's spiritual beacon, their coach is Simon Quayle, whose wife and two sons are back in Perth while he runs amok with the boys. Lanky and fit at 33, Quayle is a natural leader who is proud to have guided his team into the Grand Finals, a match they narrowly conceded under slanting rain. But here, he goes along with Stewy and Stokesy like everyone else.

As they turn onto Legian Street, Kuta's main drag, traffic is jammed. Cheap Japanese motorcycles fill the air with exhaust, which mingles in the warm breeze with barbecue smoke and the scent of incense and sweet jasmine. Music blasts from the maze of nightclubs, CD shops, and tattoo boutiques. In the days before 747s landed ten minutes from Legian Street, Kuta was an idyllic, palm-lined village, a beachhead for hippies exploring the rest of Bali. Behind resort walls, Kuta retains some of its Balinese character, but outside it has been overwhelmed with commercialism by travelers and locals looking to make a buck.

The Sari Club offers a haven from all that. The club's policy is to prohibit Indonesians from entering, which irks some but keeps out the prostitutes who crowd other Kuta bars. Constructed of bamboo, rattan, and thatched grass, open to the sultry air, the club is smaller than the boys expect. But there are several bars and two dance floors, and they fan out to explore, ordering plastic cups of potent red jungle juice, a mixture of arrack, vodka, and fruit juice. The DJ is spinning AC/DC, and 20-year-old Corey Paltridge is doing the Angus Young, hopping across the dance floor, playing air guitar on an outstretched leg. Nearby, Ben Clohessy, the team's 24-year-old vice-captain, and some others are chatting up three pretty women from Sydney. Clohessy invites them to an after-hours pool party at the team's hotel. "We'd love to," says one of the women, "but we're not wearing bathing suits, so is it okay if we swim in our undies?" With a beer in hand, Stewy leans against a bamboo pillar, chuckling to himself, knowing that he's the reason the team's all here.

Meanwhile, 200 yards down Legian Street, expats Bob Stevens and Lee Gilkes are drinking beer in the Mini bar, a dark, low-key hangout. A middle-aged, hard-drinking Aussie, Stevens has flowing hair and a ruddy complexion that makes him look like a ship's captain. A naked vixen is tattooed on his right calf, and the letters F-U-C-K grace his left knuckles. "From my angry years," he explains. Intelligent and fun-loving, if somewhat rudderless, he's been in Bali for five years, living off his savings and staying at a $10-a-night guesthouse. He greets people with a cheery "good morning" no matter the time of day, a joke that always makes him laugh. "Time doesn't matter here," Stevens says. Gilkes, a fair-skinned 34-year-old Brit with tattoos ringing his biceps, is like many of the backpackers who cross paths in Kuta. Tired of his life in the U.K., he sold some property he'd inherited from his father and bought a round-the-world ticket. He traveled to Guatemala, Mexico, the States, and New Zealand. "I've seen some beautiful, beautiful places," he says, "met some beautiful people, and realized my dream of diving and bungee jumping"—including a 440-foot plunge from a tram. But the footloose adventure changed for Gilkes when he arrived in Bali five months ago, and he decided to stay for the long term.

The most travel-friendly island in Indonesia, Bali is one of those places where outsiders immediately feel at home, where life seems simple and comforting. Maybe it's the combination of the perfect trop-ical weather, the sublime beaches, the enchanting people, and the rich culture, but many foreigners have taken up residence in homes on stilts among the emerald, terraced rice paddies. Gilkes quickly found himself at peace here; that he could live for a pittance was a bonus. Most important, within 48 hours of arriving, while at the Mini bar with Stevens, he met I'in, a young Javanese Muslim, and instantly fell in love. "Within a week we were a regular item," Gilkes recalls. "She's very beautiful, used to make me laugh all the time." But their affair eventually ended, and tonight Gilkes is thinking about Sandra, a 23-year-old Javanese he's been with for a month. They met while drinking arrack behind the post office. Sandra owned little more than a mat-tress, a plastic cart, and a big bucket for bathing, so Gilkes took her shopping. But they've begun to break up their relationship—"She's a lovely girl, but she's just too young," Gilkes says. Tonight, she's with friends at Paddy's Irish Pub, across the street from the Sari Club.

If Bali felt like paradise before October 12, many places in Indonesia—

a vast 3,000-mile-long archipelago—did not. In the past few years, Indonesia has seen substantial turmoil, which many political analysts fear has fomented militancy among Islamic extremists and other factions of society.

As a predominantly Hindu enclave, Bali is virtually alone among Indonesia's 17,000 other islands, whose 230 million residents include more Muslims than any other country in the world. Indonesian Muslims practice a moderate and traditionally pro-Western form of Islam, and they have a reputation for being friendly and refined people. For more than three decades, beginning in the 1960s, Indonesia was a poster child for Asian economic development. Growth hovered around 7 percent for years, lifting millions out of poverty. And despite a potentially volatile mix of ethnic groups, the country remained relatively peaceful, though the military's heavy hand was largely responsible for this. But the country's fortunes reversed when the Asian economic crisis struck in 1997. The currency crashed, banks collapsed, companies went bankrupt, and millions lost their jobs. Within a year, a popular uprising toppled the corrupt, longtime dictator, President Suharto, ushering in democracy but leaving lawlessness and a power vacuum at the top.

The new openness—some might say anarchy—has brought about a renaissance for extremists who were suppressed by Suharto, and who are seizing the opportunity to push their agendas. As a result, a number of conflicts have flared up across the country. There have been dozens of bombings, including a Christmas Eve 2000 attack that damaged more than 30 churches.

Ironically, the Indonesian military has served as a catalyst for the extremists. After the economic crisis, the government slashed spending, forcing the military to raise at least half of its budget on its own. To do this, the military is widely believed to engage in extortion and protection schemes, and analysts say soldiers have sowed unrest and abetted militant groups in order to elevate their own status and income. In August 2002, gunmen attacked a convoy of vehicles belonging to an American mining company in West Papua, killing two

Americans and an Indonesian. American intelligence analysts say the attack was orchestrated by Indonesian military officials who wanted to bolster the military presence in the area.

Most of Indonesia's violence has been motivated by economic and political grievances, not by religious aspirations. Yet in the past few years, analysts have grown increasingly concerned that some Islamic militants—who have long sought to transform Indonesia into a Muslim state—are looking to attack Western interests. Extremists in Indonesia view the conflicts in the Israeli-occupied territories, in Afghanistan, and in Iraq as growing evidence of a U.S.-driven war on Islam. Many feel that the Bush administration equates Islam with terrorism. Even the country's moderates are skeptical that Al Qaeda perpetrated the September 11 attacks. These moderates abhor hostility, and even those who advocate an Islamic state reject violence. But, of course, it takes only a small number of terrorists to cause a big problem.

In the weeks prior to October 12, headlines focused on a radical Islamic cleric, the charismatic Abu Bakar Bashir, whom the U.S. and other countries have accused of being an international terrorist and of leading a group called Jemaah Islamiyah, allegedly linked to Al Qaeda. This summer, a suspected Al Qaeda operative in American custody testified that Bashir was behind a plot to attack the American embassy in Jakarta. Bashir denies having ties to terrorists, but he's an unabashed enemy of the U.S. government, which he says was behind the attacks on the World Trade Center.

As a precaution, the U.S. closed its embassy in Jakarta for a few days around the anniversary of September 11. Then, on September 23, after the embassy had reopened, a grenade exploded inside a moving car near Jakarta's diplomatic quarter, killing one of the alleged perpetrators. American officials say the incident was a botched attack on U.S. diplomats. Over the next two and a half weeks, the U.S. State Department issued a series of travel warnings, including one on September 26 that cautioned Westerners to avoid "locations known to cater primarily to a Western clientele, such as certain bars, restaurants, and tourist areas."

If terrorists wanted to strike Westerners on Indonesian soil, Bali would be a good target. At any given time, there are more than 20,000 tourists on the island, among them honeymooning Americans, globe-trotting Europeans, and particularly Australians, who have to fly only a few hours to reach paradise. But their proximity to Bali wasn't a shield: On October 8, Abu Bakar Bashir was quoted in an Indonesian newspaper as saying, "Australia, the United States, and the Jews are countries that want to destroy Islam."

It is in this increasingly volatile context that, according to Indonesian police, a white Mitsubishi L-300 van owned by a student of Bashir's named Amrozi is driven down Legian Street in Kuta on the evening of October 12 and abandoned, with the doors and steering wheel locked, in the drop-off zone of the Sari Club around 11 p.m.

At 11 o'clock inside Sari Club, the DJ is spinning Eminem—"Two trailer park girls go round the outside, round the outside, round the outside . . ."—and everyone on the dance floor stomps like elephants to the heavy beat. Then a devastating explosion rocks Legian Street. The Australian federal police and the Indonesian national police later determine that the white van outside was loaded with between 110 and 330 pounds of explosives. Its detonation leaves a three-foot-deep crater and throws diners off their chairs in restaurants more than 300 feet away. Fifteen seconds earlier, a smaller bomb exploded in Paddy's, across the street, igniting flash fires inside the bar. But people in the Sari kept dancing, perhaps because the music drowned out the explosion. When the second bomb goes off, however, it's as though the *Enola Gay* dropped Fat Man on the dance floor.

First, the Kingsley boys see a white flash, as if the sun had torn through the night sky. Next comes a tsunami of energy that hurls the revelers off their feet and against the walls like bowling pins, filling the air with shrapnel and shards of brick, glass, and wood. Then the ceiling crashes down, trapping people under beams and heavy mats of dry thatched roofing. Everything goes black, and for a suspended moment, silence shrouds all of Kuta. The Sari Club is motionless, until the inferno erupts and a collective cry of agony begins. Bleeding and broken, their clothes blown off, people plead for help in at least five languages.

As Coach Quayle, Ben Clohessy, and some of the other boys come to, adrenaline kicks in, and they throw off the debris like a duvet cover. The Sari Club resembles a 19th-century slaughterhouse, but the boys, drenched in sweat and seized by panic, ignore the limbs and bloodied bodies, some the remains of their mates. They struggle over the wreckage, away from the flames, running over glass and fractured concrete, which sink like fangs into their bare feet.

Searching for an exit, Quayle and Clohessy come upon a daunting sight: a ten-foot cement wall that has somehow remained standing. There are a dozen others there, men and women, covered in soot. Some are wailing and jumping for the ledge, but it's beyond reach. Their chests, bellies, and chins become bloodied against the concrete. "Fuck, fuck, fuck, it's hot," someone shouts. So some of the Kingsley boys grab people and heave them over the wall. A woman emerges from the dust, her dress on fire. Clohessy grabs a handful of the soft cotton and tears the dress from her body. She hardly notices as she staggers for the wall. Clohessy puts his hands against her ribs and presses her high against the concrete. With one herculean push, he throws her over, and she thuds to the ground on the other side. She stumbles into the street, where a crowd of Balinese has gathered. They part as she approaches, gawking at this naked apparition wearing only a black thong, her cut flesh glowing in the orange light.

Back inside, Laurie Kerr is stuck in a crag of rubble, pinned between the fallen roof and a crumbled wall. He sees a small gap where he thinks he can lift the roofing and free himself. But the spot is blocked by a young woman who is wheezing in panic and paralyzed with fear. Kerr tries to calm her, to talk her out of the crag, but she flails, unable to move the roofing. As the fire grows hotter, Kerr stays calm enough to convince the woman to crawl behind him. He squeezes past, shoving his heavy torso through the fractured beams, and battles with the roofing. They've been stuck for more than a minute now, and the fire is on top of them, searing their skin and filling the air with the acrid odor of burning flesh. Others, trapped nearby, emit one last cry as the fire engulfs them. Only seconds separate Kerr and the woman from the same fate, but they continue to fight.

At the Mini bar, Lee Gilkes polishes off another Bintang. He looks at his watch: five minutes to eleven, still early. "Let's have another beer, shall we?" he says to a drinking buddy. Stevens is quarreling with his girlfriend and has gone home early.

"All right, mate."

They're ordering the next round and chatting with the bar girls, having "a laugh and a giggle," as Gilkes later puts it, when the first explosion goes off down the street. "What was that?" Gilkes asks, resting his beer on the bar.

"Probably a transformer again," someone replies.

"Ill go have a look," Gilkes says, but then comes the other, much bigger blast, which knocks over glasses and bar stools and throws Gilkes into his friend's lap. After a pause, debris splatters down on the bar's roof. "Sandra's down at Paddy's. I've got to go see if she's all right," Gilkes says, and he runs out of the bar. He fights his way through people on motorcycles, in cars, and on foot as they tear up the road, away from the bomb site. "Please don't be hurt, Sandra, please don't be hurt," Gilkes whispers to himself. But as he approaches Paddy's, the scene on the street is gruesome. Beneath the smoke and dust, a stew of blood and severed limbs clogs the street, which is hot as a kiln. People are crawling, rolling, and pulling themselves through rubble to escape the heat. Many are motionless. Gilkes runs past them to search for Sandra, but he's halted by the fireball, an inferno that has by now engulfed half a city block, its yellow and blue flames billowing out from Paddy's and the Sari Club on both sides of the street. A line of cars and motorcycles along the curb is ablaze, melting. He sees a young Indonesian girl in the street, maybe 19, dressed in hot pants and a sleeveless blouse. She lies placidly, uninjured except for her head, half of which has been crushed by a telephone pole.

On the street between Paddy's and the Sari, Gilkes spots a burly Westerner, bleeding badly, a piece of shrapnel piercing through his jeans and into his thigh. The man struggles, flames licking at his back, but his limbs flail like a wounded ant's. Gilkes grabs him under the armpits. "This is gonna hurt," he says, "but I've gotta get you out of here." But the man is too heavy. Gilkes hollers for some tourists who are videotaping the carnage, but they don't move. Finally, an Indonesian man appears, and they drag the injured man through ankle-deep shards of metal and terracotta roof tiles, brushing past body parts, laying him down in front of a bar up the street. There are others near Paddy's, dozens of them, and Gilkes and the Indonesian, the fire burning their cheeks and singeing their hair, do what they can to drag them to safety as well. They seize a woman who crawls out from under the fire, her clothes burned off. They return for another, a blond Australian wearing a shredded sundress and half a pair of underwear, then help three Indonesians. Gilkes grabs for the hand of one but misses: The bottom half of her arm is gone. When he throws people over his shoulder, their scorched skin sticks to his hands.

After the firetrucks arrive, Gilkes makes his way to Sandra's boardinghouse, but she's not there. He checks his place, fighting his way through hordes of travelers who are lugging their rucksacks toward the airport or the beach, too frightened to remain in Kuta. But Sandra is missing. He searches for two hours and finally finds her back at home with some friends. She's terrified; she was in the restroom at Paddy's when the bomb went off and got out before the fire spread. Gilkes holds her, waits with her until she's calm. Later, he begins drinking again. "In my neck of the woods," he says, "when something like this happens, we drink until we're legless."

Back at the Sari Club, Laurie Kerr finally breaks out of the crag of rubble. He grabs the panicked woman beside him and pulls her after him, lurching for the cement wall, where several revelers, too weak or maimed from the blast, are trapped and desperately fighting to escape. By now, the fire is intense, and Coach Quayle and Ben Clohessy, who are agile enough to scale the wall, have already bolted. Kerr struggles over as well, but he's badly burned, and blood is pouring from the back of his head.

Out in the street, a black mushroom cloud still churns overhead. Quayle, feeling the heat on his face, searches the crowd for his players. Among the black-haired Balinese, he spots the sandy-blond head of Damon Brimson. The two of them embrace. Then they see the woman in the black thong. Quayle puts his hand around her arm, trying to calm her. She tells him her name is Claudia and that she lost her boyfriend inside. She is desperate to find him. Quayle finds a T-shirt in the street and pulls it over her.

While they're calming Claudia, Quayle spots Kerr. But just as Quayle reaches him, people in the crowd begin screaming, and the terrified throng erupts, stampeding down the street. Quayle thinks terrorists are coming after them with machine guns, to kill as many as they can. The foursome tries to keep up, but with Claudia and Kerr, who is losing blood fast and turning pale, they labor along, looking behind them in trepidation as people charge past. A taxi driver offers to help, and they head for Claudia's hotel, 20 minutes away, in Sanur. But Kerr begins to lose consciousness, so they turn the car around, and as an ambulance screams past they follow, blasting the horn and careening through Bali's narrow, congested streets to the hospital.

When they arrive, scores of burned, bleeding people are piled shoulder to shoulder in an open ward. The victims far outnumber the doctors and nurses, who ricochet among gurneys, trying to revive dying patients. Quayle sees something on a stretcher, something that looks like burned wood. Its charred flesh hangs like a black web, but it's still eking out shallow breaths. It could be one of the women from Sydney who were coming to the pool party, or someone's mother, or even one of his own players. Someone locates a bottle of water and slowly pours it over the suffering body, hoping to soothe the victim's last moments.

After finding a doctor for Kerr and scanning the area for team members, Quayle and Brimson return to the taxi, where Claudia waits. Her legs are bleeding, and she's shaking, wondering if she'll ever see her boyfriend again. As the driver heads toward Sanur beach, Claudia gets increasingly desperate. "I need you to stay with me," she says, clutching Quayle's arm. "And if he's not there, I want to come back with you.

Don't leave me alone." When they finally reach Sanur, Claudia jumps out of the taxi and sprints down a dark path through a row of bungalows, screaming in German. Quayle and Brimson follow. Finally, a door opens, and out bursts her man, weeping. The two embrace, and Quayle and Brimson join them, bawling and hugging the couple as if they've known them all their lives. "It was unreal," Quayle later recalls. "Like 40 Christmases." Claudia still begs them to stay, but the boys have their own friends to find.

Arriving back at the Bounty Hotel, Quayle and Brimson are reunited with Clohessy at what's become a makeshift battle ward. Backpackers use torn sheets to bandage scores of wounded, who are lying on chaise lounges by the pool. And then comes the ominous news: It's after 1 a.m., and only 12 of the Kingsley boys are accounted for. Eight are missing, including Anthony Stewart, Jason Stokes, and Corey Paltridge. The boys camp out in front of the BBC. At first they're encouraged by reports of only three confirmed dead, but as the night passes the numbers increase: 10, 14, 15, 25. At daybreak, another batch of tourists arrives from the airport. On the BBC, the death toll is more than 80. The Kingsley boys are numb.

On October 16, David "Spike" Stewart, Anthony's father, arrives in Kuta with Andy Bridson, an old army pal. Spike, who wears a Crocodile Dundee hat, is a portly, "straight-talking Aussie with a heart of gold," as one friend says. But the victims' families are furious with Australian Prime Minister John Howard for not warning his citizens about the danger in Bali, and frustrated by how long it's taking to identify the remains. Earlier in the day, Spike made global headlines by chewing out Howard at a press conference. "My son Anthony is missing," he said. "Is it going to take you six weeks to find him?"

Spike and the others who gather in Bali to retrieve their loved ones belong to a fraternity of misery. They don't notice Bali's perfect tropical weather, the bougainvillea, or the fragrant jasmine in the air. They don't take in the sunset over Kuta beach. Instead, they pass their nights staring at unfamiliar ceilings, their days trying to discern the faces of their children or siblings among photos of mutilated corpses. They look forward to the day when they can bring their family members home from the morgue. "I often go up to the Blackwood Cemetery and have a beer with Rodney," says Spike, referring to Stewy's deceased twin. "Only now I'll have to have two."

For the Kingsley boys, there is a bit of good news: A couple of days after the blast, they found their teammate Phil Britten, meaning that seven, not eight, of the 20 had perished. Britten's name had been spelled wrong on a hospital list, so they had missed him earlier. But when the boys arrived at the hospital to visit him, he was so badly burned that they recognized only his voice.

Back in Perth, Quayle, Kerr, and the other Kingsley boys who survived—as well as the girlfriends and wives of those who didn't—spend every waking hour together. They gather at the Kingsley Pub and field media calls; the ones willing to venture back into crowds are honored at drag races and nightclubs. The city has rallied around them in one giant, communal bear hug. But even those who escaped are badly wounded inside and deeply angry at the perpetrators. "I hope they burn in hell," says Adam Nimmo, a 20-year-old forward. "I'd like to string them up."

The Balinese are also hurting, but they remain remarkably immune to anger and vengeance. Two weeks after the bombing, Lingk Widya Sari camps out on a mattress below the hospital eaves. A Hindu, she's the wife of a waiter who was badly burned. In Bali, she says, "if something bad happens, we say, 'So be it.' We just want to take care of whatever is left. What happens is God's will, and our task is to rebuild family, friendship, and business, to think about the future, not the past." In addition to worrying about her husband, Widya Sari, who is from a poor family, is anxious about money. These days, people are losing their jobs; Bali's beaches are deserted and its hotels empty.

Despite all he's been through, Spike is determined to do what he can to help the Balinese. They're "great people—they don't deserve this," he says. "When I'm back in Australia, I'm going to go on television and tell everyone to go back to Bali. If people abandon this place, then the terrorists win."

The Slipping Point

by Laurence Gonzales

Laurence Gonzales' piece for National Geographic
Adventure *tells the story of an American climbing disaster.*

Steve Boyer rode the Palmer chairlift, carrying his skis, poles, and
an ice ax, on his way up Oregon's Mount Hood on Thursday
morning, May 30. He reached the top of the lift at about 8:45. It
was a beautiful day, hardly a cloud in the sky. There'd be a lot of
climbers up there. A small man with a gray-streaked beard and professor's spectacles, Boyer looks more like a high school math teacher
than a mountaineer who has summitted Annapurna and attempted
Everest and K2. An emergency room physician with a master's degree in
geology, Boyer, 55, has been climbing Hood once a month for the past
several years, photographing the glaciers and documenting the way they
change over time. The standard route up Mount Hood's south face
takes most climbers from four to eight hours. Boyer holds the record
of 1:32 from the lodge to the summit.

Just before nine o'clock, Boyer set down his ice ax and ski poles, lifted his digital camera, and shot a frame of the entire mountain. Then he zoomed in on the summit and caught the group of climbers below it. Near the top, the standard route follows an elegant ridge of snow known as the Hogsback, which is split about halfway up by a dramatic horizontal crevasse, or *bergschrund*. Boyer made a mental note to go around to the right side of the crevasse on such a crowded day. That way he'd be out of the fall line if anyone slipped from above.

He dropped his gaze to the snow. It was unusually icy. "I don't generally put on my crampons until I reach the Hogsback," he says. "But that day, for the first time, I put them on below 9,000 feet." Moments later, Boyer looked up again at the summit. Though he didn't notice it at the time, the line of climbers he'd just seen had disappeared. The entire upper Hogsback was empty.

Tom Hillman and John Biggs had just come one mountain closer to their goal of climbing the highest point in each of the 50 states. The two men had met several years earlier at the Windsor Community United Methodist Church in Windsor, California, where Hillman, 45, is the co-pastor and Biggs, a 62-year-old retired airline pilot, was a parishioner. Soon they were taking frequent hiking and climbing trips together: Yosemite, the Sierras, Montana, Wyoming.

Like many climbers on Hood's standard route, they had started in the middle of the night with a snowcat ride to the top of the ski area. They made steady progress and reached the summit just before 8 a.m. "We could see Rainier and Saint Helens one way, and the Three Sisters the other," Hillman says.

Now they were headed down, connected to each other by 50 feet of rope. They were passing through the band of ice-encrusted rocks known as the Pearly Gates, the steepest part of the climb, when Biggs suddenly slipped. Without hesitating, he gripped his ice ax across his chest and rolled onto it, digging the pick into the icy snow to stop the fall. It was a perfect self-arrest. Gingerly he got back to his feet, and the two men started down the Hogsback ridge.

Just behind them was a party of four. Harry Slutter, a New York-based sales representative with the Hines Nursery, led the group. Next on the rope was his friend Chris Kern, an investigator for the New York appellate court. Slutter, 43, and Kern, 40, were frequent climbing partners and were particularly proud of their winter ascents of New Hampshire's Mount Washington. Slutter's friend Bill Ward, 49, was last on the rope. Ward, an experienced mountaineer who had climbed Hood before, worked at the Hines Nursery branch in Forest Grove, Oregon, which Slutter often visited on business. The two men had known each other for five years, but this was their first climb together. Ward's friend Rick Read, from Forest Grove, was the only novice in the group.

Slutter's team had met up with Hillman and Biggs during the ascent, and the men had all snapped pictures of one another on the summit. They'd talked about meeting for lunch once they got down. "It was such a glorious morning," Slutter recalls. "We were joking around up there for half an hour."

By 8:45, Slutter's group had passed through the Pearly Gates and halted on a natural shelf just above the Hogsback, where they drove the shaft of an ice ax into the snow as an anchor. The first three climbers left the shelf one at a time, each belayed by those above, until they were stretched out down the narrow ridge like beads on a string. The four men were each tied 35 feet apart on a nine-millimeter rope. Slutter, who was leading the descent, could see Biggs and Hillman just 50 feet below him. Ward was the last to leave; he pulled his anchor and started down. Now no one was attached to the mountain. But the rope still bound them together.

The team had gone only a few feet when Slutter looked over his right shoulder and saw something coming down the slope. Maybe it was Ward, at the top of the rope, or Read, who was next in line, but whoever had slipped would have had only a second or two to arrest his fall. In theory, when one member of a rope team falls, all the climbers throw themselves into the self-arrest position and collectively stop the plunge.

The theory did not work on Mount Hood that morning. Recent rains had left a glare of ice over wet snow, making it easy to fall, hard to stop. Within seconds, Ward and Read shot past Kern. Kern desperately tried to self-arrest, but the rope went taut with such force that he was yanked clear of the mountain. He flew through the air, then hit the snow with a sickening crunch.

Slutter was last in line. "I was looking at my ice ax. My chest was on top of it, and my hand was over it," he says. "Then I remember watching it ripping through the ice like it was a Slush Puppy. And I was ripped from the mountain."

It took only a second for the top team to catch up with the two Californians, 50 feet below. They struck Biggs "like a billiard ball," Hillman recalls, sending him tumbling into the air. Hillman dove to arrest himself, but a moment later he, too, was being dragged down the mountain, the pick of his ax leaving a ragged line through the soft ice.

Jeff Pierce had just ascended past the bergschrund, some 300 feet below, when he looked up and saw someone falling. "I expected them to drop, self-arrest, and start descending again," he says. "But half a second later, I knew they were coming down."

Pierce had planned carefully for this ascent. An EMT with the Tualatin Valley Fire and Rescue Department in nearby Aloha, Oregon, he was leading a group of six, including four other members of his department. The son of a well-known Portland doctor who'd been a leader in a local climbing club, Pierce had scaled Hood 12 times. His father had died of bone cancer when Pierce was 19, and the family had scattered his ashes on the peak. Now 38, Pierce was carrying on his father's tradition, introducing novices to the mountain. He had divided the party into two rope teams. On the first, he led Jeremiah Moffitt, 26, a Tualatin paramedic, and Cole Joiner, the 14-year-old son of another co-worker, Cleve Joiner. Firefighter Dennis Butler, 28, the other experienced climber in the group, led the second rope team, consisting of Selena Maestas, 27, a Portland paramedic, Chad Hashbarger, 33, the Tualatin department's fitness specialist, and the elder Joiner, 48, an assistant fire marshal.

Now six human projectiles, tangled in a mess of ropes and bristling with the points of crampons and ice axes, were plummeting toward

Pierce and his team. The climbers on Butler's rope were still below the crevasse. But Pierce and his two partners were strung out diagonally just above it. And the last of them, Moffitt, was directly in the falling climbers' path.

"I dropped and buried my ice ax," Pierce says. "I really dug in, and everyone else did, too." Moffitt was the only one hit, but that was enough.

"I felt the rope go taut, and I started to move," Pierce says. "Then I really accelerated, and I knew I was going into the crevasse." It had taken only seconds for the fall that began 300 feet above to end with nine climbers piled on top of one another deep in the bergschrund.

Though hardly the deadliest accident in American mountaineering, by afternoon the Mount Hood disaster would become certainly the most visible. And it was only one in a series of fatal accidents on West Coast peaks this past spring. A week earlier, a snowboarder had died on Hood's north side. Just the day before, three climbers had perished during a whiteout on Washington's Mount Rainier. And in June a climber would be killed in Yosemite when the helicopter that had lifted him from a ledge crash-landed in a meadow.

The Mount Hood accident in particular was a case study in chaos theory: When three groups of climbers assembled themselves in rope teams, one above the other on the steep slope, they created a system that was primed for a catastrophic change. The system reached its tipping point when one missed step by one climber promptly swept up eight others. As word of the accident reached the authorities, the effects of that slip continued to grow. Within hours, the disaster would involve state and federal agencies, three private companies, 50 search and rescue (SAR) professionals, and a half dozen Oregon Army National Guard and Air Force Reserve helicopters—one of which would crash spectacularly, producing additional casualties and necessitating an even greater rescue effort. The parking lot at the Timberline Lodge, 4,700 feet below the crevasse, would be jammed with TV trucks, and the sky would swarm with news helicopters. By early afternoon, geostationary satellites 22,000 miles overhead would be beaming images of this remote spot to viewers around the globe.

When the horrible rush of the ride stopped and silence descended, Jeff Pierce found that he had somehow landed in the crevasse on his feet, or nearly so. He had hit something hard but hadn't lost consciousness, and he seemed to be OK. Still, it was like waking in a dream. An eerie ice-blue light filtered down from the opening to the sky 20 feet overhead. Pierce looked around. A boy was gazing at him with huge, haunted eyes. It took Pierce a moment to comprehend that the boy was Cole Joiner.

"What do we do now?" Cole asked, his voice shaking. At first Pierce said nothing. He could hear people beginning to groan. Focus, he told himself; focus. "I had inspected the 'schrund before," he says. "So when I fell into it, I knew where I was. That was no big deal to me. What was a concern was how stable the floor was." The bergschrund cuts into the slope at an angle, so the uphill wall tilts overhead like a ceiling. Inside, it is a complex cave of snow slopes, weird angles, and ice formations. Jeremiah Moffitt was lying about four feet to Pierce's left. Another four feet beyond him, two climbers lay intertwined. Just past them, one climber was standing, and three more were piled on top of one another about 15 feet away, where the crevasse got deeper and narrower as it fell away into darkness. As he took in the situation, Pierce knew that the snow he was standing on might be only a thin bridge over a much deeper drop.

One fortunate coincidence of the Mount Hood accident was that many of those involved were emergency medical professionals. Pierce had actually briefed his team on what to do if there were an accident. His paramedics would treat the patient, while Dennis Butler would handle rope and extraction work. Pierce would be in charge—incident commander, in the jargon of rescue work. They were prepared for a fall and even a crevasse extraction. They just weren't prepared for one involving nine people.

When Pierce had last seen the rest of his team they'd been just below the crevasse. Now, all he could see overhead was ice blending seamlessly into sky. He prayed that they were all right. And he began shouting toward the slot of blue above.

Cleve Joiner had just watched, horrified, as his son was swept in a tangle of ropes, axes, and bodies into the crevasse. This can't be happening, he thought. His own father had begged them not to go. But Cleve had decided that, at 14, Cole was ready. Now he was struck by the terrible silence. My father was right, he thought.

He saw Butler moving up to the edge of the crevasse.

"How's Cole?" Joiner's voice sounded weak in the vast snowfield.

"Get a cell phone," Butler shouted. He was looking over the lip. "Make the call!"

Joiner had been in fire service and rescue for 27 years. There was a job to be done. He knew he wouldn't be able to help if he let his emotions get the better of him. He got his pack off and dug out his phone. Still, he needed to know: "How's Cole?"

"He's sitting up," Butler called. "I'm talking to him." Joiner felt his heart start beating again. He dialed 911. Just after he began to talk, his connection failed. He redialed, and then his phone went dead. He turned and yelled to Maestas, "Selena, get your phone." But Maestas was still lying in the self-arrest position they'd all assumed when the climbers above had come hurtling toward them. She couldn't even sit up to take off her pack. She'd found the steep slopes intimidating before the accident. Now she'd just watched her friends hurtle into a crevasse. And one of them, Jeremiah Moffitt, was also her boyfriend of the past two months. She was frozen with fear.

But Maestas was a highly trained paramedic; Joiner knew they were going to need her. He climbed up to her, removed her pack, pulled out her phone, and handed it to her. "I hadn't moved," she says. "I just repeated Joiner's call and told them I'd call back with more. Then I put the phone in my jacket and sat there."

Harry Slutter, the leader of the highest team of climbers, had been knocked unconscious when he hit the crevasse wall. He awoke jammed upside down, his ice ax still in his hand. Debris and snow were still pouring in from above. "I felt like I was drowning, breathing in all that fine snow," he remembers.

Slutter righted himself and took stock of his injuries. He was almost certain that he'd broken both his jaw and an ankle, but he felt he could function. He was more concerned about John Biggs, the retired pilot from the two-man team he'd befriended on the ascent: "I think my body was on his or his on mine; there was no separation," Slutter says. Biggs wasn't breathing, and Slutter immediately began trying to resuscitate him. Then Jeff Pierce came over to examine the patient. "He confirmed what I suspected," Slutter says. "John was dead."

Around them, the cries of the injured were growing. Slutter's partner Chris Kern was starting to scream. "I said, 'Put the pain away and hang on,'" Slutter recalls. It was something the two men had told each other when they trained together for the duathlons in which they liked to compete. Slutter could hear the voice of Rick Read, the novice climber from the top team, who was deeper in the crevasse.

"I was hoping he could hang on," says Slutter. "I had not heard anything from Bill Ward."

To Pierce, Slutter looked as if he'd been in a car wreck. But he seemed mentally alert and wanted to help. Kern was moaning again, and Pierce directed Slutter to tie Kern to a makeshift anchor so that he wouldn't slip deeper into the crevasse.

Pierce was trying to take control, but he was also on the edge of being overwhelmed. "My first thought was: I'm understaffed," he recalls. "We had nine people down in a crevasse; one more, and it would have technically been a mass casualty. I also have two people in the hole I'm directly responsible for as climb leader, and one is my paramedic Jeremiah [Moffitt], who I work with every day."

Pierce's first job was triage, assessing the condition of the victims. He had already examined Moffitt, who was groaning and asking the same questions over and over. He assigned Cole to stay with Moffitt and watch his condition. "Cole kept me awake," Moffitt recalls. "From my position, I couldn't see anything. I was just staring straight up. But I could hear yelling and screaming."

Pierce carefully picked his way through the tangle of ropes, bodies, rocks, and debris. He found Biggs's partner, Tom Hillman, near a pile of three at the deepest end of the crevasse. Just beyond him, Pierce could see that Kern was folded almost in half and horribly jammed beneath a rock outcropping.

When he'd checked all the climbers he could reach in the narrow opening, Pierce called up to Butler: "Dennis, I've got seven victims, and one is DOS." Dead on the scene. "Make the call."

Steve Boyer hadn't given any thought to the climbers he'd photographed 45 minutes earlier. The ER doctor was thinking about his climbing, his research, the beautiful day. Now, as he rounded the large volcanic formation called Crater Rock near the base of the Hogsback, Boyer met a climber coming down. "You're about to walk into a disaster scene," the climber said and kept on going.

Boyer picked up his pace. After a few minutes of speed climbing, he approached the crevasse. "There were some very inexperienced climbers up there," he says. "People who were scared on that slope, which wasn't that steep, maybe 35 degrees. But they wouldn't let go of their ice axes."

Boyer could see that they weren't helpless, though: A haul system had already been set up. Without hesitating, he climbed down into the bergschrund. At a glance he could see that at least one of the victims was almost certainly dead. Others were clearly in need of advanced medical attention. And the crevasse was like a deep freeze, Boyer noted: The injured could die from hypothermia alone.

Three people were working with ropes and victims, but to Boyer's eye, they were victims themselves. One of them turned to Boyer and began giving orders. For a moment, Boyer was confused. "I'm a doctor," he said.

"Good," Jeff Pierce responded. "Here's your patient." He pointed to Chris Kern and kept working.

Pierce now took the haul rope that Butler was feeding down from the lip of the bergschrund and tied it in to his harness. He shouted to Butler to lower him deeper into the crevasse so that he could reach the remaining climbers. He got to Rick Read first and felt for a pulse. But Read, whose voice they had heard just after the fall, now had no heartbeat. He checked Read's airway: He wasn't breathing. Pierce unclipped the man from the rope and slid him out of the way. He approached the last victim, Bill Ward, with trepidation. Pierce was a professional, and he knew what triage meant. Even if the man had been marginally responsive, the team would still have been forced to turn its attention to those more likely to live. "We didn't have enough resources, and we could easily have killed someone else trying to save him," Pierce says.

As Pierce approached, he was shocked at what he saw. Bill Ward was completely buried in snow; only his feet were showing. Pierce had to dig him out to check for a pulse: nothing. "I did a sternum rub and everything," he says. "He was unresponsive to pain, for which I was relieved."

Boyer kept calling down to Pierce, asking for more specifics on the patient's condition. He had no idea of Pierce's experience level and seemed to doubt Pierce's assessment.

"He's dead," Pierce snapped back. "I've pronounced people dead before, and he's dead."

A wilderness accident initiates two types of responses: medical and rescue. In Oregon, those roles are divided between two of the most highly regarded SAR squads in the United States.

Shortly after the first 911 calls came in from the mountain, the Clackamas County sheriff's office placed its own call, to American Medical Response, an ambulance company that operates a wilderness paramedic squad known as the Reach and Treat Team. The RATT was founded in 1988 when the booming popularity of adventure sports led to a spike in mountain injuries. The team's mission is to reach patients by any means, from foot to helicopter, and to provide life support and treatment as advanced as anything available outside a trauma center.

"Once we're out there, we're a walking ambulance," says Dave Mull, 31, a team leader. When he got the call, Mull was working with two other RATT members in a small town called Welches, about a half hour from Hood. They immediately got in their ambulance, flipped on the lights and sirens, and sped toward the mountain.

While the RATT is the medical component, the technical rescue and extraction on Mount Hood is handled by a legendary high-angle rescue organization called Portland Mountain Rescue (PMR).

That morning, when the calls went out, PMR team leader Steve Rollins was peering at a glowing monitor in his cubicle at Nike world headquarters in Beaverton, Oregon. Rollins, 27, looks like what he is: a computer-security specialist in a cube in a big glass building. But appearances are deceptive. Just a week earlier, Rollins had been lowered from an Air Force Reserve Pave Hawk helicopter into the black night to pluck a stranded climber off Hood's forbidding Sandy Headwall.

Rollins's watch read 9:08:33 when he heard his pager go off. Two cubes over, the pager of Matt Weaver, another PMR volunteer, sounded simultaneously. The two men stuck their heads out and looked at each other. "Uh-oh," they said in unison. They raced home to get their rescue gear and begin the 90-minute trip to the mountain.

When Mull and his RATTs arrived at the Timberline Lodge at 10:30, Rollins and Weaver were still a half hour away, driving as fast as they could without getting pulled over for speeding. As much as SAR is a humanitarian calling, it is also, if you will, an extreme sport. The object is to get the patient off the mountain and into the trauma system. Those who excel at SAR are highly trained, highly motivated— and at times highly competitive. Which is one of the reasons this was beginning to look like a race: Everybody wanted to get in the game.

Meanwhile, though, the elite teams from RATT and PMR were racing in the wake of a member of the Timberline professional ski patrol. Jeff Livick had been at the top of the Palmer lift at 9:30 when he got word of the accident 1,700 feet above him. A medically trained former Navy corpsman, Livick, 35, had immediately begun assembling oxygen tanks, backboards, splints, cervical collars, and any other medical gear he could find, and loading it all onto a snowcat. Then the cat began churning up the slope in a cloud of diesel exhaust.

Before Chris Kern could be lifted out of the crevasse, he needed to be hauled ten feet across its uneven floor. It was pure agony, not only for Kern but for Pierce and Slutter, too. "We dragged him sideways to get him out from underneath the rocks," Slutter says. Though they didn't know it, Kern's hip was shattered. "We had to unfold him and get his head facing uphill. We really hurt him," Slutter says of his friend.

Inch by torturous inch, they pulled Kern, who was conscious throughout the entire ordeal, into position for the lift. Pierce yelled that patient number one was coming up.

On top, Butler, the Tualatin firefighter in charge of the haul rope, had asked Selena Maestas and Cleve Joiner to climb up and help with the line. "I couldn't see who or what I was pulling," Maestas says. "But once I had patients, I became focused. I wasn't afraid anymore."

At last, they hoisted Kern into the light.

Maestas could see instantly how bad he was. He was gravely injured, hypothermic, possibly dying. "When I found out that we had three dead and three critical," she says, "I got on the phone while I was still on the haul line and dialed 911 again."

"Emergency 911, please hold."

"Jesus."

Maestas's call kept getting bounced around. Frustrated, at last she simply said: "Get us some helicopters. Now!"

Meanwhile, other climbers who happened to be on the route were converging with shovels, packs, and other equipment. Maestas stayed with Kern. She taped his feet together to stabilize his injuries. She put a sling on his shoulder, gave him gloves and sunglasses, and applied sunscreen.

Down in the crevasse, Tom Hillman, the California pastor on the two-man team, said he wanted to crawl out, but Boyer, the ER doctor, vetoed that. Hillman was getting weaker. His upper quadrant was very tender and bruised. Boyer was also concerned that Hillman may have ruptured his spleen. "Whenever we'd pull on his harness, he'd cry out in pain," says the doctor. (In fact, he had broken a vertebra.) Boyer supervised the process of hauling Hillman up, then climbed out. He and Maestas designated Hillman number two in line for an airlift.

Jeremiah Moffitt was next to come out of the crevasse. He was not as badly injured, but it still took time to pull him out. At some point during the course of these extractions, Slutter managed to drag himself out of the crevasse. "I was exhausted; I could hardly stand," he remembers. The adrenaline that had kept him going was beginning to wear off. He knelt by Kern, whose eyes were starting to roll back in his head. Slutter slapped his friend, trying to keep him conscious. "What are your kids' names? What's the name of your wife?" he shouted. "You're out of the crevasse, but you need to re-focus!" Finally, another climber came to sit with Kern, and two others began helping Slutter down the Hogsback.

All the injured were out of the hole and receiving medical attention when Cleve Joiner looked up and saw Cole pop his head out of the crevasse. Cleve choked up with pride and relief as he watched his son climb out, sit beside Moffitt, and bend his head to talk to his patient.

Pierce, the last to climb out, stood shivering and squinting in the bright sunlight. He was freezing and exhausted. There was a bloody hole in his pants; it looked like someone's crampon point had gone in there. Only now did he feel the pain. As he looked around, he was surprised to see a crowd of about 15 people. Some 10,000 climbers register to ascend Mount Hood each year, and the peak season was beginning. But a crowd scene is not what you want during a rescue, especially if helicopters are coming.

Mike Cataldo, 53, a Black Hawk helicopter pilot with the Oregon Army National Guard's 1042nd Medical Company (Air Ambulance), was giving a tour to some schoolchildren at the base in Salem at 10:05 when Major Dan Hokanson shouted out the window of the ops center: possible mission at Hood.

Cataldo went up to ops, and the major briefed him. Cataldo would be the pilot in command, flying bird number 670. Rick Chagnon, 43, would be flying the second Black Hawk, number 669. Both pilots knew that they'd be operating at high altitude and carrying weight. Together they worked out the power profile for the mission: At 10,500 feet, their Black Hawks could hover using only 78 percent of available torque, meaning a patient could be pulled off with power to spare.

The pilots had just started their engines when Hokanson radioed them to shut down. It turned out that the Air Force Reserve 304th Rescue Squadron, with its Pave Hawk helicopters, would be taking the mission. The 304th said it was better equipped for the job, but that didn't sound right to Cataldo. Though the Army Guard Black Hawks and the Air Force Reserve Pave Hawks have the same engine and airframe, the Pave Hawk carries some 4,000 pounds of additional combat-rescue gear. All that extra weight might be a problem for a bird trying to hover at 10,500 feet.

The rotors on Cataldo and Chagnon's birds hadn't stopped spinning when the major called again. "I'm going to launch you," he said. He had decided that while the Air Force Reserve was still preparing to launch, he could have his own birds on the scene, ready for the rescue. Cataldo lifted off beneath a broken deck of clouds. The time was 11:43. It would take 23 minutes to fly to the mountain.

The cat carrying Jeff Livick finally ground to a halt at about 10,000 feet, just below Crater Rock. From there, Livick and Boyd Bonney, a Timberline chairlift mechanic, began the brutal climb up the narrow Hogsback, each lugging 80 pounds of gear strapped to rescue backboards. They reached the scene about two hours after the accident. As Livick glanced around, he saw three victims down, with people around them. Someone had chopped out ledges for them to lie on. He moved up and glanced into the crevasse; there were three bodies there. He turned to the living and began distributing medical gear.

Livick started with Chris Kern, the most critical patient. He put an oxygen mask and a C-spine collar on him and applied a synthetic splint. As he worked, he called out his report. "Patient one: humerus fracture, pelvic fracture, suspected ruptured spleen, and chest injury."

Selena Maestas keyed the mike on the radio Bonney had carried up and began to make her own report to the SAR base that had been hastily established in the Timberline parking lot. There were three reds, she told them: critical patients in need of extraction. And three blacks. Then she scanned the sky: Her patient was ready to go, maybe dying. It had been more than two and a half hours since the accident. She asked for an ETA on the helos.

Maestas moved gingerly along the lip of the crevasse to kneel beside Hillman. She transmitted, "Number two patient: upper quad, possible ruptured spleen, lucid, male. . . ."

She fought for control as she crossed to her last patient and looked down at her boyfriend, who lay battered and helpless in the snow. She kept her voice steady as she recited, "Male, 26, was unconscious, conscious now, right-side mid-thoracic back pain, ribs, difficulty breathing." She couldn't believe she was talking about Jeremiah. As he smiled up at her, Maestas said, "He seems to be OK now." She put her hand on Moffitt and scanned the sky again.

Dave Mull and the RATTs reached Crater Rock about a half hour behind Livick. As they approached the lower Hogsback, they saw a man lying in the snow, surrounded by climbers, who had piled clothes on him to keep him warm. It was Harry Slutter.

"He was hypothermic, his neck was very swollen," Mull says, "and his eyes were swollen shut." Mull did a quick evaluation. Slutter's jaw was broken, and it seemed he might have internal injuries. "Every once in a while, he'd start to cry. He knew his friends were dead up there, and it was just beginning to hit him." Mull knelt down and introduced himself. "We're going to take care of you," he said. "I will get you out of here." Mull decided that he would stay with Slutter and sent the rest of his crew up to the bergschrund.

As he put in an IV line and wrapped a blood pressure cuff on Slutter, Mull mentally added him to the critical list. Now there were four reds on the mountain. It was past noon, three hours since the accident.

● ● ●

At 12:25 everyone on the mountain heard it: A helicopter, especially a Black Hawk, makes a sound unlike any other, a loud-soft, high-low, whistling thunder that creams the air until it peaks like meringue. They all turned to see the unmistakable origami-bat shape rushing up the mountain toward them.

Mike Cataldo piloted the bird smoothly up the snowfield. As he flew around Crater Rock, he could see the patients by the crevasse waiting to be lifted. He went to the spot and hovered at about 80 feet. If anything went wrong, his bailout was to turn into the westerly wind, then dive down the mountain, gaining airspeed to generate lift. But when he heard his copilot call out the power reading at 78 percent, he knew they were on the numbers.

In the back, his medic, 40-year-old Frayne Fowler, was ready. The plan was to lower Fowler onto the scene and have him orchestrate the evacuation. When the crew chief opened the door, the interior of the bird exploded with a thunderous roar. Fowler braced his feet against the door frame, one hand on the big yellow bullet of a detachable seat called the Jungle Penetrator. Then he was out in the wild air, riding the JP down to the snow.

When Cataldo lifted away, he planned to loiter nearby and wait for Fowler's signal that the first patient was ready. Then Cataldo would return and lower the Stokes litter—a metal basket used to lift patients—and hover while the patient was strapped in. Finally, he'd hoist the patient in and bring him down to the parking lot, where Rick Chagnon was waiting with bird 669 to ferry victims to the hospital. That way, they'd have a relay team to the trauma system and could get the patients off in short order.

Like most plans, this one was subject to complications: Because of the angle of the slope, Cataldo couldn't simply drop Fowler; he had to hang above while the RATTs clipped him in to an anchor. Radio communications were poor. Delays of this sort would build through the day. Finally, Cataldo returned to the crevasse and hovered with his nose pointed across the wind. He had power to spare. The litter was lowered and Chris Kern was loaded on, strapped in, and reeled up into the bird.

• • •

The Portland Mountain Rescue team finally reached the Hogsback at 12:30. Team leader Steve Rollins had arrived in the Timberline parking lot an hour and a half earlier and had immediately put together a team of four from the PMR volunteers who had already assembled. A PMR team is trained to be fully self-sufficient; the climbers stuffed special rescue packs with steel oxygen bottles, life support equipment, snow anchors, ropes, ice axes, crampons, helmets, harnesses, GPS units, prussiks, pulleys, and everything required for a crevasse rescue. If necessary, they would be able to spend the night on the mountain.

After climbing for ten minutes up the Hogsback, Rollins reached the bergschrund, where he came upon a tableau of highly motivated, amped-up rescuers, all operating effectively, if independently. There was Boyer, the ER doctor; Livick, the ski patroller; Fowler, the Army Guard medic. Then he encountered Pierce, who told him that he was scene commander. Rollins had expected to take command himself upon arrival. But it was hard to argue with results. The ad hoc team had done an extraordinary job: Pierce's crew and Boyer had extracted the victims and saved lives. Livick, Fowler, and the RATTs had brought needed medical gear and expertise.

So Rollins didn't quibble with Pierce. The whole thing was almost over. If they could just hoist these next two patients and control the crowd, it wouldn't really matter who thought he was in charge.

Down at the Timberline parking lot, the landing zone was getting crowded. The Air Force Reserve 304th had made the scene, and one of its Pave Hawks was sitting there with its rotors turning.

The plan was for Mike Cataldo and his Black Hawk 670 to make all the lifts on the mountain, shuttling each patient to a helicopter in the parking lot. But by the time Chris Kern had been transferred to Chagnon's helicopter, it was becoming clear that Cataldo would have enough fuel for only one more hoist.

Cataldo called Captain Grant Dysle, the Pave Hawk pilot, to discuss a change of plans. If the Pave Hawk could lift the third patient, Cataldo could take Hillman, the second patient, straight to the hospital. But he needed to know if the Pave Hawk had enough power for the job. "I know I asked him if he could do it—twice, in fact," Cataldo says. "I gave him the numbers: 10,500 feet, 10 degrees, and a prolonged hover with a little wind out of the west. He said he could do it." (The Air Force Reserve, which is conducting an inquiry into the accident, refused to let Dysle or other crew members be interviewed for this article.)

As they sat there burning fuel, other critical patients were waiting to be airlifted out. "I questioned it in my own mind, but I'm not going to challenge the guy," Cataldo says. Finally, Cataldo pulled pitch and headed up the mountain.

When Steve Rollins saw Cataldo's Black Hawk returning, he was still trying to get the crowd under control. At that point, he estimates, there were at least 50 people between the bergschrund and the base of the Hogsback. "When a helicopter's doing a hoist," he says, "in the back of my mind is always the possibility that something might happen, and I want as few people on the scene as possible." But the onlookers had no idea who Rollins was. Even the Tualatin team wouldn't clear the area as the Black Hawk came in to lift Hillman.

As he lowered the Stokes litter, Cataldo worried again that the Pave Hawk would have trouble doing the same maneuver. The slope was so steep that he couldn't simply drop the Stokes and loiter while Hillman was loaded on; he had to stay hooked in. "Sitting there hovering for 15 minutes takes a lot more power than just flying," Cataldo says. "I tried to pass this on to the Air Force—that it wasn't just drop it and go; it was drop it and hover."

Finally, the crew wrestled Hillman inside, and helicopter 670 rose away. Another patient was heading into the trauma system.

Selena Maestas was still at Moffitt's side when Rollins came over and told her that they needed to get off the mountain. She leaned over her boyfriend one last time. "Take care. I love you," she said. "I'll see you at the hospital." She had lost her ice ax, so Rollins gave her his and the two began to make their way down the Hogsback.

Unlike the Black Hawk, the Air Force Reserve ship came in very low, just 20 feet off the ridge, and lowered a parajumper. The PJ checked Moffitt's condition and then called the Pave Hawk back for the lift. With the bird thundering right overhead, the rotor wash was punishing. Gear began whipping down the mountain. In the open doorway, Technical Sergeant Martin Mills, the 36-year-old flight engineer, hit the joystick, and the Stokes litter descended.

"I heard the helicopter coming in," remembers Moffitt, who was flat on his back in a C-spine collar with his head taped to a backboard. "I saw the rotors and watched the hoist line as it dropped down." Livick helped lift Moffitt into the litter and secured the straps.

While the PJ checked the cable connection, Livick leaned over Moffitt to protect him from flying chunks of ice. He had to shout to be heard: "OK, you're hooked in! They're going to lift you now!" Then he waited, expecting the litter to spool up at any moment.

Down on the lower Hogsback, Dave Mull, the RATT paramedic, was still standing by Slutter, watching the hoist. This one didn't look as stable as the others. Then he heard the normal shrieking roar of the rotors turn into a very strange noise, "like a lawn mower going through heavy grass." It was the sound of rotor blades slowing down.

Everyone used the same words later: It was like a dream. "Your worst nightmare," Fowler called it. Boyer, who'd moved away from the litter, watched the helicopter slowly yaw to the right. Instead of pointing into the safety of the prevailing wind, the ship was now facing into the slope of the Hogsback. Then the nose began oscillating down and up. Says Boyer, "It suddenly occurred to me: They're going to crash."

"I felt the wind go away," Livick remembers. "Then I saw something falling." It was the hoist cable. Mills, the flight engineer, had fired the explosive squib to sever it.

Moffitt had no idea that his life had just been saved. "When the line went taut, I thought I was going to be lifted," he recalls. "But then the cable went limp. I saw the helicopter move off to my left, and then I heard people yelling."

Everyone stared, frozen, as the long refueling probe on the Pave Hawk's nose dug into the slope and the ship rolled on its side. There was a volley of rifle cracks as the bird's rotor blades hit the terrain. Then came the scythe-like sound of shattered blades cutting through the air. Rollins threw himself onto Selena Maestas, and together they landed on the far side of the Hogsback as the slabs of fiberglass and titanium whipped overhead with a wicked hiss.

"I looked over to where Jeremiah was, and thank God, he was still there," remembers Maestas. "Then I just started crying. I'd been so good all day . . . I just sat there and cried."

Down the hill, Mull watched as the colossal metal fuselage began rolling toward him. For a moment, he stood as fixed as the others, but then he had a thought: His responsibility was Harry Slutter. He put himself between the helicopter and his patient. "I grabbed hold of his jacket," Mull says. "I didn't want him to panic and run off."

Livick was standing beside Moffitt, watching, horrified, as Mills, the flight engineer, shot out the door, still tethered to the Pave Hawk. As the helicopter rolled, reeling in his tether, Mills was jerked off the snow and flung in an arc around the turning fuselage. Then he was slammed into the snow ahead of it. Livick could feel his stomach contract as the chopper rolled right over Mills. As it passed downhill, he was amazed to see Mills sit up.

But the helicopter turned again, reeling in Mills once more and rolling over him a second time. Livick realized that he'd been screaming "No! No! No!" Then, somehow, the tether broke, and Mills was released. The helicopter continued to roll, finally coming to rest just above a 30-foot drop near the base of the Hogsback.

Livick didn't hesitate. "I grabbed my skis, clicked in, and straight-lined it down to Mills," he says. Incredibly, Mills was sitting up again. Even before reaching him, Livick could hear Mills screaming "Holy shit! What the hell happened? Oh, shit!" Or choice words to that effect, Livick says.

"Don't move," Livick told him. He got right in Mills's face and shouted it again: "Don't move!"

But Mills was not quite finished: "I'm not getting in any goddamn helicopter again! Don't you put me in any goddamn helicopters, you hear me?"

Livick examined Mills and realized he might have a potentially fatal lacerated liver. (It was an accurate diagnosis.) "I kept taking his pulse and vitals, even as Mills continued to talk," he says. Mills was coded red, in urgent need of evacuation. As Livick realized that Mills was the man who must have cut the cable to save Moffitt's life, he decided that for the rest of the day, this was his job: keeping this man alive.

When Rollins raised his head from the snow and saw the Pave Hawk skidding to a stop, he knew that the disaster had just jumped another quantum level. And the PMR leader had a clear-cut job to do. He stood up and took command. Rollins had a crowd on the mountain, and he knew that more helicopters would be coming. There would be additional hoists, and he feared there would be more bodies to recover.

"At that point," he says, "the SAR base is calling on the radio, everybody's running around, and I'm acutely aware that I have responsibility for all these people who are now very amped up on adrenaline. I didn't want to violate rule number one, which is not to create more victims—which we had already obviously done."

RATT leader Mull was on the move as soon as the fuselage halted. He found the helicopter's crewmen wandering in a daze. He dug seats into the snow and got the men to sit. "There was chaos at first," he recalls, "but then the rescue came back together. And it came back together because of years of training."

Rollins put paramedic teams on each crew member. Then he called the SAR base and started relaying patient status reports. The seemingly impossible good news: Mills was the only critical patient. No other crew members, rescue workers, or onlookers were dead or badly injured. Everybody else would eventually ski down or walk off.

By 3:30, the game was all but over. The uninjured Tualatin climbers, including Selena Maestas and Cleve and Cole Joiner, had all made it down to the Timberline Lodge, where they were amazed to see the crowd of news vans and military helicopters. The Army Guard had returned and lifted off Slutter and Moffitt. Mills, with his understandable aversion to taking another helicopter ride, had been ferried down by two off-duty ski patrollers.

At last, all the injured were off the mountain. Livick heard Rollins yelling, "All rescuers: Meet for a briefing on the Hogsback in five!" Rollins had to account for everyone. As he puts it, "We take a deep breath and change gears. Now we've got a body recovery." But by then, Livick was carving turns back to the lodge. When he reached the ski-patrol room, he says, "I looked at myself in the mirror, and my eyes were huge. I was just trembling all over."

When Boyer saw that he was no longer needed, he continued the climb he'd started more than seven hours before. He moved quickly up the Hogsback and examined the place where the men had fallen. Despite the fact that a dozen people had been on the upper ridge that day, Boyer saw only three footprints on the slope. "It looked as if there had been freezing rain" that had left a slick glaze over the soft snow, he says. If a boot wouldn't break through the crust, a prone body wouldn't have a chance.

Boyer surmised that the initial fall was caused by a simple stumble. "Most people don't know how to walk with crampons on," he says. "You have to use an unnaturally wide gait, or else you'll catch one crampon on the other pant leg." In fact, Slutter and Kern's team had practiced crampon technique and self-arresting the day before. And Slutter had paid particular attention to Rick Read, the novice in the group. But the party had been moving for six hours at the time of the accident, and everyone was tired.

Boyer wasn't surprised that the fall had occurred on the descent. Beyond being fatigued, climbers often let down their guard once they've reached their goal. It's part of the natural cycle of human emotions: When we get geared up for action, especially if we're excited or afraid, the body is flooded with adrenaline and steroids; once the goal is met, the chemicals of emotion are metabolized and our focus, which was sharp in the goal-seeking phase, gets blurry.

Compounding this is the simple fact that descending is technically more difficult than ascending. During the climb, the foot is planted before any weight is shifted. The opposite is true on descent, making a climber's grip less stable. At about 45 degrees, the uppermost section of the Hogsback is not highly technical. Still, a fall here would need to be arrested almost instantly. And Boyer believes many of the climbers on Hood place far too much faith in their ability to self-arrest.

The risks of the terrain were exacerbated, not remedied, by the use of ropes. In tests performed in June 2001 on Mount Rainier by the Mountain Rescue Association, a group of experienced climbers dug into a snow slope with their ice axes in the full self-arrest position. Then their ropes were loaded to see how much weight each could hold. The climbers felt back pain or that they were going to break loose under as little as 277 pounds. One climber falling on a few slack feet of rope will produce far more force than that.

At the time of the fall, none of the three groups were anchored to the mountain. Like dozens of other teams on Mount Hood every day, they chose to move together, roped but not belayed. Boyer often takes beginner climbers up Mount Hood. But, he says, "we never move simultaneously on a slope like that." Instead, he leads the climb, and then, attached to a solid anchor, belays the other climbers, just as Slutter's team had been doing until minutes before the accident. Having passed the Pearly Gates, the group evidently felt that the terrain was moderate enough to handle without a fixed belay. In retrospect, of course, the safest strategy would have been to continue to belay one another. But failing that, Boyer says, the team as a whole would have been safer if they had unroped entirely. "A rope without fixed protection is a suicide pact," he says.

By linking themselves, the climbers had created a tightly coupled mechanical system. As they ascended the mountain, they put energy into the system. The higher they went, the more energy was available for release. Moving together on an icy slope, they gave that system its hair trigger.

By the time Slutter and Kern realized that their partners above them had fallen, there was no chance to save them. Since the men were spaced about 35 feet apart, Ward, the highest climber, would have been about 70 feet above Kern, who was second from the bottom. So Ward had to travel 70 feet before he passed Kern, and then another 70 feet before the rope between them went taut. The energy released in that 140-foot plunge was explosive. Kern believes he broke his hip not when he fell into the crevasse but when he slammed into the slope after the rope yanked him through the air.

Nevertheless, once the fall began, the climbers did their best to stop it. Slutter managed to stay in the self-arrest position all the way to the bergschrund. "I went down the mountain on my chest," he recalls. Tom Hillman, the California pastor on the next team below, had more time to get ready. "I prayed, because I knew that I'd have to arrest five people," he says. "I remember the ice ax ripping the ice all the way down to the crevasse."

The two men took a pounding in their desperate attempts to arrest. In the hospital, Slutter discovered he had several bruised ribs and a concussion, in addition to his broken jaw and ankle. Hillman had muscle damage in both shoulders, along with a hairline fracture of one vertebra. (Both men have recovered rapidly, and Slutter is already planning a return to Oregon for a reunion with some of the rescuers and other climbers involved in the incident. Hillman, for his part, has decided to give up technical climbing—four peaks short of his goal of reaching the highest point in each state.)

Collectively, the efforts of these men clearly slowed the fall of at least some of the climbers and probably prevented far worse injuries. "I have to believe the effort that Tom Hillman put out, that Chris Kern put out, that I put out, changed the outcome," Slutter says, "even if it was just saving our own lives and reducing the injuries to the other people on the mountain."

To rope up is a serious decision. Without ropes, an individual who falls may be able to self-arrest or, at the very least, will avoid taking others with him. But to most climbers, the rope is more than a safety device. It's both a real and a symbolic commitment to a partner. Hillman raises a rhetorical question: Given the chance, would he have considered cutting his rope? For him the answer is clear. "No. There was no question what I had to do as a member of a team and as a friend."

While Boyer pondered the cause of the fall, Cataldo, Chagnon, and other pilots were analyzing the Pave Hawk crash. Those who had seen the accident and the news footage felt they knew just what had happened.

"He was doing what we call 'settling with power,' " Chagnon says. A helicopter rotor turns at a constant speed, he explains. When the pilot pulls for more lift, a gearbox increases the angle of attack of the blades. Think of putting your hand out the window of a speeding car: If you tilt the leading edge up, your hand rises; it wants to fly. But just as the wind will push your hand backward, it will also slow the blades. So the transmission automatically adds the right amount of power to keep the blades turning at a constant speed.

Because the main rotor is spinning counterclockwise, the fuselage wants to turn the other way. The tail rotor prevents that by adding a counterforce. So every time the pilot adds power to the main rotor, he also needs to add power to the tail rotor to keep the bird pointed straight ahead.

This all works fine in normal flight, but when a helicopter hovers, things get complicated. If the helicopter sits suspended in one place for too long, it can produce a vortex, a spinning column of air much like the whirlpool in a blender. Eventually, that vortex can start sucking down the helicopter. "You're flying in your own downdraft," Chagnon explains. To counteract it, the pilot needs to pull more power.

That's why Chagnon and Cataldo were so concerned about their power reserve: If a pilot who is starting to settle tries to pull more power than the helicopter has, the rotors begin to slow down,

Chagnon says, and the helicopter just settles more. It's a vicious cycle: "More power, more settling. You've maxed out."

The best move when settling with power is to fly out of the vortex and gain lift from forward speed. But when a helicopter begins to run out of power, the tail rotor loses effectiveness, too. So the bird begins to turn to the right. Chagnon believes this is what happened to Dysle, the Pave Hawk pilot. "Once the nose had turned right, he had nowhere to go," says Chagnon. "He was facing into the mountain. At that point, it appears he decided to back down, which just wasn't going to work. His refueling probe went into the snow, he tilted over, and his rotors struck the snow. And that was that."

With the Pave Hawk crew forbidden to speak, Dwayne Troxel, a recently retired Pave Hawk pilot who had flown with members of the downed crew, helped explain the Air Force Reserve point of view. "If Dysle hadn't had the patient on the cable, he'd have been able to fly out of it," says Troxel, 52, who is now an SAR coordinator for the Hood River County sheriff's office. Still, he concedes that the Army Guard pilots have a point about the Pave Hawk's being heavy: "The Air Force has a tendency to overload helicopters. And that could definitely do it, with the limited extra power, his weight, the high altitude." Pilots and flight engineers are supposed to calculate their power profile for each mission, he says. "But it was going to be close, there's no question about that. If there were a significant change in wind direction, that could have gotten him."

Indeed, the Army Guard pilot and crew chief who lifted out Moffitt late in the day reported that the winds had picked up considerably since midday. On the other hand, as Chagnon puts it, "I hope the Air Force, while they're doing their investigation, will come and ask us why we had four Black Hawk extractions that day without any problem and a Pave Hawk extraction that resulted in a crash. I hope they'll ask us what the wind was like. I flew up there, and there was wind, but not much. Anyway, he's the pilot in command. If he can't handle the wind, he shouldn't be there."

• • •

Night falls on Mount Hood like a family photograph growing old in the attic. The great reaches of the Cascades conduct a slow fade to candle-wax gray as the cloud deck boils and flags snap in the freshening breeze. Pink sunlight tops the clouds.

By 5 p.m., rescuers Mull, Rollins, and a few others had dragged themselves down past Crater Rock, where two snowcats were waiting. Glancing back up, they could see the fresh PMR technical teams working the haul system for bringing out the dead. Already, families were gathering at Timberline Lodge. The rescuers watched the crush of activity far below as they headed down—the media, the police, and the flickering lights of a still-crowded landing zone.

The Forest Service kept the Mount Hood Wilderness Area closed for a week, and in the end, the Air Force Reserve asked the Oregon Army National Guard to come in with a twin-rotor Chinook helicopter to lift the battered Pave Hawk off the mountain.

The injured were all out of the hospital within a week. Technical Sergeant Mills, the Air Force Reserve flight engineer, was treated for a lacerated liver and a broken ankle. Chris Kern, with his broken hip, faced a long recovery back home on Long Island, but he hopes to return to climbing. Of the critical patients, Jeremiah Moffitt sustained the lightest injuries, just as the rescue experts had surmised: a concussion, bruised ribs, and a bruised hand. He would be back on his mountain bike within a month and plans to climb Hood again with his girlfriend, Selena Maestas, and some of the other members of the Tualatin team.

Weather moved in, and heavy snow covered the scars of the accident and partially filled the bergschrund. On a sunny day three weeks later, Boyer ascended Mount Hood again. As he set out, he could see three dozen climbers strung out along the Hogsback. Most were climbing in the classic fashion: roped together, moving without anchors, their fates linked to those above and below.

Five Who Survived

by Steve Howe

Many wilderness-lovers wonder how they'd fare in a survival situation. The five people profiled in this article found out. Steve Howe compiled these cautionary examples for Backpacker.

Eric Tucker

THE NOT-SO-SHORT CUT
MISSING 9 DAYS
EMIGRANT WILDERNESS, CA
5-DAY LOOP HIKE

BAD KARMA: Changed plans, left trail, poor navigation, injury, passive signaling
GOOD KARMA: Well-equipped, well-provisioned, stayed hydrated, rationed food, never-say-die attitude

"I don't know how my shoulder got dislocated," recalls Eric Tucker. "But I landed on my feet. If I'd hit my head, the whole thing could have turned out a lot worse."

Things were bad enough. Tucker lay at the bottom of a narrow ravine with a broken left ankle, a sprained right ankle, torn knee ligaments, and a dislocated right shoulder. He was far from any trail, and search efforts wouldn't even start for a week.

The 28-year-old computer engineer from Mountain View, CA, had changed plans on day 1 of a 5-day, 50-mile loop through California's 113,000-acre Emigrant Wilderness. After his chosen route from Kennedy Meadows toward Big Sam Mountain kept disappearing in the rocks, Tucker worried that he'd lose it altogether, so he turned down a small creekbed he thought would intersect the main trail up Kennedy Creek.

Bordered to the south by Yosemite, the Emigrant is a sparsely timbered landscape of steep granite domes that roll over into lake-filled meadows and narrow, glaciated canyons. Tucker's creekbed shortcut dropped sharply, then choked off at a 45-foot, three-tiered cliff. "It looked like the last thing I had to get down before I was in the clear," he recalls. Tucker figured he'd toss his pack down to the first ledge and scout one level at a time. But his pack bounced to the bottom.

"At that point, it would have been better to turn around," he reflects. "I'd have been dehydrated walking out with no water or supplies, but my legs would have worked."

Tucker was climbing to his pack when he greased off water-slick holds and fell 30 feet to the base of the cliff. For 5 nights, he holed up on a rocky ledge, rationing his food and wincing as his shoulder popped and ground toward realignment. Fortunately, he'd landed next to his pack and a small trickle of water.

On the 6th day, Tucker was healed up enough to move toward a more visible location in the valley below. Hanging his pack off his good arm, he clambered 20 feet down the slope before his shoulder went out again. "Now I couldn't even get back up to where I'd started because I couldn't use the arm for balance in the ravine," he recalls. "I got really discouraged because there was no water right there. I was scared I'd die from dehydration."

On the morning of his 7th day, Tucker's shoulder was better, and he made it back up the slope to water. The first helicopter appeared on day 8. "I thought, 'Great! I'll just wave my big yellow poncho and they'll see me.' But they didn't," he explains. Over the next several days, four helicopters flew directly overhead, but none spotted him.

That same afternoon, Tucker finally reached the valley floor, but the trail he'd expected had vanished. "That was another bad time," he remembers. "I felt I couldn't trust the map, but now I know I misread it."

Tucker pitched camp and built the first of numerous signal fires. "I should have been working to make more smoke," he says, By now he was 4 days overdue and the target of a massive search effort. More than a hundred ground searchers were combing the Emigrant.

"When the 'copters didn't see me, I began to think seriously about getting myself out," says Tucker. Despite stabbing pain in his ankles, he spent the next 5 days limping from camp on short forays, scouting for possible exit routes back through the cliffs he'd fallen down. Finally, a day after rains pounded the Emigrant, Tucker found a way through talus and rock bands to the ridgetop. There, he located the trail he'd been seeking.

On the way out, Tucker shuffled past 12 or 15 hikers in small groups. "I didn't want to inconvenience them," he reasons. "And by now I was determined to get myself out." It took him 6 hours to reach the busy Kennedy Meadows trailhead, 2 weeks after he'd left it. Search operations had been called off that morning.

PROFESSIONAL OPINION

California State SAR Coordinator Matt Scharper calls Tucker's shortcut "a very typical mistake in rugged wilderness environments. Because it's physically easier, victims often head downhill through steep terrain, then get in trouble at the rollovers. Eric saw those 'copters only because that was the path they followed for refuel. Nobody was looking where he was, relatively close in."

David Whittlesey
Bugs, Beer, And Broken Teeth
Missing 6 days
Grand Canyon, AZ
24-day raft trip

Bad karma: Foodless, gearless, injured, cold weather
Good karma: Bic lighter, plentiful water, built shelter, kept trying

"I was in the river when I came to," David Whittlesey recalls. "It was so cold. I remember crawling out of the water, spitting out pieces of my teeth."

Just minutes earlier he'd been finishing up a 3-week solo raft trip down the Grand Canyon. The 45-year-old construction contractor from nearby Prescott was an experienced wilderness oarsman, but it was mid-November. The canyon bottom received only a couple of hours of sun each day, and night temperatures hovered near freezing. Only half an hour in the 50 Fahrenheit waters of the Colorado River would make a grown man hypothermic.

Whittlesey had cleared more than 100 rapids on his 270-mile expedition. All the hard stuff was behind him. "I figured I'd be home in no time, eatin' cheeseburgers," he recalls with a wry grimace. Then his boat hit submerged rocks in 232-Mile rapid and flipped. He managed to get the 1,500-pound raft to an eddy and rig a pulley system to right it, but his anchors failed.

Whittlesey next tried to pole his overturned raft to a beach where he could unload it, but the current pulled him into 234-Mile rapid, where waves swept him off the slick rubber bottom. Chilled to the bone, he needed to get out of the river. "As I scrambled to shore, the raft kept going, and I thought, 'Oh my god, what have I done now?'"

Whittlesey frantically scrambled up a cliff to see if the boat would eddy out. A handhold pulled loose, and he fell over backward. "I somersaulted down the slope, then went over a 10-foot drop into the water." On the way down, he hit the cliff edge with his jaw and blacked out.

Whittlesey woke up floating in his lifejacket. The raft was gone. His sandals had been sucked off. "The rock punched a hole through my chin," he says. "And the blow shattered four teeth, one of them down to the nerve." Crawling from the water, Whittlesey found himself perched on a long cliff that rose straight from the river. Downstream, he could see a small beach where he might rest and recover. As he scrambled along the crumbling wall, a rock rolled over his foot and broke two toes.

Finally, his luck changed. "As I was working around this outcropping, I looked up and saw a can of Miller Lite wedged in a crack, probably by the big floods of 1983. Caloriewise, they say there's a sandwich in every can, so I scored it."

When Whittlesey reached the alcove, it was raining and cold, and he was dressed only in shorts and a T-shirt. He built a windbreak out of driftwood, then dug a pit, gathered bunchgrass and made a nest. Then he found his saving grace: a Bic lighter. "If it had gotten washed out of my pocket," says Whittlesey, "I wouldn't be alive." He immediately made a fire and heated rocks that he buried in the sand beneath his nest.

This late in the season, Whittlesey saw no other rafts. He tried flashing flightseeing planes, using his rescue knife as a mirror. Eventually he drank the beer. "It was really, really rank," he recalls. "But it was nourishment."

Two days later, he swatted a lizard with some bunchgrass. "I just broke it in half and swallowed it whole," he recounts. Next came a sizable grasshopper. "It was a pleasant surprise, sweet and salty. The legs and claws are a little rough going down, but the taste was quite a treat.

"It's fascinating what your mind does," Whittlesey says. "I knew that dying of hypothermia feels like going to sleep, so I began to get very little sleep, worrying it would be permanent . . . I was getting really depressed, thinking maybe I wouldn't get out. My firewood was almost gone. I didn't want to become an anonymous body, so I took a piece of driftwood and scratched out a message to my family. I always wrote one day ahead, just to give me hope."

Finally, Whittlesey heard the thump of helicopter blades. "They came downstream, right at river level, looking for a body," he recalls. "And there I was, jumping around, waving my arms, crying hysterically. It was the only time I really lost it."

PROFESSIONAL OPINION

According to ranger Ivan Kassovich, incident commander for numerous Grand Canyon rescues, "The best insurance policy is one trustworthy person who knows not only where you were going and when you were due out, but understands your activity and what your contingency plans are if you run into trouble."

Keith Nyitray
ALASKA GRABS YOU
MISSING 26 DAYS
BROOKS RANGE, AK
8-MONTH EXPEDITION

BAD KARMA: -50 Fahrenheit temps, ends-of-the-Earth remoteness, no search initiated
GOOD KARMA: very experienced, ultra fit, emergency prepared, mentally tough

"I was on a downward emotional spiral," Keith Nyitray recalls. "I wasn't making my miles. I was waiting for a plane to come over, hoping for rescue, but when I didn't hear one, I'd get depressed."

Curled in his hastily scraped snow cave, 240 miles from the nearest Arctic village, Keith Nyitray had good reason to worry. It was -50 Fahrenheit and howling. Tree line—with its promise of shelter and fuel—was 100 miles distant. Fortunately, his prospects weren't entirely bleak: Nyitray was anything but a typical backcountry victim.

The Long Island native had moved to Alaska at age 20, after summiting Mt. McKinley. He'd pioneered routes in the Alaska Range; he'd become an EMT and an incredibly experienced wilderness soloist. Each summer, he trekked 270 miles, one way, to his homestead in the Revelation Mountains north of Lake Clark National Park. Each fall, he built a log raft and floated out. "I was spending up to 10 months a year alone in the bush," he recalls. "When something grabs you, it grabs you, and Alaska did me."

Only days before, Nyitray had been canoeing down the Noatak River, enjoying the homestretch of an 8-month solo traverse of Alaska's immense Brooks Range. Then, on October 10, winter blew in a month ahead of schedule. "People up here still wear T-shirts saying 'I survived the winter of '89,'" he says.

Nyitray was as prepared as any trekker could be. He'd already overcome a broken ankle and a dogsled epic to get this far. He had the experience, the physical and medical training, and a "10-pound emergency and first-aid kit." But none of that was much help; the Noatak froze solid almost overnight.

He alternately dragged and paddled his canoe for 10 days, past berg-filled channels and slush-dammed suck-holes, until thermal "katabatic" winds descended from Howard Pass. "I went to sleep in calm weather at 10 Fahrenheit and woke when 60 mph wind gusts slammed into my tarp at -30 Fahrenheit," Nyitray recalls. "That storm lasted 3 1/2 days."

Nyitray abandoned his canoe and began a desperate, 100-mile march over frozen, snow-drifted tundra. "My goal was Arctic treeline," he says. "There'd be shelter, firewood, and game to hunt." He also expected to find a cabin. "Fire suddenly became my ultimate survival tool," he remembers. "During the day it was go-go-go, but I often spent more time collecting and burning willow than I did hiking, and at minus 40, that heat bubble is only about 2 feet from the flames. My back was always freezing."

Nyitray's food ran low, until all he had left was a little rice. He carried a shotgun for emergencies and self-defense, but the animals had migrated to more-sheltered country. Breakfasts were weak tea.

"I was following fox tracks along the river," he recalls. "Because they could smell places where anglers had cleaned their fish prior to freeze-up, leaving the guts and heads, but they couldn't dig through the ice to get them. So I ate those, and occasionally I'd have a bit of wolf-kill slurry."

The grisly meals were barely enough to keep him going, and Nyitray's mood plunged along with his blood sugar. He began hoping for a rescue from nowhere. "I realized I was on a very slippery slope," he says. "I finally told myself, 'There will be no plane.' I didn't know if I'd lose fingers or toes, or if I'd have to eat my dog, but I decided I'd do anything to survive."

When he could move, Nyitray could keep warm and focus on progress. When forced into inactivity by storms or darkness, he resorted to mental escape. "I'd just put aside all my anxieties for the night and deal with it next morning, compartmentalizing the overwhelming heaviness of my situation," he says. "At first I fantasized about all-you-can-eat buffets, but that became depressing, so I began to visualize how to expand my cabin. When I finished those renovations, I began writing a historical romance novel in my head . . . the main character like me— with a beautiful native woman. I called it 'Arctic Eves.' "

Nyitray began looking forward to nights huddled in his heavy winter bag as his only mental and physical escape. The bag was thick enough to keep him alive, but not warm, and it was starting to fall apart from scorching and sparks. Frostbite began nibbling at his fingers and toes. "I was like a three-fingered person," he remembers. "I had my frosted fingers wrapped together, so manipulation was difficult."

In early November, 26 days after winter blew in, a skeletonized Nyitray finally reached treeline with a badly abscessed tooth and frostbite on face, fingers, and toes. There, he found a fully stocked cabin and, with radio permission from the owner, holed up for 3 weeks, eating, healing digits, and doing dental surgery on himself. Rested and restless, he ventured back into the darkness of an Arctic winter, hiking 140 moonlit miles to the village of Noatak, then 60 more to the Bering Sea at Kotzebue, and the end of his journey.

PROFESSIONAL OPINION

One Alaska veteran told us, "Nyitray's actions were borderline suicidal for any normal person. But this is one tough hombre who clearly prepped himself for Arctic disaster through years of hard wilderness training. It just goes to show that big ambitions can kill you if you don't acquire appropriate skills and experience over the course of tougher and tougher trips."

Paul Nelson
OLYMPIC NATIONAL PARK, WA
MISSING 11 DAYS
5-DAY HIKE

BAD KARMA: Poor route finding, underestimated terrain, lost map
GOOD KARMA: Well-equipped and provisioned, rationed food, gathered food, kept trying

"I was hanging from cedar branches, feet clawing for footholds, trying to lower myself down this overgrown cliff," Paul Nelson recalls. "There were waterfalls to both sides and a 75-foot drop," he says. "If I'd let go, I'd have fallen the whole distance."

The 38-year-old poet, community activist, and jazz deejay from Auburn, WA, had set out on a 5-day hike through the Appleton Pass-Sol Duc River country of Olympic National Park. It's some of the wettest, steepest, most tangled mountain terrain in the Pacific Northwest. And now, after a series of mishaps, he was hopelessly lost, short on food, a week overdue, and face-to-face with impassable cliffs.

On his 3rd day out, Nelson had diverged from his planned itinerary by joining up with two hikers headed for the Bailey Range. But he dropped out the next day, unable to maintain their pace. After consulting another party about cross-country routes back to Appleton Pass, Nelson tried to locate a little-used route. Soon he was floundering down the choked drainage of Cat Creek, jumping pourovers and wading waist-deep in the stream whenever the brush got too thick.

Realizing he was heading the wrong direction—east rather than northwest—Nelson climbed the slopes above, attempting to gain a view. Finally he settled on a route up steep talus toward the precipitous ridgeline north of Cat Creek, knowing it was the right direction, if not actually the correct route.

"I was basically clawing my way up the mountain," Nelson recalls, "grabbing trees and pulling myself up." His map and journal were wedged in the thigh pocket of his cargo pants, but the zipper wouldn't quite close over them. During his struggles, both fell out. By nightfall of Day 6, Nelson was wedged against the slope behind two large cedars, halfway to the Cat Creek/Schoeffel Creek ridgeline . . . totally lost.

After another day of hand-to-hand combat with dense undergrowth and feeling the telltale signs of dehydration, Nelson found a snowfield in a protected north-facing pocket near the ridge crest. "I realized this was a chance to chill out and rehydrate. I had four meals left; I started eating just one a day, along with all the blueberries I could find."

Daunted by views of endless rainforest and the risks he'd already taken, Nelson sat tight for 3 days. He made an SOS on the snowfield from rocks, logs, and sticks, then delved into a book of Walt Whitman's poetry. "That lust for life helped inspire and buttress me," he says. "One line in particular had a strong effect: 'Those who love each other shall become invincible.' I wanted to get back to my loved ones."

By this time, Nelson was 2 days late, so his partner alerted the park service. But overdue hikers are common in the Olympic rainforest, and Nelson had refused to get a permit. "It was a political statement," he admits sheepishly. "Here we are subsidizing all this logging, and they're charging people 2 bucks a night to sleep out. It's a statement I don't make anymore." His wife finally convinced authorities that Nelson needed help, and they rallied 40 searchers and several helicopters to comb the area.

Down to his last meal and facing cloudy skies, Nelson abandoned thoughts of aerial rescue and moved off the ridge. He thought he was making for Cat Creek, but he was actually weaving through cliff bands down into the small, choked canyon of Schoeffel Creek. Look at a map of the area, and you realize he'd just crossed the steepest, nastiest ridge in miles.

"Looking back, I'm a lot more scared than I was at the time," Nelson recalls. "There was the overgrown cliff, and I remember one huge boulder with a 25-foot drop off the back. It seemed like the only way down. Tree branches reached halfway up the drop, and I thought I could jump, grab the branches, bend 'em over, and drop to solid ground. Fortunately it worked."

A helicopter found Nelson's SOS later that afternoon, but it took another day to spot him in what reports called "incredibly hazardous terrain beneath a 300-foot waterfall." He was standing on a rock in Schoeffel Creek, scraped, bruised, and 14 pounds lighter when a helicopter winched him out.

PROFESSIONAL OPINION

"Paul didn't plan his adventure very well," says Dan Pontbriand, park service operations chief for the Nelson search. "But you have to give him credit for getting out of some very sticky situations. He kept his head. He maintained a positive attitude. After 4 days, I'd guess only about 5 percent of lost solo hikers survive, and Paul broke that mold. He even had food left. He climbed to open ridgeline where he could signal, and that's what really saved him, because if folks hug a tree here, we'll never find 'em."

Douglas Dent
THIS IS THE MIDDLE OF NOWHERE
MISSING 4 DAYS
STEIN WILDERNESS, BRITISH COLUMBIA
8-DAY TRIP

BAD KARMA: Poor navigation, stormy weather, remote location, large search area

GOOD KARMA: Well equipped, good attitude, active signaling

"I kept hiking in the snow and fog going from cairn to cairn," Doug Dent remembers with remorse. "And then they disappeared."

The 52-year-old attorney from Vancouver, Canada, was on the next-to-last day of an 8-day, 55-mile solo trek through the Stein River Valley, a remote, rugged mountain landscape about 200 miles east of Vancouver, BC. Maps contain this notation: "You are 2 days from any help in any direction. This is the middle of nowhere."

Dent had been an avid hiker for 5 years, and he'd taken precautions before heading into the wilderness, packing extra food, clothing, and emergency gear. With one exception: He had been scheduled to take a map and compass course before the trip, but it was cancelled.

Dent's route began on the dry eastern flank of the mountains. "As you move west, you move into rainforest," he explains. "You follow the Stein River for several days, then climb onto a ridge that takes you out toward Lizzie Lake." This plateau raised and condensed the incoming clouds, creating a misty fog that saturated everything, including Dent. On the evening of his 6th day out, the mist turned to wet snow. "I could see only about 10 meters," Dent recalls. Benighted at ridgetop by the rising storm, he huddled in his tarp, slowly getting soaked. "Next day I got up and continued all day, still in fog and snow."

That's when the cairns ran out. Dent overnighted again on the ridgetop, but resolved to descend to a campsite at Tundra Lake the next morning. "My question was, 'Do I descend off the ridge to left or right?' I chose right because I thought I saw a trail down there." He should've gone left.

Dent was now a day overdue, so his son Greg reported him missing. Searchers knew that finding him would be difficult. Numerous timbered canyons and weather-catching peaks would complicate movement and communication, and even the trailheads were remote.

"It was a tough search," recalls Martin Colwell, search coordinator for Lion's Bay SAR. "In these mountains, you rarely get more than 30 searchers who are experienced enough to deploy. And they have to go back home in a couple of days. The farther you get from city centers, the tougher time you have keeping the search going."

A complete advance basecamp was set up. Three planes began combing the area. Helicopters ferried ground searchers to various drop points. Everything was slowed by a lack of communications. "We had only one satellite phone to talk to headquarters in Pemberton," Colwell explains. "And it had to be recharged periodically."

Meanwhile, Dent had struggled down a steep creekbed, finally reaching the valley but finding no trail. "My recollection of survival info was that you're supposed to locate a clearing, light a fire, and stay put. So I pitched my tent, started the fire, and dried out my clothes and sleeping bag, which were soaked. I decided I was lost. I just had to wait."

For 3 days he sat tight and kept his fires going. "I heard planes overhead and even fired off a flare, but they didn't see it. When the planes grew fainter and I could tell the search was moving off, I began to think maybe I'd die if I stayed here. On top of that, the weather had warmed and my little patch of open beach was disappearing as the creek rose."

Next morning's weather cleared, so Dent decided to relocate his trail. He found it after backtracking up the ridge. "I eventually reached tree level about noon," he remembers. "From then until 5 p.m., I probably waved my jacket at a dozen planes." He'd already reached the Tundra Lake campsite when he heard a chopper coming. "Knowing I needed something bigger to get their attention, I dug out my blue sleeping bag and started waving."

"He was pretty tired and scratched up when we found him," says Colwell. "But otherwise he was in good condition." That evening, heavy storms brought rain, snow, and fog that would have shut down the search. But Doug Dent had already found his way back.

PROFESSIONAL OPINION

"The Dent search was as remote as any we've ever done," says Colwell. "It definitely taxed our abilities. Fortunately, he realized he would never be found where he was camped and made his way back into our search area. Doug needed more navigation skills, but he made smart decisions and took care of himself after getting lost."

6 Dumbest Things To Say In The Wilds

1.   I'll take this shortcut.
2.   You go on ahead.
3.   I'm sure there'll be water.
4.   Let's climb. Those clouds aren't even close.
5.   That summit doesn't look hard.
6.   Keep going. We're bound to see something familiar.

acknowledgments

Many people made this anthology.

At Thunder's Mouth Press and Avalon Publishing Group:
Thanks to Will Balliett, Sue Canavan, Kristen Couse, Maria Fernandez, Linda Kosarin, Dan O'Connor, Neil Ortenberg, Susan Reich, David Riedy, Michelle Rosenfield, Simon Sullivan, and Mike Walters for their support, dedication and hard work.

At The Writing Company:
Taylor Smith and Nathaniel May took up slack on other projects.

At the Portland Public Library in Portland, Maine:
The librarians helped collect books from around the country.

Finally, I am grateful to the writers whose work appears in this book.

permissions

bibliography

The selections used in this anthology were taken from the editions listed below. In some cases, other editions may be easier to find. Hard-to-find or out-of-print titles often are available through inter-library loan services or through Internet booksellers.

Anson, Robert Sam. "The Journalist and the Terrorist". Originally appeared in *Vanity Fair,* August 2002.

Canby, Peter. "The Forest Primeval". Originally appeared in *Harper's,* July 2002.

Case, David. "Terror in Paradise". Originally appeared in *Men's Journal,* January 2003.

Finkel, Michael. "Little Sister, Big Mountain". Originally appeared in *National Geographic Adventure,* November 2002.

Frump, Robert. "Man-Eaters". Originally appeared in *Men's Journal,* January 2003.

Gonzales, Laurence. "The Slipping Point". Originally appeared in *National Geographic Adventure,* September 2002.

Grosz, Terry. *A Sword for Mother Nature: The Further Adventures of a Fish and Game Warden.* Boulder, Colorado: Johnson Books, 2002.

Heath, Chris. "This is Not a Rodeo Story". Originally appeared in *Men's Journal,* December 2002.

Howe, Steve. "Five Who Survived". Originally appeared in *Backpacker,* September 2002.

Kerasote, Ted. "A Thin White Line". Originally appeared in *Outside,* April 2003.

Langewiesche, William. *American Ground: Unbuilding the World Trade Center.* New York: North Point Press, 2002.

Mawdsley, James. *The Iron Road: A Stand for Truth and Democracy in Burma.* New York: North Point Press, 2002.

Pelton, Robert Young. "Kidnapped in the Gap". Originally appeared in *National Geographic Adventure,* June/July 2003.

Ramo, Joshua Cooper. *No Visible Horizon: Surviving the World's Most Dangerous Sport.* New York: Simon & Schuster, 2003.

Singer, Natasha. "These Pants Saved My Life". Originally appeared in *Outside,* October 2002.

Weselake, Evan, as told to Mike Grudowski. "Avalanche: A Survivor's Story". Originally appeared in *Men's Journal,* April 2003